CW01498784

This book is dedicated to Debra Hiltz, Donna Salzano, Tammy Dove, and Ann Meemken
Special thanks to Tracie Podger, Susan Ward, Nancy Pracht, and Joanne Swinney for their tireless patience with social media support, and to Joanne for allowing me to brainstorm my ideas during the writing of this book. You are all amazing and I am eternally grateful for your support.

MISSING BEATS

K. L. SHANDWICK

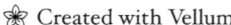

When I started writing just over three years ago, I never dreamed I'd be able to write a book. This book is my thirteenth book. Being able to continuing writing has only been possible by my readers and supporters. Please find me on social media, follow me on by signing up to my newsletter and find out the latest from my works in progress, or just a place where you can hang out with me. If you read my books please leave a review, it helps indie authors to be more visible on social media. Your thirst for my books is what keeps me writing. Thank you for your faith and support for what I do. To my loyal readers who have read everything I've written, I'm truly in awe of your support and to those of you who are new to me, I hope I don't disappoint.

PROLOGUE

$\mathcal{I}$ had loved Kane Exeter since I was six and a half years old; I just didn't know it until later. We met for the first time in Germany when both of our fathers served as military personnel stationed overseas.

Kane was an alpha boy even then; his thought processes were head and shoulders above his peers. He was always taking charge and organizing everyone.

As he grew up, that natural leadership combined with his smart as hell brain, had taken him to places I could only dream about. Kane had no time for girls back then so I counted myself privileged that he was my friend.

The reality was that he saw me as one of the boys when they were a goalkeeper short for the barracks under nine's soccer team.

It may be clichéd to say, but Kane and I just clicked. My brother Matt, who was nine at the time, and my twin brother, Jacob, were his best friends until he started calling around for me to hang out with him—about six months later—without my brothers.

Both of my siblings attended band practice and Kane didn't play, so he hung out with me instead. It's strange how things turned out. They

1

practiced their musical instruments religiously and it was Kane who became a rock star.

Being around him as a kid was effortless, and as young as we were, the special bond that formed between us made us practically inseparable.

Somehow we instinctively knew what the other was thinking and had an easy friendship that kept us close. He was my god as an impressionable little girl and he always made me laugh.

Although my name is Josephine, my family called me Josie, but Kane, he always called me Jo. In my head, I heard that as the boy's name, Joe. It fluffed my seven year-old ego that he thought of me as an equal—one of the boys as it were.

Looking back, we had a pretty secure and idyllic lifestyle on our military campus until the notice came for our fathers to return to their USA army bases, tilting our small world on its axis.

We had no idea then how quickly our little lives would change. No one really thought much about us kids when we were suddenly transferred back. Our endings were abrupt and without closure to those we'd become attached to. Not being able to see Kane every day after that felt like a bereavement to me.

I knew from those left behind, that promises made to keep in touch with them rarely transpired once people departed and moved on. They were never heard from again.

Mom told us, in a matter-of-fact tone, that the army couldn't afford to care about the effects on individuals and that our country and its people had to be protected. She said sacrifices had to be made. I was never sure if that was something she was told, if she'd made it up or if it was something she believed, but because of the nature of our fathers' work, Kane and I became emotional casualties of war in our own right.

When we packed up and headed back to Maryland there were tears and promises made that we'd see each other often.

Although we were in the same state and the intention was there at the time from our parents, the next time I saw Kane was when he was almost twelve years old. Kane's father, Samuel, had become a fallen hero during a later tour of Iraq. We traveled to Baltimore to see him and his mom.

As we pulled up at his house, nerves tore at my tummy. Part of me wanted to catch the latch on the car door and run to find him, while another part was dreading our reunion because I was afraid I'd say the wrong thing and make him feel worse than I imagined he was already feeling.

When I entered his sitting room my eyes were immediately drawn to Kane's tearstained face. An instant pang of sadness shot through my body and left me in shock at the sight of him.

The reality and my imagination of how he'd look were poles apart. His grief-stricken, tired appearance had ravished the golden-skinned little boy I remembered, draining him of any color.

My aching heart almost broke with how sad I had felt once we found ourselves on our own in a corner of the room and he let his tears flow unchecked again. Hot tears stung my eyes while the lump in my throat grew bigger and I did the only thing I could have managed at that moment, hugged him—tightly.

Kane hugged me back like he never wanted to let me go again, clinging so forcefully I struggled to breathe normally. I felt everything he didn't say in that hug, not just physically, silent distress seared my soul.

"It's so good to see you, Jo. I've missed you every single day," he sniffed, stepping back one pace to look at me. I'd never seen this version of Kane. Heartbroken and lost. His voice warbled from his grief. He looked so fragile.

"Me too. I've missed you too. I'm so sorry about...I love your letters," I said, quickly holding my hand out for him to take.

The change of subject to something safer worked to a point, and I was glad because he stopped crying and gave me a sad smile. Skirting around the topic of his dad, at that point I made eye contact, the pained look he had, grabbed my heart and squeezed it tightly.

"I feel I know all your friends from how you write about them, but it makes me feel sad and miss you more. I've wished for something to bring you back to me," I said, before quickly realizing it was a stupid thing to say given the circumstances. "I mean...I didn't wish for—"

"Oh, I know. It's not your fault...I just...miss him," he said, cutting across my inept attempt to recover from the idiotic timing of my comment. Fresh tears rolled down his cheeks, dripping off his chin. I realized that I should have finished my sentence before about his dad.

Reaching up, I held his face between my hands and wiped his tears again. I just wanted to do something to comfort him.

Looking into those huge, blue eyes, brimming with tears made me cry again. I'd spent almost a whole week before the funeral anticipating that moment with him, and when it came I'd hated it.

Helplessly watching someone you love suffer like that is possibly the hardest thing to bear. It felt so much worse because I had to do it in a room full of adults that were all solemn and dour. The fact that I was only going to be there for one day made it even worse.

The last thing I had wanted to do on this earth that night was walk away from him again. That wasn't my choice; I had only turned ten years old and had no say in the matter.

Years passed and life went on without Kane, but I always had a thousand memories of him stored at the back of my mind.

Chapter One

HEDONISM

"Why Hedonism for a band name? Well, Louise...it *is* okay to call you that, right, honey?" he asked, with a twinkle in his eye and a sexy-as-fuck smirk on his face. He reached over and placed his hand on her knee and she giggled uncontrollably.

"Of course," she replied, slightly breathless, her hand rising to rest at the center of her bust.

The music show presenter's body language was embarrassing as she squirmed in her seat, obviously loving the interaction between them.

It was plain to see that she was unable to stay still while the rock star she was interviewing seduced her with his tongue to the point where I thought she was going to climb over and straddle him.

"Well for those who don't know, hedonism means the pursuit of happiness—sensual self-indulgence. I'm all for indulging in anything that makes me feel good—and it's a sexy name. We're a sexy number one band that sings songs about sex, so we changed the 'I' in hedonism to the number one. It suits us perfectly, don't you think?" he continued, leaning back and placing his arm along the length of the sofa without an ounce of embarrassment.

Goosebumps stopped me in my tracks. I hadn't seen my childhood friend since the day of his father's funeral, but I had never forgotten him.

It was a pure fluke that I caught his appearance on the show. I had only just put the TV on and had been about to curl up on my over-sized, squishy sofa for another exciting Friday night of chick flicks and popcorn.

Scrolling through the channels I had suddenly hit the music channel and was immediately drawn to his image on the screen.

Looking very different, yet somehow incredibly familiar, Kane Exeter—*my* Kane Exeter, larger than life was sitting on a red, TV network studio sofa.

A zap of electricity ran through my body and jolted my heart. It stalled momentarily while I caught my breath until it raced wildly in my chest again at the sight of him.

I turned up the sound and walked closer to the television. Capti-vated, I listened to what he was saying.

Oozing sex appeal and charm, he was flirting outrageously with the attractive female presenter while talking about his first big tour with his newly formed rock band, Hedonism.

During the interview the presenter began running through all the places we could see Hedonism on tour, and when she mentioned Balti-more, Maryland, I almost fell through the floor.

Excited beyond words, my mind went blank and missed the date she gave because I'd been so pre-occupied when he mentioned that he'd be in my home state.

My heart skipped a beat when I heard he was going to be in my town and I stood rooted to the spot, completely paralyzed to see him after all these years.

The last time I'd seen him he was a grief-stricken young boy, and I'd been unable to shake that image of him in my mind ever since.

I'd always thought him a handsome boy, but the adult man-hunk version of the boy I once knew was so freaking hot I couldn't tear my eyes away.

Inked artwork covered the golden skin on his tight, muscular upper arms and shoulders as he sat back with one leg crossed over at the knee, completely owning the biker boots he wore.

Muscular legs in his tight-fitted jeans matched the same muscle structure of his arms and shoulders. He looked so strong and fit and not at all how I remembered him.

It was plain to see that Kane had taken care of himself. He'd turned into the guy no woman would pass in the street without checking out. His whole persona gave the vibe that he was a self-assured charmer.

I stood mesmerized watching the screen, staring in shock while a hundred different emotions from hate to love, and frustration to elation wreaked havoc with my mind.

My aching heart pounded wildly and filled with longing just from hearing his name again. I couldn't stop looking at him. He was so attractive—strike that, he was beautifully handsome and jaw-droppingly sexy.

A dull ache formed deep inside of me, longing to be close to the boy I used to know—fame and looks had nothing to do with that particular void.

Tears welled in my eyes and my throat constricted. All those years I had missed my friend, I'd kept him in a tiny corner of my heart, and suddenly there he was, in my face as some famous guy living a life a million miles apart from the ordinary life that I led.

Next thing I knew I was sobbing like some lovesick teenager still staring at him having fun up there on my fifty-inch, flat-screen TV. I was bawling my eyes out because I never did get my closure with him.

Suddenly the interview was being concluded as Kane continued to flirt outrageously.

Changing position, he sat slumped back in the seat with his legs open and one arm behind his head, like he was talking to a buddy in his den. His torso looked ripped in his tight, white T-shirt and as he smoothed his other hand down his torso and rested it unconsciously over his groin, the presenter's hungry eyes followed it. I could see he wasn't aware of what he'd done, but the presenter certainly was.

When I looked back at her she was biting her lip; she barely managed to say goodbye to the viewers, her focus returning to Kane.

Instantly, a music track of theirs began to play and I eased myself back onto the arm of the chair and continued to watch in disbelief, totally enthralled by his amazing voice and fluid movements while he sang about drinking bourbon and fucking red-headed women.

When the song finished, the next spot on the show was a band I didn't know, and as quick as he'd come into my life again he was gone. I missed him, immediately.

Switching channels, I found the old Bridget Jones movie I had thought about watching. By this stage I was restless and couldn't concentrate on anything since I'd seen the boy that had left a hole in my world.

Switching off the TV, I laid flat on my back on the sofa, closed my eyes and let my mind drift back to the past. His smile, the way he used to nudge me conspiratorially when he was teasing one of my brothers, like we were members of some secret club—memory after memory of the things we shared came flooding back.

One memory stood out more than all the others. It was the night our parents agreed to a camp out in our back garden. It was safe because we were surrounded by soldiers, and to us it was a huge adventure—until darkness fell.

All four of us lay in the tent and Matt, told a story about a bear eating some campers. I got scared and wanted to go home.

My brothers teased me for being a girl. Kane defended me to them and he hugged me tightly after that because I was afraid of the dark—I felt safer because he did that.

Then there was that day we'd all bought ice creams and a swarm of ladybirds stuck to mine.

Jacob thought this was so funny, but Kane had shared his ice cream with me after I refused to pick them off and eat mine like Jacob had suggested.

I must have fallen asleep because the buzzing of my cell, on the arm of the sofa near my head, woke me. Groggily, I picked it up and swiped to answer without looking.

"Hello, gorgeous, how is your weekend going?" When I heard Elliott's voice it raised a sleepy smile.

"Hi, how has your day, been?" I loved the way he always wanted to know about me.

My previous two boyfriends only spoke about themselves like I wasn't that important. With Elliott, he wasn't just playing lip service in his greeting; he always genuinely wanted to know.

"You first," I offered.

"You first," he insisted.

"Ah, well, it's been lazy. In fact, you woke me up. I was taking a nap."

"Can't have me there so you're dreaming of me, eh?"

I'd have liked to have said yes, but I was honest to a fault and I had been thinking about Kane right before I'd fallen asleep so I skipped the question. "When do you fly home?"

"Tuesday. Why? Are you missing me?"

"Sure," I answered, honestly. Elliott was a really nice guy. A straight-forward guy, and we'd been getting on well together until his company had sent him overseas to fix a problem with a huge construction project they were involved with in Europe.

"Did you know it's our six week anniversary today?"

"It is?" I queried as I did a quick calculation in my head. The fact that he knew this information was endearing. I had only had sex with Elliott twice since we'd been together. I liked him. I liked him a lot actually.

Elliott was mature—almost thirty—and for a guy of his age it was unusual to find that he had no hang-ups or previous messy relationships.

After he'd left college, he traveled extensively before settling down in a career. He was funny and sweet, a romantic, and he had rocked my world between the sheets.

When I had been introduced to him at a party, I had thought myself lucky that he was interested in me.

"You're still waiting for me, right, Josie? I mean I know we're fairly new and our relationship had just gone to the next level when I was sent to this godforsaken hole. I'd hate to lose out on you because I really like you," he stated frankly.

"I haven't been dating anyone else, I'm looking forward to you coming home," I replied with conviction.

"I'm relieved to hear it, honey. You're a beautiful girl. I can't wait to get back and pick up where we left off."

I felt myself blush at his inference. We were good together and I had started to miss him while he'd been away.

"You've gone quiet...did I say something wrong?"

A nervous giggle escaped and I cleared my throat. "Mmm, no you didn't...I just don't know what to say to that."

Elliott gave a hearty laugh down the phone, "It was good wasn't it? Who am I kidding, sex with you is awesome. I'm hard here just thinking about what I did to you, and it was almost a week ago."

A twinge pulsed between my legs and I wriggled uncomfortably, changing position. His words were turning me on and a small thrill of excitement ran through me.

"I was worried the timing of this trip would cool things between us," he admitted.

"Same here," I agreed. He was a handsome guy and I was sure he wouldn't be short of company while he was away. We'd left it that we were free to see other people while he was gone.

Personally I hadn't been happy with that. When he'd suggested it, I had felt obliged to agree. We were new and we hadn't had the opportunity to discuss us being totally exclusive.

I had been honest with him when I told him I had a long-standing date night arranged with Michael—a colleague from work, who had invited me to his sister's first night performance of a play.

"Dare I ask—Michael?"

The fact that he'd asked made me think he'd been concerned. "Sure. We went to the theatre, had a great time at dinner then I drove home alone.

I explained I had started a new relationship and that I liked you, and although he was disappointed, he was happy that I'd found someone to take care of me...I mean, his perception of what we are, not mine."

"No? You don't want me to take care of you?"

"You know what I mean, he has me married off already, when it's still...new, you know?"

"I'd be happy to take care of you, Josie. I'm a little bit in love with you already," he said in a quiet voice.

My heart squeezed, I was touched, and although I couldn't tell him I loved him back at that point, I knew I was emotionally invested in what we had.

"Thank you, let's just see how it goes, shall we? I may start to irritate you in another couple of months," I said, making light of his comment. "Anyway, what about you? Have any of those pretty French ladies snuggled up to you?"

"Had some company yes, but I kept my cock in my pants if that's what you're asking."

"Nice to know. And yes, I was asking." Oddly enough I didn't feel jealous and I was relieved he'd answered honestly.

Since we were early in our relationship and didn't have too many people in common, we ran out of things to say.

It was late for him as he was six hours ahead of me anyway, so I used that as an excuse to conclude the call. I felt much better for having spoken to him and decided a long soak in the bathtub was in order before I tried again with the movie.

Chapter Two

CELL SHOCK

Steam filled the bathroom as I filled the tub and inhaled deeply. The vapor burned my lungs but the ache felt strangely pleasurable.

I undressed and began to step into the bath. I had barely dipped my toe in the water when my cell rang again. Thinking it was Elliott calling back, I swiped to take the call and stepped into the bath.

"Did you have to wait until I was wet and naked to interrupt me?"

"If that's the case, Jo, then yes, and as always my timing is perfect for conversing with naked women," he said, in that same flirtatious tone I'd heard on the TV.

My heart stopped momentarily. The tingle from the lack of oxygen to my fingers and lips were reminders to breathe while I stood paralyzed by the sound of his voice.

Gasping, I sucked in a long breath while my heart flipped over inside my chest and bounced up into my throat. "Kane?" I asked, my voice barely a whisper. "Kane Exeter?"

"One and the same, Jo. Don't let me interrupt your wet nakedness...please continue," he crooned, with a smile in his voice.

Stuttering for words while my heart found its rhythm again, I half-crouched down toward the bubbles, not sure whether to get out or stay in there as my brain struggled to compute that he was actually calling me again after all these years.

"No...no. You're not interrupting. I mean I wasn't doing anything."

"Well, sure sounded like you were doing plenty from this end with your 'wet and naked' comment."

"I thought you were my friend," I blurted out, as my shock turned to hurt when I remembered that he'd abandoned me all those years ago.

"Damn, I am, remember? And I want to be *the* friend you're wet and naked for. I'm jealous." His flirtatious comment made him laugh.

Blood rushed to the surface of my skin but I ignored the sudden heat, and asked, "Is it really you?" My voice sounded hesitant, but with good reason after all this time.

"Who?"

"Kane?"

"Of course it is. God, it's good to hear your voice, honey." The way he said that felt like it was my fault we had all those lost years. Suddenly I was furious.

A rush of anger knotted my stomach and tightened my jawline. After all those years of no contact or communication apart from one birthday card, Kane had cut me dead.

"You'd have heard it a lot sooner if you hadn't dropped me from your life, Kane." My clipped tone was bitchy and harsh.

"Ouch. Don't be like that, baby. You were only ten years old, Jo, I was twelve. Life took us in different directions, and when Mom died I had to cut contact for my sanity. You were a link to my Dad and all the hurt I felt around that time. I had a tough few years following the loss of my parents. I don't expect you to understand, but I had to do what I did to get by. My counsellor insisted."

"So after twelve years you want to pick up where we left off? Or did you want something in particular?" *A few hours earlier I'd been sobbing on the sofa about this guy, and like some miracle he calls me as if he's telepathic. And what do I do? My first conversation with him in twelve years, I just about tore him a new asshole on how he had let me down.*

"You sound so pissed off, Jo. I'm really sorry, babe. I never meant to hurt you. Cutting everyone from my past was the only way I could keep a handle on things. Losing my Dad almost killed me. Samuel Exeter was *my* hero, Jo, not just the country's." My mind pulled the image of his grief to the forefront and my anger instantly ebbed away with that.

"Okay. I can accept that even if maybe I don't get it. I was really hurt. Devastated, Kane. Your parents died, but from how I felt at the time it was like you had too."

"Shit. I'm sorry, Jo. I was an angry kid back then. Life just kept kicking me in the balls and I was bagged with all the advice and strategies everyone wanted me to follow. I'd have done anything not to feel that horrible feeling of hopelessness."

All the hurt he had experienced was evident in his voice, and by the time he'd finished talking, any hostile feelings I had toward him had vanished.

"Sorry," I offered, feeling ashamed for only thinking of myself. "I am happy to hear from you. What did you call for? Why now?" I hated that I hadn't just said something more giving.

"Maybe this wasn't such a good idea. Did I leave it too long? I knew it might be, but I want you to know it took guts for me to pick up the phone and call you. I've wanted to...many times."

A pang of sympathy shot through me, mainly because his tone wasn't the flirty one that the call had started out with.

A stony silence hung between us and I realized that this may be my one and only chance for us to make amends. *We hadn't spoken for twelve years. What if he never rang back?*

"Kane, you're right. I am really, *really* pleased to hear from you. I just have twelve years of being angry and frustrated at you to get off my chest," I stated honestly.

"As you are naked, babe, you can get anything you like off your chest...just so long as I can watch," he said, slipping into the humorous, flirty tone he'd had on TV. "And for the record, I'm all for great angry make-up sex." I giggled because his frank comment was so unexpected, it embarrassed me a little.

"So where are you?"

"Is that a where are you, come right on over for the angry make—"

"No it damn well isn't," I answered giggling.

"Shoot, it was worth a try. To answer your question, I'm in Boston."

"Boston?" I repeated.

"Yep, but we're playing in your neck of the woods in a couple of days, and I figured as I had some downtime before the gig it would be the perfect time for a make-up session with you...without the sex of course...or with. I'll take you either way...or every which way," he said softly.

I could hear a smile in his voice, and even though I should have been embarrassed because we really had nothing in common apart from our childhoods, I couldn't help but feel flattered that he'd even bother to flirt with me.

"When...I mean...no to the sex, but I'd love to see you. When are you here?" My heart raced with excitement while my head had a hundred and one different things going on at the same time. I didn't know what to think.

"On my way to the airport later tonight, honey. Although, I wish I was there right now, with you being wet and naked and all," he chuckled, continuing with his flirtatious banter.

I felt my face flush and more than one pulse between my legs. I was confident it was all show and when he arrived I'd find him nothing like the guy on TV. After all, we were innocent kids when our friendship had blossomed.

"I see you've mastered the art of flirting?" I said, and was glad he couldn't see me when I said it.

By that time my neck was bright red right down to my breasts, and my cheeks were burning. The effect of his sudden call felt surreal, like it was all too much to take in.

"So where will you be staying when you're here?" I asked, wondering if I had anything suitable to wear to visit a swanky hotel.

Then I had a mild panic attack about how I didn't want to show up at a hotel and ask for Kane in case they thought I was one of his groupies.

"Jesus, Jo, what the fuck happened to you? Where did that quick witted soulmate go? You used to know what I was thinking."

Soulmate? Using that word took me by surprise. I'd never have thought he viewed the connection we had in the same way as I had.

15

Suddenly, I was scared; my feelings were a jumble of excitement, apprehension and anticipation. I knew he was joking with me, but the thought that Kane wanted to see me again after all this time gave me an infestation of butterflies that warranted a fainting fit at the very least.

"Do I need a hotel or do you have room for me there? I can crash on your couch, I'm not fussy."

Stunned I pulled the phone away from my ear and stared at it. I hadn't seen Kane for over a decade, and although we were close as kids I knew nothing of the rock star he'd become. I figured he had probably become accustomed to a lifestyle my tiny apartment couldn't compete with.

Suddenly, I feared we were so different we probably didn't have much to say to each other. *What if we had nothing in common these days? Do I want to be stuck tongue-tied in my own apartment with a virtual stranger?*

"You want to stay here? In my apartment? With me?" My disbelief came across in my voice, adrenaline fueling a slight tremor in it. I was sure my heart rate was at the very least, one hundred beats faster than usual.

"Jeez, you make it sound like a mass murderer has asked to stay, Jo. It's me, Kane Exeter, the kid from way back. I don't have much time in Maryland and I don't really want to spend it waiting for you, or you for me because we're in different places. It would be great to sit somewhere I know the press won't find me and catch up on all the news about Matt and Jacob as well as yours. I was pretty sure you'd be up for that, but I guess I never thought about the time lapse," he said as his voice trailed off.

"How did you get my number?"

"Your Mom. It was lucky your parents were still at the same address. I had my PA dig up the number and I called your Mom. So anyway, you've got my number now that I've called you.

Your Mom told me you lived alone so I figured you may like to catch up on the lost years, give me some company, and we could just hang out."

"Are you sure you wouldn't be more comfortable in a hotel?" I was uncertain I would know what to do with him after a few hours.

"Would *you* be more comfortable if I stayed in a hotel?" Kane asked, throwing my question back at me.

I'd thought about him for years and cried like a baby when I watched him earlier on the interview, so even though I had a million reservations and I wasn't usually a risk-taker I answered, "Stay. I'd love you to stay. Don't expect luxury. my place is pretty minimalist. I'm on a tight budget."

"Jo, baby, I'm not going to notice what your place is like. I'll be too busy staring at you after all this time."

I felt myself blush scarlet again, but I knew he hadn't meant that in any romantic way.

My heart skipped another beat and a small thrill ran though me just the same. If he continued to flirt like that I knew I'd have to change my underwear more regularly. There was no doubts about it, if flirting was an Olympic sport, Kane Exeter would be a medal contender.

"Can you pick me up at the airport? It would be less noticeable than a driver with my name on a placard. If not, I'll need your address. I don't have that."

God. He wants me to meet him? I figured he was being overfamiliar considering the time that had passed, but the familiar feeling was still there despite the years. "Sure I'll meet you—"

"Great I'll text you the details. Oh, and Jo...I think I'll need a picture. You probably look way different to the last time I saw you," he said with a soft laugh.

Just before I'd climbed in the bath I had caught sight of myself in the bathroom mirror. I had looked dreadful. Puffy eyes from crying, limp straggly hair, and no make-up. Since his call I had blushed so many times I was sure I looked like a hot mess.

"Okay, I'll send one as soon as I've finished my bath." I was trying to sound casual but my mind was racing ahead to the flat irons and make-up job I was going to be doing straight after our call.

I placed my cell on the vanity unit when we'd finalized the details. I exhaled heavily. still very much in a state of shock.

Sinking down into the water, I ducked my head until my face was the only part of my body that wasn't submerged.

Bubbles crackled around in my ears until they dispersed while the steady sound of my heartbeat pounded through my body. Then came two seconds of calm while I adjusted to the silence of lying there.

After that, I slid myself back into a sitting position when the impact of what had just happened hit me again and my mind went into overdrive. I had to prepare.

As soon as I'd shaved almost everything, except the hair on my head, I washed that hair and spent another two hours making myself date-ready for the selfie picture I had to send to the drop-dead gorgeous, pantie-melting, rock star who was coming to stay.

Straightening my hair, I stared blankly into the mirror wondering if I'd dreamed the whole thing up, but with that thought my cell vibrated on the countertop and a flight number flashed across the screen.

When I opened it I was stunned to see his flight arrived at 5:45 am. Less than eight hours away by that time, as it was already 8:10 pm.

Fourteen selfies later, where I'd pouted, smiled, tried to look casually attractive and failed miserably, I finally sent one that was less than perfect but the best of a bad bunch. Kane answered immediately with one word. *Boner.*

It was a few seconds before I realized my jaw was hanging and I had just about managed to swallow my heart back down to my chest.

Adrenaline flooded my body and the blood swished loudly in my ears in reaction to his flirty response. Excited and petrified, I could barely breathe.

Kane used to love shocking me as a child, but weirdly I had heard his voice in my mind as I read that word and I could hardly think of anything else all evening—not his boner—just Kane.

On autopilot, I began to clean and polish while I reflected on how his life had changed. I had a great deal of sympathy for him.

First his dad had been killed, then his mom died in a tragic accident less than a year later. I instantly connected with the emotions I'd felt the day my mom told me about it.

At the time my heart had splintered into pieces at the thought he'd been left alone.

We never knew his mom had passed until after the memorial service because no one ever contacted us; it was an acquaintance of my dad's that told him.

Last we'd heard he went to live with his mom's brother and his wife but I had no idea where. I guess, like he said, his cross was too much to bear, and cutting us out of his life limited his grief in some odd way.

After that day, I'd heard nothing from him for ten years and initially I grieved the loss of Kane from my life for a second time.

For several years there wasn't a day that passed that I didn't think about him at least once.

Then out of the blue on my twenty-first birthday, he sent a card to my parents' house. I had stopped thinking about him by then, but receiving that card, and knowing he still thought of me enough to know it was my birthday, had been the best gift ever.

It was the day after my birthday before the depression set in and his card left me feeling frantic because it had a Baltimore postmark on it.

To know he was still close by after all that time made me slightly crazy for a while. I'd spend hours searching the faces of every man on the streets in the hope of bumping into him one day.

It had never happened, and that handwritten envelope and card are still ranked amongst my most treasured possessions to this day.

A visual flashback to the image of my hands shaking as I tore the stark white envelope open, my little heart soaring when I saw the small, dusty pink birthday card inside. *To Someone Special,* the heading read.

On the front of the card the image was of two small children, a dark-haired boy and a little blonde girl, hugging. It could have been us back in the day.

Inside he'd written; *I saw this card and thought of you. I hope you have a fabulous day on your twenty-first birthday. I miss you, love, Kane.* I miss you. As soon as I read those words I dissolved into a blubbering mess.

Turning the card over, I expected a number or something, but there was nothing else. He left no way for me to contact him in return. The impact of the loss I'd felt all that time ago, after his mom had died, was fresh again.

A knock on the door brought me out of my reverie and I turned to stare at the bathroom door.

Wrapping my bathrobe tightly around me I headed to the front door to look through the spyhole and saw a delivery guy standing there with a big basket wrapped in cellophane.

I opened the door and the basket was laden with luxury booze, chocolate, and other assorted goodies in it. "Jo Carmichael?" he said, looking puzzled. I guess he was expecting a man.

"Yep, short for Josephine," I smirked, signing his little machine with a squiggle that was totally illegible. I told him to wait and closed the door, grabbed my purse, and took a ten-dollar bill back to him.

Smiling, he left with a whistle, in the direction of the broken elevator as I closed the door.

A small, red wine glass embossed company card was attached. *I'm guessing you weren't expecting any guests, but these aren't for you, they're M.I.N.E. Hands off, Carmichael. Don't even look at the malted balls, I've counted them.* His comment made me grin widely. He was still as funny as ever.

My heart squeezed again because he was reminding me of the times when my mom gave us a box of malted balls. He'd insisted on counting them out evenly to all of us. His gesture lifted some of my reservations and I was happy Kane may be back in my life.

However, I was also nervous and wary. I wanted answers to some questions, but I prayed if we worked it out, this time he'd be back for good.

Chapter Three

FROM A DISTANCE

*R*ain splashed noisily on the windshield of my car as the wipers swiped rhythmically back and forth. I glanced up at the dark sky.

Daylight was still a couple of hours away. I was on my way to the airport and I hadn't had a wink of sleep.

All night I'd been thinking about what I would say to Kane, until my emotional state was in meltdown.

Gripping the steering wheel with my sweaty palms, I flexed and closed my fingers trying to keep myself calm.

Adrenaline surged my anxiety every time I thought about his pending visit, causing my heart to flip-flop over and over again.

The arrivals lounge was packed with vacationers and business people, all mulling around either waiting for someone or trying to arrange rides home. I'd never been in a commercial airport as a civilian.

I'd always been part of relocation packages, so my tickets and baggage were handled by my dad. Actually, I'd never been out of Maryland again since we'd returned.

Stretching on tiptoe, with my heart in my mouth, I craned my neck, tilting my head from side to side as I searched frantically with each batch of new arrivals entering the hall. *This is crazy, what if we hate each other as adults*

The wait was killing me a little more with every second that passed. And the nerves in my belly made me want to pee. I'd arrived at the airport two hours before his plane touched down because, well, I hadn't seen him in such a long time.

Eager wasn't the word to describe my feelings, but they were mingled with apprehension and worry that I may have been too provincial for him since he'd become a rock star. I wasn't cool, I wasn't trendy, and I had no idea about bands and music.

The most conversation I'd ever had in regards to my opinion about songs was when I shouted over the DJ in a club to Candice, telling her that I liked the song.

Yet, there I was at the airport fangirling, and I couldn't remember a time when I'd felt so nervous—ever. My heartbeat was so erratic, calm one minute and racing the next.

Not even the fact that it was an ungodly hour of the morning could douse my excitement.

A long line of grey, tired faces passed me by. Passengers of all shapes, ages and sizes entered the arrivals hall looking exhausted from their travels.

I stopped looking for a moment when my eyes fixed on someone and I almost had a stroke as my nerves kicked in while butterflies danced in circles around my bladder.

When I looked back, someone of the same height and build as him came walking through the double doors pulling a heavily laden luggage cart.

Relief and disappointment washed over me in equal parts when I realized it wasn't him. I went back to looking.

Seconds later, there he was, striding purposefully out of the arrivals entrance looking not only fresh, but even more handsome in person than he'd looked on TV. With his head bent, he looked warily around him.

A thrill ran through me. Perhaps that was because I hadn't seen him face-to-face in all those years, perhaps it was a true fangirl moment, who knows.

I took a few precious seconds to observe him tugging his baseball cap down over his eyes to preserve his anonymity, while he scanned the crowd looking for me.

The moment he found where I was, there was a slight falter in his step before he came striding across the concourse toward the barrier.

Kane's whole face transformed from the don't-fuck-with-me expression that seemed to be his only protection in that moment, to one of sheer delight as he came closer.

Hesitantly, I stepped toward him not really knowing what to say. He grabbed my hand and squeezed it possessively as we walked the length of the steel crowd-control barrier together.

All the while he was smiling and staring directly into my eyes.

As soon as there was nothing between us, he dropped the heavy leather holdall he was carrying and pulled me tightly against his hard muscular chest.

"C'mere, you," he said gruffly, smiling down at me warmly. I looked up at his face that was only a few inches from mine and the twinkle in his eye said he was ecstatic to see me.

"Damn, look at you, Miss Hot Pants. You're stunning, baby. How did I ever let you get away?" he teased as he bent forward and placed his mouth close to my ear.

Embracing me again in a tight bear hug, his strong, warm hold brought a wave of deep-seated feelings that swelled up from the core of my body.

My throat constricted tightly as tears sprang to my eyes and I swallowed several times in an attempt not to let them flow.

It's hard to explain, but as soon as he held me like that, it made me feel whole. Like all those years since Germany there had been something missing.

Ever since I'd known Kane, I'd been drawn to him in a way I'd never known with anyone since. It confirmed something I had denied all of those years.

Kane Exeter was the boy that I had never let go. Bonding to him the way I had all those years ago must have had a huge influence on me because I'd never truly let my deep feelings go. He had never let me down until he cut me off at ten years old.

Somehow, Kane the boy had touched my soul in a way I couldn't describe, and no one else had ever come close since.

Yet, at the same time, the moment he hugged me as Kane the man, I feared that somehow he'd be the man who would break my heart.

My hands clung desperately to the back of his blue, button down shirt as I felt the warmth of his hard muscles flexing and the heat from his body radiating through the thin cotton material.

Rocking me from side to side where we stood, he said, "It's been far too long, baby, but now that I'm here with you it feels like I'm home." His gruff tone cracked a little and I realized I wasn't the only one loaded with emotions.

Pushing me to arm's length; his piercing blue eyes twinkled as the stark overhead lighting caught them. They roamed leisurely over my body and back up to my face where he silently held my eyes in a soul searching gaze.

Sexual feelings stirred inside me making me blush even though I sensed he was trying to get a rise out of me. Seconds later he gave me another sexy smile.

"Damn, Jo, you have no idea what you do to my heart. I've missed you so much," he admitted huskily, pushing my head to his mouth and kissing it reverently. It all felt too much.

Wrapped in his warmth I couldn't help but be that girl and inhale the bare skin on his neck. So manly and clean, his musky scent collided with a hint of his cologne. It was so enticing.

Before I knew what I was doing I had risen onto my tiptoes and kissed his cheek. His chin had a few days of unshaven growth and felt velvet soft against my lips.

Stepping back, he grinned and I could see the boy in him again as he grabbed my hand tightly and picked up his bag. "Let's get the hell out of here before someone recognizes me."

Tucking his chin in his chest he glanced furtively to the side and led me toward the multistory parking lot as if he knew where he was going. It turned out he did, it was the only parking at that particular airport.

The way he took control of the situation was definitely the same way I remembered him to be.

Memories of the boy I once knew flashed back in my mind as his firm grasp tugged me alongside him. Kane had been an alpha boy for as long as I'd known him. That hadn't changed.

Sliding into the passenger seat of my old red Chevy, Kane twisted his body and slung his holdall onto the worn cracked leather seat behind him.

Turning back, his eyes searched for mine and we stared at each other for a moment too long.

My heart fluttered and I felt myself blush like crazy while nervous feelings zipped through my body and pulled at my core.

The involuntary squeeze of my thighs made me look away as I fumbled and pushed the key into the ignition while he reached over and pulled the seat belt around him.

Kane's distraction gave me a moment to mentally gather myself, and once I heard him click it in place, my eyes flitted across just at the same moment he turned to look at me again.

"God, this feels great," he admitted as he adjusted himself in his seat and spread his legs wider. My eyes fell to his groin for a second just like the woman on TV's had and I suddenly had all the sympathy in the world for her trying to interview him in front of millions.

I was tempted to reach out and touch him, but looked up and stared straight ahead instead while I struggled to keep my hands to myself by gripping the steering wheel.

Turning my head, I glanced at him. "What does? Being in my Chevy?" I teased, trying to appear casual when inside I felt like someone had emptied my intestines into a blender.

I turned the key and fired the engine, my eyes riveted to the front so as not to show him how unnerved I was by his presence.

"Well yeah, I'd prefer the back seat though," he said, flirting outrageously with a cheeky grin. I shook my head and couldn't hide the smile at how opportunistic he was. He hadn't lost that since he was a kid either.

Kane laughed and shook his head at my smile, dipping his head just a little. I loved that look, it was an unguarded shyness and I imagined a rare sight to anyone who knew him.

"Nah, what I mean is home state and being right here with you—

it's where my heart is." He gave me a warm smile and looked directly at me.

I scoffed at his comment because if that were the case why had he never been in touch before now?

Out of the corner of my eye I saw him reposition himself to the side and lean his elbow on the back of his seat turning slightly toward me. He held his head in his hand and watched me while I drove. I was self-conscious but tried not to show it.

When I saw him crack a grin it almost melted my panties. A sudden surge of electricity coursed through my veins and I told myself to behave, because I wasn't used to fangirling, nor was I used to having anything other than platonic feelings for Kane.

My brain and my heart appeared to have a very short neuropath as far as Kane Exeter was concerned.

With every mile of the six mile journey home our conversation became less stilted as he told me what he'd been doing with his band.

Kane made me forget that I hadn't seen him in so long. His banter had me cracking up in laughter and by the time we reached my apartment I was feeling a little more comfortable at the prospect of spending time with him.

Kane's confidence was as high as I remembered and when we entered my home he didn't stand on ceremony when he spied the basket of goodies on the kitchen counter. It was the most decorative and fanciest thing in the whole apartment.

"You didn't open it yet?" he asked as he turned, looking puzzled.

"It wasn't mine *to* open," I stated flatly.

"Damn, Jo, you never used to do anything you were told. What happened to you?"

"You said it was for you, remember?"

"Oh baby, this is going to be fun, me giving you orders and you doing what I tell you," he chuckled as he snapped the seal on the Jack Daniels bottle and searched my cabinet for whiskey tumblers.

Pushing the glasses against my ice dispenser, two cubes of ice clinked their way into both glasses before he made his way over to the sofa with them like he owned the place.

"Wow, this couch is incredible, Jo. I'm gonna love it here. I don't know why you were worried about me staying. It's a cute place, and you've made it feel incredibly comfortable."

Placing the tumblers on the table he sat down and exhaled heavily. "God, this is amazing." His eyes glanced around the room while I stood in a daze watching him.

Since we'd entered my home I hadn't spoken and I hadn't moved. He left me speechless while I stared at the amazing whirlwind actions of the gorgeous guy I couldn't believe was here.

Kane continued to make himself at home and chatted like it had been yesterday since he'd seen me.

Within minutes he'd reached down and loosened his boots, toed one off and tugged at the other before standing again, shrugging himself out of his brown leather bomber jacket.

"Come over here and sit beside me," he said, patting the sofa. Suddenly my nerves were back and my heart flipped over in my chest. I didn't know if I *could* actually move at that point.

Drawing in a deep breath I focused on exhaling slowly. I was self-conscious he was watching as I took off my jacket and shoes.

Kane watched my every move. "Jesus, Jo, you'd make a fortune in a strip club. I've never seen a girl take off her outer clothing that slow before." I gave him a wide-eyed smile but thought inwardly, *I bet most women undress like their clothes are on fire while you're standing watching them.*

I took my time—stalling by grabbing some chips, even though it was breakfast time, as I tried again to control my nerves and look cool.

Kane looked away and began to pour the whiskey into the glasses but glanced back up as I neared him. "You're having a drink with me, babe. I don't care if you don't drink. The last thing I wanna do is drink alone."

I felt it was pointless explaining it was almost 7:00 am. After all he was a rock star. It was probably his normal bedtime so I waited patiently beside the sofa feeling awkward while

Kane screwed the top back on the bottle, maintaining eye contact with me and giving me that grin that made me weak.

As soon as he had a hand free, he grabbed mine and pulled me down gently onto the sofa beside him.

Twisting to grab the drinks from the table he turned toward me and handed me one. Gazing directly into my eyes he smiled slowly.

It felt like a seductive move and frightened the crap out of me. I had a boyfriend. "To old friendships rekindled." We clinked our glasses together before he threw his head back, the generous measure of amber liquid sliding down his throat. I sighed with relief that he wasn't making a move on me.

No sooner did I feel safe, he sat forward, placed his empty tumbler back on the table in front of him and leaned back into the sofa, sliding his hand around my shoulder, taking me with him.

All of a sudden I felt panicked and my resolve wavered—it all felt too much. Why would he want anything to do with me? *If I had really meant that much to him he'd have stayed in touch all these years.*

"So tell me all your news? What does Jo Carmichael do for fun?" he asked, stroking his thumb absent-mindedly across the material of my thin cardigan over my shoulder, and waggled his brow suggestively. His gaze was intense and I was so captivated. For a moment I almost swallowed my tongue at how hot he was.

The heat in my cheeks made me feel like some beacon in the fog, and I could tell by the wicked smirk he gave me he'd noticed it as well.

If I had known him just a teeny bit less I'd have called him a prick for behaving the way he was, all familiar, like we were more than just the acquaintance status we had, but I knew him just enough to know he wanted to make me feel uncomfortable.

His teasing of me was legendary. I swallowed a sip of whiskey and decided I'd have to be as shocking as him to make him back off.

"Hmm, sometimes I go dancing with a few friends. If I'm horny and drunk enough to find a guy attractive I bring him back here get him to fuck my brains out. Apart from that, not a lot," I said as matter-of-factly as I could and took another sip of my whiskey.

"Sounds like a normal night for me," he responded, straight-faced.

"You pick up guys to fuck you, Kane? Good to know," I retorted, and thought how smart my remark was.

"No guys, not yet anyway," he said without smiling, leaned forward and poured himself another drink. That response—I had no clue what to do with.

"So what do you do for fun?" I prompted, in my effort to shift the attention away from me.

Turning with the bottle poised to pour, he said, "Playing with my band, hanging out with cool chicks like you, and writing music. What else is there? Music, sex, and good conversation. It's what makes life worth living."

"So there's not a permanent girl in your life?"

"Yep," he said. I felt instantly deflated despite my 'not going there' pact I had made with myself. Sitting back against the sofa cushion he took a deep breath and turned his face toward mine. "You."

"Jeez, you are in a worse state than I thought if I'm the permanent girl. This is the first time I've seen you in twelve years, Kane," I responded, relieved because I knew he was joking. Then I felt uncomfortable that I was relieved. I was an emotional mess.

"I know...I'm sorry about that, but my life was totally wrecked when my mom died," he said, sounding remorseful. His sad expression made me want to kiss him. Not a passionate kiss—one to comfort him.

We both stared at each other in a long silence; then his lips slowly curved upward in a smile. "You've always been in my heart, Jo. If you cut it up into little pieces you'd find Jo Carmichael in almost every one. I adored you as a kid."

"And now?" I heard myself say with confidence. *What the fuck are you fishing for by asking that?*

"And now, I'd like to get closer to you again."

I swallowed roughly and almost choked. My mouth had gone dry.

"Huh. So you want to be my friend again? Do you think because you are a rock star it gives you a free pass to pick people up and put them back down again when you say so?" I was surprised at how curt I sounded.

"We're already friends, Jo. We just haven't seen each other in a while."

"A while...try more than half of my life, Kane. Friends do not discard people because it suits them."

"I know...and I'm sorry." Staring intensely into my eyes, I believed he was.

"Why? What do I have that no self-respecting rock star should go without?"

"Genuine friendship. I know you're not there because I'm on my way up and if I fall on my ass you'd still be there. You know how hard it is in this game I'm playing?"

"No, Kane, I don't, and I don't really care. Life isn't a game for me. It's hard work every day just to make ends meet.

Living independently means living from pay check to pay check. Some months there is something left over for a treat, some months there isn't quite enough to pay the rent."

"Do you need money, Jo? I'm happy to—"

"No. I don't want your money, Kane. I'd never want your money. I want your respect. You don't get to wander back into my life with your rock star swagger and your sexy-as-hell body and think I'll roll over."

"So you think I'm sexy, eh? And I'd never expect you to roll over. I'm the kinda guy that takes charge...if you know what I mean." He smiled his heart-stopping smile; the one that shows the dimple on his cheek and makes him almost irresistible to me. It made me realize I'd have to be stronger.

"Kane, stop that. What I'm trying to do here isn't easy. It's harder for a woman than a man to live independently. We struggle to find people to take us seriously in the workplace so earn less and work twice as hard for promotion. Except I work for my dad, and despite all his talk about equality in the work place, he's passed me over for promotion twice in favor of ex-servicemen like himself. Respect me and I'll do the same for you. You don't get to waltz in here and fuck with my emotions all over again. I'm not that glassy-eyed little kid that followed you around anymore. This is my life and it's not always easy, but I'm getting there. If you're back permanently, great, I'm stoked about that, and I've waited for twelve years for this day, but if you ever cut me out again, we're done."

"Got that loud and clear," he said as he cupped the back of my head and drew it to his lips. They pressed softly against my forehead as his cell began to ring, breaking the tender moment we were having.

Shifting to fish his phone from his front jeans pocket he checked it and stood up abruptly. "Sorry I have to take this," he said, before he wandered over to the window.

"Hey. How is he doing?" he asked. His face suddenly expressionless as he listened to the caller.

"Alright, keep me up to speed with any changes," he demanded in a clipped tone, and then hung up.

"Sorry, one of our security guys was injured after a gig in Phoenix last week. He had to wait for the swelling to go down and had reconstructive surgery on his ankle today."

"I'm sorry."

"Why? You didn't do it, did you?" he stated, as he gave me a smile that softened the way he'd been looking at me. "Quit apologizing for shit that's not your fault, that's the Jo I remember."

Slumping back down beside me he nudged my shoulder with his. I smacked his arm and he caught my hand, bringing it to his lips, kissing it softly. Another look passed between us and I quickly pulled my hand away like he'd bitten it.

I shot to my feet because the way he caressed my hand had felt too intimate and I had to put some space between us. My mind was stuck on the fact that I wasn't dealing with the kid I once knew, but a guy who knew women like the back of his hand.

"Do you want breakfast? I can scramble some eggs and make some toast," I said, busying myself in the kitchen. The way he continued to stare at me intensely before he answered knocked me off kilter. I had hoped my offer of breakfast would buy me some breathing space.

Chapter Four

BREAKFAST

"Scrambled eggs and bourbon...hmm...I'll pass, but I could manage a few rounds of toast." Turning away he poured yet another large whiskey into his tumbler.

"Kane, it's not even 8:00 am yet and you've had half the bottle. Do you have a drinking problem?"

"Nah, technically it's still my night. I haven't been to bed yet, and besides I'm a little intimidated by you," he said, grinning wickedly.

"By me? You're the one with the rock star tag, the sexy songs, and the hot band. It's me that should be feeling inadequate," I replied as I moved around the kitchen making toast and coffee.

"From what I can see, you're *definitely* not inadequate. You're as sexy-as-fuck, Jo. I'd do you in a heartbeat."

My hand stopped from beating the eggs and I stared, open-mouthed, at his comment. My heart catapulted from my chest to my throat then dropped to my belly before slamming against my ribcage.

"You did not just say that." I gave him an incredulous stare.

"Sorry, that thought just slipped out, but why fight a great connection?"

"You're not being interviewed now, Kane...there aren't any cameras in here," I stated, feeling awkward again.

"You've been watching me on TV?" He smirked after he said that and his eyes narrowed. "So you don't find me attractive? Maybe you need to drink more, like you said." He looked at me and chuckled.

"I was being crass, Kane. I don't do casual sex. Besides, I'm in a relationship." I had to shut his flirting down because he was hard to resist and Elliott was the perfect weapon to hide behind.

I turned away to take the butter from the fridge, and to catch my breath before turning back. Pouring the filtered coffee into the filter, I closed the lid and flipped the switch on.

When I looked directly at Kane I caught the disappointment on his face. He held my gaze and sat forward on the couch, clasping his hands between his open legs. I figured he looked a little bit taken aback by my news. Obviously, my mom hadn't told him that part of my life.

"Well fuck," he said quietly. "Where the hell is he? Why did he allow you to drive in the middle of the night to pick up a guy like me? I'd be all over you if you were mine, babe. What kinda guy is he? He should be taking better care of you."

"Elliott is overseas right now. There was something urgent that only he could deal with. He'll be back on the third. I'd just finished talking to him last night when you called."

"So he was the lucky guy you were wet and naked for, and he wasn't even in the country? Well hell, I'm jealous. I guess I left it too long and missed my chance," he muttered, in a mock deflated tone.

"It's just as well I remember how you were when we were kids. I can take the conversation we've just had seriously, but I'm not so easy to get a rise out of these days, Kane." I shrugged his comment off as I continued to butter the toast.

Pouring black coffee into two, white ceramic mugs I admitted to myself I couldn't read Kane as well as I did when we were children, and I wasn't confident what was fact and what was his sick sense of humor.

I made my way to the table and placed the stacked toast in front of him, and instead of sitting back down beside him on the sofa, I chose to sit on the floor on the opposite side of the low table.

"Drink the coffee," I prompted.

"Yes, ma'am." He nodded and chuckled while reaching for the Jack

Daniels bottle again. My hand covered his, "No, Kane, coffee," I said sternly, because I was concerned at how quickly he had drunk what he had.

Slowly he took his hand off the bottle and picked the mug up, cupping his hands around the warm pottery and hugging it close to his mouth.

"So...how serious is it with Elliott?" he enquired, his blue eyes looking straight into mine.

"We're still new—six weeks, but he's been away for almost one."

"You're into him?" he asks quietly.

"I like him a lot, yes."

"Is it love?" His inquisitive eyes pierced mine, holding the gaze a little too long so I looked away.

"Hmm...I still have to think about that so I guess I'm not there yet," I answered honestly, looking at him, even though I wasn't completely comfortable answering that question.

Kane stared at me in silence and our connection was awkward because his face was expressionless. It was hard to read what he was thinking.

"And he's not back until after my gig on Monday night?" he queried.

"No. The third of December. Wednesday."

"So we have two days together with no interruptions?" Raising his brow, my heart flipped over at the suggestive wide-eyed stare he gave me and I had to dig deep. I was no pushover with men and normally I saw past all the bullshit, devious ways they had, but they weren't Kane.

My heart ached for the boy I knew, and feared for the man he'd become. Somehow I'd have to resist him and be careful not to blur the lines of our adult friendship.

"To do what?"

"Have fun. Can I take you to a club?"

"No, Kane. I don't want to be classed as one of Kane Exeter's groupies."

"I'd never let them do that to you," he said, sitting forward on the edge of the sofa with a concerned look on his face.

"And how would you stop that, exactly? Any woman you are with from now on is going to be tagged with that label. You're naïve if you think otherwise. Plus, I have Elliott to think about."

"Will you tell him I'm here?" I thought for a moment and decided I would. If Kane was back in my life it would come up sooner or later. The connection we'd had as kids came up one night when we were talking about our childhoods over dinner, so Elliott knew how strongly Kane's friendship had affected me.

"Of course. I don't keep secrets, and you and I are just friends, right?"

Kane closed his eyes a fraction too long before opening them wide to stare back at me. "Right," he agreed. After he accepted we'd hang out at home, we began to reflect on our pasts and ate every crumb of toast before I yawned, stretching my arms above my head.

"Wow, those carbs have sapped the last ounce of energy I had. We need to go to bed," I said.

Kane's slouched position on the sofa looked pretty mellow, but his head snapped around in my direction.

"Lead the way," he said, giving me another trademark smirk and caught my hand in passing. I pulled it back sharply.

"I meant you there and me in my bed," I replied, gesturing with both hands to the sofa and giggled.

"Ah, gotcha. Can I just say that this friendship is not very beneficial right now?"

The way his voice rose in question made my core tweak with interest. It felt uncomfortably wrong that I should have such feelings when I was with Elliott.

"Kane, there's the door, I'm sure you'd find plenty of women to take up that offer," I quipped, gesturing my thumb in the direction of it.

"True. All true, I'm afraid," he replied, with a wry grin. "Pity my sights are set on the unavailable," he scoffed, winking at me and my heart raced again.

"On that note, I'm going to bed. If I were you, I would too."

Without waiting for a reply I stood up to head for my bedroom, but before I could get far he stood up as well and pulled the hem of his shirt out of his jeans.

"Sure. Now there's an offer I can't refuse. Lead the way, babe," he dared, with a cocky swagger in his voice. Glancing back, I gave him a puzzled stare. "What? You said you were going to bed, and if you were me I should too. So..." Holding his hands out he paused, sporting that flirtatious grin of his again.

"I meant the sofa, Kane." I smiled at him and shook my head as I passed him by. "Really, those moves of yours are ancient, it's a wonder you get into any woman's panties with lines like that."

"So teach me. What do I have to say to get into yours?" he provoked, catching my wrist and holding it firmly.

The way he hit on me like that took me by surprise, and although his line was corny, it had turned me on to think that in some way he really wanted me.

"Enough, Kane. I'm tired. Get some sleep and I'll see you later," I asserted firmly, walking over to the linen closet. I handed him a clean comforter, sheet and pillow. "Bathroom is the second door down the hall. See you when I get up." I was surprised at how he had made my stomach tense in all the right ways.

Kane was sexually confident and because I knew enough about him, he wasn't coming off as leery. If anyone else had behaved the way he had with me, I'd have run a mile. Getting into bed with that thought, I pondered, *what if I didn't stop feeling so attracted to him?* How would I control the feelings he stirred in me.

Someone was talking when I woke up and initially I lay listening, trying to get my bearings, and remembering that Kane was out there in my sitting room. He was obviously talking to someone on the phone. His tone seemed pretty curt when I heard, "Sure I'll tell her when she gets up."

I slid out of bed and padded into my bathroom, turned on the shower and stepped under the warm water allowing the powerful shower jets to bring me back to life. I had no idea what time it was, but I was thirsty.

After I'd gone to bed, my heart wouldn't stop pounding as I mulled over the conversations we'd had when Kane had flirted outrageously about having sex with me. I found myself fantasizing what it would be like to kiss him.

With the same thought creeping back into my mind in the shower I quickly shrugged it aside, turned off the faucet and reached for the towel.

Once dried, I grabbed my bathrobe and wrapped it tightly around me.

A knock on the bedroom door startled me and I spun in the direction of it just in time to see Kane pop his head around it. "Coffee?"

"Thanks, I'll be right out," I explained, tugging at the ties on my robe to ensure they were secure.

Kane had his cell phone hooked up to a laptop and was busy typing when I walked into the open plan kitchen.

"Hey, you look great," he complimented, before looking back at what he was doing. I looked like a drowned rat with my blonde hair wet and straggling from the shower.

"Coffee's on the counter. Black right? Like this morning?" He'd taken note how I liked my coffee. "Elliott called by the way," he mentioned with a sly smirk and continued to type. "I told him you were still sleeping." My heart stopped for like a millisecond.

"You answered my cell?" I shrieked, my high-pitched question showing how stressed I felt about that.

"Sure. It was loud and you were asleep. Would you have preferred I cut off the call?" I wasn't sure why I felt guilty. We were only friends after all. Unless maybe, it was because I'd let my mind wander in the wrong direction about Kane.

"What did you say to him?"

"I told you what I said."

"And that was it? Nothing else?"

"Well, no. He asked who I was and what I was doing in your apartment while you were asleep. I explained I was in town for a gig and you had kindly agreed to put me up."

"Yeah, like he'd really believe that, Kane. He's not stupid. Why would a rock star forgo staying in a fancy hotel to stay in a dingy apartment?" I asked, before realizing I'd spoken the truth.

"I don't really know. I was wondering that myself. Do you see any orgies going on here? Jesus, Jo, we're friends, aren't we? That's what friends do; spend time together. Call the guy back for Christ's sake. I never said anything wrong. Just told him how it was, that's all!"

Elliott was doing the same, having company, he'd told me that already. The last call we'd had he'd talked about getting a little more serious but we weren't exclusive yet, there was no firm commitment talked about.

I picked up my phone and called him back as I wandered into my bedroom for some privacy.

"Hey. You rang?"

"Indeed. Kane Exeter is staying at your apartment? I thought you weren't in touch anymore?" His angry tone pissed me off.

"Listen, Elliott, I had as much of a clue about this as you did. He rang last night after I got off the phone with you and told me he was playing in town. He asked if he could come and spend some time with me."

"And after twelve years you said, sure come on over."

"Pretty much. We were close friends once, Elliott."

"Open your eyes, Josie, no woman is just 'friends' with Kane Exeter."

"What does that mean?" I asked indignantly.

"The guy is a serial seducer. I've seen him in action. He could charm the panties of the most frigid of women."

"Well we both know I'm not frigid, Elliott, and thank you for the vote of confidence," I said, livid that he could make such a snap judgment about either of us.

"Did he tell you he wished me luck in keeping you?"

"Elliott, if you knew him like I did once, you'd know he was testing you."

"To my limit," he huffed, exhaling heavily into the handset.

A long pause killed the conversation before he spoke again.

"Right. Spend time with him, Josie. Do what you need to do with him. I'm not happy that you took another man into your home as soon as I was out of the picture. I need to know if you are worth my time or whether Kane Exeter will always be on your mind. I heard the way you spoke about him that night when we had dinner at the Drake Hotel."

"What exactly are you getting at, Elliott? Because I'm damned if I know!" I thought his reaction was absurd, but the anger in his tone sounded possessive and more than a little demanding.

"I don't share, physically or emotionally. Spend time with him. I should be home on Tuesday. Call me then if you're still interested." Click.

What the! I stood, staring at the cell in my hand like he might pop out of it and shout I'd been punked. I wondered what the hell Kane had said to Elliot, because it was only last night that the guy had told me he thought he was falling in love with me, and now he shut me down like that.

I flung my bedroom door wide and stomped angrily toward Kane, waving my cell at him. "You're an ass, you know that?"

"Correction, a fine ass," he replied with a soft chuckle as he closed the lid on his laptop, giving me his full attention.

"This is no laughing matter, Kane Exeter. Elliott just broke up with me. On the fucking phone no less. You've only been here a few hours and my guy has ditched me already?"

"He did? Woo–hoo," he cheered in a humorous tone, but when he saw how hurt I was his whole demeanor changed and he cleared his throat. A genuine look of concern in his eyes told me he hadn't known I was serious before. He threw his hands up and his brow knitted. "Really? What the fuck did he do that for? What the hell is wrong with that guy?"

"That's what I'm hoping you can tell me. We were fine on the phone until you spoke to him and suddenly we're on a break?" I shrieked. I felt pretty pissed at him.

Kane huffed out a sharp breath and stood up. "Jesus, Jo. How old is this guy? Sixteen?"

"Almost thirty," I answered with a note of sarcasm.

"And he's calling all the shots because he's a control freak? Has he never dealt with a partner or lived with anyone? There's something off about that. Trust issues or something." His lips formed a thin line as he walked over to where I was standing and held me by my upper arms.

My skin tingled where he touched and distracted me for a second until I saw him bending to my eye level as he stared seriously into my eyes.

"Jo, I swear to you that I said nothing that should have made him react like that." Conscious of his warm, firm grip on my arms, I felt the power of conviction behind what he said.

To confirm his belief he squeezed my arms a little tighter. "Come over here and sit down. I'll re-enact the whole damn call for you," he retorted in exasperation as he tried to convince me.

Moving me toward the sofa, he positioned me in the center of it and picked up my cell from the countertop. He made a big deal of laying it on the table where it had been before I went to bed. I bunched my brow wondering what he was doing.

Seconds later he started singing the ring tone on my phone, "Run The World" by Beyonce, and began to dance like she did in her music video, gesticulating wildly at my cell phone.

His behavior was so unexpected and his animation so comical that a reluctant chuckle escaped my throat. I was so damn mad at him but couldn't help the smile that curved my lips.

Fully immersed in his task, he sang the first verse then turned his head pointedly at my bedroom door making exaggerated glances in the direction of it and then at the phone. He placed his index finger to his lips as he still sang, and pointed down at my cell.

By this time, I was struggling to keep my face straight and bit back a grin. Next, he picked up the phone. "Hello. It's me..." He answered the phone singing the first words of Adele's song 'Hello' and I couldn't restrain my laughter even when he raised an eyebrow.

Continuing like the pro he was, he stood to his left with the phone to his ear and asked, "Who's that?" Then turned to the right and answered himself, "A friend." Turning back to the left he said in all seriousness, and a low aggressive tone, "A fucking friend?" I was almost breathless with laughter and I don't know how he contained himself, but he remained resolute in his performance, alternating sides to represent both parties of the conversation. "No fucking, just a friend," he said in a growly voice, then added for my benefit, "Although I may have added that knowing myself as well as I do, I would have been a willing participant, but that fucking someone was difficult when only one of us felt that way."

"You said that?" I asked in disbelief. I sat open-mouthed digesting that information.

"Sure, do you want to hear the rest or not?" His face was deadpan while he stood with his hands on his hips.

"Sorry, continue," I urged, waving my hand, totally enthralled by his re-enactment. I definitely had a better idea why Elliott was so pissed off. If I'd been on the receiving end of Kane's call and thousands of miles from home when such a charismatic rock star was with my partner, I'd have been pissed off as well.

"Elliott then became all caveman and said something like, *she's mine*, and I replied, oh oh oh oh oh oh oh oh oh...because I was trying to stay with the Beyonce theme. He called me an asshole after that and told me to leave you the fuck alone. Oh, then he said again you were *his* girl, and that I should get the fuck out of your apartment. So...I replied...good luck on keeping Jo with an attitude like that. Where's your sense of humor?"

There was silence between us for a second then his eyes met mine and he shrugged his shoulders giving me a wicked grin. There was no remorse whatsoever in what he had done. He wandered slowly toward me and sat gently on the sofa beside me.

"I may be wrong, but I think that's the point where he hung up on me. I can't be sure because the coffee had started overflowing as I poured extra water in the top of the machine after finding it a bit strong earlier. I placed your phone on the side to deal with that. So I guess he really doesn't have a sense of humor. How could you want to be with a guy like that, Jo? You were always a fun girl. He must have something going for him. Does he have big dick?" He nudged my shoulder with his and chuckled. My face grew red with his question and he spoke again to cover my embarrassment.

"Listen, like you said, It's a new relationship. If you really like him and he likes you, he'll be back. And if he rolls over and plays dead that easily, he's got no place in my girl's life, capish? Frankly, if you don't want him after that, I'd be overjoyed. No guy should ever treat you like you are an object."

Chapter Five

CHINESE

It was 2:00 pm and I was starving. Gurgling noises were coming from my stomach and when I caught sight of myself in the mirror in the hallway, I flinched at the sorry state I looked. I padded through to the kitchen and opened the fridge, which was embarrassingly empty.

I grabbed some cookies from Kane's luxury basket and had just taken a bite when there was a knock at the door. Without hesitation Kane jumped up and looked through the spyhole.

"Damn, Jo, I think it's that dude from the phone call. He has an axe," he joked, as he opened the door.

A delivery boy with a large box of Chinese food was standing in the doorway. "Fuck me. Kane Exeter," he announces in a startled voice at finding the rock star in my apartment.

"Sorry, dude, I'm tapped out with this chick, she's insatiable." He grins wickedly looking over at me. I buried my head in my hands mortified he would say such a thing. "Can I take a rain check on that offer?" he asked, continuing to insinuate he'd be up for that.

The poor delivery guy didn't know what to do with himself. He obviously thought Kane was serious.

"That wasn't an offer, dude, it was a figure of speech," he mumbled as he passed over the Styrofoam cartons of warm food. Kane chuckled and explained he was only busting his balls as he pulled a few new crisp fifty dollar bills from his wallet.

Shoving them into the delivery boy's hand, the teenager gasped, "Thanks, dude, much appreciated. Can I have a selfie with you?"

Kane obliged, both of them doing that rock salute thing with their fingers and their tongues sticking out for the photo. Once they were done the teenager muttered, "Have a nice day."

Mirroring the guy's parting words Kane closed the door with his foot and carried the boxes to the countertop. "Chinese okay? I wasn't sure what to get because we skipped breakfast," he muttered while pulling out carton after carton of food.

"Did you invite someone else?" I questioned, because I couldn't imagine all that food just for the two of us.

"Nope, I figured we could have some for lunch, pick at it later, and if there's any left we could eat it for dinner. If not, I'll order something else." He surprised me by his willingness to eat leftovers considering how wealthy and exposed he must have been to the best cuisine, especially as he attended fancy parties and music industry dinners.

If I'd been nervous about how the day was going to go after Elliott's call, I needn't have worried. Well, not about the first part of it anyway.

Eating tons of Chinese food and reminiscing about our childhood had brought Kane and I closer in one day than I'd imagined it could.

By the evening our years apart had mostly slipped away, each of us filling the other in on what we'd been up to and who had been our main influences in life.

Mine were mainly authors as I was an avid reader in my spare time, whereas Kane had gone to live with an uncle who was in a band, and when he was old enough his uncle had taken him along to his gigs.

Being a part of that scene had cultivated his love for rock music, and deciding he loved that kind of environment, he tried his hand at singing.

A few small gigs later some guy approached him with an offer to be the lead singer in his band. The rest is history. Andrew Store was the lead guitarist in his band, and once he'd found his final member in Kane, their band Hedonism was formed.

When Kane talked about Hedonism his eyes shone with excitement. His enthusiasm for what he did oozed from every sexy pore on his body.

His facial expressions and stories made me feel like I was a part of what he'd been doing, totally mesmerizing me by his ability to recount a lot of what had been happening in a female friendly way.

I'm sure that some of what went on, actually a lot of what went on, wasn't something he'd have been able to share with me unless I'd been a horny guy. References to groupies and tales of things that had happened were no doubt tamped down for my ears.

Gradually, the spotlight fell on me again, so to speak, and my life felt extremely dull in comparison. I'd worked in the office at my dad's security firm from the day I'd left school at eighteen years old.

After almost five years I was still a PA to a shitty manager that my father thought walked on water, all because he'd been a navy seal.

I figured he must have been amazing in that role because if that part was true, from my personal experience of him, I knew it was possible to be a hero in one job and an ass in another.

The money Dad paid me was pretty decent for someone with only a high school diploma. Without a college degree, any other job outside of my dad's company would have been less money for my paygrade.

As the evening wore on our conversation made its way around to talking about his parents.

That subject definitely wasn't easy for him, but Kane said it helped to talk to me because he didn't have to explain everything leading up to what had happened with his father, I already knew.

When he told me about his mom, the anguish and sorrow on his face from the memory of that time gutted me and I wept openly. I couldn't imagine how difficult life must have been to have no parents by the age of thirteen.

Any anger I held in my heart about him not contacting me dissipated during that conversation and all my self-consciousness disappeared.

My knee-jerk reaction to him sharing that harrowing time was to crawl onto the sofa and cradle his head in my arms. I kissed the top of his head, just like he had mine, and forgave any hurt he'd made me feel. It was nothing compared to the hurt he'd carried himself at the loss of his parents.

Minutes passed where we didn't speak. I stayed holding him that way in my arms, inhaling the scent of him and absorbing every conceivable trace of him into my lungs.

My head was filled with memories, good and bad, until my knees ached and I had to change position.

"Thank you, no woman has just held me like that without motive since my mom died," he said, with a slow smile. "You have no idea what that just did for me, Jo." Lumps formed in my throat, one after another, and I fought hard to swallow each one down and not become the focus of the moment.

"Anytime. Please don't cut me off again now that I have you back. I couldn't go through that again...I won't go through that again. Losing contact was painful, Kane. My life wasn't easy for a long time after your letters stopped, but I understand better why it happened," I said, smoothing the soft, thick hair on his head. I stared into his beautiful, sad blue eyes that were so dull and full of painful memories.

Sitting back on my heels on the sofa, I saw his mouth twist in thought as his hand reached up and cupped my face. "I can't believe you're right in front of me, Jo. Having you here...touching you like this has soothed an ache in my heart that I've carried with me all this time." I could feel the sincerity in his words by his wistful tone of voice and the way he gently grazed my cheek with his thumb.

"Why now? I mean if your band hadn't been playing in town, would you ever have reached out?"

Closing his eyes, Kane swallowed hard and I watched his Adam's apple bob up and down before his eyelids slowly opened, looking at me with a sad half-smile.

"God knows I wanted to see you; many times, but I guess I felt bad for what I'd done and perhaps I needed the right excuse, something that would help me be accepted again. I don't know, Jo, maybe I never felt good enough. I left it so long that I couldn't see you being able to forgive me for what I had done. That definitely held me back. Often, I'd play the likely scenarios of how you'd react in my mind...and every time you'd reject me. Up until now I never thought my heart could take anymore hurt, so that pretty much kept me away."

"Oh, Kane, did you think I was the kind of friend that would do that? I loved you so much then. My heart still aches when I think of what happened...having you here it still does...just like it did the last time I had to leave you."

"I still love you, Jo. No matter how much time has passed I've never stopped loving you. I never forgot you. I've carried that little girl in here since the day we parted all those years ago in Germany," he admitted, pointing at the center of his chest. Suddenly my throat tightened and I swallowed back tears again.

Reaching out I pushed myself up off the sofa and headed over to the fridge. "I think I need wine," I stated, trying not to let myself get completely overwhelmed by his admission.

Pulling the fridge door open I was glad for a moment where he couldn't see me.

Taking a bottle of cheap Pinot Grigio from the door storage compartment, I turned to him and asked, "You?" as I gestured at him by holding the bottle where he could see it.

"Just a glass and ice, there's still some JD here. Although, would you mind if I took a shower first?" he asked. I then realized he was still wearing the same clothes he'd worn when I picked him up at the airport.

"Oh jeez, I'm sorry. Sure, you can use my bathroom. The shower in the other bathroom isn't working properly."

Walking to the linen closet I pulled out two clean, fluffy towels for him while he sifted around in his holdall for his washbag.

Handing him the towels, he started off down the hall then turned to look at me. "Thanks, Jo...for letting me spend time with you."

I nodded, unable to speak because my throat was clogged again. I realized that even though Kane was becoming a huge star, there probably weren't many people who really got him the way I did. He had remained humble so far and I was in awe that I'd mattered that much to him for him to come back and make amends.

Every minute apart had been worth it if it had helped him deal with his parents' deaths in some way.

Almost an hour after he'd gone to shower he came back to the sitting room looking incredible. It was the second time in twenty-four hours I'd almost choked. I had kind of expected a fully clothed version of the sexy, hot, rock star that wandered back from the bathroom.

Wrapped in my powder blue towel his smooth, inked, torso was cut and ripped like something one would see on a Greek statue: six-pack abs, tight pecs, and a defined V in the muscle group running from his waist to below the towel.

I dragged my eyes away from the towel and tried to focus on the hot ink markings all over his arms. A huge Native American tribal tattoo covered his left shoulder, the bold ink etched perfectly against his golden shiny skin.

My eyes fell to the towel again, noticing it was not wrapped very tightly around him. *A girl can only take so much teasing.* I could see a definite bulge in the front. I was about to look away when he caught me looking.

"Busted," he said, grinning. "Things change and people grow, Jo." He pulled the towel tighter, the way he brazenly outlined his genitals shocked me. "Thank God, they grow," he chuckled, looking down at himself.

My eyes automatically followed his gaze and I realized what he'd done before he took his hands away. "Sorry, the rock star in me snuck out for a minute," he said, looking sheepish. "Did I turn out the way you imagined?"

How the fuck am I supposed to answer that now? Damn, I'd never have imagined him to look like that. No one could have imagined that level of perfection. Silky, dark brown hair; strong jawline; gorgeous mouth with incredible lips, and straight white teeth.

Attractive didn't begin to describe how he looked. Menacingly broody with his dark eyebrows, and lashes contrasting with his ice-blue eyes—his look had alpha etched all over it.

Perusing him caused more than a few strange twinges in-between my legs with every lingering look between us. He wasn't a pretty boy in the least, he was handsome.

Stunningly handsome; the kind of attraction that made you want to pull up a chair because your legs would be tired from standing so long.

Everything he wore fitted him to perfection. His commanding looks, his assertive personality, his popularity and his amazing talent.

"What makes you think I imagined how you looked?" I asked, a little breathless at the intensity of his gaze.

We stood a few feet from each other but it felt too close. I could feel when the heat crept into my cheeks again because I was lying through my teeth. Of course I'd done that—many times. None of my images even came close to how he looked and that made me think I had a very limited imagination.

"Oh come on, Jo, you must have," he said with a wicked smirk as he held onto my gaze. "With the connection we had as kids, I know you did. You've crossed my mind thousands of times. I used to lie in bed and wonder what you looked like, pictured that smile." He grazed his finger across my lips.

"I loved how your nose wrinkled in distaste at something you didn't like...wondered how that looked now, how you dressed, what your voice sounded like now." He stopped and swallowed, then said more quietly, "I wondered if you had cut your hair...I'm so happy to see you kept it long. I've always loved how it hangs down your back," he admitted, unabashedly.

I felt my whole body respond to his intimate words about his thoughts and it took me a couple of seconds to realize what his finger was doing and the air in the room seemed to thicken between us. What was happening had nothing to do with two old friends getting reacquainted anymore. It was something far more than that. I just didn't know what.

Feelings stirred inside me that I had no right to feel. I was with Elliott. My shame began to fight with my feelings, and as if he knew, Kane snickered at my embarrassment and smiled affectionately.

"Come here," he murmured, in a volume that was barely above a whisper. Coaxing me toward him, he held out his hand. "I don't bite, Jo," he mocked, and my heart rate shot through the roof as I took a step closer to him.

Barely a foot of air separated us when he reached down and took my right hand, placing it over his heart.

My fingers tingled and my core pulsed as my hand became trapped between his pecs with his palpable heartbeat and the warmth of his soft palm. Such a small gesture, but the effect of him holding it there felt calming for some reason.

Spreading my hand on his chest I wallowed in the smoothness of his skin from the shower. I could smell the clean fresh soap from my body wash mingling with the minty toothpaste on his breath. I wanted to wrap my arms around him; no, I wanted to climb inside to experience everything about him.

Commanding my attention, he spoke, "As long as this beats in my chest I'll remember you, Jo. Can you feel it? You have been in my dreams so many times over the years I feel like I'm dreaming now," he murmured as he continued to hold my hand against his chest. "Did you ever dream of me?"

Glancing up at his face, he was a good six inches above me. The deeper meaning in his conversation wasn't lost on me. I nodded slowly, a pang of sadness jolting my heart. "Yes," I whispered. "I did, but they weren't dreams I'm eager to recall. I used to worry about you when I was younger and I guess some of those transferred into my subconscious at times. They weren't dreams, Kane, they were nightmares."

The magic of the moment we had been sharing was disrupted by my honesty. A look of dismay flitted across Kane's face.

Closing the space between us completely, he pulled me flat against his chest. My cheek rested on his hard pec muscle and my heartbeat rose instantly in reaction.

Strangely, for all our years apart; that moment was the most comfortable I'd ever felt around him. Bending his head nearer to my ear, his grip tightened and his large hand splayed over my back. "God, I'm so sorry, I had no idea—"

"Stop, it's fine. It's just that we used to be so honest with each other. I didn't want to start lying now."

Kane took a deep breath, breathing me in just like I had done with him each time we had hugged or comforted each other. He showed no sign of releasing me from his arms.

The familiarity we shared during those moments felt pretty

unnerving. One day I had watched him on TV, flirting for sport with beautiful eye-candy on a music channel, and the next, he stood in my sitting room wearing nothing but a towel, telling me things about his feelings that I had no idea what to do with.

Stepping back, I created some distance between us again and folded my arms.

"Look, Kane, I'm happy you're back but all this talk is pretty seductive. This is me, Jo. The girl you saw on the same level as you from our childhood. So why do I get the feeling you are trying to seduce me?"

I had no idea if what I was saying was the right thing at the time, but I was falling for the same things I had mocked him for in my head when I had seen him play the woman on the screen.

"And why do I get the feeling that you would be uncomfortable with that, Jo? We're not kids anymore. Look at us, we're both consenting adults, and we have a mountain of history together. I came to see the girl I loved from my childhood, but since the moment I heard your voice I had this longing to get to know the woman you became. I want to mend fences with you and have you back in my life."

"I am back, Kane, so you don't have to try to seduce me. I know how charismatic and charming you are. I see through your wit and flir-tatious teasing; they were some of the things I loved about you, but please...don't play with me like that. Not now."

"Is that what you think I'm doing? Who says I'm playing? When you sent me your picture my dick twitched in my pants and the skin on my balls tightened. It felt almost orgasmic, babe. You think I get that often?" He shook his head. "Standing here with you right now...I don't know what this is, but all I want to do is kiss you. I'm trying hard not to do that, babe. I don't want to ruin whatever this is. But...if I'm honest, it scares the shit out of me because I'm normally a no-ties kinda guy. I'm a musician in a band, I fuck and duck. I'm going to be out on the road in a few days' time and girlfriends have never been a priority. I've never found anyone I wanted to be with. Yet, I'm standing in this moment with you...missing you already, and I just got here. So... help me out, Jo, because I really don't know what the fuck is going on here."

Chapter Six

JUDGE AND JURY

Is he playing me? Everything was suddenly too serious and I pushed back. "Whoa. Where did that come from?" Kane was messing with my sanity and I knew I'd be ruined if I didn't get a grip on my feelings.

"I get it, there's something intense going on for the both of us right now, a flood of memories to a time when we were innocent and safe. That's bound to make us think that things were better than they actually were, but I'm not going to climb into bed so you can fuck me."

"Damn, Jo. How well you know me, eh? You'd rather believe what you read than find out who I am? Maybe you and Elliott do deserve each other, 'cause you're both just as quick to make judgments about me."

His comment took me back, I'd said virtually the same thing to Elliott earlier, but I felt that Kane was way ahead of me at playing mind games.

"You're good, Kane, I'll give you that. You had me believing that you were here for me. That you wanted to make up for lost time and get close to me again. Or wasn't that the plan at all? Did you think...oh I know, I'll ring that little chick I used to know from when we were kids, it'll be fun to fuck her and less effort than picking up a groupie while I'm in town? Well I have news for you. You can gather up your shit and get the fuck out of my apartment. I'm not a fuck and duck kinda girl. You got the wrong woman for that, Kane."

My whole body shook with temper at the thought I was being played. I stood with my hands on my hips breathing deeply while I tried to prevent myself falling apart in front of him.

I was mostly angry at myself for allowing him to get under my skin and romanticizing our reunion. It had to be that otherwise what he had said wouldn't have mattered so much. I was no match for the adult Kane Exeter.

The level of intimacy he had built up over the previous five minutes had me in no doubt he would have crossed the line between us. If I hadn't come to my senses in time I may well have let him.

"Jesus, Josie," he said, running his hands through his silky dark hair. My gaze caught the flex of the various muscle groups on his body as they rippled when he moved. I was annoyed with myself when another kind of ripple altogether ran through *my* body.

Rarely had he ever called me Josie and that made me hesitate for a second as I heard the frustration in his voice. The last thing I wanted was to be turned on by him, but as furious as I was I couldn't help but drool at how appealing he looked.

When he turned and our eyes met again, his expression was the nearest to shame I'd ever seen. He then shocked me as he did something that stopped me dead in my tracks.

Kane dropped his towel and walked away from me toward his holdall, crouched down and pulled out a fresh pair of jeans.

My eyes were riveted to his strong, muscular back and the amazing contours of his body from behind. Shaking his jeans out, he threaded one leg in then the other. He slid them slowly up his calves to his thighs then slowly over his perfectly defined ass, pulled them up and turned to face me as he buttoned up the fly.

Walking back over to me he put his hand out to touch my shoulder and I shied away, moving out of his reach altogether and sat on the sofa. He followed and slowly took a seat next to me.

The pained look on his face said it all and he closed his eyes for a second. I don't know what it was but something in the look he gave me made me feel ashamed. When he opened his eyes, he bit his bottom lip giving me a sad smile.

"Jo, I'm truly sorry. This isn't at all how I wanted this to go," he explained, shaking his head. "I came back to find you because after all these years I know I did the wrong thing by dropping you from my life. You were one of the best pieces of my childhood, and as young as I was, you have been the only girl with a place in my heart since then. Your sweet face is the one that's always risen to the surface with every happy childhood memory. The last thing in the world I want to do is fuck with your feelings."

Nothing I could have said would have been the right thing at that moment. If I had spoken I would have confessed to everything I had felt since the moment he hugged me at the airport.

"Maybe you're right, maybe this thing in my head is a fantasy and I've taken this opportunity to play it out. You know what? Maybe we should just get drunk and forget this whole damned conversation."

My heart sunk in disappointment, yet I understood. Why would he be attracted to me when there are so many other better looking girls out there on his wavelength?

For a moment I thought about continuing with my demand for him to leave, but without the added stress of him standing in a small blue towel and nothing else, I 'd relented because I wasn't ready to watch him walk out of my life again without us being in a good place.

I knew I'd never be ready to do that. So I backed down and stupidly thought getting drunk seemed like the only action to change the course of our day.

I'd noticed that both bottles of expensive white wine amongst Kane's goodies had made their way into the fridge, so I grabbed a bottle and lifted two, long-stemmed glasses from the side cabinet.

While I was doing that, Kane searched my cabinets for some snacks.

A pout confirmed that he came up with nothing much as I usually hit the store on payday for luxuries. I would eat them in the first week and the rest of the month I lived on mircowave popcorn as a treat.

Deciding to start on another carton of cold noodles, Kane sat cross-legged, Indian style on the floor by the low table.

Joining him on the floor, I knelt down beside him. Once again, after a couple of glasses of wine the tension I had been feeling ebbed away and I began to relax.

After an hour we were on much safer ground when his stories had me rolling around laughing. Descriptively, he recalled funny situations he'd been in with his band and his storytelling was so amazing I felt as if I were there.

When I poured the last of the wine into our glasses, Kane stood up, swayed unsteadily then reached over and grabbed his phone.

Giggling at him trying to focus on the screen, I watched as he pulled his cell to his face and closed one eye, tapped a number out then lifted the phone to his ear. "What's this address again?"

Without even asking what he wanted it for I gave it to him; he relayed it line for line to whoever was on the other end, followed by, "Two bottles of tequila, two of white rum, and two bottles of JD. Chips, nuts and whatever the fuck you think we need for a party. Nah, fuck, no drugs...that shit fucks with my artistic flow," he snickered, before he hung up without giving credit card details or anything.

Staring down at me he smirked crookedly. "While the bar's being restocked I'm just gonna..." He gestured his thumb toward the bathroom and I watched him from the weird angle where I was sitting on the floor as he staggered away, bounced off the wall and disappeared from sight.

I smirked, feeling pretty mellow and drowsy so I lay back and stared up at the ceiling for a few seconds before closing my eyes, happy that we had gotten past the weird shit.

When I felt the vibration of his footsteps I opened my eyes and saw him nearing me. Grinning sheepishly, he stated, "Sorry, I had to make yellow."

"Eww, thanks, I hope you washed your hands," I mumbled. Crouching down beside me he drew his finger down my wrinkled nose, in another intimate gesture. "See, that's what I was talking about..." He didn't finish his sentence as he fell back on his ass beside me.

For a minute he had tried to sit up again but gave up and rolled onto his side to lie beside me. Feeling spaced out I turned my head to face him.

"Remember the day we went to that meadow and lay on the grass like this watching the clouds floating by in the sky?"

"Oh. My. God, yes! We had an argument because I saw a rhino's head; you saw a unicorn and Jacob told us it looked like a cauliflower with a giant penis," Kane exclaimed and we both laughed hysterically, more because we were so drunk and found it funnier than it actually was.

We were both creased with laughter and at one point we ended up rolling into each other. We both stopped laughing at the same time and had another weird moment where we stared into each other's eyes for what seemed like forever.

Eventually, I blinked and broke our trance as Kane reached up and took a strand of my hair between two of his fingers.

"You turned out gorgeous, baby," he said as his eyes roamed over my face. He pulled a strand of my hair to his nose and inhaled deeply. "We're so drunk, right?" he said, chuckling.

Drunk didn't begin to describe the state we were in, but unfortunately even blind drunk he was still the sexiest guy I'd ever laid on a floor with.

I figured he wasn't expecting an answer so I said nothing and lay there staring back at him. "This is so fucking surreal...me here with you. Lying on the floor of your apartment," he added, as he flashed me his million-dollar smile before his expression became serious again. "I missed you, Jo, but now that I'm here, I realize I missed so much with you over the years. We were special together...don't you think?"

"We were kids, Kane, but yeah it was a special time. Seeing you again...it's weird. Great, I mean, but I have all these weird feelings meshing together, and I'm not sure what to make of them."

"Exactly! I couldn't have said it better myself, it's like I want to hug you...protect you, but seeing how hot you are, I have a tense feeling in my gut and my balls, but in the best possible way. Like I want to sit you on my knee and rock you...that kinda feeling."

Once more the weight of his stare gave me butterflies. "But I can't lie, Jo. I've had a half chub since I knew I was going to see you again and a boner for most of the time since I hugged you at the airport," he said, chuckling at his own description.

"It's true...it's like all the blood has rushed to my cock and can't find the exit." My heart did somersaults, flattered by his comment, but heat flushed my face because it felt wrong. I hardly know him. *Where is the kid I knew, because this guy is way too dangerous for me?*

"Stop it. I think you're romanticizing the situation or you're just horny," I replied, and leaned over to swat him. He continued to stare at me and I weirded out before trying to move away, but as drunk as he was, he grabbed my wrist, rolled me onto my back, and climbed over me on all fours.

"Still as slow as ever, Jo." The sloppy version of his pantie-melting grin made my stomach clench. "Remember how we used to play fight? We always ended up in this very position." He gestured at our position and waggled his eyebrows.

"Yeah, that's because I let you win," I said, trying to save face and ignore his suggestive smirk.

"Oh, so even then you wanted to be beneath me," he joked. "Interesting." Another weighted stare took my breath away until I realized I was holding it and exhaled heavily.

"You're sick, you know that." I said it like I was bored, but giggled when he started tickling me making me breathless. As abruptly as he had started to tickle me he stopped, his face taking on the same serious expression as before.

"Fuck. You're so beautiful. Can I kiss you, Jo? If you had been any other woman I would have done it by now, and more," he laughed softly. "But...since it's you, I'm asking." Dropping his forehead to mine I found the intimacy of his action and the intensity of the moment one too many for one day.

The desire in his eyes was burning hot. Alcohol definitely impaired my judgment because even though I knew it was a terrible idea, it had only taken a split second to decide that I wanted his kiss more than air or any possible consequences we faced afterward.

Taking a deep breath before replying, I wallowed in the private closeness we shared, never wanting it to end.

A sharp knock on my apartment door made me jump. I banged my head against his and the floor, while Kane cussed and rolled back onto the floor turning away from me.

Clumsily, Kane rose to his hands and knees, using the table to stand upright, and staggered to the door.

The distraction brought me to my senses as I struggled up onto my hands, sitting up while he dealt with another delivery guy. I figured he must have an account somewhere because he never paid.

Closing the door, he carried the two cartons of alcohol and snacks over to the kitchen counter. I was glad for the breathing space, and although I was deeply disappointed we hadn't kissed, I quickly figured God was looking out for me. I was sure if he'd kissed me in the state I was in we would have gone all the way.

Stumbling to my feet my instinct was to go to bed before we did something we, or at least I, would regret in the morning.

"No more for me, I'm—" A wave of nausea lurched up from my belly and made me retch. Staggering past Kane I headed for the bathroom as my stomach rolled over inside. I barely made the toilet bowl before Kane reached the doorway.

"Ah, shit," he mumbled as I felt him move to stand beside me. "You really are a lightweight drinker, huh?" he affirmed as he scooped my hair and pulled it into a ponytail. Three more bouts of sickness and I'd about spewed myself inside out. My eyeballs and throat stung.

"Well, if I'd known asking to kiss you would make you vomit, I'd have kept that question to myself," he joked, trying to make me feel better as he rubbed my back.

Moving to the sink, he grabbed my toothbrush, put paste on it and handed it to me. I stood up and turned to face him.

Kane chuckled while he looked at me, swiped his thumbs above my cheekbones and said, "Look at you. You've got mascara down to your knees, Josephine Carmichael." He said it like I was a child. He also appeared to stay steady on his feet while he tended to me. I was in awe of that with the amount of alcohol he'd put away during the day.

"Maybe we should get you to bed," he stated, his concerned eyes still inspecting me as he continued to clean my face. "And I think I should stay with you. We don't want you choking on your own vomit." I vaguely remember protesting but then I must have passed out.

Chapter Seven

MODESTY

*U*ncoordinated and slow, I rolled onto my side. I only managed to get so far when I was stopped by the weight of a strong arm over my waist and froze. My naked waist.

Sliding my hand up to my breasts I cringed. A horrible feeling formed in the pit of my stomach when I realized they were exposed.

Racking my fuzzy brain, I vaguely remembered some of what happened from the night before. Lying quietly, my heart pounded while I had a silent freak out about the blank spaces in my memory, and the hot rock star sleeping and curved alongside me in my bed.

When I moved my legs another shockwave hit me.

It was worse than I thought because I was almost totally naked except for the small, blue satin thong I was wearing.

Reaching behind me I touched his thick, hard penis and pulled my hand away like I'd been scalded. Confused and mortified, I lay paralyzed on my bed wondering what the hell had gone on between us.

Nothing clicked into place before Kane stirred as he changed position and cleared his throat.

"We didn't fuck, if that's what you're thinking," he said flatly, huffing out a long sigh.

The tension in my body began to dissolve and I exhaled heavily, until I remembered my state of undress.

"Thank, God I feel like I've been in a train wreck this morning," I said, feeling relieved. I turned to look at him.

"Then you feel how you look," he muttered, chuckling as he dug in his heels and sat up on the bed with no finesse whatsoever. "Amazing rack, Jo," he commented, with a lingering look at my body. My hands immediately grabbed my breasts as I remembered I hadn't worn a bra the day before. The top I had on had a low back so I'd gone without.

"Did you take my clothes off?" I asked in a high pitched voice.

"Had to, baby, you'd puked all down the front of your T-shirt...and mine."

"Yours?" The vague memory came back about barfing into the toilet, but Kane had been behind me.

"Yeah, right after you brushed your teeth you turned to face me, puked all over the two of us and passed out."

"Oh my God, I'm sorry," I groaned, mortified.

"Don't be. It's a normal day at the office for me. With the way the guys in the band party there's always some chick that can't hold their liquor."

Wriggling over to the edge of the bed, my eyes roamed the room for something to cover my modesty. I had to make do with a cushion as it was the only thing I was able to reach at the end of my bed.

As I stood I hid my ass with it because the string of my thong was the only thing between Kane's eyes and my butthole.

"Jesus, girl, I don't know why you're bothering with that. I've committed your ass to memory. It's a fucking peach," he said, with a naughty laugh. "I fell asleep a happy man last night."

"Really, Kane?" I asked indignantly.

"Okay, I'm sorry. I take full responsibility for you getting shit-faced and puking all over me last night. But I did get to strip you almost naked and lie beside that hot, tight body all night. The only downside was the raging boner that almost made my nuts explode because I couldn't touch you," he stated as his eyes slowly raked appreciatively up and down my body.

I turned to face him, covering up as much as I could with the cushion.

"I'm going to have a shower," I declared as I began to walk backward toward my bathroom.

"Good idea, am I invited?" He was relentless. I stared at him like he had sprouted a horn on his head but kept stepping in the direction of the bathroom while Kane lay in bed laughing heartily at my effort to leave the room.

Once I had made it in there it never occurred to me that there was no lock on the bathroom door and five minutes into my shower, Kane wandered in scrubbing the scruff on his chin.

Standing on the other side of the glass partition he began to urinate into the toilet. I was been washing my hair and was rinsing it when I opened my eyes and saw him standing, not three feet away, watching me shower as he peed.

"Get the fuck out," I spat as I curled up trying to hide my modesty.

"What? You're only naked, Jo. I had to pee. My cock was aching and I was busting. Do you know how hard it is to pee with a boner?"

"Couldn't you have gone to the one down the hall?"

"For Christ's sake, baby, it's not like I haven't seen you naked already," he reasoned as he looked at me like I was the one with the problem.

Turning the faucet off roughly, I grabbed the white towel on the peg outside the cubicle and wrapped it around me.

"You are not the guy I used to know, Kane Exeter. He'd never have wanted to embarrass me the way you are doing right now."

"What the fuck is there to be embarrassed about? You took a shower and I had to whizz. You wouldn't have wanted me to end up with an infection from holding it too long, would you? And to be honest, Jo, why would I go all the way down the hall when I can just come in here?" he asked impatiently.

"You have been mind-fucking me since yesterday, Kane, I don't appreciate it."

"Me neither, baby, but I've been trying to play by your rules. All I wanted was to come and find my friend, but it's kinda hard not to notice how hot you've turned out. I'm a red-blooded male with a high sex drive that hasn't been laid for three days." He stepped past me into the shower and turned it on.

Grabbing my body wash he began stroking the soapy suds all over his body. I stood there, my mouth gaping open, feasting my eyes on his beautiful toned body.

He hasn't been laid for three days? "Well I haven't been laid for almost a week and I'm not behaving the way you are." As soon as I said that aloud I felt shocked at myself.

Stopping what he was doing, Kane turned to look at me. "Damn. These days my ball bag would burst if I went that long." I couldn't help smiling at his unexpected response. "Oh, you think that's funny, huh?" he said, snaking around the glass cubicle and hauling me back in beside him, towel and all. Seconds later my back hit the cold tiles on the wall.

I screeched loudly, nudging forward as he ducked me under the warm water. He pushed me back against the wall and caged me in with his strong arms. The thrill of his grip and the way he had handled me was exhilarating. I'd never felt so scared and excited at the same time.

The reality of us standing there, him naked and me wrapped in a wet towel, but together, made my heart thud erratically in anticipation.

If any other man had treated me like that, I'd have hated it. But I sensed that even with all those years missing between us, Kane would never do anything to me that I didn't want. *What the hell did I want?*

"Tell me you don't want me to kiss you and I'll leave you alone, Jo. Better make it quick. We have a window of opportunity to do this. What's it gonna to be...yay or nay?"

The course of any future relationship as friends hung in the balance. I wasn't sure what I wanted. A platonic friendship that would last however long, depending on Kane's commitment, or stepping out of that childhood relationship and demanding more from a new one?

Glancing up at him I stuck with my policy of being honest. I couldn't lie and tell him I didn't want him to kiss me, because since the first time he'd mentioned it I had thought of nothing else.

Bending his head close to my ear as the water splashed around us, he softly whispered, "Your silence tells me you can't lie. You want this as much as I do." Softly, he pressed his lips to the side of my cheek. "Since the moment I saw your picture this is all I've wanted to do."

Kane's mouth leisurely paced its way down my neck, peppering small kisses from below my ear to my shoulder and back again.

A shiver ran down my spine and pulled at my core while tiny explosions of ecstasy detonated at every erogenous zone in my whole body. I had never felt anything remotely close to the chemistry I felt with him and his mouth had yet to touch mine.

"You taste incredible just like I knew you would," he husked roughly, as he continued to lavish me with unhurried kisses. His heavy breath wafted with desire along my collarbone and back up to my neck.

My body hummed, sagging further against the wall as my resistance slid from every pore.

"Kiss me," I whispered desperately, while my hands crept up his arms and tangled in his thick, wet hair, the smell of my body wash products familiar and uplifting. I wasn't strong enough to hold back from what I had been resisting.

Pulling his head back to look at me, he gave me his slow sexy grin. I melted right there in the shower. "With pleasure. Even though I didn't know it, I think I've waited half my life to do this," he whispered in a seductive voice that was almost lost with the noise of the shower.

Piercing blue eyes centered on my lips, his thumb grazed them while he licked his own. I couldn't wait another second. I leaned in and pressed mine to his and sighed involuntarily with relief. Kane chuckled against my mouth before his tongue became more demanding and he swiped it, pressing along my closed lips, parting them.

I moaned with pleasure and sagged even further until his arm pulled me closer and a hand clasped loosely around my throat in a sensual sweep that sent my desire soaring to a new level. Within seconds our bodies were entangled and our kiss was frantic.

It was almost like we were making up for all the lost time we'd missed with each other, but in a new and exciting way. Kane reached between us and pulled my towel away, covering my naked body with his.

The sensation of his hard masculine presence almost made me wild with desire to have more of him.

"Tell me to stop," he mumbled as he cupped my breast and took my beaded nipple into his mouth, sucking hard.

"I...I can't," I panted breathlessly from the passion in his grip and the way he seemed to be devouring my skin, pinching and nibbling his way over my shoulders and breasts.

"Then I won't, but you need to be sure you want this," he warned.

"I do, please—" I never got to finish my sentence as he scooped me up and wrapped my legs around his waist.

Stepping out of the shower he carried me back to my bedroom, dripping wet. I felt his hard length, and something metal, brush against me as he carried me.

Reaching the bed, he threw me unceremoniously onto it and pried my knees roughly apart.

"I need to taste you, Jo, I just need to do this, babe," he mumbled as he kissed his way slowly from my calf to my knee, all the way up to my pussy.

The tension in his shoulders made his arms vibrate a little with every peck of his mouth on my skin. I anticipated a soft, gentle lick for that first stroke like I was used to when a man went down on me, but with Kane, his technique was powerful and devouring in every sense of the word.

Kane's hot wet mouth covered as much of my pussy as he could before his tongue dove deep into my entrance while he sucked hard.

The ecstasy I derived from that one sudden action almost made me come.

Once he'd fed his initial desire, his tongue circled slowly and then lashed at speed against my clit before he slid his tongue gently up the length of my seam.

Every time I thought I could handle what he was doing he switched it up making me moan like I'd never done before.

The level of pleasure I felt was something I'd never felt had before. I'd only had two partners in the past before Elliott, but none of them had ever played my body like a sexual instrument with the expertize that Kane did.

"I've never wanted to fuck anyone as much as I want you, Jo. Do you have condoms here?"

"In the box in the drawer," I answered in a voice laced with the same desperation and urgency that matched his.

Stopping briefly to grab one from the box, he ripped it open with his teeth and rolled it down his thick, veiny, length and I balked at the size of it.

Kane was bigger than any man I'd previously been with and when I realized he had an apa, and two small round piercings on his skin on either side of his cock, I almost freaked out. I had missed that when he'd dropped his towel before.

When he saw the shocked look on my face he laughed aloud. "Trust me, it's amazing, you'll love it."

Reaching down, he grabbed my legs under the knee and pulled me toward the edge of the bed. We were both still damp from the shower and the tacky feeling between us as his skin stuck to mine added to the whole experience.

Suddenly, he pushed my legs straight and flexed my hips up toward his face where his mouth connected with my wet heat. That one move stole my breath.

Lavishing his tongue in my entrance again he let out a long moan of appreciation before he spread my legs wide and slid the tip of his cock from my clit all the way down to my entrance.

Strumming his fingers skimmed down my inner lips and sunk deep inside. "Fuck, you're dripping wet, babe. You ready for me?" he asked, with a glance that turned into a locked stare. The heat in his eyes almost ended me.

Taking me in one long glide made me gasp for air. Kane grunted and stilled for a second while I adjusted to his size. He was huge and I was extremely wet.

After he pulled back and sunk deep again I was ready for more. Just as well really, because he rode me hard for around ten seconds before he slowed his pace. He was right about the piercings. I loved them.

No man had ever taken me in the way Kane did. I loved the way he commanded my body with such demanding control. He left me speechless and breathless.

Kane smiled and there was something about it that made my heart stutter sluggishly in my chest. He was heartbreakingly stunning. His eyes half closed with lust as his hands wandered reverently up the sides of my ribcage and over my breasts.

I squirmed when he looked down at me from above and turned my head away because the connection we'd shared at that moment felt almost too intimate. He caught my face roughly by my chin and turned me back to look at him.

"No, don't do that, look at me," he said in his seductive, commanding tone. I thought he was God's gift to women before, when I'd seen him on TV—that was nothing like seeing him the way he was with me in that moment. The way he directed my body affirmed such a notion.

By that point I didn't care whether I was his fuck and duck or not. To see him in all his masculinity, with all the bullshit stripped away and his behavior so raw and dirty toward me was something I'd remember forever.

"I know what you're thinking," he mumbled, in his low serious tone as his pace slowed to a gentle rock.

"You do?" I asked a little startled, while my eyes tried to read his. I had my doubts he would ever have guessed my last thought.

"You think I'll be gone tomorrow and this is a time-filler for me, right?" he replied softly, leaning over me to place his forehead on mine.

Something about that particular gesture as he was entering me was so intimate it felt like more than casual sex. It moved me and brought a lump to my throat.

"Isn't that exactly what this is?"

Kane snickered as he leaned back to brush some strands of hair from my eyes. "I'd hate to think that, Jo. Is this what it is for you? Your chance to fuck a rock star?" His tone was questioning as he watched my face intensely, waiting for my answer. I struggled to accept it was anything else. We weren't the kids we once were. This was different, but we'd only just met again.

"I don't know what this is. The only thing I know for sure is that it's happening," I answered honestly. Having casual sex went against everything I normally stood for and how I'd given into him so easily confused me.

"Damn straight it is, and I'm going to give you the ride of your life, whatever happens after is your call," he warned as he ground himself deeper inside me.

I had thought he was a cocky bastard for using a line like that, but as it turned out he wasn't lying. Forty minutes later, I thought I was going to pass out from the way he had rocked my world. I'd never been taken so many times and in so many positions.

I had lost count of how many times he'd made me come. My screams were primal and unguarded. When he came I was in no doubt. His animalistic growl could have been heard down the apartment hallway.

Pulsing rhythmically inside me, he leaned over from his position behind me and held my back tightly to his chest. I could hardly breathe and when we collapsed sideways on the bed he was spooning with me.

"Hot damn, baby. Best ride of my life," he stated, panting. His voice sounded gruff. I was embarrassed when he slapped my ass then rubbed the sting away while I lay quietly trying to catch my breath.

I was exhausted from how my body had been stretched and bent to its limits as he'd turned me every which way he wanted to take me. A few minutes later I had just about recovered when his breathing gradually slowed and became heavy and deep. Kane had fallen asleep.

I rolled off the bed carefully so that I didn't wake him and headed back to the bathroom to clean up.

Guilt and shame had replaced any positive feelings I'd had about what we'd just done. I had never had a one night stand before. I stared into the mirror and noted the raspberry-colored bite mark on my neck. *What the hell were you thinking?* I hadn't thought at all, it was more about what I'd felt.

Immediately I thought it had been my biggest mistake. Kane wasn't some lame guy I could forget, he was the boy from my past, my one-time best friend, and he was a rock star that was frequently splashed all over the press. *I'm screwed.*

Chapter Eight
REGRETS

wo hours later, Kane came padding out of the bedroom stark naked, stretching his arms above his head and looking every inch the delicious rock star, not to mention he was sporting another large erection. "Hey, Jo, are you okay?"

I felt desperately self-conscious again and chided myself for being such a pushover with him. Struggling to keep my eyes on his face, I answered truthfully, "Erm, yeah, I'm just not used to doing a one and done event, is all. I'm not that kind of girl, and I feel like a slut for making it happen."

Concern clouded his eyes, and he frowned. "Look at you. There is absolutely nothing slutty about you, Jo. Get that out of your head right now, you are a stunningly beautiful and desirable woman, that's why that happened between us," he said as he stroked my hair.

Kane gave me a soft smile of reassurance as he leaned on the arm of the sofa beside me and crouched down to be face-to-face next to me.

"This has got to be the weirdest weekend of my life. Not only do I have a rock star sleeping on my couch and in my bed, but I let him screw me with his seductive persuasion like some desperate backstage groupie."

Looking hurt, Kane's eyes pierced mine and his angry expression told me I'd offended him. "Is that what you think? You got fucked by a rock star? That's how you read what happened here? I seduced you? This is me, Jo. Kane Exeter, the guy you used to know. Not Kane Exeter of Hedonism. I thought what happened back there this morning was a real-life mutual attraction. I'm fucking offended that you're sitting there thinking that I had to persuade you to do that."

Standing up straight, he paced the floor, his muscles flexing with every frustrated stride before he spun around to face me again. His dick slapped on his leg and my eyes went straight to it. "Eyes up here, Jo, look at *me*," he said, sounding angrier than I'd ever heard him. "I asked you. I fucking sought your permission. You know how many times I've had to do that? *Once*. You may not have been in my life, but I remembered how we were together as kids enough to know that you wanted that to happen every bit as much as I did. The way you were spinning in there, you loved every minute of what we did, so don't sit there full of regrets like you're better than me, Josie, it's not fucking cool."

Watching how furious I'd made him wasn't easy, but a teeny bit of me couldn't help but feel pleased, at least it showed me that having sex with me had really meant something to him.

"Maybe I'm just naturally suspicious, but my life was going fine until yesterday morning. I'm a normal girl from a no-nonsense family. Strict upbringing and ingrained morals, Kane."

"Right, and that means you'd rather have a guy that gets you off once in a while, and gets pissed because you have an old friend look you up?"

"It seems to me that Elliott was right on that score, Kane. We never kept it platonic, did we?"

"I'd never have done that if he hadn't have broken up with you. Believe it or not, I don't have to fuck other guy's chicks, Jo. I get plenty of pussy offered to me every day without those kinds of complications."

"Well...and doesn't that make you sound like you can take the moral high ground?" I shouted back.

Kane rubbed his eyes with his thumb and forefinger then turned and went into the bedroom while I sat wondering what he was going to do next.

My heart felt heavy that we were fighting, especially after the connection we'd shared a few hours before.

Nothing he said made me feel better, and no matter what, I could hardly ignore the fact that he was still a rock star with a playboy reputation.

Reappearing in the clothes he'd changed into the night before he stuffed his belongings into his leather holdall. "As I'm obviously making you feel uncomfortable, I'm just gonna check into a hotel. Here are a couple of tickets for the gig on Monday night, and a couple of backstage passes. I'd love to see you there. Despite what you think, Jo, what we did this morning actually meant a great deal to me, but I think a bit of space is in order for you to work out that remorse you have going on."

And there's the line he uses to validate leaving. I'm just another one and done fuck to him. I knew everything he had been saying was too good to be true. Standing to face him, I dragged up the gutsiest performance I could muster and scoffed, "Sure. Whatever. See you around, Kane." It came out sounding downright bitchy.

Kane's eyes narrowed as he looked briefly toward the door then back at me. "I hope you come to the gig, Jo. I'd like you there. Maybe when you've had some time to think about this, it won't seem so weird for you," he offered.

Picking up his bag he slung it over his shoulder, hesitated and looked longingly at me before reaching for the doorknob. "I've loved seeing you again, babe, and I don't regret what we did or being here with you. Despite what you think, I really am taken with you. You're more beautiful and wonderful than I imagined in my mind. Take care," he mumbled as he turned the handle forcefully and pulled the door open.

A second later he stepped out into the corridor and closed the door softly behind him, leaving me alone.

I felt totally demolished once he'd gone. Watching him leave broke my heart all over again. All those years I'd wondered about him, lost sleep thinking about him, worried about him, and I'd convinced myself that our second chance at friendship had been blown out of the water because we'd let sex get in the way.

Tears rolled down my face as my heart crushed under the weight in my chest. I wiped my runny nose on my shirt sleeve and a sob tore from my throat at what we'd done.

My feelings were that there was no going back now, we'd ruined our second chance to be friends.

Kane had only been back for a day, but I felt his loss like a gaping hole in my life as soon as he'd left the apartment. *Girls like me never end up with guys like Kane. I should have known better.* Curling up on my sofa, I buried my head in my hands and sobbed loudly.

Exhausted from crying, I dozed off and was awoken by my cell playing my Beyonce ringtone. I knew I had to change it because I had the images of Kane's re-enactment associated with the song.

Glancing at the screen I saw it was my friend, Candice, from the office. "Hey, Candice, how are you?" I asked in a croaky voice.

"I'm good...what's wrong? Are you okay?" she replied sounding concerned.

I considered shrugging off her concern but I felt so desolate I found myself pouring out the whole sorry story.

"You slept with Kane Exeter? Fucking hell...you fucked Kane Exeter? Kane Hedonism Exeter?" she shrieked in disbelief. "That's the Kane from when you were kids?"

"Yeah, that's him, and I'm not proud of it, Candice."

"No I can hear that, but jeez, he so frigging hot, Josie. What was he like, I mean a guy like that would know what he's doing...sorry, I'm not being that great of a comfort to you, but hell's bells—*Kane Exeter*. Damn, he is the finest man I've ever seen." I had to give her that, but I wasn't encouraging the conversation.

When I didn't reply she picked up on the silence and cleared her throat. "Sorry I just got so excited for a moment," she mumbled in apology. "So are we going to his concert Monday? Did he give you tickets?"

"What? No, of course I'm not going."

"Why not? His band is amazing."

"I don't want to see him after what happened."

"Well I can understand that, but that's all in your head. Kane's a rock star, he's used to fucking beautiful girls every day of the week and all day long, if you believe the article in the Celebrity Stud, magazine. So why should you feel awkward? Tell me he gave you tickets."

"Candice!" She mumbled her apology for being insensitive and tried hard to make me feel better and somewhere along the line our conversation turned.

I wasn't sure when that happened but by the end of the call I had agreed to go to the concert and take her with me. I hadn't told her about the backstage passes because I already knew there was no way I was turning up after his gig to see him like some groupie.

Afterwards I felt less than happy about what I'd agreed to. My mind flitted to Elliott. He'd been right to be cautious about Kane staying with me.

I wasn't sure why, but I had a sudden urge to come clean with him burned in my brain, and stupidly, before I'd had time to think through what to say, I called him on his cell. I knew he said we weren't together but to my mind I had cheated, whether it was right or wrong, I had to come clean.

"Hello, Josie," he answered in a curt polite tone.

"Hi, Elliott, I need to talk to you."

"Josie, you don't have to tell me, I can hear it in your voice. You slept with him, didn't you?"

"It wasn't supposed to happen, I mean, I didn't—"

"Mean to fuck my rock star buddy." He was rightly incensed and his voice was laced with sarcasm.

"That's not fair, Elliott, I'm trying—"

"Not fair? I'll tell you what's not fair, Josie. It's not fair that my boss sent me to this godforsaken place, that I left you thinking we were so good together. Five weeks it took me to get you into my bed. *Five weeks* and I was happy that we took things slowly, because I had told myself that you were worth it. I was beginning to have deeper feelings for you and all it's taken is my absence for less than a week and an old friend who rocks up at your door to end all of that. So you know what? I went out last night and got laid as well. Don't think you're the only one that has needs or wants."

"And that will fix this, yeah? Two wrongs don't make a right, Elliott." I was mad as well by then, and wondered if he was one of those crazy guys who broke up with a girl just to screw someone else so he felt he was doing no wrong. "I rang to come clean and apologize to you, Elliott."

"What for, Josie? To make you feel better? I told you we're not together anymore. Do what you like. I'm done. You're definitely not the girl I left behind, or maybe you were, I don't know, maybe you just hid it well."

Swallowing roughly, I knew I'd made yet another mistake, and from the irrational tone Elliott had, I knew I'd hurt him as well as myself. "I'm truly sorry, Elliott, I guess there's nothing left to say," I mumbled and hung up feeling less than proud of myself for what I'd done. *What the hell is wrong with me?*

~

For the rest of the day I beat myself up by going over and over my relationship with Elliott and my short time with Kane. Elliott had been safe, but with Kane's connection to happier times as a kid and the excitement of having him back in my life, I guess my judgment was way off.

To look at them both there wasn't a lot of difference between them. Roughly the same height, hair and eye color, and they were both handsome men, but it was like Kane shone in comparison.

The way he was put together was ultra-sexy and he had this magnetism that was missing in Elliott. I guessed it was lust that had clouded my vision even when I knew it would end badly. That night in bed I could still imagine him here with me and for that reason alone, sleep avoided me.

As I made my way to work the following morning, Kane Exeter still dominated my waking thoughts. He was the fourth man I'd slept with, and I knew, by the way he'd consumed me, and with the chemistry we shared, that he'd probably ruined me for anyone else.

With my limited intimate knowledge I sensed I would never experience anything else like it and would struggle to find that kind of connection ever again with someone else.

"Morning, Josie," Jacob greeted. My twin brother was chatting up the new receptionist as I entered the building.

"Morning," I mumbled back, still preoccupied about Kane.

"Jeez, Josie, you look rough, if I didn't know you better I'd say you'd been partying hard this weekend."

Jacob was the first to say that to me that day, but he definitely wasn't the last. All day long people commented on how tired I looked and by the time I was ready to leave, I was sick of listening to it.

Candice called as I was packing up for the day. "All set? I'll meet you downstairs, I just have to drop some mail in the post room that's urgent," she told me.

"Just about to change into my jeans, I'll be there in five."

Swiping my screen to close the call out, I scooted down the hall to the washroom and changed into a tight-fitted, aqua blue T-shirt, some blue skinny jeans and kitten heels.

Once ready, I stuffed my work attire into a hanging bag, hung it on the back of my office door and headed toward the elevators to meet Candice.

"Hey, sexy lady, you look fabulous," she said, greeting me with a warm, friendly smile.

I didn't feel fabulous but welcomed her encouragement because I was so nervous about the gig and being in the same place as him again. I had almost called her several times during the day to back out.

Candice chatted all the way across town about work and I was happy to listen because inside I was a mess.

Anxiety wasn't something I suffered from usually, but the feelings that were running amok in me were worse than sitting in the dentist chair awaiting root canal treatment.

By the time we reached the venue I was definitely having second thoughts about going in there. I reassured myself that nine thousand people was a good cover to hide amongst.

I prayed that the seat tickets we'd been given would be set back in the midst of the crowd.

Candice grabbed the tickets out of my hand and began to walk along the concourse. "Wow, these are in section A. That's almost stage level. We're going to be up close and personal with the band.

"This is so freaking cool." I shuddered at the thought, unhappy about Kane possibly seeing me sitting there like nothing had ever happened between us. That was the message I figured I'd be sending to him.

Suddenly I felt weak-willed at allowing Candice to talk me into being there and dragged my heels behind her.

After a few moments she noticed my reluctance. "Come on, Josie, in a venue of nine thousand plus, he's not going to notice you. Just enjoy the band and take it for what it is. He owes you a fun time after all that shit with Elliott."

I almost said he'd already given me the fun time. However, once she had validated my entitlement to be there, and we'd found our seats, I began to relax—a little.

We were right at the edge of the stage and as the microphone was in the middle I figured that he'd be so busy over there, running up and down the runway that ran through the middle, that he'd have no idea I was even in the venue.

"Damn, we should have got some drinks. Wait here I'll run to the kiosk back out on the concourse and grab us something," she said, shuffling past me. I watched her running up the stairs to the walkway above.

When she left me alone I looked around, my eyes scanning all the expensive technical equipment on the stage and I tried to figure out how Kane's band had afforded all this kind of gear before they were famous. Especially when a cheap electric guitar cost a couple of hundred bucks.

There was nothing cheap about anything that I could see and I had to take my hat off to Hedonism for their celebrity status. They had only been around for about eighteen months and this was their first tour after cutting their album. I knew that because I'd heard Kane tell the TV presenter.

A commotion behind me turned my head. Candice had come back, wiggling her way past a couple of good-looking guys with our drinks. One of them offered to help. She fluttered her eyelids and gave them a coy look, saying, "Sorry, boys, we're groupies for the band."

Personally, I could have punched her because that's exactly how Kane had left me feeling after our passionate session the day before. "Thanks, Candice," I mumbled sarcastically.

"Well would you rather they hit on us all evening while you sit and ogle Kane?" she asked, like she'd done me a favor to shut them out. I let her comment slide and sat back in my tiny seat. Suddenly, the lights dimmed and I settled down to watch the warm up band do their set.

The poor opening act never even got an introduction. They just wandered out on stage, strapped on their guitars and immediately began to play a series of fast riffs that didn't sound particularly in sync.

All the technical jargon I learned came from Candice's commentary. I didn't know much about music, but even I could tell their timing was off.

The lead singer saddled up to the mic looking like he could do with a good wash and shouted his way through the first song. I wouldn't go as far as to say I was entertained by his performance, but he tried too hard and it showed.

"They're great, aren't they," Candice gushed after slating everything about them. I stared at her wide-eyed because it seemed like we were both hearing something completely different.

"If you like someone screaming their way through some badly written lyrics and trying to murder the concept of music—yeah, great," I answered, in a voice heavy with boredom.

"Damn, Josie, get yourself straight. It's hard work being with you tonight," she huffed, continuing to stamp her foot in time to the bad music.

The band finished their set without another word of complaint from me, and personally, when they had finished it was the high point of their whole performance. I stared around at the seats that had yet to be filled for the main band and wondered how many of them had heard of the band that had just played.

Maybe they had and that's why they had dined late or had chosen to hang around in the bars until Hedonism took to the stage.

Once again, Candice went to get more drinks and I sat watching the technicians tweak the equipment on the stage, before the lights dimmed and the crowd roared in appreciation for Kane and his band.

My heartbeat accelerated to the point where I could feel the strong pulse in my neck without thinking about it.

This time I had expected an emcee to mention their name, but once again there was no introduction, just a sudden burst of noise.

I felt like I'd been ripped from my seat, the vibrations of their bass reverberated up through my feet and resonated in my chest as the guitarists played clever, fast, riffs that complimented one another as far as I could tell.

The difference between both bands was stark. The musicians that formed Hedonism were effortless music-makers and the sounds they made were awesome.

The flow of one instrument to another sounded seamless and as I listened to the drum percussions accompanying them, it was the glue that made their music gel into a rhythm. As a listener it drew me in and hooked me to the tune.

Kane was standing with his back to the audience, mic in hand as he gestured in time to the beat the drummer was playing until the intro was complete.

Turning to face the audience he began to belt out a song I'd never heard before, but it would appear I was the only one who hadn't heard it, judging from how their fans reacted to it. Kane's voice was incredibly smooth and charismatic. The way he moved on stage had me staring open-mouthed.

Watching his hips moving from side to side and gyrating occasionally was seductive and delighted every woman in the crowd.

Scanning the audience, women everywhere were losing their shit, screaming and swooning at the rock star on the stage.

The same man who was so seductive he'd made me reckless and left a stain on my heart.

I became aware my heart was pounding fast and hard at his ability to turn on a whole arena full of people, both male and female, who hung on his every word and did exactly what he told them. And reluctantly I gave into my feelings and was mesmerized during the ninety minute performance, when I became a spellbound and loyal fan of Hedonism.

Nearing the end of their set, Kane came across to the side of the stage we were near and looked up at where we were sitting. Shielding his eyes, it was clear he was looking for something or someone.

I almost ducked because I felt embarrassed, and the last thing I had wanted was for him to see me and think I was fine after how we'd left things.

I wasn't okay, but none of that mattered because once he'd seen us he'd probably figured I'd had second thoughts, because thanks to Candice, I had turned up. So what did that say about me and what message did that give him?

Chapter Nine

FANGIRLING

When they left the stage at the end, to rapturous applause, I felt more than a little bereft. I thought, *that's it. It's all over between us*, and I felt so sad I had wanted to cry.

Blinking back tears forming, I stood to leave, but Candice tugged at my sleeve insisting that they would be back for an encore.

My initial reaction was that I couldn't go through that feeling I'd just had again, but I sat patiently waiting for them with a renewed, sudden eagerness to see him for a few minutes more, knowing my life would never be the same but would continue without him.

My heart sank to my belly for the tenth time that day and I asked myself if I would be happy not to see him again. The answer to that was no.

Panic tightened my chest that this was it—that this may be the last time Kane Exeter and I were in the same room at the same time.

Tears welled in my eyes as the guy next to me tapped my shoulder. I turned to see him pointing toward a thick-set man in an immaculate black suit who was standing at the end of the row.

Pointing at me, he gave me a come here gesture with his hand and I stood slowly, edging past the two men who were seated at the end of the row, to see what he wanted. Even though I kind of knew what it was already.

"Ms. Carmichael?" he asked, shouting close to my ear as Hedonism began to sing their most famous song. "Mr. Exeter said he's very glad you decided to come and he'd like to see you backstage after the show. If you'd like to come with me," he said as he nodded toward the exit at the back. I felt relieved that he wanted to see me but confused about prolonging the agony of our goodbye. I had never been so indecisive in my life.

Either way, once I went home it would be over. I squeezed past the two guys and nudging Candice, I nodded toward the security guy and shouted in her ear that we were going backstage.

I groaned as I observed Candice become overly animated, as she shook and cussed with excitement, picking up her bag and jacket as she turned to go.

Following the guard, I was sure Candice and I had very different feelings about the invitation to meet the band. It felt like a walk of shame for me as we wandered down the dimly lit stairs and along a never-ending passageway before we reached a large seating area.

The smell of weed was so thick I was getting high just from standing in there.

"Take a seat and help yourselves to drinks, they'll be through in a few minutes," the broad bodyguard said with an easy smile. He left us in the room full of people.

Amongst the smattering of men were five beautiful, waiflike, play-boy-bunny-type females, with rocker chick groupie written all over them. All of them had their eyes trained on Candice and me as a series of sly smiles passed between them.

After trading some duck lips and attitude stances between them-selves, the tallest one, with the biggest fake tits, sauntered over in our direction with her hands on her hips.

"Are you two competition winners or something?" Her snarky manner did nothing for me. I think she was trying to intimidate us. Candice took exception to the way she spoke down at us. "No we're not. Josie has been personally invited here by Kane."

The way she had said it had made me feel dirt cheap, like I'd been picked out of the crowd to entertain him, and from the look on the groupie's face, that's exactly what she had thought as well.

"How sweet, just like the rest of us," she said in voice loud enough for the others to hear, and twisted her body in the direction of the other women.

They all raised their long-stemmed wine glasses in salute and heat rose to my cheeks, mortified as to what they thought we were doing there. I looked down at my feet before willing myself to make eye contact with the skinny groupie again.

The fake smile that had been there before was gone, a scowl in its place as she regarded me with narrowed eyes.

"Take it from someone with first-hand experience, Kane Exeter is a sexual animal, he'll devour you. I actually passed out the first time he did me," she gloated, like she was proud of that fact and smirked in the direction of the others.

By that point, they were all standing in a conspiratorial huddle staring at Candice and I like we were the shit on their shoes.

Even though I didn't think for one minute Kane and I were going anywhere, it pissed me off that she thought she had rights over him. She had thrown down a challenge and I don't know why, but I felt it my duty to wipe the smirk off her face.

I had years of attending an all-girls school, and I had learned exactly what to do with women like her.

"Well then, I believe it's you that's no match for *him*. Sorry to disappoint you on that because I'm still fully conscious and here, aren't I?" I gestured at myself by sweeping my hand down the front of me. "And for the record, I never pass out. And I hate to burst that skanky bubble you've surrounded yourself with, but I think he's nowhere near finished with me." I giggled nervously, not believing I'd uttered such a thing and hoped I looked much more confident than I felt.

Glancing at Candice, her eyebrow was almost in her hairline as she stared speechless at me for once. "Shall we sit over there, honey? The air over here is pretty stale."

Tipping my chin in the direction of the white leather seating on the other side of the room, I spun on my heel and began to head over in the direction of it.

"Fuck, Josie, that was surreal. I've never heard you talk like that before, you've always been such a lady. You sounded so badass." Candice giggled hoisting her bag up onto her shoulder.

At that same moment the band members flooded the room, their energy making the room buzz. I recognized the lead guitarist and the drummer as they came in still high from the performance or it could have been drugs, I'm not sure, but they looked deliriously happy.

"Fucking A, that was sick! Best gig we've ever had," the long-haired guitarist said. "Cole, dude, you were on fire, we rocked the house." The drummer held up his hands in mock adulation and slapped the guitarist whose name I had gathered was Cole by that time, on the back.

Kane came wandering in, dripping in sweat, chatting animatedly to the guy beside him. My breath hitched and I squeezed my thighs together as an electrical current pulled at my core. Shirtless, he looked so freaking hot as he dried off his chest and underarms on the T-shirt he'd already stripped off.

Of course at that moment the bimbo that had been harassing me moved in for the kill. "Kane, honey, you were absolutely awesome," she said, winding her arms around his waist and staring adoringly up at him.

Looking past her to me, his strong hand gripped her forearm and I saw the color of her skin go pale where his fingertips dug in.

Pulling her away by her forearms he gave me his winning, sexy smile that I had always loved, even as a child. It lit up his whole face.

Not once did he take his eyes off me while he removed her hands from his body. Once he was free of her, he headed straight across the room toward me.

"You came," he said, with a hint of disbelief as he towered over me, offering me an outstretched hand. "Indeed," I returned, conscious of the harem in the corner drawing daggers at me. Twisting his upper body, he turned to see what I was looking at and snickered, "Don't mind them. They're an occupational hazard."

Leaning down further to grab my wrists he pulled me up to stand closely in front of him. Too close. My eyes met his naked, sweat-glistened chest and I wanted to lick it.

The intimate position forced me to tilt my head up to look at him. He looked down at the same time and our faces were inches from one another's. Kane's warm breath wafted over my face and my eyes dropped to his lips for a second.

My arms slid to my sides, but he hadn't lost his grip, it felt sexy and threatening at the same time. Everything about him was too alluring; his scent, the way he looked into my eyes and the sound of his deep, sexy voice. It just wasn't enough for me—I wanted to taste him.

"So happy you're here." His smile widened showing his perfect white teeth as he released my wrists and grabbed my face. Closing the space between us his lips touched mine and I felt myself sag toward him.

"Hi, Kane, you have me to thank for that, she needed a helluva lot of persuasion." Candice's voice interrupted the moment and he pulled back just enough to look at me.

"Is that so?" he asked, grinning wickedly as he smoothed my hair down. "I love a woman who plays hard to get. They're my favorite flavor."

"Then I failed epically on that one," I mumbled and stepped back when I thought about how easily I'd fallen for his charm.

"It happened, Jo. Own it. And personally, I'm okay with what we did. I'm glad it happened because it was pretty incredible and there's nothing we don't know about each other now. Come with me."

I glanced to the groupies, sure they had heard our conversation, but before I could resist he'd flung his arm around my shoulder and ushered me past everyone.

As I passed the group of women I heard one mutter, looks like Kane's found another magic pussy."

Crashing to a halt, Kane stopped and turned to face them. "Watch your fucking mouth, you hear? This woman is worth a thousand of you, she's my closest friend," he growled.

My heart raced at how protective he sounded. "If I hear another word said against her you'll all be walking home. I don't care how good you think you are at sucking dick, girls like you are dime a dozen, fucking remember that."

He took my hand and tugged me through a doorway into a dressing room with what looked like a red leather barber's chair and lighted mirrors.

Seating me on one of the chairs he wheeled a stool over to sit on and face me. Sitting down he took my hands in his and squeezed them slightly.

A thrill ran through me at his caring gesture and a smile played on his lips.

"Hey. I'm sorry you had to deal with that. Those women get out of hand sometimes."

"But they are an expert fuck, right?"

"The guys in the band use them, sure. They're not doing anything those girls don't want to happen. It's a lifestyle they lead."

"But they're there for you as well, right? I mean how can you even condone something like that? You fuck them as well, don't you?" I couldn't keep my distaste and hate for demeaning women from the tone of my voice.

"I'm not proud to say I have in the past, but not lately."

"No?"

"I was seeing someone and I was trying to stay faithful to her."

"Trying? That means you weren't?" I asked, feeling disappointed at both the facts that he'd been seeing someone that meant that much to him and that he wasn't able to resist temptation.

"No I was. Three months until you," he answered, giving me a meaningful smile.

"You mean you cheated on her with me?" I said as I tried to pull my hands away, but he gripped them tighter and held them firm. Shocked at his revelation I was disgusted with myself for falling for his seductive charm.

"That's not what happened, I never cheated on anyone. She sent me a text telling me that she'd never be able to accept my life on the road. Although she loved me, she said she didn't want a relationship with a guy who spent half of his life on a bus and had women falling over themselves to offer me easy sex."

"Smart woman," I agreed, with a note of hostility in my voice. "When was this?"

"Almost a week ago."

"So a few days before you flew in from Boston? And I ended your so-called dry spell?" I asked, giving him a pointed stare. I was so mad at myself.

Kane grinned sheepishly and gave me a soft chuckle. "Well, when you put it like that, yeah, you did...but in my defense, there was something going on between us from the moment I hugged you at the airport. The sexual tension was killing me, but you did a great job of hiding those signals."

"So you thought you'd get me drunk then make your move?" I asked, feeling gutted as I searched his face for the truth.

"Oh no, baby. You're not pinning that one on me. You were the one to get the wine, remember? I drank a whole bottle of JD trying to keep my dick in check and then we had all that wine, hell I even ordered more booze and even after all of that, I couldn't sedate it enough to stop wanting you. Fuck...I still want you now."

"No. Stop. This wasn't why I came here. Candice was right. It took a lot of persuasion to get me here, but I came because I didn't want to leave this on bad terms, and as lame as it sounds, I'd still like us to be friends again...if we can. I don't want to fall into bed with you every time I see you, Kane. Sex comes with emotion and relationships in my world, it isn't a sport."

Kane let go of my hands and cupped my face in his palms. "I wouldn't expect anything less from you, I understand, Jo, but I'm not sorry I crossed the line. How could I be sorry when you gave me my biggest high? I won't ever forget how that felt between us." I was trying so hard to remain resolute but he said the sweetest things that made my body tense and pulse in all the right places.

"It may have escaped your notice, but your world and mine are at opposite ends of the spectrum, Kane. I'm not the kind of girl that's okay with this ram and run rock star lifestyle, and all its excesses. I'm homey and comfortable, the kind of girl who's happy with my ordinary day-to-day life. Your girl was clever to give you up before she got in too deep. We should never have had sex."

Staring sharply at him as I tried to stay cool, I watched as Kane's lips pressed into a line and his thumb gently stroked my cheek.

When I remained still he sucked in a deep breath and sounded deflated as he let it escape his lungs. "Okay, fuck it. I'm tired, Jo. Have it your way. It's not going to be easy, but friends without benefits it is," he conceded in a slightly regretful tone.

Even though he was agreeing to what I wanted I felt an odd twinge of disappointment that, just like Elliott, he hadn't fought harder. *My emotions are so fucking contrary at times.*

"Come on, there are people I'd like you to meet." Standing he shoved his stool away with the back of his knees and grabbed both my hands pulling me to my feet.

Entwining his fingers between mine he clasped his other hand possessively over them and my heart ached a little that things couldn't be different between us.

Tugging me along with him into the room where the others were, he wandered over to the group of musicians that were mulling around drinking beers from their bottles. "Cody Myers, meet Jo, this is the best friend I was telling you about."

"Oh, so you're the elusive Jo, Kane's been filling us in on."

Instantly blushing I became self-conscious, I wondered if he'd told them he'd slept with me. Kane must have noticed my awkward glance and came to my rescue.

"I told the guys I was headed down to see you as we were playing in Maryland remember?" It must have been obvious I was wigging out, ashamed that we'd had sex.

"Yeah it's been good catching up," I mumbled, wondering if that was the extent of his conversation about me. I'd have liked to think that Kane would have respected me enough not to talk about me in that way, but I couldn't be sure of the adult version of the boy I used to know.

Zander Hull, the drummer, came wandering across, beer in hand with a salacious smile on his face, "Who's this little beauty? Not thinking of keeping her all to yourself were you, Kane?"

"Where's your respect, Zander? Jo's not a groupie, she's special to me."

"Just like Debra was last week, right?" he scoffed, and continued to rake his eyes up and down me like he was undressing me.

"Jo and I were friends as kids, she's the one I told you I was coming to see in Maryland when I was flying from Boston," he added.

A spark of recognition flitted across Zander's eyes and his mouth formed a silent 'O'. "Oh yeah, I remember. You're the kid from Germany, right?" Zander looked stoned, like he'd wouldn't remember his own name at that particular moment, but I only realized how anxious and knotted my stomach was when it relaxed after he'd said that.

I don't know why I expected special treatment; after all, just like hundreds of other girls, all I'd had was a one night stand with Kane.

I muddled through various conversations for the following hour feeling like a fish out of water, and although Kane had tried to include me in every conversation, I still felt awkward and out of place.

The moment when Cody walked over and selected one of the five girls and stated he was going to get laid, I knew I was done trying to be something I wasn't and that was my cue to get Candice and I out of there.

Kane was distracted when he was called over to settle an argument and have his picture taken by some VIP's that were connected to the venue.

Candice and I were left talking to someone else who was promoting the band and I glanced over at Kane who was the center of attention.

If only he wasn't so good looking and living the lifestyle of a rock star. As soon as I had that thought I knew I was in danger of becoming emotionally invested in a way that was dangerous.

I took that as my cue to leave, and grabbed Candice by the arm. "Come on, I'm done, let's go." Candice initially resisted, riveted to her spot like her feet were made of lead as she gave me a wide-eyed look like a whiney child that may have burst into tears at any moment. She huffed heavily.

I knew she thought I was spoiling her night and I read from her expression that she was far from done with the whole scene. "Fine, stay, but I'm out," I warned, letting go of her arm and turning to head for the door.

"No wait, I'm coming," she replied, with a tinge of regret. "Don't you think you should at least tell Kane we're leaving?" I never answered her, just kept walking, slightly too fast and with purpose, until we were outside. Running alongside me she cussed when she stumbled in her heels. "Jesus, Josie, where's the fire?"

"Sorry, Candice, none of this is your fault, but I really had to get out of there. Did you see how indifferent Cole treated that girl in there?" Without waiting for her to answer I continued, "We're *way* different to those girls, Candice. That's a part of Kane Exeter's lifestyle I don't want to be caught up in." The emotion in my voice was thick, like I'd cry any minute. I turned and resumed my hurried pace down the sidewalk.

"Jeez, Josie, slow down my feet are killing me in these shoes," she whined, but my need to be clear of Kane overrode anything my friend had going on. I continued with my speedy walking pace until I saw and hailed a cab.

Once inside the cab I sagged into the seat. There was a horrible feeling in the pit of my stomach because I couldn't really fault Kane, he'd been great with me.

Any hang ups between Kane and I, were mine. It hadn't given me any satisfaction to run away like that and I felt heartbroken.

Kane had come back, but there was no way I could have seen myself in that life. Mine was too orderly, regimented.

I swallowed back the lump in my throat just as my cell began to play the familiar tune that took me right back to Kane in my sitting room, and I searched my bag for it. His number lit up my screen and my heart squeezed.

My chest felt tight and I considered not answering, but if I hadn't I'd have been going back on our agreement to stay friends.

My bruised heart ached because I knew that as soon as I heard his voice, it would suck the last of my strength I had mustered to leave him back at the venue in the first place.

"Jo...you went without saying goodbye? That suggests to me you feel more about us than you're prepared to admit to." His monotone voice sounded deflated.

I considered his answer carefully. "Maybe I do. Maybe it was too dangerous for me to stay?" My answer came out as a truthful question for the both of us. Candice sat forward and faced me with a shocked expression.

"Come back, Jo. We'll talk. I only have tonight, we fly to Boston tomorrow," he urged, in a tone that suggested he really wanted me to.

"I can't do that, Kane. I don't belong in your world. I know nothing about music or bands, and seeing how Cole dealt with that woman—"

"Cole's a dog, Jo. Any woman is fair game to him—"

"And you, Kane? What about you?"

"I won't lie. I've had my share...more than my share, but if I was in a relationship, I wouldn't stray—"

"How can you know that? We're too different. The past couple of days have been too weird for words. I'd never have had a one night stand with any guy...yet I did that with you of all people. I'm ashamed of myself."

"Perhaps if we'd met for the first time as adults, without all the history we have, you wouldn't have this mental block about exploring a relationship with me."

"A relationship? Kane have you been doping on something? We both know that's never going to happen. We're too different now. You have the world at your feet and I'm still finding my way in mine."

"So leave it. Come with me, Jo. Let's find out if what I think we could be is possible."

"Stop, Kane. It all sounds too easy. You're being ridiculous now. You show up after twelve years and we have one mind-blowing sexual encounter, and you think I'm going to drop everything to be with you? That may seem normal for your lifestyle, but it's grossly abnormal in mine. Let's not make this any harder than it is already," I pleaded. "I hope you enjoy your tour, have fun and stay safe. I'll text you my email, you already have my phone number. Keep in touch and I hope when you have some downtime you'll come and see me again."

"So you thought it was mind-blowing as well?" He said, ignoring everything else I'd said. I heard him snicker. After he was met with silence, he exhaled slowly, "Ah, my little Jo, you're breaking my heart." Another long pause between us ended when he gave up. "Okay, like I said before, have it your way. I'll miss you, baby, and I'll definitely keep in touch. Be happy, girl, you deserve it. I love you, Jo—"

The line went dead and I stared at the signal because it had dropped off and I never got to respond to those words or to say goodbye.

My heart sunk, feeling desperate and depressed that I never got to hear what else he would have said. I missed those final last words, whatever they may have been. I wondered if he had thought that I'd ended the call deliberately. I considered calling him back, but decided it would have just prolonged my agony.

Before Friday night, my life had been pretty level. My existence wasn't exciting, but it had been ticking along nicely, until Kane dropped back into my life like he'd fallen from the sky.

I stared out the window thinking there hadn't been enough time to fully process all that had happened and that's why my feelings were in conflict. The route the driver took us on passed Candice's place first.

Ten minutes after we'd dropped her off I'd made it home in one piece on the outside, but in millions of tiny fragments on the inside.

It had been the strangest three days of my life and if a fortune teller had told me that Kane Exeter would pass through my life like a force 5 tornado and would leave me with a much bigger void than he had when I was ten years old, I'd never have believed it.

I was furious with both Kane and Elliott, but most of all with myself.

There was one thing I knew Kane was right about. I wanted a guy that was willing to fight for me and Elliott had given me to Kane on a plate like I couldn't make my own decisions.

Whether I liked him or not, if Elliott wasn't willing to respect my friends, male or female, would I be happy with that? *We're not together now anyway*.

Chapter Ten

JEALOUSY BURNS

itful is the best way to describe my night after the concert. Suddenly I was left with nothing but to pick up the threads of my life and I really wasn't relishing in the thought of starting another romantic connection in the future. I woke and turned to see the clock on my nightstand, realizing I had overslept.

Throwing back the comforter, I darted around like a crazy person, putting myself together to hit the streets on time to catch my train to work. I ran all the way down the block with people looking in the direction I came from like I was being chased.

By the time I reached the station platform I was a hot mess, heaving heavily, puffing and panting from the exertion just as the train was pulling into the station.

I thought my day was improving when I saw one seat unoccupied when I entered the car. I flopped into that seat and took my cell out of my pocket and texted Candice to prepare the files for my morning meeting with my father and my awkwardly strict boss.

There was a text from Elliott waiting for me, and my level of guilt for what I'd done quadrupled as soon as I saw what he'd written.

Josie, you bring out the best and the worst in me. Please forgive me for my ridiculous behavior yesterday. It was stupid. I was so frustrated about being so far away from you. I remembered how you spoke about Kane from your past and I had an idea what he meant to you. That made me insane with jealously. Knowing that he was with you and I wasn't there to defend my position cut me to the bone. I'll be home on Wednesday. Please say we can talk then. Love you. x

Tight, suffocating feelings stole my breath, and just when I thought I couldn't feel any worse, I had. Before Kane had come back, Elliott had made me feel safe and secure.

Okay, he wasn't Kane Exeter with his rock star magnetic personality, but he was pretty fucking hot in his own right.

Elliott had dark brown hair, brooding good looks, six feet three inches, and with a well-honed body from hours at the gym. He also had gorgeous, blue-colored eyes like Kane's and I had felt proud walking out with him. He may not have been a rock star but he had his fair share of heads that turned in his direction.

I willed myself to stop thinking about him and tried to focus on not getting killed by the distraction on my cell phone as I made my way across the street from the station to the office.

My boss, Lester Marling, was waiting by reception when I entered the revolving doors and as soon as he saw me strode over and started to challenge me before I'd even drawn a breath to speak.

"You were supposed to be here an hour ago. Early meeting at Hollings Industries ring any bells?"

From the stunned look on his face it was clear he was shocked that I'd completely forgotten. It would have been pointless to make an excuse. I had such an honest face that I'm sure if I'd tried to lie it would only have backfired and I'd have appeared more of an ass.

At least I had sent everything over to Candice last thing on Friday, and noting the files tucked under his arm, I knew he'd received them that morning. I inclined my head in the direction of them and did my best not to show my utter incompetence by saying, "Ah, I see Candice followed my instructions and put them on your desk, I knew I'd be running a little late this morning."

Checking my wrist watch, I continued, "However, we still have fifteen minutes, so let's make our way over there before the competitors snatch the contract." Taking charge I sounded more confident than I had felt.

From that point on my day got progressively better and it wasn't until it was time to go home that I thought about the text from Elliott again.

Calling him was pointless; I'd done the dirty with Kane and figured I'd burned my bridges for any hope of any real reconciliation with him after something like that. I'd been weak and stupid to have fallen for Kane's lines, but guys did that all the time with women, and I kept telling myself I hadn't cheated. It had been Elliott's choice to push me away.

It just so happened it hadn't taken that much of a push for me to fall into the arms of Kane with no real resistance. *Jesus I'm a mess.*

Pushing both men to the back of my mind, I entered my apartment and no sooner had I placed my purse on the kitchen counter, I heard my cell vibrate.

Ignoring it, I made my way to the shower to wash away the grime of the day. Only after I was rocking my baggy cotton PJ's did I pull my cell out and check who had called.

My heart leapt into my mouth with excitement and once it settled back in my chest it thumped wildly in an erratic beat at the sight of Kane's missed call.

My mind went blank because he had tried to call so soon again after our conversation when I was in the taxi. I sat trying to pull myself together again and wondered whether to call him back. I never had to make that decision because my cell rang again.

This time the excitement I had been feeling was instantly snubbed out by the guilt that followed when I was already swiping to answer Elliott's call.

"Hey," I said, sounding pretty meek.

"Thank God, you answered me. I was scared you wouldn't talk to me again after my jealous spat with you a couple of days ago."

I couldn't believe how serious he sounded and how guilty I felt again about what I'd done. He had been nasty on the phone before, but he had told me he'd slept with someone as well. I couldn't feel hurt about that because it was his revenge borne out of anger.

The heavy feeling in the pit of my stomach had risen to my throat and tears stung as I prepared to discuss what happened with Kane. I may have had a fling with him, but essentially, I wasn't that kind of girl. To lie to Elliott would have made me just that.

"You had every right to be wary, and after I'm honest with you, I'll understand if you never want to know me—"

"Stop. I don't want to know what happened. I only have myself to blame for the way I behaved."

"No. Don't do that. Don't take responsibility for my bad decisions. Own your own."

"So it was a bad decision? That you slept with him?" he asked, even though he'd said he didn't want to know.

I stared straight ahead in my sitting room at the blue chair over in the corner and knew I had to say the words to him that would probably kill any relationship we may have still been able to salvage.

"Yeah, and I do regret it...I can't lie to you, Elliott, no matter how much that hurts—"

"It's my fault. I gave you to him—"

"That's a ridiculous statement, you don't own me."

"Is it? I shouldn't have told you to spend time with him? What if I hadn't behaved like a crazy caveman?"

I smiled nervously because that's exactly what Kane had called him. "Then perhaps the outcome would have been the same, then again, perhaps it wouldn't have been. I can't know that now."

"Do you love him?"

"I think so...yeah I do...but it's...complicated." I knew I risked hurting him by saying it, but I couldn't deny how deep my feelings went for Kane.

"Complicated? How? Do you love me?"

Silently, I stood and pondered my answer. I knew I liked Elliott before Kane came back, but once again, the fact that I'd had to think about it told me it wasn't love, yet.

"Kane has been in my heart since I was a child. That kind of bond runs deep, I'm not *in* love with him nor am I there with you yet, I'm not the kind of girl that falls head over heels for someone. It's how someone acts, my romantic relationships are cultivated over time."

"And that's why you love Kane?"

"I don't know. I love him because I think I've always loved him. In love with him is different, Elliott. Like I said, I'm not in love with either of you."

"That's a very honest answer, Josie. Do you think you could fall in love with him? With me?"

"I'm sure I could...with both of you, but I don't feel I deserve you after what happened, Elliott."

"Is he coming back? Are you seeing him again?"

"I hadn't planned on that. We didn't arrange...well I didn't..."

"So for him it was what? Curiosity? A slow night? I'm trying to understand where he's at with you." His comment about a slow night stung.

"He suggested more...I told him that I wasn't a fit for his lifestyle."

"So even if you had those feelings you wouldn't pack a bag and run away with him?"

"I can answer that question honestly right now because he offered that to me and I'm still here," I stated. *I wonder how many women would have taken him up on that.*

A strained silence fell between us. "Are you still there?" I asked, a short time later.

"Yeah, I was thinking," he inhaled deeply and sounded deflated when he exhaled. "Can we...try again?"

I didn't know what to do with his question. "Really? You'd want that...even with what I just told you?"

"From the sounds of things it was sex. Sex that should have scratched that itch you both had about each other."

Is that what it was for Kane? For me? "And that doesn't bother you?"

"Yeah, it bothers the fuck out of me, but it would bother me more if you weren't mine," he said in a sad tone. My heart squeezed tightly, aching from how my choice of actions had affected him.

We spent the following hour and a half going around in circles with the both of us beating ourselves up about what had happened with Kane. Then he suddenly mentioned again about us trying again.

I didn't feel deserving of that, but I owed it to Elliott and myself to find out if we could be as good as I thought we might have been, had Kane not showed up.

Before i answered there was a question I had to ask and I'm not sure if I would have, had Kane not tried to call minutes before.

"What if he came back? What if Kane called me and still wanted to be my friend?"

"Like I said before, Josie, I don't think any woman can be just friends with Kane Exeter, but we'll figure that out if it happens. All my life I've waited for the right person to come along. Somehow, I felt that was you. Get this straight in your head, I refuse to be a doormat but I'm willing to try again with you, if you think I'm worth it." My heart shattered with the sadness in his statement and tears sprang to my eyes with his unguarded comment.

"I don't deserve your forgiveness, but think I'd like that, Elliott," I said, my voice barely a whisper.

"Then...I will see you when I get home. If you change your mind for any reason, call me."

"Thank you, for giving me another chance. Most men wouldn't."

"Josie, if my thirty years has taught me anything, it's that the heart wants what it wants and neither you nor I can force it to feel what it doesn't. I called you today because I can't deny what's in mine. My head on the other hand wanted to fuck you over so badly, but my heart hurts like a bitch, so the only way to make that ache go away is to let the love that's been developing for you override all those thoughts."

The way he forgave me just like that hit me harder than any harsh words he could have spoken. My throat closed so fast I felt like I was suffocating. Elliott had shown me that his love could be unconditional and I knew it was more than I should have expected.

"Okay, Josie, I have to run. I love you." Elliott never waited for a reply before he hung up.

I wandered over to my sofa with my phone still poised at my ear then I threw myself face down and allowed all my guilty feelings for what I had done to surface and spill out in my tears.

After what had happened I felt undeserving of a guy like him, but I wasn't going to squander my second chance even though he'd forgiven me too easily. If it had been me I knew I'd never have forgiven him.

Kane tried to call me again that night—twice, but I switched my phone to silent, and even after he left voice messages I made my mind up not to listen to them.

I had to focus on my future with Elliott, and although the draw toward Kane was overwhelmingly strong, his way of life was so far removed from my own that I figured I'd never belong.

It hurt me to think that, but once I had settled on that fact, I knew I had to do my best to forget, keep my distance for a while and hope that time would bring the horny feelings I felt for him under control. *Infatuation isn't the same as love.*

Being with him after all these years had somehow screwed with my judgment and I convinced myself it was possible that what we'd felt had gotten mixed up with feelings of better times from our past. I figured my feelings were just deep-rooted fairytale desires and fantasies.

They were nothing like the love and devotion that I believed was possible in Elliott's voice earlier that evening. I used his words as my focus to concentrate on what could be my own reality if I allowed it to be

All of that was easier said than done when I slipped between the sheets and my first thoughts weren't about Elliott sharing my bed, but the memory of Kane being there and all the feelings I'd felt while he'd held me in his arms. I cried and I hoped that one day those memories would fade.

Chapter Eleven

EVERYWHERE

The day seemed to drag as I waited for Elliott to get back from France, especially when there were four messages on my phone from Kane that I hadn't listened to.

I found myself staring at the message icon on the top corner of my screen and I knew I was scared to hear his voice because I'd been trying my best to forget him, yet somehow he was everywhere in my thoughts.

For example, the day he left I had stripped the bed and changed the sheets throwing everything into the washing machine.

Days later they were still in there because I couldn't bear to see them. I worried that every time I saw that comforter I'd forever be reminded of the sight in my mind's eye of my fist twisting a handful of it while Kane went down on me.

That one morning with Kane was never far from my mind. When I had decided to tackle the laundry, pulling the wet bed clothes from the machine, I had a visual of Kane's beautiful face lying on the comforter with a sensual smile on his face and raw passion in his eyes as I rode him. I was right, that vision would never leave me. The image was so overpowering that I immediately went to my phone and checked my voicemail.

"Hey, gorgeous, I just thought I'd call and say, hi, but you must be busy. I'll try again later." It was a pretty standard message but the sound of his voice and him calling me 'gorgeous' made my heart flip over in my chest. I shrugged off that feeling and tapped to listen to the second.

"Damn, I missed you again, beautiful. We're leaving Boston and heading over to Michigan tonight, call me if you get the chance."

Clearly, Kane had no idea I had shunned the first message.

"Three messages and no callback. Do me a favor and give me a quick buzz so that I know we're good."

It was the first sign that he had begun to realize I wasn't returning his calls on purpose.

"Jo I refuse to leave it like this. Why won't you at least talk to me? Call me... please...just pick up the goddamn phone." From the frustration in his tone it was easy to hear how annoyed he was that I hadn't responded.

Kane had probably never had that happen to him with anyone else, but the sound of his sexy tone pleading with me sent a shiver of excitement running down my spine.

An hour later I was still thinking about him—still had the sound of his sexy voice in my head even when my cell rang again. Elliott's picture was smiling up at me from the screen so I swiped to accept and placed the phone to my ear.

"Hiya, honey. Just landed in Dublin. I can't believe that this time tomorrow night I'll be back. Question is; would it be too soon to come over and see you?"

My heart didn't race in the same way as it did when I heard Kane's voice, but I refused to allow his flirtatious, seductive ways to prevent me from moving on with Elliott.

"Tomorrow night? I'd love it, Elliott. I can't wait to see you. Should I make dinner?

"No, I'm not letting my girl go to all that effort when she's been working all day. What say we get take-out...Chinese good with you?"

My mind immediately wandered back to the food that Kane ordered and what happened during the subsequent twelve hours and the best I could do was nod before I remembered he couldn't see me.

"Sounds amazing. Anything that stops me from cooking is the best choice of take-out," I managed to respond.

After talking for a few more minutes he finished by talking a little dirty about what he wanted to do when he saw me again.

I didn't respond to that because it had only been a few days since Kane had been in my bed and the last thing I wanted to do was to make another mistake.

Most girls would probably have been shouting from the rooftops if they'd spent a night in bed with Kane Exeter, but not me. I wasn't proud of myself.

No sooner had our call ended, Candice called. "Kane called me. Kane fucking Exeter called...*me*," she shrieked hysterically. I could hear her hyperventilating and told her to breathe. I had done my best to ignore my feelings, but my heart was in my mouth because he clearly wasn't going away.

"He asked me if you were sick. I told him normal life had resumed and that you were looking forward to Elliott coming back. After several cussed words he called Elliott a son of a...anyhow he just about flipped and said to tell you he's flying in from Kentucky on Sunday. Honestly, Josie, he sounded so freaking hot, with all that aggression in his voice—it gave me goosebumps that made my nipples tingle. Have you heard that alpha male thing he has going on when he's pissed? It made me squirm in my seat. Do you think he's looking for a re-match in the bedroom?"

"Don't be ridiculous. He probably just wants to mess with my mind after you told him about Elliott."

"Oh yeah, wonder how Elliott will react if he does turn up at your place? If there's any chance of that happening, I'd buy a ticket to see it."

I groaned as my heart weighed heavily in my chest again, that feeling had become familiar. "This can't be happening to me. Of all the times Kane could have come back, he'd waited until I was in a relationship I wanted to be in."

"Elliott is what you want?" Candice's pitch was almost near hysteria. "Hmm...Kane Exeter or Elliott Packer? I mean...don't get me wrong, Elliott's a good looking man, but Kane? That ass? Those tattoos? The way his eyes twinkle with that sexy, dimpled smirk and that smooth as soft caramel sauce voice of his? He could croon me to sleep any night of the week or stare into my eyes or...just fall asleep beside me. I'd settle for that," she sighed dreamily.

"It isn't the falling asleep that bothers me, Candice. It's just all the waking hours when he's around," I mumbled, putting my head in my hands.

"Ah-ha! So you *do* have the hots for him. I knew it."

"Stop doing that. Stop encouraging me to do something I'd regret for the rest of my life," I admonished.

It was bad enough that I was struggling to get my life back on track without my best friend trying to push me back toward the man who had sent it off kilter in the first place.

"Is this my choice or yours, Candice? Because if it is, I choose Elliott. He's funny and warm, loving and steady. Kane is spectacular and so fucking sexy...he's the fantasy every woman has, but that's not real life...it's just like you with Jason Bourne," I reasoned, hoping I'd explained myself well enough for her to back off.

"Yeah, and if it was my choice between Jason Bourne and Elliott? What choice? I would so drop my drawers for a badass actor like Jason Bourne."

"Correction, Candice, that's exactly my point, Jason Bourne is a made-up character; Matt Damon is the man behind him. So you see where I'm coming from? Jason Bourne isn't a real person," I said as I rested my head back on my hand that had been gesticulating the whole way through my analogy.

"No, Josie, I don't, for starters Kane *is* real. Oh-so-real," she sighed, then giggled like a dreamy fangirl. "Second, I don't give a rat's ass who Matt Damon plays; whether it's Jason Bourne, the nerdy guy from *The Informant* or whatever character, I'd still do him. Have you seen his body? I wouldn't mind lying under that...at all," she said excitedly, then laughed at herself. "What I am saying is that Kane is...*Kane*. He's a rock star, but he's himself. What you see is what you get. So that flirty, kinda dirty vibe he has going on is exactly the same guy on and off stage. He fucks for fun and why shouldn't he? He's so hot he probably needs to get off a couple of times a day at least, just to relax, with all that testosterone running around that hot, ripped and tatted body of his."

"Candice! That's quite enough. What in the hell has gotten into you?" I shouted, pissed at the way she was making me drool. Hearing her talking about him like that affected me on a personal level and stirred feelings between my thighs that made my pussy ache. I felt jealous that she was lusting after Kane.

Suddenly my mind wandered and I was remembering the way his big, strong hands splayed widely as they scrolled leisurely over my body—like he was memorizing every curve. How I came alive when he'd touched me, the way his fingers and tongue had teased my flesh, giving me pleasure as he took me to the edge of ecstasy, and held me there.

There were vividly clear memories of the weighted stare in his darkened, lust-filled eyes that warned of a turbulent ride as he pushed himself roughly inside me. I closed my eyes for a second to relish in that particular thought.

My panties were soaked and my mind was firmly back to that time in the bedroom replaying the erotic scenes we created during that one morning of free love we had together.

Closing my eyes, I tried to shut out the images in my mind's eye, but that only made them more vivid. Seconds later I was off my sofa and walking over toward the kitchen area. I pulled open the fridge and I tried to shake off the heat between my thighs and put those unnerving thoughts out of my head.

"Are you still there?" Candice's voice pulled me out of my daydream.

"Yep."

"Well it sure as hell isn't Matt Damon, I think I may have noticed if he was," she said, and continued to laugh loudly. I had to backtrack to the last thing I'd said to Candice to realize her smutty joke.

"Listen to me. Kane is my fantasy guy, Elliott's my reality. If you really care about me, believe me when I say that Elliott is what I need in my life. That one time with Kane was a mistake, and I'm really thankful that Elliott has given us a second chance. He's a good man."

"Listen, Josie, I get it. You were brought up with a father who still has a stick up his ass from his time in the military—that and the fact you know squat about music or the lifestyle he has. I bet it isn't half as sensational as they say it is in the media. You are a sweetheart but you need to let your hair down and take a risk or two."

When I made no response Candice didn't force the issue any further and decided that she'd rather spend the night stalking Matt Damon's page on Facebook than arguing with me. *And she wondered why she was still single. If she's waiting for Matt to come knocking on her door, then she'll be disappointed, because he's already married.*

After our conversation I was even more determined not to call Kane back and managed to convince myself that after a few weeks the strong feelings I had about him would fade as quickly as they'd arrived.

What I felt was happening was just a stupid infatuation. I felt like a sixteen-year-old having a crush on a rock idol, but the difference was that I didn't have to imagine what it would be like to sleep with him, because I already knew.

Craving a much needed distraction from the melancholic feelings that were setting in, I knew there was only one thing for it.

Delving into my hall closet I pulled out my vacuum and cleaned the apartment within an inch of my life.

Two hours later I had finished and was so exhausted I had a shower to soothe my muscles.

Nothing seemed to help, but by then my mind was all over the place about facing Elliott again.

When I went to bed my heartbeat kept faltering with every new obstacle I saw coming and it filled me with dread.

The nerves in my belly had begun to take over. I wasn't crazy enough to think that when Elliott came home that I was going to get off lightly with what had happened.

On my way home from work, Elliott called to tell me he'd be at my apartment by 6:00 pm. He was already in a cab on his way from the airport.

My heart rate pounded in anticipation of what he'd say once I saw him. I felt dreadful and filled with shame because it had taken me no time at all to do what I had with Kane.

I made it home fifteen minutes before Elliot, and when I heard his firm knock on the door I nearly fell through the floor, anxious about facing him.

"Hi," he said, smiling as he leaned against the doorframe when I opened the door for him. He looked even better than I remembered and I hesitated before I opened the door wider for him to enter.

Stepping forward as I stepped back, Elliott's hand grabbed hold of my cardigan and pulled me swiftly toward him, his other hand gripped my waist and pulled me closer as his face stopped a couple of inches from mine.

"You look amazing...and smell even better than you look, if that's possible." My heart raced at his sudden move. He dipped his head and landed a small kiss with his soft lips on the side of my cheek.

I heard him inhale and felt shy and awkward when he appeared to behave like nothing had happened.

Previously, I had always felt at ease around Elliott, but to suddenly have him in my apartment and remember what had happened with Kane had created a barrier between us for me.

Pushing him away gently I made my way over to pick up the take-out menus I'd left on the counter before he arrived.

"Should we order take-out now? It will take around forty-five minutes to arrive, this is the peak time for orders," I asked, creating a diversion because I was unnerved by his nonchalant calm approach.

"Sure, let me look," he said casually, holding his hand out for me to give him the menus.

After we'd ordered dinner I made a big deal of choosing the wine we eventually opened. I was stalling for time, and when I could no longer avoid sitting down I knew we were going to deal with the elephant in the room.

My heart thumped irregularly and another attack of nerves set in. I felt like I was going to vomit.

"So, Kane Exeter. I thought I'd throw his name out there because he's been in the room with us since the moment you opened the door for me."

Staring at my hands then at the floor I was suddenly dumbfounded. There were no words I could say that would make what I'd done any easier, and when I couldn't meet his gaze he broke the silence that had grown between us.

"He was very lucky I was so far away, Josie. The way he spoke to me on the phone—"

"That's just how he—"

"Don't. I'm trying to be tolerant about what happened, to save what we had, Josie, so don't fucking defend the guy. He moved in on my girl. You did tell him about us, right?" When I looked up and saw the hurt look in his eyes I had to be honest.

"Of course I did, and he...we would never...I mean we'd never have done what we did if...you hadn't—"

"Really, Josie? Is that how you want to play it? You'd never have let him fuck you if I hadn't been upset and told you to go for it? Do you always do what you're told?"

Tears sprang to my eyes, my windpipe crushed by the onslaught of raw emotions I felt, and even though I had been beating myself up about it, I still couldn't articulate the embarrassment and shame I had growing inside of me.

I couldn't face the discussion I knew we had to have, all because I had the humiliation of knowing how weak I had been as soon as he'd turned his back. It wasn't as if Elliott had chosen to go away—it was his job.

"Did you come here to see how distraught I felt about the mistake I made?"

"Do you regret it happened?"

"With every bone in my body," I said quickly.

Elliott sat staring, his eyes ticking over my face, studying me—searching for the truth. I had regretted it. Given the time again I wouldn't have let myself get lost in Kane's web of seduction and intrigue. Curiosity killed the cat, and I knew all too well what that particular proverb meant.

I bowed my head and stared into my lap, wondering why Elliott had even come. He deserved more than I had given him, and for a moment I wondered if this was his sadistic way of pouring more salt into my already open wound.

Gradually, I forced my head up to look straight into his eyes and the hurt that was evident there had a greater impact than any words he could have possibly chosen to tell me how wounded he felt. My hands rose to cradle his face and I held his head.

"You can't imagine what this feels like for me...how sorry I am. There aren't enough words to say that, Elliott. And if, now that you're here, you feel this was a bad idea to come and try to mend what we had, I don't blame you. I can't undo what I did, and if you can't forgive me then it's no more than I deserve."

"If you had the choice between me and Kane Exeter what would you do?"

I didn't know his motivation for asking that question at that particular point but I said, "I choose you."

Chapter Twelve

HIGH SCHOOL CRUSH

he compassion in his eyes was more than I could have wished for when he said, "I've been in your shoes once myself, Josie. When I was nineteen I had a long-term girlfriend I'd met in high school and we'd been messing around for months but we never got past second base. Her father was a big hitter in the city and she was groomed for MIT College, whereas I wanted to study construction and civil engineering nearer to home. My father wasn't too healthy and my mom was kinda flitting between taking care of him, my elderly grandmother and working two jobs. Then there was my kid sister as well, so when I had an offer from college right here in New York, it seemed like the best solution at that time. Anyway...I digress. Katie Lawrence was everything I ever wanted in a girl; funny, sweet, smart, and a kick-ass sassy bundle of dynamite. On the other hand, I was this quiet, unassuming little nerd that she took a shine to." He smiled a little wistfully before looking slightly embarrassed by his self-depreciating description.

"What I'm trying to say...badly, is that I never saw Katie for four years, but like your Kane, I never forgot her either. Four years after we both graduated I ran into her at a wine bar in the city one Friday night after work. We were both with our respective partners at the time and although a lot of time had passed there was still this...spark that hadn't quite gone out between us. Our other halves were totally oblivious to the signals that passed between us during our conversations that night and as the time neared for us to leave I found myself becoming more and more agitated at the thought of walking away from her again. When the time came, I was reluctant in winding up our impromptu double date, and when the bar was closing Katie slid a note into the back pocket of my pants. I'm not trying to hurt you when I say this, but I can still remember her slow, intimate gesture to this day."

At first I thought that was exactly what he was trying to do, and I have to admit, his words were like he was giving me a taste of my own medicine.

I was surprised at how jealous I felt by the way he spoke about his past love. It was like he still carried a torch for her. However, the more he disclosed the easier it was to see there was definite purpose to his story.

"For three days I held that note in my hands resisting the urge to call her, and by Tuesday evening it was burning a hole in the inside breast pocket of my jacket.

Looking back, I knew from the moment I tucked it in there when I got home, that I was going to see her again. By 3:00 pm the following afternoon we were wrecking a bed in a little backstreet hotel on the Upper East Side and I was balls deep inside her."

Pulling away from me, Elliott stood and paced in thought. He looked a little uncomfortable at sharing this part of his past.

"You see, she was my one-time thing...the little piece of kryptonite that I hadn't seen coming and I had absolutely no willpower or the want to resist her. After that day, I wanted her so badly that I completely neglected the great girl I had, to regress to my past because I believed that Katie was everything I wanted in my life. For weeks I ignored Carly, and no matter what she did, I couldn't even pretend to give her the time of day. Eventually, she packed her bags and decided she wasn't prepared to live with the shell of the guy I had been before Katie had walked back into my life."

"Why are you telling me all of this?" I mused, thinking he'd tell me that I had done the same to him, but I was way off the mark.

"Because it wasn't until after she'd gone that I came to my senses and decided that Katie was my fantasy, and the more I thought about it the less I liked myself for what I had done. I was weak and had thrown away a great relationship for the idea of something that wasn't ever going to be my reality. Katie rang me a month later to say her and her guy were moving to California. Never once did she mention what happened that night, and the fact that she could carry on like nothing had happened made me wonder if I was the first she'd been unfaithful with."

"So I'm Katie? I mean you think I'm just like her?"

"No, Josie. I'm saying that I hate what happened but having been in a similar position I can hardly blame either one of you for what happened."

"Just like that? No questions?"

"None. It would drive me fucking nuts to hash it over again. You answered what I wanted to know on the phone. As long as you've drawn a line under it then I have to let it go because I don't want to make the same mistake of destroying something good, and your honesty shows me how remorseful you are about letting that happen. We can only go forward from here, and like I said when I called you, the thought of losing you hurt. I realize what we have is pretty new, every new relationship has its rocky patch...this one was a doozy for sure, but I'm willing to try to put it behind us if you can."

"Elliott if I could have a do-over—"

Without letting me finish he placed his index finger over my lips. "Shh, no more," he whispered as he knelt down beside me by the sofa. Taking my head in his hands he leaned forward and pressed his lips into mine in a soft kiss. Leaning back, he gave me a sad smile. "It may take us a while but we're gonna make it," he said, with no hint of a smile. The seriousness of his expression made my heart ache and I leaned forward to kiss him softly on his closed mouth.

"Thank you, Elliott, I don't deserve you," I said in a small voice when I pulled back.

"Yeah, you do, Josie. Like I said before, the heart wants what it wants. What happened wasn't planned—at least not by you. Stuff like that...the draw is so strong that we're kinda powerless to resist it."

Our moving conversation was really poignant and I watched his face, unable to fathom what was going on behind his eyes.

He was hurt I was in no doubt about that but he had risen above that feeling to give me another chance to be happy with him.

Deep down I felt I should have said more, but anything else I said would just have prolonged our discomfort so I remained silent and waited for him to lead the way.

Fortunately, my apartment doorbell rang and Elliott rose to answer it leaving me staring at his back and wondering how I deserved someone as good as him in my life.

As it seemed to be a growing theme with me and men, the food arrived and life was a little easier for the distraction.

Soon afterward we were treading safer ground with our topic of conversation shifting to his work and his trip to France.

Kane made me laugh at some of the translation mistakes he'd made and by the time the food was done I had managed to push Kane to the back of my mind and listen to Elliott's dulcet tone with his mellow, quite refined accent for a native New Yorker.

Listening to him speak gave me the chance to study him again and I enjoyed watching his gorgeous, even facial features, the way he ran his fingers through his hair habitually, and the way he devoured the food from the Chinese cartons spread over the low table beside the sofa.

Every time he licked his lips I felt mine curve in a small smile. I had a fascination for his mouth, his lips in particular, and the way his tongue smoothed over them made me want to kiss him, but there was no way I was pushing anything like that between us.

I had been in the wrong and wanted to make sure if we were taking things forward it had to be at Elliott's pace. I had no rights as far as benchmarking how that happened.

By 10:00 pm Elliott was beat. He'd been traveling for almost thirteen hours from his construction base in north eastern France to New York via Paris and Dublin, and had come straight to me from the airport.

When he mentioned that he was tired and had to go to bed my heart leapt to my throat at the thought of him staying the night.

I wasn't ready for any intimacy between us so soon after being with Kane and felt cheap, but was relieved when Elliott stood, grabbed his jacket off the chair, and began to shrug himself into it.

"I'll call you, and we'll maybe meet up on Friday. I have a couple of days work ahead in the office and a meeting at 9:00 am tomorrow. Don't worry, Josie. We'll be taking this slowly; neither of us are in the right frame of mind for anything more than we have at the moment. It'll happen when it happens, so don't stress yourself. We'll get there," he said, bending to give me another closed-mouthed kiss. Stepping back, he drew his fingers down over my lips and gave me a small smile.

"Get some sleep. I'll call you tomorrow," he confirmed, then opened the front door. Just before he stepped out into the corridor he turned and placed his palm on the door again. "You look great by the way, Jo. I never got the chance to tell you how beautiful you look tonight." He gave me the first genuine smile I'd seen that evening. "I'll call you," he said again as if to reassure me, and picked up his suitcase to leave. I watched him as he walked down the corridor toward the elevator but he never looked back.

I stared down the narrow hallway for a while after he'd gone. And when I stepped back inside and closed the door quietly, I wondered what I'd done to deserve such a man.

There was nothing stopping him from finding someone else, yet despite what he knew, I was still the one he wanted.

Taking the food cartons from the table I threw them into the trash while my mind replayed all the things he'd told me. I was thankful he'd gone home because if he had pushed me for anything sexual I know I'd have rejected him.

I was in no fit state to jump into bed with any man. No matter how much I wanted to make amends.

Just before 6:40 am my cell vibrated on the kitchen counter and fell off it onto the floor.

The sudden noise woke me and for a couple of seconds I was startled by the strange noise until my mind recognized the sound.

I slid out from between my crumpled cotton sheets and squeezed around the half-open bedroom door and into my open plan sitting room.

As I'd suspected my phone had vibrated its way off the kitchen counter and was lying on the wooden floor.

Luckily, it had fallen screen up and when I picked it up the last number displayed was Kane.

My stomach sank as depression set in because I couldn't face another day of turmoil between the two men tugging at my heartstrings.

Instinct told me to call him back because I assumed if I continued to ignore him, he would only find another way to reach me. He'd already shown me that by contacting Candice.

The last thing I wanted was him showing up unannounced at my apartment especially since Elliott and I had decided to iron out the huge kink that had messed up our fledging relationship.

Willing myself to press his number on the screen was no simple task. Adrenaline rushed through my veins and squeezed tight at my chest.

My whole body shook in anticipation of hearing his smooth, familiar voice and I hadn't even hit the green handset icon to make the call.

Plucking up my courage I swiped his number and my heart raced to the point where my breathing was shallow and much quicker than usual.

That click—when it connected, registered with me that I had to talk to him and knowing that had made me feel weak.

I gripped the granite counter, my fingers blanching against the cool, smooth surface and it offered me no comfort as the call began to ring. Less than one ring later Kane answered.

"About fucking time, baby. You've been avoiding me. I gotta see you on Sunday. I've got four days off. We should talk—"

"It's pointless, Kane. Our lives are never going to meet in the middle. You agreed. There's nothing to talk about, Kane. Elliott's home and we both want to try again."

"He's a prick, Jo. Look at what he did to you. The fucker blew you out because I was visiting you."

"No, Kane, Elliott had a sixth sense about us and he was right."

"So, if he had this...sixth sense or whatever you want to call it, how come he didn't put up more of a fight and at least try to prevent what we did?"

"That's his story to tell, Kane, not mine. Let's just say he had his reasons."

"That's it? So I rock up and bang his woman and he's cool with that?"

"Seriously, Kane. Hello? This is the woman you *banged,* you're talking to her, remember?" At that moment I had never felt less valued.

"Damn, sorry, baby, I'm only trying to say that if you were mine, I'd have been on the next fucking plane, work or not."

"And you were the one that said *he'd* come across all caveman."

"Shit, this call isn't going the way I wanted it to go," he said, sounding full of regret. "Meet me?" he asked hopefully.

"No, Kane, I can't do that."

"Why not?"

"Are you fucking insane, you know exactly why not." I sounded irritated.

"Because you don't trust yourself around me?"

"Yes. I mean no, jeez...what I mean is that Elliott and I are working it out, Kane."

"And you're prepared for us never to be in the same room again to make that happen?"

His question was met with my silence. Was that what I meant? *Is that what Elliott wants from me? That isn't what he said on the phone, but was that what it was going to take to help us both forget?*

"Kane, you and I both know what happened was pointless—"

"It was? Why don't you try being honest with yourself, Jo? It was probably the least pointless thing I've ever done in my life." Kane's voice held so much conviction. I almost choked.

"Stop. Just stop the fucking endless Ferris wheel ride you've put me on. I'm at my limit. You and I are made differently. Our views on life are too different now. I won't allow you to mess with my mind. I've made my choice. It may be hard for you to understand, and I know you're probably not used to being second best, but I choose Elliott."

Chapter Thirteen

BACK OFF

"So that's it? You're just gonna settle for someone who doesn't rock your world the way I can?"

"Will you get over yourself, Kane? Why can't you accept that I don't want to be with you? Don't you want me to be happy?"

"Of course I want you to be happy, but you are denying what you feel for me. I saw how you looked at me, Jo. I think you are making a huge mistake."

"No you were the mistake, Kane."

"Not fucking buying that, Jo. Not for a minute. I know I'm gonna sound like a dickhead when I say this, but I'll say it, because we're all about honesty, right? Well I am, anyway. I've been with hundreds of girls. Hundreds...and none of them made me feel like you do."

My heart skipped another beat to know I meant more than a simple lay, but the same barrier existed as before—he was a rock star and that statement said so much about what my life would be like if I were to try and go there.

The thought of sharing someone with hundreds, and no doubt thousands of girls in the future wasn't something I'd even begun to contemplate.

"So I'm this week's magic vagina? I'm flattered by your comment, but that doesn't turn my head in the least. I love you, Kane, I'll always love you, but not in that way."

"Liar. When we were in your bed you seem to have forgotten that it takes two to make that kinda chemistry. You think a guy with my experience wouldn't notice something like that? The way I lit you up when I slid inside you still makes my dick twitch eagerly. Your whole body came to life in a way I'd never seen in any woman before...or since." I felt like I'd been stabbed in the heart. I remembered Elliott's comment about being with someone to get back at me but it had nowhere near the same devastating impact of Kane's disclosure.

"Did you hear that 'or since' statement right there? It's been less than a week since we..."

My voice tailed off because the jealousy coursing through my body stiffened every muscle and I hated him for turning my world on its head while he appeared to breeze in taking my feet from under me and going right back to living the life he had before.

"And that bothers you? Because you taking that guy back bothers me. Why did you do that? What kind of guy takes a woman back that has feelings for someone else? I'll tell you who...a desperate one."

"He's not desperate, and you're one cocky son of a bitch."

"Not cocky, confident, there's a difference."

"Not from where I'm standing."

"Alright, Jo, have it your way, I'll bow out and back off. I can't force you to want me. Back when we were kids you were open to taking a risk now and again, what happened? You know, you were right about one thing, we're not kids anymore, and if my parents taught me anything it was that life is short. Think about that while you stay with your safe bet and have your mundane, soulless relationship with Elliott. You're choosing the life you like instead of the one that sets you on fire."

Click. The line went dead. The effect of his harsh words and the furious tone in his voice was a shock to my heart. Hate toward him built deep inside for how he'd ended the call. I was an emotional mess even when it was supposed to be what I wanted.

Lying on the sofa I bawled my eyes out for hours until all the fight I had left in me was back and I was furious with Kane Exeter. *What the fuck did he know about me, anyway?* Not a lot. The way my life had been since he'd cut his contact with me had been ticking along nicely until he'd showed his face again.

Both work and my personal life had been pretty even. Work hard, get promoted...eventually. Save hard, find independence, learn not to be a fool with my heart and snag a nice guy, a good looking guy with a sound background, like Elliott.

Then Kane fucking Exeter had decided to come and disrupt my equilibrium, creating dissatisfaction within me where it hadn't existed before.

A scream of frustration tore from my throat as I began to prepare myself to face a day in the office and I shoved all thoughts of Kane firmly to the side.

My one night with a rock star was exactly that. An insane, never to be repeated experience. For one night only.

Contracts and invoices kept my mind from my personal life all day and I was particularly thankful that I had such a demanding boss for once.

There was no time to let my mind wander as he set tasks and assigned more projects to me to prepare for approval. It wasn't until I arrived home and sat in a warm bath to soothe my aching bones that I heard from Elliott.

"Hey, how're you doing?" he asked in a calming voice.

"I'm good...tired. My boss ran me ragged today. You?"

"Same...although, I did make some headway on the building project finally, so it was worth the effort."

Elliott cleared his voice then asked, "How did you feel after I left yesterday?"

"Better, even though I don't deserve it." My comment was met with silence which felt like a knife twisting in my stomach, but what had I expected him to say?

"Can we do dinner on Sunday?" he asked, hesitantly. I was oddly disappointed because the night before he had mentioned Friday, but I let that slide as I was quietly relieved, figuring the extra couple of days was exactly what I needed to get my head straight.

"I'd like that. Where did you have in mind?"

"The Drake?" My heart stuttered in my chest because that's where we had our first date and that fact wasn't lost on me. I must have taken too long to answer because he added, "Yeah, it's where we began so I thought it was as good a place as any." It was as if he'd read my mind.

Once we'd arranged our dinner date our conversation carefully avoided anything that may have sparked any emotive discussion, and ten minutes later our call was done.

I lay back in the bath wondering if we'd ever have the natural care-free feeling we'd had before Kane showed up. I worried that if we couldn't get that back whether reuniting would be a waste of time.

For the rest of my week life was pretty uneventful. I'd kept my world small, refusing an offer of drinks after work with Candice, and had closed her down the one time she mentioned my love life.

I had become an expert at avoidance to anything she said that would open that particular avenue of conversation.

All in all life at the office and at home became a little more sedate as the days passed.

Occasionally, my mind ticked over thoughts about Kane and Elliott before I mentally forced myself to put any notion of Kane to one side. He'd pretty much done me the best favor he could have when he had ended the call.

It had gutted me but it gave me the fire to fight the good parts of seeing him again. Hanging up was pretty symbolic because it was almost akin to what he'd done before, when he simply cut me off all those years ago.

By Saturday night, the horrible nerves in my belly were back, and I was apprehensive. I wasn't sure how dinner with Elliott was going to pan out because he hadn't called me all week after the call on Thursday. Us trying to take things slowly wasn't helping me to feel any sense of security.

A passing thought made me wonder if Elliott was thinking the same.

Torturing myself I sat with my phone in my hand wondering if I should call him to confirm the dinner date and decided it was ridiculous for me to be this worried about something that was supposed to be my future.

Deciding whatever would be would be, I turned on the TV and tried to find a movie that would take my mind off things.

Some things just can't be avoided because when I thought I had, lo and behold, there was Kane sitting on another fucking sofa, a blue one this time, headlining a prime time TV chat show. He looked so damned sexy and lickable.

My reaction was instant, I wanted to mount the TV on the wall to get at him. *It's a test. It has to be. He's so fascinating to look at. Life is so cruel sometimes.*

"So where to next? Where do we have to alert the city authorities of the sudden influx in restraining order applications?"

The male interviewer asked smugly and chuckled while the studio audience screamed in appreciation when Kane smiled seductively and winked at the camera.

"Maryland. I have some urgent personal business to take care of back there," he said, smirking sexily as he ran his hands through his hair.

My gaze fell to my hands for a second as I languished in the memory of the luxuriously silky feel of his amazing dark hair running between my fingers.

One thought triggered another, his strong hand winding my hair around it as he pulled it tightly and extended my head back to kiss me.

Shit! I groaned out loud. He wasn't even in the room and my thighs squeezed together to soothe the pulsing ache of desire for him. And damn, the Maryland comment was almost missed because I'd been objectifying him again. *Well he isn't coming back here!*

Turning the TV off, I threw the remote down and made my way to the fridge. I grabbed a bottle of wine—*there's no way I'll get through the night without a little Dutch courage after the feelings he just evoked while I was simply sitting in a chair and he was hundreds of miles away.*

I pulled up my brother Matt's number, looking for some normal male company, and when I reached him I was out of luck when he told me he was about to go into a Broadway show with his latest squeeze. Smirking, I ended the call and thought *it must be love because he hates musical theatre shows.*

It was 11:30 pm when I drained the last of the wine from the bottle into my long-stemmed glass and realized I'd drunk every last drop. And it wasn't even the standard sized bottle I usually took a week to drink. It was the larger economy one I'd use if I had people to dinner.

Feeling brave and very drunk I decided to call Kane back and give him a piece of my mind for fucking up my life.

Fumbling for my phone I scrolled down through the last incoming calls and found his on the sixth number down. It rang twice and a woman with a Southern accent answered.

"This is Kane Exeter's phone. Kane can't come to the phone right now because he's a little busy...Oh God, yeah, there...right there," she moaned loudly in ecstasy. I think I threw up in my mouth a little at the sound of her.

I felt distressed and quickly cut the call. I threw my phone toward the far end of my sofa like the damn thing had burned me. I sat in shock staring at it like Kane was somehow going to be able to see my reaction from inside it.

What did I expect? I wasn't sure but not that. I was mortified I had allowed myself to sink so low. *Well you definitely dealt with that well. Good job, that told him.*

Slouching further down on the sofa in my drunken state, I was too numb from all the alcohol to have any real feelings or even think straight after that. I couldn't even cry. He didn't deserve me to anyway, he'd moved on to groupie number six hundred and whatever. It's what I wanted, right? And I have Elliott.

～

When I woke with my neck in an awkward position, I had the sudden recollection of the night before, despite the fog from the alcohol. I cringed feeling sorry for myself as I tried to move. I felt like death.

Stretching out, every muscle in my body felt stiff and my mouth felt like someone had been stuffing flour coated cotton balls in there.

Standing up took more skill than I expected and after swaying a little I made my way to my bathroom. I winced when I saw the state I was in.

My teeth and lips were stained red from the wine, and my stomach felt like someone had inserted a lead balloon in it.

If anyone had seen me like that they'd have staged an intervention and dragged me off to rehab. *Who said I couldn't party like a rock star? One night of that is enough to last me a year, yet I've managed to be carelessly drunk twice in the space of a couple of weekends since Kane showed up.*

I frowned, an instant ache in my chest because I was so damned bad at trying to do the right thing.

Thinking of Kane made me wonder if I'd dreamed the whole phone call thing, but when I saw my cell lying where I'd thrown it, depression set in and I prayed that by some miraculous intervention he wouldn't know I had rung.

Glancing at my screen confirmed that miracles rarely happened because he'd tried to call me back. Twice.

My dry mouth seemed even more parched and my throat closed with emotion at my stupidity of opening the line of communication again between us.

The familiar message icon was showing on the left-hand side of the screen. I placed my cell, screen down on the table, ignoring the message and I headed to take a shower. I tried to convince myself I'd feel better afterward. I didn't.

All it achieved was to dilute the salty tears from the warm spray as it ran over my face.

The feeling was a mixture of suffocation and drowning as I stood, face up, and tried to wash the memories of the past week away. I thought that for someone who had previously been particularly well-balanced, some of my more recent decisions had been less than sound.

Denying the feelings I had for Kane, I was determined to give

Elliott my full attention from that point on. I blamed the wine for my lapse in judgment and used the rest of the day to preen myself ready for dinner with him.

When I left the sanctuary of my small apartment to meet him for dinner, visually I bore no scars of my induced alcohol coma from the night before.

Inside I felt like a train wreck; a big one, and I was still suffering from a hangover. However, as I sat in the cab on the way to the hotel I was hoping to give Elliot the girl that caught his eye the first time we met.

There was nothing more I could have done with how I looked that evening. The attention to detail I'd worked hard for took hours, but had looked effortless.

The Stella McCartney dress I had chosen to wear was as sexy-as-hell. Midnight blue velvet with a plunging neckline and a bare back.

The material started just above the dimples at the base of my spine and accentuated every curve beautifully. It was the best fitting dress I'd ever owned and I knew the dress turned heads.

I had debated whether to wear it or not because I wasn't sure if it made my appearance overtly sexy given the circumstances, but once I'd tried it on there was nothing else that compared. It was unlike me, but I had to power dress to give myself some courage.

Elliott's reaction to how I looked was worth all the effort I'd made. He greeted me with a wide smile and eyes that couldn't hold my gaze as he appraised what I wore.

"You look stunning, Josie," he gushed his approval as he led me into the restaurant. Placing his warm hand on the small of my back, he gently stroked my skin with his thumb.

A small shiver ran up my spine as the maître d pulled out the chair for me then for Elliott. His strong palm brushed across my lower back before he dropped it to his side and took his seat after I had taken mine.

At first things were a little strained between us, each of us remaining on safe, mutual ground as we spoke about work and movies, all the while ordering food and drinks. Elliott scowled at the waiter for talking to my cleavage rather than to me.

"I almost covered you up with a napkin there," he said, without a hint of humor in his tone.

"Well…I suppose if I wear something like this for you, and you take me out in public, someone is bound to look."

"If I stab them in the eye with my fork do you think they'll get the idea I don't like it?" he questioned, in a tone that was a little less aggressive.

"Next time, I'll wear a sweater," I said deadpan, thinking the dress had been a stupid idea.

"Don't you fucking dare. Your breasts look amazing in that." I glanced around as heat rose to my cheeks ensuring that no one had heard him.

Normally if a guy said something like that to me he'd be wearing the drink and I'd already have called a cab home, but it was Elliott sharing a private joke between us. *So why does it still feel wrong?*

"How was yesterday, did you do anything exciting on your day off?"

I sipped my wine, and took my time, for several reasons. First, the smell of it made me want to vomit because I was still hung over, and secondly, I had been a little excited when I called Kane before the woman answered. And most of all, I didn't want to lie. The conflicted feelings I had been experiencing were killing me.

"Stayed home, watched TV, drank some wine and fell asleep," I said, missing out the part where I was completely wrecked and called Kane, interrupting his groupie sex.

"Sounds relaxing."

Having my toenail extracted with rusty pliers would have been more relaxing. "What about you, did you do anything good?" Shifting the focus away from me was the best plan I'd had all day.

"Yeah." Elliott looked past me and I turned to see what he was looking at but there was only a waiter passing.

I giggled when he didn't expand on his answer. "Are you going to tell me what you did?" I asked, smiling at the expressionless look on his face.

"Met up with a friend that came to town and I ended up getting home at 10:00 am this morning," he said, fingering his silverware as he ran his index finger up his wine glass collecting the condensation.

His honest answer pissed me off. I had been torturing myself at home while he'd been out partying with one of his buddies. I knew I had no right to feel the way I did because of what I'd done. We were supposed to be starting again. *But then again, I had called Kane so what gives me the right to put my foot down?*

"And where is this buddy now? At home still recovering from the excess?" I asked, trying to keep the annoyed tone from my voice.

Elliott stared at me with an intensity that riveted me to my chair. "She's flying back to California. She's been here for two days." The way he delivered the bombshell was callous and I knew it was meant to sting. It had stung.

Everything he'd said to me was a lie. Elliott hadn't forgiven me at all, he obviously wanted revenge.

Chapter Fourteen

ATTRACTING ATTENTION

Oh my God! What am I doing here? When I began to rise from my seat Elliott grabbed my wrist and pulled my arm down so that I had no choice but to sit back in the chair.

"Don't start acting like the wounded party, Josie, you're the one who fucked the rock star remember?" The icy tone of his voice gave me chills, but I was damned if I was going to let him humiliate me.

"How could I forget when he was so much better than you?" I spat back, wanting to hurt him for punishing me the way he was.

"Really? You have no idea what I'm like between the sheets, I gave you the dumbed down version. We were new remember? I don't know what you're getting your panties in a twist for, I spent some time with Katie...and damn it was a good time, and now we're even."

You think? By that point I didn't care who was looking, how I was dressed or if I ever set foot in The Drake Hotel again.

The way I'd tormented myself for letting him down had been unnecessary, because for the previous two days he'd been screwing his old flame in some skanky hotel while I'd been denying the best sexual encounter of my life in my efforts not to disappoint him again.

"Let go of my arm. Let it go right now," I growled in a low voice and glanced nervously around me.

"And if I don't?" he sneered, looking at me menacingly.

Grabbing the table cloth in my fist, I raised an eyebrow. "You want to humiliate me, Elliott? Then I guess I'd better make it worth it. Let go or I'll be attracting a whole lot more attention—"

"Damn, baby, so glad you came." All of a sudden Kane was standing beside me and from the scowl he had on his face he'd obviously seen the frightened look on my face as he quickly surveyed the scene.

"Is this guy bothering you, baby?" Glancing up in confusion, first at Kane, then to Elliott, I wasn't sure who was the most shocked to see Kane, him or me.

Everyone in the restaurant had fallen silent when they realized Kane Exeter was there. Most of the patrons had taken out their cells to capture the moment.

"They didn't call my room to let me know you'd arrived so I came down to check. Have you been waiting long?" His comment took me by surprise and I couldn't understand why he had been expecting me.

Elliott's grip had gone slack the moment he'd seen Kane and as soon as I'd noticed this I pulled my hand free. I stood up, almost too close to Kane, and although I was relieved that he had intervened, I had no idea what was going on.

Looking around the room I was aware of the other diners watching us. I was in no fit state to deal with either of them by that point.

"Here take my seat, you two deserve each other, I'm out of here." Shoving my way past Kane, I was disgusted that I had let myself get into such a position between two men. This happened to other girls not me.

In my haste to leave, my velvet dress caused friction against the starched white, cotton table cloth, displacing everything on the table.

All eyes were on me as I fled the restaurant to the sound of Kane calling my name.

When I saw at least three people taking pictures of the scene, I about died of shame over the whole sorry chapter in my life.

By the time I reached the street a yellow cab was parked close to the sidewalk at the side of the hotel.

Hurriedly, I flagged the driver so that he wouldn't drive off. I slid into the seat and closed the door feeling relieved to be out of there.

When I looked through the restaurant window I saw Kane still standing by the table. Elliott was out of his seat squaring up in confrontation with him and I felt a new level of shame while I mumbled my address to the taxi driver.

My eyes were fixed on the scene and I continued to watch the mess I'd made until we pulled away from the curb and I lost sight of them.

Fighting back tears I called Candice. "Hello?" I said when I heard her voice. I couldn't attempt another word after that because I was an emotional mess. My throat constricted and I swallowed painfully.

"Are you there, Josie? Has your phone called me from that huge ol' purse again?" she asked, laughing.

"Sorry, I'm here..." Again, I struggled and as if Candice sensed it she asked, "Where are you, Josie? Are you okay?"

"Going home," was all I could manage.

"On my way," she said intuitively, knowing I needed someone with me. I closed my eyes in relief that she hadn't asked any questions. Her apartment was only ten minutes from mine and I knew she'd arrive there before I did.

Candice had a spare key and could let herself into my apartment so I wasn't worried about her hanging around outside in the dark.

Knowing Candice would be waiting for me was comforting and I sagged back into the black leather seat, letting the tears I'd been biting back stream down my face unchecked.

Paying the cab driver, I avoided eye contact with him. I walked quickly inside my building when I saw my next door neighbor, Barney, leaving at the same time. He gave me a friendly greeting as he passed me.

I wasn't in the mood for small talk and ignored him, and quite frankly, the way I had felt, he was a prime candidate for a kick in the balls, because my hate for all men felt real.

I pressed the button incessantly for the elevator, taking my frustration out on the poor thing because it was either that or punch the wall and swear like a sailor.

The ride up to my apartment seemed slower than usual, and just as I reached my apartment door my cell began to play that stupid Beyonce ringtone I'd forgotten to change.

Since Kane had gone I had set my phone to vibrate and I must have knocked it from vibrate to ringtone again without realizing it.

Thinking it may be Candice I pulled it out of my bag and saw that it was Kane. *What the fuck? Why can't he just leave me alone? Why was he even there?*

This was all too much to deal with. I placed my key in the lock, but Candice beat me to it by pulling the door open before I could use the key.

"Thank God you're okay. Where were you? What happened?" She grabbed me and hugged me tightly before pushing me to arm's length to look at me. One look at my face had her backtracking. "It's okay, you don't have to answer. It has something to do with Elliott, right? It *was* him you were meeting? Where did you have dinner?"

"The Drake," I offered, taking off my coat, and still trying to get my feelings under control.

Jesus, and Kane turned up, right? Oh man, I bet that was a blood bath. No wonder you can hardly speak with two hot men fighting over you."

Candice's tongue sure needed surgery to render her mute some-times. "How the hell did you know Kane was there?"

"Because he told me on the phone he was coming back to speak to you on Sunday, remember? Naturally he'd stay at the Drake. God I should be a detective or something." I had forgotten about that. It went some way to explaining why he wasn't as surprised to see me as I was to see him. *Talk about a clusterfuck.*

Candice led me over to the sofa and I toed off my shoes before climbing onto it in my dress and hugging my knees.

"It's a fucking mess. I'm a mess. What the hell did I do? Who knew I was such a slut? I'm humiliated."

Sitting down gently beside me, Candice listened as I poured my heart out about Elliott, Katie and my telephone call to Kane when I heard his groupie sex.

"Damn girl, you certainly have been through the wars." I glanced up at her and the strange look she gave me made me feel disgusted with myself all over again.

"What?"

"I'm just thinking that you are actually human...like the rest of us after all. Not only did you fuck up, Josie, but DAMN you did it in style," she said as she laughed.

I was hurting inside but reluctantly I had to give her that, I had messed up with rock star style.

Candice poured wine into two of my best long-stemmed glasses and handed me one. I swirled the red wine around in the glass.

"Not only am I fucking rock stars I'm turning into an alcoholic," I said, and stared into the glass.

Candice giggled and took a long swig of her wine. As she did there was a forceful knock at the door. She froze like a statue and held her glass still. "Are you expecting anyone?"

I stared at the door and shook my head.

Candice jumped up and turned the light off, plunging us into darkness. I almost jumped out of my skin when her mouth appeared a hair's breadth from my ear.

"Shh. Maybe it's Elliott. He might see the light through the spyhole," she advised in a whisper.

"Jo? Open the door; I know you're in there." Kane's low tone sounded frustrated.

Candice squeaked loudly, "It's Kane Exeter." As if I didn't know his voice.

Her tone was totally fangirl, even in a stage whisper. I had thought it may be him at the first knock, but I didn't want to face him after I'd told him I chose Elliott and what he had put me through at dinner.

Suddenly I burst out laughing at the absurdity of the whole idea of everything that had happened during the previous week. And Candice, being the true friend she was, immediately joined in.

Lying curled up on my sofa in the dark, in my best dress, I was hiding from a rock star in my own house.

The more I thought about it the worse my laughing fit became until Kane pounded irately on the door again. "I don't know what it is you're finding so fucking funny, Jo. Open this goddamn door before I kick the fucking thing in." Cautioning me in a furious tone stunned us both and we fell still and silent for a split second until Candice snorted and laughed even harder.

Breathlessly she heaved and said, "Josie, I think there's a rock star at the door."

I burst out laughing again and without another warning we heard a loud bang as my lock came flying into the room.

Kane stood in the doorway, his silhouette backlit by the subtle yellow glow of the corridor lighting, looking every inch the rock star. I couldn't help remembering how amazing he had looked the week before when I watched him on stage at his gig.

"Glad you're enjoying the drama of this. Are you having fun? What are you, fucking twelve?" he asked, sounding more pent up than a heavyweight boxer preparing to fight.

Candice snickered in the dark and another laughing fit gripped her again until she was breathless and all I could hear was her gasping for air.

We were still in the shadows and every second that passed where Kane hadn't reached for the light became funnier than the last. Tears rolled down my face as I laughed hysterically at how I'd screwed myself over.

Eventually Kane reached out for the switch by the door. When flicked the switch the light bathed the room, and Candice rolled over cracking up again in a new bout of rhythmic laughter that looked like she was having a fit on the floor.

Kane was as furious as hell and stalked over toward me, stepping over Candice's body that was curled on the floor. He grabbed me firmly by my upper arms and yanked me off the sofa. Scooping me up in his arms he strode into my bedroom, carrying me over his shoulder.

As we entered the room he swung around to close the door narrowly missing my head connecting with the wall. Without talking he dropped me unceremoniously onto the bed and placed his hands on his hips.

"What the fuck are you laughing about? Do you realize I almost got arrested tonight because of you? What the fuck kind of stunt was that you were trying to pull back there running off and leaving me to deal with that crazy fucker? I stepped into help you and you ditched the scene."

Watching the stormy color in his eyes as his jaw ticked with natural aggression made him ten times hotter.

"Don't waste my fucking time, Jo. I flew from Kentucky all the way over here on my days off to meet up with you."

"And I should be grateful about that? A meeting takes two people to arrange, Kane. Has no one ever told you that? I never agreed to meet you. I didn't even know you'd be at The Drake. And let me tell you, your tone and bulldozer tactics aren't necessarily winning me over. Why did you come back anyway? You are exactly like I thought you'd be. It's not like I've been your last or anything. You'd fuck anything that moves—anytime you can. You turn my stomach—"

"And you turn mine. What the fuck, Jo? You'd settle for that piece of shit guy who takes you somewhere public to humiliate you? Telling you he fucked his old girlfriend for a couple of days to get even?" I looked at him in shock as he nodded. "Yeah he told me what he did to you."

"At least he knew the name of the woman he was fucking, Kane? Can you remember the name of yours from last night? Did you even ask her?"

Kane's eyes darkened; a mixture of fury and confusion in them. "I never fucked anyone last night," he stated.

"Liar."

"I've never lied to you. I never fucked anyone last night."

"How come I got the breathy whore on the line telling me you were busy...oh God, there...right there," I said, mimicking what I'd heard.

"Ah, I see. That. Sorry to disappoint you and kill my reputation, but that wasn't me."

I snickered and shook my head. "Don't tell me...she was pleasuring herself and talking to herself at the same time, right? And she just happened to have your phone with her...yeah...that makes sense." My sarcasm didn't hide the jealous tone in my voice.

"No actually, that's not it at all. When you called we were on the tour bus on the way to the airport. Cody, the dirty bastard, was giving oral to some groupie. They were stoned, Josie. My cell was on the table near where they had been sitting and I was in the John. I never knew you had called until I picked up my cell as we left the bus, and when I called you back, I got sent to voicemail.

Candice's voice interrupted us. "Guys if you don't need me anymore I'm gonna head home. Can I just say one thing? Kane, when you kicked the door in like that...that was fucking hot. The way you lifted her up and dragged her off to her room...mmm...got any friends that are single?" she asked, giggling from the other side of the door. Kane's face softened instantly.

"Night, Candice. I owe you one."

"Can you be more specific on the one part please?" she asked hopefully.

Kane snickered and the way he smiled and rubbed the back of his neck was cute. It was the first time I'd ever seen him embarrassed.

"Erm, got my hands a little full right now, Candice, but I'll see if I can set you up with one of the nicer guys in the band," he chuckled.

"Really? Well...cool." She sounded flustered and I smiled at her request backfiring like that. "Okay, well you might want to come and do something with the front door after I've gone because I'm sure someone would love this big-assed flat-screen TV of yours, Josie."

Kane turned and opened the door to check out the damage. A softly spoken conversation took place between him and Candice, but even when I strained my ears it still sounded like mumbles to me.

I stood up from the bed and began to make my way back into the sitting room in time to see Kane closing the door and shoving my heavy oak cabinet in front of it.

"That should secure it until tomorrow morning and I'll call a locksmith.

"Sorry but you'll have to move that again, you're on the wrong side of the door and there *is* no *we*, I'll get it fixed tomorrow."

"Oh no you don't. Not this time, Jo. I'm going nowhere until we've ironed this out."

"What is there to iron? You want to fuck me again? Is that what it takes for you to leave me alone? If so have at it. Come on...in the bedroom right now. I'm yours for the night. Is that what this is about?"

"Don't tempt me, Jo. You have no idea what I'm capable of." The gravelly low tone told me I was trying his patience or turning him on.

"Why not? I don't have a boyfriend now, right? You helped me out of that relationship, remember?" Kane stood motionless and stared me square in the eyes.

The intensity of the moment fueled my anger further, and I snapped. I wanted him. More than I wanted life so I decided...well I didn't consciously decide anything—I just acted.

Chapter Fifteen

BRAZEN

"*H*ere...take what you want. You have my permission. You said you wanted my permission to touch me or kiss me before, well...knock yourself out."

Kane shook his head and gave me that sexy smile, the one that makes me want to get naked. So I did exactly that, but the way he stared into my eyes was so intense.

Conflicting feelings flitted across his face and his piercing blue eyes narrowed in question at my sudden change of heart.

He didn't move or blink once when I began to slide my dress over one shoulder, exposing my smooth bare skin in the most tantalizingly slow way I knew how. I swallowed roughly at my brazen, seductive move.

As soon as I repeated the action on the other shoulder the heavy velvet material fell away from my body and cascaded down my legs to pool at my feet.

Stepping gingerly out of it and to the side, I stood motionlessly in front of him and tried to emit the confidence my act appeared to portray. My thin, blue lace thong was the last barrier between my nakedness and modesty.

Kane's eyes feasted slowly over my breasts, up my collar bone and continued to my long, platinum blonde hair that was still pinned up in a bun. I knew it exposed the nape of my neck which had been his focus during our foreplay that other morning.

His eyes locked onto mine for a second then followed the direction of my hands as they reached up to find the pins holding my hair in place. I knew he enjoyed tangling his hands in it before.

Seductively, I removed each of the three pins holding the arrangement, one at a time. My hair fell loose in three sections, one over my right breast, one down my back, while the last of it fell in line with the other at the front and covered my left breast.

My eyes never left him and his never left me. Watching him take in every move I made was exhilarating because I saw the way my body was visually stimulating him.

The adjustment in his stance was notable as his spine grew stiff, his feet spread further apart to ground himself, while both of his hands hung down by his sides and curled into fists.

When I had taken my hair down I saw him crane his head from one side to the other like the strain of holding it up on his shoulders was suddenly too much.

The way he grazed his bottom lip with his teeth then stopped to bite into the plump flesh was more than a suggestive move for how he felt. And when his gaze finally settled on my face, his eyes looked intensely into mine. They were almost black with desire as his pupils had swallowed up almost all of his blue colored irises.

The way we connected gave me the most incredible feeling of intimacy I'd ever had.

"I'm not going to touch you." His tone was different...lower. My heart ached longingly with those words, even when we both knew he was lying.

"No? I'm disappointed. It's a pity because I'm so frustrated with the games you men play that I may as well join in and fuck who I want, when I want." I had sounded so convincing that I knew there was an element of truth in what I had said in that moment.

"And you want me? Is that what you're saying, Jo? Is that an admission that you want more with me?"

"Who doesn't want to fuck a rock star?" I answered, mocking him.

"You have all the moves, the confidence with girls, you're all dirty, whorish bastards in your behavior, and us girls know we're getting someone who knows what to do with that six-inch appendage between your legs. Flashing that grin that makes me weak at the knees." Kane shook his head and snickered at my reply.

"Nothing six inches about me below the belt buckle. Eight is more like it...and the way I stretched that sweet little pussy of yours, it's a wonder you've forgotten about that so easily."

My pussy clenched at his dirty response because I hadn't forgotten at all. I ached all over after being with him last time. In fact it was one of the reasons I had been denying the connection we had, because it had felt too good.

True to his word he hadn't reached out to touch me. I knew that it was up to me to call all the shots and briefly wondered if I could really carry on with what I'd started.

At the same time I already knew, that for me at least, there was no turning back.

Finding the courage, I walked over and stood inches in front of him, my eyes instantly connecting with his once again.

The devouring, hungry look burning in his eyes gave me courage. I smiled slowly, stuck my thumb in my mouth, and sucked it sensually.

Inhaling deeply through his nose his gaze dropped to watch my cheeks hollow. His lips parted slightly while his breathing became notably heavier. I could smell his cologne all around me and although it was subtle my senses were heightened, excited by how I was turning him on.

When I pulled my thumb back out, it popped. Kane's serious, lust-filled eyes darted back to mine as I watched him come undone right in front of me.

Stroking the wet, swollen digit across his bottom lip made him swallow hard and loudly, encouraging me to push my thumb into his mouth.

Like the opportunist he was, Kane instantly sucked on it with force. The lace of my thong became drenched in my warm desire. The sensation felt like it might well have melted from the warm wet feeling against the bare heat between my thighs.

Glancing down at the slate grey, button down shirt under his casual black jacket, he popped my thumb from his mouth and I moved my hands to his abs, toward his pecs then up to his shoulders, assisting him with removing his jacket.

My fingers trembled slightly as they found and began to undo each small, darker grey button on his shirt with due care.

As I worked my way down from the collar I was rewarded when it exposed a little more skin with each one.

Pushing both sides of the shirt wide, I took in the thick, inked pieces of art that completed his torso to perfection. I pulled the rest of his shirt free of his jeans from front to back.

Whatever was going on in Kane's mind was a mystery, but I knew from his reactions that he was definitely not immune to me.

Studying his normally silky smooth skin, I noticed his pecs were covered in pinprick goosebumps, his nipples were drawn together in tight, dark, erect buds. His anticipation of my touch rolled off him in waves, and occasionally, his pecs seemed to flex in tight little spasms.

Noting a change in his breathing when it grew heavier, I reached for his belt buckle.

Hastily his hand snapped over my fingers, his serious dark glance seemed a little more than intimidating as he shook his head.

"Enough, you've had your fun. You think I'm gonna stand here and let you get me all riled up—prick tease me, then you'll ask me to leave? I'm not into mindfucks, Jo."

"Me neither. I'm not playing games. I'm tired of thinking about what everybody else will think. I just want you to forget everything."

Kane studied me more intensely and when I held his gaze and stared him out without backing down he chewed the side of his mouth in thought.

Slowly his hand fell away to his side and he stood silently waiting for my next move.

His frustrated expression changed the instant I dropped to my knees and sat back on my calves, reaching for his buckle again. A delicious smile lit up his eyes and his erection grew in front of my eyes.

Unbuckling his belt, my fingers slipped behind his waistband and I smiled when a small shiver trembled through his body. I glanced up and my breath caught in my throat as the look of a starving man stared back at me.

Opening the first button on his fly gave me a glimpse of a small smattering of dark hair. I couldn't resist running my fingertips over it.

As soon as I felt it the urgent feeling that ran through me had me frantically scrambling to hold his cock in my hand. I leaned forward and kissed the tip slowly and when I drew back I saw a bead of pre-come that glistened.

Swallowing nervously, I licked my lips in preparation of taking him into my mouth. I was surprised when his arms swept down under my armpits and stopped me.

"Don't, I'll fuck your mouth hard and come if you take me in there. I don't want to come unless I'm inside you." Effortlessly, he hauled me up off of the floor and onto his waist.

Instinctively, I wrapped my legs tightly around him and I felt the length of his erection slide against the material of my wet thong. Kane growled and moaned a low throaty sound in reaction as he buried his face in my neck for a second. Almost as if he needed a moment to find his control.

Seconds later he shuffled across the room chuckling as his jeans were still around his ankles. He sat with me on his lap on the nearest chair he could find. His strong, warm hands palmed up my thighs and his callused fingertips kneaded the globes of my ass when he reached them.

Softly, his mouth trailed a sensual path as he explored my sweet spots; first gently on my neck, then with more pressure as he licked and nibbled at my skin as he tasted me.

When his mouth reached my left nipple he engulfed it sucking forcefully. I gasped and moaned loudly when the sensation stole my breath and threw my head back enjoying the feeling.

It was ecstasy, and my pussy clenched with need. In that moment I felt his hunger and wanton desire. I was more alive than I ever had been.

"I can't wait, I need to be inside you, Jo. Are you on the pill?"

I shook my head no and he reached down, tugging his wallet from the back pocket of his jeans.

Pulling out a row of gold packaged condoms, he shook them out and tore one off, discarding the other five carelessly to the floor.

Leaning back, I became mesmerized as he expertly rolled the thin see-through barrier down his shaft. I tried to ignore how many times he'd done that before to have been so adept at it.

It wasn't long before I was distracted from that thought when his fingers sunk between my legs and rubbed gently over the soaked thong I was wearing.

"Fuck, you're drenched, you smell so fucking sexy," he groaned as his fingers slid under the edge of the tiny piece of material and basked in the wet heat of my slit.

Kane's hungry mouth found mine, our tongues tangling in a sensual kiss at first that kept my juices flowing. It became devouring when two thick fingers parted my outer lips and another slid along the wetness and breached into my entrance.

Slowly, his finger moved in and out, like he was savoring the moment, memorizing the sensation of how much I wanted him.

In one swift movement, he curled it upwards and probed deeper and faster with expert confidence. I moaned loudly with pleasure and he slowed the pace, while his other hand slid up and squeezed my breast.

A softer, needy moan escaped my mouth and entered his before I broke the kiss, and allowed my head to rest on his shoulder.

He kissed my neck, his breath heavy as he began nibbling on my shoulder.

Drawing his finger back he slipped a second in, curling both upward anteriorly toward my G-spot. I almost lost my mind when his efforts went back to a slow tease as I neared the edge of a blissful release.

"Please," I whimpered, in a soft whisper while he snickered into my neck.

"Since you begged me so nicely," he chuckled softly as he began to move his hand again with a little more commitment. His fingers rubbed my nub and stretched my pussy in preparation for his girth. I was so turned on that I arched up and ground myself against his knuckles.

Groaning into my neck he muttered, "You like that?" Already knowing the answer from how fast I'd been losing control.

"Mmm," I moaned, continuing to gyrate my hips in my effort to increase the speed. He pulled his fingers away and brought them up to my face, drawing them across my lips.

The weight of his dark, sexy stare almost stopped my heart. His face was close, his breath becoming my air before he stuck one of his fingers into my mouth.

"Can you taste that sweet pussy of yours? How fucking amazing is that? It's like sweet syrup, baby. Fucking incredible," he said, smiling salaciously then groaned as he pulled it out of my mouth and stuck all three of his fingers that he had inside of me, in his mouth.

I watched him lick and suck at his fingers while his cock nudged and bounced against my belly in reaction to my taste.

"Can't wait," he said, pulling my thong to the side and opening my legs wider.

Lifting me into position against the tip of his cock he gripped both hips, his fingers digging into my flesh while he sunk himself quickly inside me.

There was no teasing or the chance for either of us to catch our breath before he took me so fast from the moment he slid in up to the hilt. Despite the fact I was soaked it had still taken a moment or two to adjust to the size of him, but when I had, it was the most thrilling experience of my life.

"Damn you are like no woman I've been with before," he muttered and then grunted heavily as he rode me hard.

In less than two minutes my whole body was fizzing with the sensation he'd built inside me. His hands wandering up and down my body then back to my butt as he lifted me on and off of him. He held me tightly anticipating the build. "Do it," he said, before I felt the peak rising.

My legs and hips quivered as he kept me on the edge while every single cell in my body lit up in a single connection that culminated in the most blinding orgasm of my life. I had no control over my body as it shook, the ripples of orgasmic waves taking over my nerve endings.

I'd never known a man to read my body the way Kane seemed to be able to. When I came, one orgasm flowed and ebbed, but I barely had time to catch my breath before the next began to build. I was no longer in charge of my bodily functions.

Kane Exeter controlled every fiber of my being. His musky, manly smell that mingled with his cologne invaded my nostrils.

I relished in the heightening of all of my senses, the slight taste of whiskey and mint on his breath, the feel of his hands as they learned and teased all of the sensitive sweet spots on my skin, the sight of his eyes boring intimately into mine.

There was an unspoken promise in the way he looked at me that said he was not only inside me, but all around me, his body, mind and soul knowing me inside and out—effortlessly. In that moment he had taken ownership of me.

When he'd made me come for the third time he pulled out, stood and shuffled around.

Placing me on the chair, he ran his fingers through his hair. I realized he had come at some point, but I had been in such a haze of my own that his orgasm was lost on me. "Damn, Jo." He smiled salaciously again and shook his head.

"Remember you started this." Glancing down he pulled the condom off, tied it in a knot and unlaced his converse shoes before reaching down and pulling one off and then the other.

Placing the used condom inside one of his shoes and not on the floor, he grabbed the other five as he stepped out of his jeans and tore another gold square off of the strip.

My gaze fell to his cock and it was still as ridged as it had been before.

In seconds Kane had rolled on another rubber and scooped me up off of the chair. Carrying me over to the kitchen counter he placed my bare ass on the cold, shiny granite and I screamed in shock.

Leaning over he grabbed a knife from my cutting block and fear ran through me.

It must have shown on my face because he scoffed, "Hey, no." He gestured at the knife and continued, "I may get a little freakish between the sheets, Jo, but I'm not into S&M." Sliding his finger under the string at the side of my thong he cut one side and then the other.

When he pulled the small patch of silk out from beneath my legs, he cussed and squeezed the wet material tightly in his fist, raising it to his nose.

Kane took the deepest breath I'd ever seen anyone take and I was sure he'd pass out before he had the chance to breathe out.

I only realized I had been holding mine watching him when he raggedly exhaled. "Mmm," he hummed. "Fucking amazing, babe." His husky voice sent another thrill through me.

Placing his closed hand on the granite still clutching my thong, he pushed my legs wide apart at the knees with one hand then dropped the thong and shifted his weight on both hands to hold us. His behavior since he'd sat me on the counter had me both turned on and shy that he was acting so scandalous.

Reaching over he hastily gripped my thong again, clutching it tightly in his left hand as he dipped his head between my legs and peppered slow, leisurely kisses up my thighs.

Adjusting, I arched my heat toward his mouth but he taunted me by ignoring the cues in my body. Just when I had about given up on my efforts, his mouth clamped over my pussy and sucked hard while his tongue delved deeply inside me.

I swear I came inside a minute and cried out in a way I'd never done before. I heard it echo around the room but couldn't be sure whether it was that or Kane's groans of appreciation that were the loudest.

Chapter Sixteen

INTIMACY

Stepping back from me, Kane wiped his mouth with the back of his hand and grinned in a way that had my whole being and every sense alight again in seconds. I was exhausted but elated at the same time.

Wrapping his hand around his cock he stroked it up and down as he came closer again.

Carefully, he lifted my legs and rested my calves on his hips. I felt the tip of his cock being drawn down along my slit.

As soon as he reached my entrance, he leaned over me, his forearms caging my head in as he dropped his forehead onto mine.

The intimacy in the way he seemed to see my soul as he slid slowly inside will be etched deep in my mind forever.

When he'd taken me in that unhurried way, deliberately watching my reaction, a wave of emotion washed over me that became overwhelming.

Without warning my throat closed in protest at the nearness. When he swept my hair tenderly from my eyes with his thumbs it was more than I could bear. Tears pricked my eyes and his face softened.

"Shh. Don't cry. It's beautiful, Josie. Can you feel this connection between us?" He wasn't expecting a reply from how quickly his mouth covered mine.

I was glad because I didn't want to admit that I could. That would have meant I'd have to deal with him leaving because of his work and all the reasons I'd been putting up a fight not to fall for him. And I knew I had anyway.

When he broke the kiss, another soft, intimate smile curved his luscious lips as he looked down at me from above. Rocking into me slowly, he dipped his head and peppered small kisses in a heated trail down my neck and collar bone.

My warm skin was alive with goosebumps. The tingling sensation just under my skin from how his touch commanded my body to respond was insane.

I became lost in my desire until he pulled back from me changing position.

The warmth that had been radiating between his body and mine was an instant loss. I shivered with the change of air over my damp skin and when he saw this, his hands reached up just under my armpits and he dragged his nails gently down both sides, sending ripples of ecstasy from my toes to my scalp.

Kane continued to love me tenderly for the following hour, whispering how much he had missed me during that past week, how difficult it had been for him to get me out of his head, and how insanely jealous he'd felt when I had said I chose Elliott.

At that point he stopped and stared at me meaningfully then asked, "That was bullshit, right? He was the safe bet?"

Until Kane said it I hadn't realized that's exactly what Elliott was after being with Kane, but I thought trying to be with Kane I'd be setting myself up for a future of heartbreak and jealousy.

I could be sassy when I wanted to be, and I was no pushover, but the taste of being around those groupies at his concert made me even more certain that the constant challenges to our relationship, if we had one, would get old quickly.

No matter how much I felt for Kane, I knew I couldn't tolerate living like that day after day.

Chapter Seventeen

RUN AWAY

Waking the following morning wasn't nearly as awkward as I had imagined it might be.

Kane was still asleep and I lay facing him, memorizing all of the finer details on his beautiful face. The rate of his deep, steady breaths were only around ten a minute.

Before long watching him wasn't enough and I had to reach out and place my hand lightly on his hard belly. Still deep in sleep he moaned slightly and shifted on the bed, my heart thudded rapidly as I took the opportunity to explore the rippling contours of his incredible defined torso with my shaking fingertips.

"Yeah, I'll run away with you. That's what you just wrote there, isn't it?"

My hand stilled immediately and my heart rate raced at the sound of his voice. I glanced up to see him looking directly into my eyes with a sleepy smile on his face.

Damn he's beautiful first thing in the morning. I was busted checking him out.

"You wish," I teased, giggling because there was no point in even trying to deny what I'd been doing. Kane Exeter probably got that reaction from women a lot.

Who was I kidding, by now it was such a regular occurrence he probably expected women to do it, either as foreplay or aftercare.

"I do." *And right at that moment I wished I was one of those free spirited girls who could just surrender to what they felt and just run with the experience.*

I figured I could never let Kane know that was how I felt because he had been extremely persuasive as a child. If I had learned anything from my short amount of time with him, Kane the adult was lethal.

Therefore, I knew if I had shown even an inkling of interest in his suggestion, I would have found myself on his tour bus, and to everyone looking on I'd have been regarded as flavor of the week in Hedonism's groupie harem by the month's end.

Turning on his side to face me, he sighed heavily and reached out to stroke his fingers lightly over my shoulder. "Am I going to be disappointed, Jo?"

Glancing at his face made my heart ache, my heart said no, but in the cold light of day, my head was calling the shots. "Sorry."

Kane stared at me for the longest time. "So we're just friends and you don't want more, except that you definitely didn't behave like someone who wanted to keep things platonic last night."

"Don't. Please..." I placed my fingertips over his lips and he instantly kissed them.

My heart squeezed and splintered inside my chest because I was denying what it really wanted. "It's better this way. We can be friends for the rest of our lives, Kane. I was weak both times we've had sex, but this...thing between us...is infatuation and lust. If we continue down this road, it'll end in an acrimonious shit-storm."

"As new as this is...what we're doing here...I fucking know this is more than you're willing to admit to, babe."

"That's not it at all. I'll admit you make me feel...wanted... desired, and sexy. Definitely sexy. You'll never know how much that flatters me, and tears my heart apart at the same time, Kane. But when I look at your lifestyle I just know instinctively that I'd hate it. My life has revolved around rules and boundaries, barriers and doing the right thing. It's what's made me the way I am. You'd be happy but I wouldn't. Our lives as adults are so far apart that I know we could never meet in the middle. I wish I was the kind of girl that acted without caution, but I'm not. Josephine Carmichael from Germany, is long gone; I learned about risk and consequence long ago."

Kane shook his head and I read the sad disappointment on his face. I knew he thought I was simply the type to just give up without trying, but that wasn't it at all.

The decision I had made to deny the urge in that moment took every ounce of strength in me.

Taking the hard decision to protect my feelings and our friendship for the future may have seemed boring but one of us had to keep our feet on the ground.

"Maybe our lives turned out differently, Jo, but deep down we're still the same people we were when we were kids."

"No, I don't believe that. Circumstances and experiences shape us; it robs the innocence and replaces it with the stark realities of life."

"Well aren't you a bag of delights? What the fuck, Jo? You're twenty-two years old. For fuck's sake, live a little."

"I was trying to do that when you bulldozed your way back into my life."

"And you resent me for fucking up your mundane relationship with that lanky asshole who wanted to publicly humiliate you? Looked like I got there just in time if you ask me."

Kane threw back the comforter and stood up by the side of the bed.

"Believe it or not, Jo, I really like you. Put it this way, I've never flown across the country to try and build something with a chick before, but I hear you. We're friends until the next time we meet up and fuck each other's brains out while you deny what it means to you. I'm gonna get a shower, then I'll catch a flight to New York. Some of the guys are up there for a couple of days. I may as well go party with them since you only want to be friends. My downtime is precious these days."

Suddenly I felt horrible and Kane looked hurt as he tore his eyes away and walked into my bathroom banging the door so hard, I jumped.

Grabbing a clean T-shirt and some yoga pants I pulled them on quickly and went out into the sitting room, leaving him to shower.

My cell was lying on the table and I swiped it off there and switched the display on to see the time.

My mom, Jacob and Matt had all called me, but I had a rare Monday off work and we were going to lunch to celebrate my dad's fiftieth birthday, so I knew why they were calling.

However, Candice had tried to call me five times. She either wanted the low down on the night before or something was wrong.

I hesitated on whether to call her back, but I knew she'd only keep trying. I figured the best way to placate her would be to confirm that Kane was still with me and tell her I'd call her later.

Candice's phone barely rang once before she answered. "Holy Christ, Josie, have you seen the news? You are all over it. Elliott has sold the story about you cheating on him with Kane." I didn't reply and stared into my room in a dream-like state thinking I'd imagined what she said. "Are you still there, Josie?"

Nodding slowly, my mind was blank. I had nothing to say and I realized there were tears running down my face. "Do you want me to come over?" Candice asked when I hadn't answered. Still I said nothing, too shocked to form a response. "Right, I'll be there in ten. I still have an hour before I have to be at work," she stated, as I wandered absent-mindedly into the sitting room.

Call me a coward, but I couldn't begin to think what people thought of me. I shouldn't have cared anyway. But I did. Everyone would know how weak and cheap I was sleeping with a rock star.

Slowly, I sat on the sofa and stared out of my window, the grey December weather, with its relentless drizzly rain and dark menacing clouds, fully reflected my mood. *How do you recover from the scrutiny of a bunch of horrible bloodthirsty gossip journalists?*

There were no thoughts in my head as I sat there for several minutes just absorbing how stupid I'd been.

Hearing the door creak from my bedroom, my head turned automatically at the sound to see Kane walking through it, fresh from the shower. He was fully dressed, and already wearing his jacket as if he were ready to leave.

"Fuck, I forgot about that," he said, gesturing his head at the cabinet and my busted door.

Turning to look at me he stopped exactly where he was as his foot faltered while he assessed the scene of my crying before he rushed over and crouched down beside me. "What's the matter? Why are you crying?"

My throat closed tightly. I had no words for how I felt, both from the thought of saying goodbye to him, and from the news I'd learned. I felt disgusted with myself.

Unable to talk, I just waved my phone pathetically at him and shook my head. Glancing at my phone he looked back at me, eyeing me with concern.

"Tell me what's wrong? Did someone upset you? Did that fucking asshole call you? Did someone die?" he asked in an incredulous tone.

A loud sob tore from my throat and I became inconsolable.

"Tell me what the fuck is wrong, Jo. I can't help you if I don't know what's going on in there."

Candice's voice called out from the doorway, "Let me in, I can't get the door open."

Spinning on his heel he ran across the room and pushed the cabinet away from the door, Candice rushed in and pushed past him, heading straight for me.

"Damn, Josie. Please stop crying—will somebody tell me what the fuck is going on here?"

"You're what's going on. You, Josie and Elliott are all over the gossip mags and the internet."

Nodding, his head he looked at the floor. "The fucking restaurant... don't worry, Josie, they didn't get much. Whatever they said is pure speculation—"

"Not when Elliott is out there selling his story about being the victim it isn't." Candice gave Kane a nasty sneer like she had a bad smell up her nose and Kane's brow creased into a scowl.

"Did he, the motherfucker? I'll fix this, Jo, I promise."

"Yeah, just like you fixed the door, huh?" Candice retorted and pulled out some tissues, handing them to me.

"Just go, Kane. Don't make this any worse." My plea hurt him. I saw that plain as day in his eyes.

"I'll get someone—" he started to say, but I cut him off.

"Leave it, I'll get it fixed."

"I'm not fucking leaving you like this—"

"If you care anything at all, you'll get out of here and leave me alone, right now," I replied, adamant that's what I needed.

Kane shoved his hands deep into his pockets and looked helplessly back at me. "Please, Jo..."

"Go," my voice whispered.

Walking over to me he crouched again, hugged me tightly and his warmth surrounded me. He inhaled deeply, remembering my smell and placed a soft kiss on my head. "I'm here, please Jo, don't do this."

I had started to sound distraught, and Kane quickly realized there was no reasoning.

"Alright I'm going, but I'm here when you need me, I'll call you from New York." When I remembered what he had said he was going to do there, I felt annoyed he'd toy with my feelings.

"No. Don't, I'll call you in a few weeks," I said, sobbing for too many reasons to think about.

Turning away from me he walked to the door and turned back to look at me. "Are you sure you want me to do this?" I said nothing because I wasn't. But Kane took my silence to mean I was. "Take care of yourself for me, Jo," he urged with a sad smile. Seconds later he was gone.

Candice acted like my guardian angel that day, calling in sick, and fielding questions both from the press and our friends.

Honestly, I couldn't have asked for anyone better to guide me through the ordeal. It didn't stop me from having to face my family at my father's birthday dinner though.

Luckily, by that time, Kane's publicity guru had waved his magic, spinning an entirely different slant on the event by painting Elliott out as a threatening Neanderthal caveman who didn't like that I had a male friend.

It was crazy how they had managed to turn the tables back on him less than the six hours since he'd sold his story.

Strangely enough, my family thought it was funny—all apart from my father, who had the measure of me, but didn't ask questions in front of the others.

That's not to say he let the whole episode slide because as soon as we were alone he asked how much of the event was true. I had to be honest with him, and he thanked me for being so.

I knew he liked Kane as a child and I also knew he knew how sad I'd been in the past when his contact stopped.

It was embarrassing admitting to spending time alone with Kane, which was as far as I was prepared to go,—my moral standards had slumped to an all-time low, but I wasn't prepared to add lying to my dad to the list of mistakes I'd made that week.

Chapter Eighteen

SOCIAL MEDIA

or the following three weeks my life felt pretty unsettled. I missed Kane more than I missed Elliott which was weird considering the amount of time I'd spent with each of them. Post-relationship, or non-relationship as in Kane's case, depression had set in and Kane never called.

Candice and I remained holed up in my apartment, when not at work, safe with my shiny new lock watching weepy chick flicks, eating pizza and with me crying regularly.

After a few days of this, I felt brave enough to check out my social media notifications on my way to work. They were mainly private messages from people I'd gone to school with wanting to meet up or find out what Kane Exeter was like. Some called me a whore and a few were supportive. I clicked onto my newsfeed and was paralyzed with shock when I saw Elliott's status on my timeline.

"This is Elliott's sister, Marian, I am posting this to inform you that Elliott died last night as the result of a car accident. Final arrangements will be posted when Elliott's body has been released for burial. Our family is devastated, by the loss of our wonderful son and brother. Please, can we ask for privacy in our grief. We will post the funeral arrangements in due course.

A sharp zap of electricity hit the center of my chest as tears blurred my vision. I sat in a stunned silence, staring at the outline of my cell phone unable to comprehend the shocking news I'd just read.

Elliott was dead and all I could think about was that I'd hurt him in his final days of life.

"Excuse me, Miss, are you okay?" I glanced up to see a middle-aged woman watching me with concern.

Choked with emotion, tears rolled down my face and the only thing I could do was gesture my cell at her. She turned her head to see what I had been reading and her eyes closed in horror after she read it. "A relative?" she asked gently.

"No. Ex-boyfriend," I sniffed.

"Okay, where were you going?"

I looked up to see where we were and answered, "Next stop. Work. My office is just around the corner from the station."

"I'll come with you."

"No...it's fine. I'll be okay. It's only a few minutes away. You've been really kind already," I said, taking the tissue she gave me. I didn't deserve her sympathy.

"Are you sure it's no problem—"

"Thank you, honestly, I'll be stronger on my own, but thank you for helping me," I offered as I wiped my eyes with a tissue before blowing my nose on it. I gave her a watery smile of reassurance.

The train arrived at my stop and I went through the motion of getting off, conscious that I was attracting attention because I'd been crying...was still crying.

The look on people's faces as I passed them in the street wasn't lost on me.

I made it to the office reception and my silent tears became wailing sobs as soon as I was in the safety of the building. The blonde receptionist Jacob had been hitting on for the previous week came around the circular desk and rushed toward me. I waved her away and hit the elevator button.

Fortunately, the car was already on the ground floor and opened immediately. I pushed the button for the 27th floor and leaned back against the car wall, trying to catch my breath in my tight grief-stricken chest.

The reception staff must have called up to Candice after I got into the elevator because she was standing hugging herself at the elevator door with a worried look on her face when they opened.

"Jeez, what the hell happened to you, Josie? What's wrong?" I pushed past her because my throat was so tight and I was afraid to speak the words because I knew they would tear me apart.

Holding onto my silent grief had been the only way I'd made it as far as the office, with twenty-five yards from the elevator to my office I knew I'd only make it if I continued to do the same.

Placing my bag on top of the filing cabinet, I slowly walked around my desk and slumped heavily in my chair, placing my head in my arms on my desk and sobbed even louder.

By this time, Candice was beside herself and paced back and forth in front of me. "Josie you have to talk to me. Did someone die?" Briefly, I looked up at her and nodded, put my head back in my arms and wailed loudly again.

"Oh. My. God. No."

Taking my cell out of my coat pocket, I passed it to her. "Facebook, Elliott." It was the best I could offer her. A period of silence was followed by, "Dear God, that's terrible for him and his family. You don't have to go to his funeral or anything you're not together anymore."

"That's what makes it even worse. He died and the last thing I told him was that Kane was better in bed than him," I sniffed as more tears came.

My father came into the office and when Candice told him why I was so upset he sent me straight home. He wanted to send Candice with me but I couldn't have coped with her trying to make me feel better all day.

Dad put me in a cab himself, kissed the top of my head in sympathy and sent me on my way. He looked hurt that I was upset, and I felt horrible.

The hardest part was I couldn't even contact Elliott's sister because I had no idea if she would even want to hear from me. He had over a thousand friends on his account.

The last thing she needed was an ex-girlfriend popping up to complicate an already harrowing situation for his family.

Grief had taken its toll on me and as soon as I got home I collapsed into bed. I must have sobbed for hours, my brain going over and over the previous week.

Eventually I fell asleep exhausted. It was late when I woke in the darkness.

My initial thought was calm then I remembered the clusterfuck I'd fallen into and my short-lived sedation fell away and was replaced by an aching heart and a horrible feeling in my gut.

Nothing I thought of made me feel better, nothing I thought of would bring Elliott back or undo what I did with Kane either.

I had allowed the gap in my childhood heart to be satisfied by welcoming Kane back into my life, but the adult version of my heart was in conflict because it confused our feelings from that time, and I'd let them override my feelings of what I should have done and not crossed the line with Kane.

Elliott's death wiped me out for a good couple of weeks. Dad even gave me leave from work. Apart from the grocery store delivery boy, I wasn't accepting callers to my home.

Candice called daily to check in but respected my pleas for time and patience to help get my head straight again.

Almost four weeks after I heard the news about Elliott my life began to return to some semblance of normal.

I had stopped stalking his social media page after it had been removed two weeks after he died, but had read every heartfelt message his friends had written. I couldn't bring myself to write anything.

Apart from the ending we'd had, he had been a nice man toward me. I was surprised I hadn't received a nasty inbox from his family.

Being on my own again, with no social life to speak of, was great news for my manager who insensitively voiced that he'd seen an upturn in my productivity since my boyfriend was out of the picture.

I gave him a pointed stare and shook my head, but it would have been pointless to have thought of a clever retort to his comment as he was the kind of guy that had a knack for dishing out the insults but was immune to incoming responses.

Leaving his office, I caught Candice by the arm on the way down the hall. "What say we hit the wine bar on 47th Street and have a few drinks? I've missed my best friend these past few weeks."

"Sorry, Josie, but I have a date with a hot water bottle and a couple of Tylenol. This period is murdering me slowly," she added as we left the building together.

The impact of her words hit me like a wrecking ball. In my head my mind was busy doing the math as I quickly recalled events and dates of the last one that I'd had.

It had been around eight days before I'd slept with Elliott and roughly days fourteen and twenty of a cycle since I'd slept with Kane—I was around eight days late. *Oh. My. God.*

"Have you heard anything from Kane again since he left?" It was as if Candice had read my thoughts.

"Not a word. I guess my assessment was right in the first place, our lifestyles just wouldn't fit. I can't believe I allowed myself to have casual sex with him like that," I said, feeling embarrassed at my admission and quietly freaking out as I thought about heading in the direction of a pharmacy to buy a pregnancy kit.

"Maybe it was that for him, but not for you, Josie. I haven't forgotten the stories you told me about how close you were as kids. Did a part of you wish for more? I mean...I can fuck any guy I'm attracted to and move on, but you...you aren't made like that at all. Everything is emotions and feelings. I mean we only need to take Elliott as an example; you were with him what...six weeks? And you only had sex once."

"Twice. We had sex twice."

Okay, twice in six weeks—"

"Five—he was away for the last one."

"Whatever, you liked the guy and you didn't get down and dirty for a whole month. You're twenty-two years old and the guy was almost thirty. You weren't kids playing house."

"Well, I was lucky to make it twenty-four hours with Kane," I mumbled.

"Exactly. In your case that's because you were already emotionally invested in the guy. All that history between you has brought you both to where you are now. Time was short too. Neither of you had much of that to cultivate the feelings you were having, and Kane being the kind of guy he is just took what he wanted."

"No, he didn't do that. He asked permission. That was something he spelled out to me. He asked if he could kiss me. Twice he told me he wanted to, but he asked if he could."

"Well, hell, he must have been scared he'd upset you if he asked that. I've never had any man care enough to ask that question. The moment has just been there and they've gone for it...or I have," she said and laughed.

"I guess so. Anyway, I'm not holding my breath about hearing from him again."

"Really? Well I wouldn't be too sure about that, Josie. I saw the way he was looking at you."

"To be honest I was probably staring at him in the same way. It was weird seeing each other after all that time. Hugging him made me feel whole. Like a part of me had been missing all those years until he touched me. It was like finding a favorite toy I'd lost a long time ago."

I entered the pharmacy noting that Candice was still with me and strolled down the aisle until I came to the display of pregnancy kits.

There were so many of them my first instinct was to grab one of each because I wanted the one that displayed not pregnant or negative in the boldest letters.

Candice laughed, "Kane Exeter would most definitely be my favorite toy if I suddenly found myself alone with him."

Taking a deep breath, I had something else that was on my mind and I figured that I couldn't keep it to myself for much longer. "I'm done with men, Candice...what I mean is...I didn't realize it until we started talking, but I think I might be pregnant.

"Oh. My. God. Seriously? Whose is it? I mean that sounded insensitive but given that—"

"It's Elliott's. I mean it's most likely his, but I feel like such a slut because I had sex with them both a week apart."

At twenty-two I still felt embarrassed buying a pregnancy test kit. I had no business having a child when I hadn't fully matured myself. Candice stayed with me all the way home.

My mind swirled in circles about what I would do if the innocent looking box containing the small plastic thing in my purse affirmed my suspicions.

It was ridiculous to accept the concept that such a simple action as peeing on a stick could change my whole life as I knew it.

Flashing me a sympathetic smile when we entered my apartment, Candice hugged me. "No matter what...I'm here for you, okay?"

Nodding I headed straight to the bathroom. There was no point in delaying, it wouldn't change the outcome and by the time I'd arrived outside my building I had already prepared myself for the answer I didn't want, but knew was a distinct possibility—I was pregnant.

I wasn't wrong and five minutes later I waved the stick at Candice nodding and burst into tears.

Chapter Nineteen

MOVING

*R*ubbing my back, Candice shushed me, then leaned away to look at me for a minute. "Will you keep it?"

"Yeah, of course I will. I just need to pluck up the courage to tell my parents because I won't be able to do it without them. I can't stay here. I can't afford to. It's just not feasible without a partner, and with only one bedroom it wouldn't be long before the baby outgrew the space."

"So come and live with me. My house has a back yard and you can pay me what you can afford. You can have the whole of the upstairs and I'll have the rooms I normally use downstairs. We can share the kitchen, and you'll have a built-in babysitter."

"Thanks for the offer, Candice, it's amazing, but I think I'm going to need to move back home for a while. These past few weeks have been pretty epic as far as fucking my life up goes. I'll head over to my parent's place tomorrow as it's Saturday. It'll give us plenty of time to talk about things."

"Wow you're so strong. It would take me at least a week to pluck that kind of courage up." Candice continued to offer awesome support like the amazing friend she was, and by the time our evening was over and she'd left, I felt terrified but more positive at facing my parents.

That feeling lasted all of an hour until my cell phone rang and I noticed Kane's number. It was the first time he'd called since he'd left my apartment weeks ago.

I had debated whether to answer it but swiped to accept it because I was a fool.

"Hey, gorgeous, how is life treating you?"

"Good thanks." I heard myself lie cheerfully. *So much for honesty.*

"Sorry I haven't been in contact, life on the road is insane."

"I can imagine," I replied, as thoughts and images of those groupies sprang to mind. Jealousy raged in me but I swallowed it down and forced myself to accept he still had to live his life his way. I'd chosen mine.

"I've thought about you all the time, though," he added. I wasn't convinced. It had been three weeks since he'd called.

"So what have you been up to?"

"Oh, just this and that, nothing exciting. Same as last time I saw you," I lied again. "You?"

"Well, we've played in some pretty exciting places; Boston, Washington State, Seattle, San Francisco, Los Angeles, and we're headed to San Diego right now. It's been incredible, the people we've met, and parties we've had have been amazing."

I felt sick. The lives we led were complete opposites.

"Can you fly down for the weekend? I'd love to see you again."

"To San Diego? No," I answered, feeling frantic about coming to terms with my news. I decided right there and then not to talk about being pregnant with him, figuring that in time his contact would fizzle out and we'd go back to occasionally writing an email or talking on the phone.

Kane's band was becoming too big to play too many concerts near home so the chances of seeing him would reduce over time anyway.

"I thought we were going to do more to keep in touch."

"We will, but I can't just hop on a plane and head across country, Kane. I have a job and a life here."

"You have the weekends off, there's nothing stopping you," he said with a small chuckle.

Because I'm pregnant and my life is upside down. "I already have plans for the weekend with Candice and I'm not dropping her to fly somewhere on your say-so."

Eventually Kane accepted that he wasn't going to get his way and moved past his invitation. We chatted for another hour about the band, his life on the road and more stories about the places he'd been.

~

The tone of that conversation was how each and every call we had went between us. He kept in touch monthly at first and as if he had a sixth sense his calls always came right after my pre-natal check-up appointments.

After speaking to my parents I gave up my apartment when I was four months pregnant. It was hard moving back in with them and Jacob, and even though my parents weren't thrilled about it, they were extremely supportive.

I knew that Elliott passing away had made them more sympathetic to my circumstances than they would have been otherwise.

By that time, Kane and I had formed a less angsty relationship, and caught up via Skype calls and by phone occasionally, but due to time differences we mainly corresponded by email.

Kane would send selfie pictures in the places he visited, and usually kept me up to date with his band news.

It surprised me how much I wanted to know about Hedonism and what he was doing and I replied with questions almost immediately to him.

I looked forward to hearing from him and couldn't help but compare my small existence to Kane's life, which sounded big, filled with excitement, thoughts, and opinions.

The content was just as detailed as the letters I remembered from when we were kids. Only the subject matter was undoubtedly more adult in nature.

I missed him, but I was living with my decision because I had bigger things to think about and as I prepared for my twenty-week ultrasound scan I saw yet another article that linked Kane's name with another female celebrity from the music scene.

While I was reading I saw that she liked the same things as he liked. It had made me ache inside. She was different from the model types and movie starlets he'd been linked to before.

I wasn't sure if it was coincidence or because I felt disappointed, but she seemed to be in most of his public photographs and as his band had been growing in popularity every day they seemed to be everywhere. It was hard to ignore what he was doing.

Hedonism wasn't the only thing growing, with each passing month my belly stretched and my life became all about my baby growing inside me.

Stepping into the sonogram room, I slipped on the gown and lay on the couch while the sonographer squirted a transparent blue-tinted gel on my baby bump. She smiled and turned to her machine explaining she'd be taking some measurements and collecting information for my medical records.

Going on she told me she would then explain what she saw, tell me the sex of the baby if she could see it clearly and take a picture for me to keep. Even though I'd insisted on going alone, I was excited about seeing him or her on the screen.

Her gentle smile turned serious as she began to draw diagonal dotted arrows with small x's and clicked to record the various parts of my baby's bone structure and abdominal circumference.

The sonographer had only taken two measurements before she replaced the conductor wand back in its holder on the machine. "I just need a minute, be right back."

No matter how nonchalant she looked, I knew instantly there was a problem.

Adrenaline fueled my body and my heart rate spiked through the roof. I stared at the image of my baby, frozen on the screen and felt panic roll from the pit of my stomach to my mouth.

A wave of fear ran over me and squeezed at my heart. Just as I was about to climb off the couch to demand an answer a tall blond man, in half spectacles, entered the room followed once again by the sonographer.

"Josephine, this is Professor Gevers, the consultant on call. He's just going to check the sonogram for me. Your baby's heartbeat seems a little irregular and sometimes a bit fast, so I just want to get him to check it out to reassure both you and myself that I'm not missing anything. Everything appears to be fine with your baby so far, but it's better that the professor checks it out before you go home."

She fell silent while I stared at the side-on profile of the distinguished looking doctor as his eyes narrowed.

Studying the screen, while my baby's heartbeat became audible again, I watched him concentrate his skill on the chambers of my baby's heart with my own heart lodged in my throat.

I held my breath as fear brought pins and needles to parts of my body.

After what seemed like an age I became light-headed and thought I was going to pass out. He turned to me with a pained look on his face and I gasped at his expression as he handed the conductor wand back to the sonographer.

"Josephine...may I call you that?" I nodded, too afraid to speak. *He can call me anything he wants as long as he tells me my baby is okay.* "Josephine, I'd like to use a more detailed ultrasound called a fetal echocardiography and have a second opinion. There are concerns about the baby's heartbeat at present and Lindsey was very diligent in picking up on the subtle changes in heartbeat rhythm and rate. It may also be necessary to run some other tests to exclude any other abnormalities."

Swallowing hard I fought back my tears and nodded, the doctor's face was stoic while his assistant's softened in sympathy when her eyes met mine.

I tried to stay strong, but wished at that moment that I'd brought someone with me. I knew the likelihood was that there was something wrong with my baby.

Three hours later the doctors were pretty sure my baby had a congenital heart defect called Transposition of the Great Valves or TGV as the doctors kept referring to it as.

The following few hours was the start of the most harrowing emotional journey I could ever have imagined. It was one I would never have wished upon anyone else—not even my worst enemy.

Bombarded with information, the doctors had gone through every possible scenario about the likely outcomes, syndromes and afflictions my baby could possibly have wrong with her.

During the counseling session that followed I had been offered the opportunity to terminate my baby before the rest of the results were concluded.

Somehow I'd made my way to the subway and was heading in the direction of home. Dazed and frightened, with my eyes raw from crying, I was so scared for my baby's life.

Initially, I blamed myself and all the alcohol I'd consumed at the time when in all likelihood she was only forming.

Professor Miriam said that it was more likely that there was a history of this in my or my partner's family. Shame stung again when I thought that I was carrying a sick baby and I knew nothing of Elliott's family.

In my heart I didn't believe that Kane was the father, but I did know that he was an only child and no one in his family had ever been sick like that as far as I knew.

Suddenly I didn't want to go home, I couldn't go home...not in the state I was in.

Staring down at the leaflet that was supposed to make me feel better and inform me to make a massive life changing decision like that, I pulled out my cell, and as soon as I got to street level I rang the one person I thought would listen without judgment. "Candice, I need to come over."

$\sim$

"So is it hereditary...this condition? I mean *you're* okay? Is there any heart illness in your family? Oh God, sorry, this is awful, me firing questions at you, but I'm trying to get a handle on what you told me so that I can offer you advice." Candice's eyes were narrow, her brow worried for me.

"Something about the baby's arteries and veins being the wrong way around, so instead of taking the deoxygenated blood to her lungs and returning oxygenated blood to her heart it just puts out the same because it's not wired up right."

"Show me the leaflet again." Taking it from me, she twisted her lips as she read over the horrible condition my baby would have to deal with. We'd all have to deal with, when she was born. I sat passively watching her while my heart squeezed tightly in my chest.

"Okay it says that some babies are diagnosed in the womb but most when they are born. Babies with your baby's condition have the main vessels in the heart the wrong way around. So oxygen poor blood gets pumped around the body instead of oxygen rich blood. I've heard the term 'blue babies' before; that must be what they mean. Like their lips are blue and stuff."

I knew that Candice was trying to help but her explanation was making me more apprehensive than when I had first found out, or maybe the information had sunk in more when she mentioned it.

"This says they are okay in the womb and grow normally because the oxygen supply comes from you through the placenta. After they are born they are given artificial hormones to keep the valve open that normally closes and switches to breathing air like us."

Tears spiked in her eyes and she swallowed audibly. The way she looked at me was worse than how the sonographer had.

A heavy weight crushed my chest. "The baby will need a major operation by the time it's three weeks old, Josie." Even Candice whispered the fate of my baby in horror and I burst into tears again.

Candice sat hugging me for the longest time, rocking me back and forth and rubbing my back. It didn't soothe me at all and I doubted nothing ever would again.

Eventually she held me away from her and looked directly into my eyes. "Right you need time to think about this, Josie. I'm not going to pressure you one way or another. This is your baby. That means all the decisions fall on your shoulders, but I think you need time to mull it all over. Read and get advice then decide what you feel is right for you, Josie. Now, I need you to pull yourself together and call your mom, tell her I invited you for dinner. She's going to ask how things went today, hon, that's up to you what you tell her."

I felt like I was in another dream-like state and went through the motions of calling my parents and being cheerful, telling them I had a picture to show them when I went home the following day. I did have a picture at least so it wasn't all lies.

Chapter Twenty

IMPERFECTIONS

True to her word, Candice didn't press me one way or another, but I already knew what I was going to do. If my daughter was inside me fighting for her life, then I was going to stick with her every step of the way.

I was scared about how I was going to achieve that with the strong family I had, where sickness was seen as weakness. I wasn't sure, but I figured I could keep my news to myself until that no longer mattered.

When I told Candice she called me brave. I wasn't that sure that brave was the right word for doing nothing and letting nature take its course.

The tests came back one by one with no further defects. I preferred them to be known as imperfections, we all had those and that was the word I'd chosen to give what they were testing for.

I drew strength from every negative result they gave me and at the time, I continued going through the motions of normal life in a daze.

My baby continued to do well inside me. She grew in keeping with the age of the pregnancy and I had kind of detached myself from thinking about how sick she was during the day. It was the only way I could keep up the pretense that everything was fine.

It was during the long nights that I fell apart. The weeks turned into months and gradually I had become conditioned to face the future I was given. I had learned to live with the fear inside me as if I were living in a dream.

I did everything I could think of to try to be healthy, resting whenever possible, and doing the bare minimum at work.

The doctors kept a close watch on me, and I had a birthing plan that was organized with military precision. I already knew the date she'd arrive if I got that far, because they would deliver my baby by C-section two weeks before the due date and take her to the Neonatal Intensive Care Unit to offer the life-saving care she would need.

The only way I can describe what was happening mentally was that I had detached from the horror of my baby's condition because it was the only way I could cope.

Being home wasn't half as bad as I thought it would be. Jacob and I became closer again, but not close enough that I wanted to share my news.

Maybe it was that I didn't want to admit that my baby was flawed and ruin the excitement they had about the new addition to the family. Or maybe it was that with every passing day I felt closer to the possibility of facing the prospect of seeing her for the first and perhaps the last time.

Denial kept me going, that and positive thoughts. Jacob was a great distraction and often caught me up in his enthusiasm about the impending birth, he had even decorated Matt's old bedroom as a nursery.

That weekend he took me to pick out a crib, all the things I'd have done with my partner had I had one.

Doing that just about killed me because I didn't know whether my baby would live long enough or be healthy enough if they operated on time, to come home and sleep in it.

The pregnancy seemed to go fast, perhaps because I wasn't prepared for what was to come.

My belly grew huge and with only a day until Thanksgiving I

dreaded the scrutiny of my family who had nothing better to do for the holiday than focus their attention on me and my unborn child.

Living the life of an expectant father vicariously through me, Jacob took me on regular shopping sprees to ensure his niece had the best of the best from the moment she was born.

It was during one of those trips with Jacob, to buy more items for his niece, that Kane called me.

When I saw who was calling I ignored it. Until that point Kane's communication with me had been my private business, but when he rang for the third time, Jacob became suspicious because I wouldn't answer it.

"Who don't you want to speak to?" Jacob questioned, his brow bunching worriedly as he gave me an intense look.

Had he been anyone else, I'd have lied, but Jacob was my twin. He'd always been able to call bullshit on anything I said that was untrue. "Kane."

"Kane who?"

"Kane Exeter."

"Holy, fuck. Is he still in touch? I thought we'd heard the last of him after that restaurant stuff. Answer it. What does he want?"

"I don't know. He calls or emails about once a month," I told him, leaving out the part where I *had* actually slept with him.

Kane had been a little more sporadic in his contact than I'd confessed to, but regular enough for it to even out to about once a month. I had never told him I was pregnant, what had happened to Elliott or even that I'd moved back to my parents.

Nothing seemed to matter except living in the moment with each phone call. I never lied to him, just didn't expand on the truth.

Kane had asked on every occasion whether I had someone new and I had answered honestly that I didn't. And every time I said that he said, "Well, you know where to find me when you come to your senses."

The story that Kane's team quashed in the papers seemed to be long forgotten by my brother, and thankfully my cell stopped ringing.

Distracting Jacob, I caught the store assistant's attention and became very interested in the selection of diapers she had directed me to.

I thought I'd got off the hook but as we stacked the trunk with all our purchases, I slid into the passenger seat and my cell rang loudly again in the confined space.

Jacob looked at me through narrowed eyes as I rummaged in my bag and pulled it out. It was Kane again, but I couldn't ignore it once Jacob knew who it was.

"Hey," I said, my heart beating out of my chest as my belly flipped over.

"Hi, Jo, where has my girl been? I've been trying to call you." Warm feelings washed through me at the sound of his soothing low tone.

"I'm out shopping with Jacob," I answered honestly as my hand shook holding my cell to my ear. I was acutely conscious that Jacob was watching me.

"So, you'll be back soon? I'm in town for four whole days as the band have a break for Thanksgiving weekend, but I got to your apartment and a strange Dude answered the door. He told me you'd moved, but he wouldn't tell me where."

My cell fell from my hand and I caught it, glanced at Jacob and swallowed roughly.

I'd been stupid to think I could keep my condition hidden from him forever. "I don't know that it's a good idea, Kane, I'm staying at my parents' place."

"Damn, I knew things were tight, but you were so proud, I didn't want to push the money side of things. I'd be happy to help you move back to a place of your own."

I was stunned by his suggestion. It wasn't as if I'd accept a gesture that grand from one of my family let alone a guy I once knew as a kid.

"No. It's fine. I'm happy to be back there with Jacob and my parents around me."

"Can I come over? Don't worry I'm not inviting myself for dinner or anything. I'll just book into The Drake Hotel, it's only about half a mile from your parents' place, right? I've hired a car so I could pick you up, we could go there and catch up."

I knew I was sunk. Apart from being pregnant and not mentioning it, I was hideously fat and frumpy, ugly as sin with my big belly and my tent dresses, and he had been all over the press with leggy models and film starlets.

Chiding myself, I wondered why I was bothered about any of that. It wasn't as if we were a couple or anything.

"No. You can come to my parents' house. Do you have the address?"

"Yeah, it's in my address book on my phone. I sent you a birthday card there once, remember?"

Of course he did, how could I ever forget when it's the first thing that catches my eye every time I open my memory box.

"Okay," I said reluctantly. "I'll see you there." I could have cried.

"I can't wait to see you again, baby," he gushed excitedly.

My heart stuttered in my chest because I knew he was in for a shock and was about to find out how close he was with that baby comment.

"So he's coming over tonight?" Jacob asked, trying to extract the details from the one-sided conversation he heard.

"Yeah." My tone came out flat—depressed.

"You don't sound too happy about it. This is the same Kane you moped over for years as a kid, Josie. What are you worried about? Do you think because he's a famous rock star he's changed?"

"Maybe."

Jacob looked at me and smiled. "Listen, you look amazing. He's going to freak when he sees how beautiful you are. You're the only pregnant woman I've ever seen that hasn't put an ounce of weight on anywhere but your belly."

"Thank you, but you're my brother, Jacob. It isn't your job to tell me I'm not fat."

"I'd be the first to tell you if you were, you're my twin, remember? People judge me by your standards." Winking, he smirked and turned to poke my belly gently. Jacob never noticed how quiet I was after that, chatting easily about how things were when we were kids, but he said something that sent a shock straight to my heart. "Dad once said to

Mom that he wouldn't be surprised if you and Kane ended up together."

"He said that?" I asked, probably a little too quickly.

"Yep, the day we were leaving after Kane's dad's funeral. You were hugging Kane and Mom said something like, *'Aw, I hate seeing those two like this.'* Dad looked to Mom and said something like, *'Don't worry, I wouldn't be surprised if they find their way back and end up growing old together.'*

Tears welled in my eyes as I sat staring out the window. My throat instantly clogged with emotion and an array of feelings inside that covered everything I felt was unfair in life.

We had reached my parents' driveway before I had recovered my composure. There was a strange car already parked there.

"Wow, he must have got here before us." Jacob nodded at the car as he switched off the engine.

Turning to look at me, he saw my distress when the porch light shone into the car. I tried to drop my gaze to my lap to hide my tears, but not quick enough for my brother.

"Damn. Don't do that. Why are you crying?" Taking his sleeve, he wiped the tears on my cheek nearest to him, while I swiped at the other one with my fingertips.

Overwhelmed by my situation, I sat silently as my throat constricted again, and the best I could do was shrug because I had no words for how sad I felt about my sick baby growing up with no father.

Hearing his voice again during that journey home, I finally accepted that I had felt more for Kane the last time I saw him than purely a platonic friendship. I had previously passed those feelings off as infatuation, but months of getting to know each other had taught me differently. *If only things were different.*

Jacob sat quietly and waited while I gathered my strength. I reached out and squeezed his hand letting him know I was ready. He clasped his strong fingers tightly around mine, and smiled affectionately. "That's my girl, ready?" I nodded and he pulled the handle, opened the door and ran around the hood to help me out my side of his low ride.

Everything felt hopeless but I had gotten used to hiding my true feelings so as soon as we stepped out of the car I dug deep and put on a brave face. Having hormones running riot whilst being pregnant wasn't helpful.

As we entered the house I heard Kane before I saw him, the low timbre of his melodic voice carrying down the hallway from the sitting room and my heart flipped over in my chest.

Formal greetings and soft laughter told me he had only arrived moments before us.

When we reached the doorway, Jacob was in front of me allowing me to observe Kane's eyes searching past him. The moment his eyes met mine his smile became wider and his eyes softened in appreciation.

Getting out of his seat he began to make his way over to us and I saw his shocked reaction as his jaw dropped open the second he saw I was heavily pregnant.

Wide eyes were replaced with confusion as it flitted through his expression. By the time he started to speak his expression was blank and unreadable.

"Damn, Jo, look at you." I didn't have to look. I felt the weight of my condition and situation with every second that passed.

"You look radiant," he managed to say in a soft voice, while his eyes raked over my ample breasts and down over my swollen bump. I was conscious all eyes were on me just like the last time I was in a compromising position around him, but this time, I was the center of attention, not Kane.

"All the times we've talked, texted, and emailed, you've never mentioned you were having a baby. This is big news, *big* news, baby."

If Kane was angry or had any other thoughts, he never showed them, and I was sure that was for my family's benefit.

I didn't respond and Jacob grabbed my coat at the shoulders helping me take it off before I walked over to the mint green, velvet sofa my parents had had since I was a child and curled up with my feet tucked under my butt.

Mom instantly went into hostess mode and took orders for coffee.

Gesticulating to my father in the direction of the kitchen she asked if he would get the mugs ready.

Jacob greeted Kane, slapped his back and they shared a man hug before Jacob headed upstairs to the nursery with the bags we'd brought home.

Chapter Twenty-One

DISCLOSURES

Spinning his head in my direction after watching my brother leave the room, his eyes darted to mine, searching my face before his serious, concerned stare locked into mine.

"Fuck, Jo. Is it mine?" Kane asked in a careful, low tone as soon as we were alone.

His steely blue eyes pierced mine willing me to tell him the truth. "No." I answered, because if she was his then my life would be even more complicated than it already was.

"So, mind if I ask who? How far along are you?"

"Thirty-five weeks or so isn't that right, Josie?" Jacob answered for me having re-entered the room as Kane asked the question.

My eyes searched out Kane's as Jacob continued to move stuff around in preparation for dinner, and after a few seconds I closed them to shut out the way Kane's stare penetrated my thoughts. His eyes held my gaze like they'd squeeze the truth from me.

"It's Elliott's?" His voice barely hid his anger.

I nodded. Even when I was unsure in that moment.

"And he didn't come back for you?"

"Elliott died," I said, my lip quivered as I said it.

"Holy fuck, I'm sorry, baby. When? How...I mean, what happened?"

"Car accident just after we—why are you here, Kane?

"Why do you think? Do you know how long you've been on my mind? But I stayed away to give you the space you needed to figure out what you felt."

My heartbeat pounded in my chest from his continued scrutiny. I jumped when my mom called out to Jacob to help them in the kitchen.

"There's nothing here for you, Kane."

"You're sure? I thought if I gave you that time—" Kane pondered what else to say. Suddenly he reached for my hand and pulled it onto his lap. Placing his warm hand over mine felt too comforting and I felt emotions beginning to rise.

"Well this should help take that thought away." My head nodded at my huge bump.

"A kid? You think that having a kid would make me feel differently about you? I've thought about you every single day since I came back. We may have been kids once, Jo, but since I spent that weekend with you, I've barely had a day's peace in my mind thinking about you."

"Really, then you've done a great job of consoling yourself if the media is anything to go by."

"True, I have. I'm not a monk, Jo. I'm a guy with needs, and a lifestyle where free love is a given for any musician who wants it."

I stared pointedly at him because his honesty stung. I said nothing for what seemed like minutes then shrugged and said, "And that's exactly why I turned you away. Anyhow, that's all in the past, it's none of my business what you do with your life."

"No? Then why does me being with other women affect you so much? Your face shows more envy that you realize. Can you say you don't want me at all? Do you feel anything for me?"

"Oh I care, I care like you have no idea, but this is all we have and this is all we'll ever have. I have a child to take care of, a huge responsibility, and you're in a rock band. In my world those two things are not compatible. If I stepped into your life we'd be eaten alive. Dealing with those groupie sluts night after night would wear me down."

"What are you talking about? You can be wherever you want. I'd always come home to you. I tour for two months of the year. That's it. I have already said I won't do any more than that. You can work with

175

us, travel with us, you don't have to come to every gig we play, Jo. This is your dad talking. All the indoctrination of what life is really like and how we shouldn't go chasing rainbows, right?"

"Can you even hear yourself? We barely know each other now. We knew each other once, Kane. The kids we were, are not who we are today."

"You're right, we're not, but I still know you, Jo. I still *want* to know you."

"For how long, Kane? Until you fuck me out of your system? Is that what this weekend visit was about? Take a good look at me. How fuckable do I look now?"

"From where I'm standing you are as beautiful as ever, being pregnant doesn't change that."

We sat silently once again, my mind blank of thought as my mom came into the room carrying a tray laden with tea and coffee, sandwiches and brownies. I pulled my hand away and clasped my hands in front of me.

I could have cut the atmosphere between us with a knife, but my mom was oblivious to it. "So tell us all your news, Kane, we're dying to know what celebrities you've met. You've been linked with some gorgeous girls, honey, are you dating one of them?" I sneered at Kane and rolled my eyes like my mom had just proved my point.

Kane sat up straighter on the sofa and Mom handed him a cup of coffee. "No one special, Maxine, it's just the management's way of gaining extra publicity for the band."

"So you haven't been out with any of them?"

Kane cast a guilty look to me then back to my mom. "Well, yeah a few, but like I said, no one special." He glanced nervously in my direction again. His honesty was killing me with every disclosure.

"Oh, which ones?" I'd never been so close to telling my mom to shut the fuck up like I was at that moment.

"Does it matter?" he asked quickly, his eyes darting back to me with an apologetic look in them. "Anyway, a gentleman never kisses and tells," he added, and I felt a massive relief to have no faces to go with his admission.

My dad asked him a few questions about where he'd been and how the band felt about playing in front of that many people. And Jacob had a few questions of his own.

I sat quietly listening and my baby was so active that I unconsciously began to rub my bump.

Kane's eyes homed in on my hand then glanced up at my face and gave me a sad smile that unnerved me.

After an hour Jacob went to get ready as he had a date. Mom asked Kane where he was staying then invited him to come for Thanksgiving dinner the next day.

My heart leapt when he said he'd like nothing better, but ached at the same time because in a way I felt he was prolonging my agony.

All evening he never took his eyes off of me, and eventually, I couldn't fight the longing I had to be hugged tightly the way he had cuddled me when we met at the airport all those months before.

If I'd had the foresight to see what would happen, my life may have turned out differently. It was before my life became the complicated car wreck I was trapped in. *And who knows, Elliott may still be alive. No. It wouldn't have mattered whether I'd slept with Kane or not, Elliott may still have died and I'd still be carrying his baby.*

I felt the familiar feeling where my throat closed as my emotions tightened in my chest, and I knew I had to get out of that room before I lost it and began to cry.

Rising to my feet, I sighed heavily and put on my best weary face. "Sorry, guys, I'm worn smooth, I need to lie down for a while."

Kane jumped to his feet. "Can I help?"

I scoffed, "Help me to lie down, Kane? I think that's one of the few things I can still do independently these days, I'll see you tomorrow if you're here."

"Oh, I'll be here. Wild horses couldn't keep me away. Rest well, beautiful," he replied.

Breathing deeply, I barely made it out the door before tears spilled at my situation.

I felt sorry for myself and finally admitted what I'd been denying for the last eight months. I had fallen in love with Kane, despite all the warning signs that it was a terrible idea.

I told myself it was infatuation because of the myth I'd built up in my mind after all the time we'd been apart was my protection mechanism. Truth was I'd given my heart to him as a child.

Once I'd left the room I chewed myself up about what the likely conversation was between him and my parents then decided none of it mattered.

Whatever he told them would make no difference to how I felt about the crush I had on a rock star.

Kane wasn't exactly father material for my baby, and his lifestyle was something I couldn't tolerate.

Trying to fit into his world wasn't something I had time for, and no matter how we felt it could never last.

My focus had to be making the best future for my baby and ensuring she was kept safe and well. I'd made a huge mistake in life, but that didn't mean I didn't want the very best for my baby.

I slept fitfully and woke feeling like I had a hangover. My eyes were puffy from crying and lack of sleep, and I had heartburn. *Great.*

Easing my way out of bed, I straightened my aching back and rubbed my belly as I padded barefooted over to the window.

Both my father and Jacob's cars were gone but Kane's car was still in the driveway.

As my mom was picking up my grandmother for Thanksgiving dinner, and Jacob had the early morning shift in his job as a firefighter, I knew they would all be gone for several hours.

As soon as I got past the shock that Kane was still downstairs I hit the shower, dressed in some maternity jeans and a bump hugging electric blue top.

I opened my bedroom door to go downstairs. I could smell the strong aroma of turkey basting in the oven.

Entering the kitchen, I saw that my mom had left me a list of instructions of when various things had to be turned on to cook. I followed the first things on the note to the letter while I waited for the coffee pot to fill.

All the time I was working in there, the anticipation of Kane coming in gave me butterflies.

With each minute that passed I became much more excited at the prospect of seeing him, so when I'd completed my tasks and made the coffee I was disappointed when he still hadn't shown his face.

Our sitting room door squeaked as I slowly pushed it open and my eyes were immediately drawn to him and my heart softened at his sleeping form.

Kane was lying flat on his back in nothing but a pair of Calvin Klein, black boxer briefs. His hands were raised above his head and the comforter he had been sleeping under was crumpled on the floor.

The sight of him lying like that was sexily enticing. It made me salivate even though I was heavily pregnant and sex had been the last thing on my mind.

Taut lean muscles lined his abdomen, every contoured ridge rippled and formed together to make his perfectly sculpted six pack torso. He was the last man I'd been with and he was even more handsome and desirable than I had remembered.

Quietly, I walked over to the seat directly opposite where he lay, *this may be the last time I ever see him like this,* and allowed myself to indulge in the luxury of studying his heartbreakingly beautiful features while he slept.

With each rise and fall of his chest, I fell a little deeper in love with him. With every breath he took, I wanted him more.

With every soft sigh his body exhaled, the memories of his touch while he slid inside me became more vivid in my mind.

I sat staring in amazement as his shaft became erect in his boxer briefs and knew that at some point in the not too distant future he'd wake up.

Less than five minutes after that thought occurred he did. Slowly his eyes fluttered open and before he even spoke he captured my heart once more with a lazy smile.

"Morning," he mumbled, smiling sleepily as he reached inside his boxers to adjust his rigid cock. "Have you been awake long?"

"Long enough to follow my mom's instructions for lunch and make a cup of coffee. Want one?" I'd been objectifying him and the instant his eyes met mine I had felt myself blush.

"Yeah, I could drain the pot. Your dad got me on the whiskey last night after your mom went to bed."

"Makes sense. I wondered why you were still here when I came down this morning."

"Did you have a good time sitting there watching me sleep?"

My first thought was to lie and say I had just sat down but I figured honesty was our thing so I told him the truth. "Yeah, best excitement I've had since I went to the cinema to see Fifty Shades of Grey."

"So you were imagining me tying you up with rope, me whipping your ass, cuffing you to a pole, and doing all that kinky shit to you? Good to know, I'll make a note," he smirked wickedly, and sat up with his legs open, leaning back into the sofa.

My eyes darted to the stiff cock in his pants, and my pussy clenched. I felt angry with myself.

I had no right feeling those things. I had a sick baby inside of me, and a life that was already mapped out ahead. But being with Kane was the first time I'd felt almost normal since the hospital had given me the devastating news about her.

"Oh right, yeah, can we do that today, please? We have at least an hour before my parents get back," I asked, joking as I rubbed my heavily pregnant belly.

"Don't think I don't find you as alluring as I did back in March, baby. It would take more than you carrying a baby to turn me off you."

"Very rock and roll, fucking someone else's baby momma, Kane."

"Stop that! Don't make it sound so fucking sensationalistic. You're not a cheap slut. What I meant was the fact that you are having a child makes you no less appealing to me."

"That's sick. You want to fuck a pregnant woman?"

"No, Jo. That's not what I'm saying at all. Stop twisting my words. You got me wrong, baby. Whatever state you were in wouldn't change the way I feel about you."

"Ha! So I'm in a state? You're definitely not wrong about that. And what exactly do you think you are feeling, Kane, because we only had a one-time thing?"

"Twice, and that was your call, not mine. You skipped out on me, I asked you to come back, remember? And the second was entirely down to you. You initiated that."

"Yeah, and you left for New York the next day."

"I had a job to do there and that's where my band had gone."

"And so did I, Kane. But that's not why you went. You said you may as well go party with them. The fact that you never contacted me for a whole month afterward says a lot as well."

"Fuck. You infuriate me. I went because you told me you were sure we should be just friends. I said that because I was pissed. What did me not calling you for a month say?"

"Out of sight, out of mind?"

"Wrong. I was giving you space. I offered you to tour with me after the first time. That's how much I wanted to find out if what we had was worth pursuing. You refused and spun me some bullshit about being too different then you cut me off and I figured what I was pursuing was a dead end. When you blew me out after using me the second time, I figured you were done and we were going to do the friends thing because that's what you told me."

"No...no, I never cut you off that first time, my signal dropped, or yours, and I figured we were done anyway. I wasn't about to run away with you, Kane. I made one sound decision in my life at least," I said, looking down at my swollen tummy. "Can you imagine how that would have played out, when you found out I was carrying Elliott's baby?"

"It doesn't matter to me who the father is. I'm here and he's no longer around. I don't care...that baby is a part of you, Josie."

I stared in disbelief. "And you'd just pick up the slack and start taking care of me and Ellie? Just like that?"

"It's a girl?" he asked quietly, his face softening.

"She is, and you think I'd place my daughter in your fucked up immoral world of drugs and corruption for however long we lasted?"

Kane winced, hurt by my response, and if it had been just me, then maybe, just maybe, I'd have caved at that point, but my reality was my responsibility to my sick, unborn daughter and nothing else mattered.

Being with Kane would have brought instant relief from the provision of her physical needs, but at what cost to her emotional ones? I had to go with my gut and stay strong.

My own wants didn't come into it anymore. *Besides, Ellie was sick and once he knew that I'd probably never see him again.*

"Fuck. Have it your way. I get it. You don't want me. You have a hate thing going on with musicians, but you are making judgments about things you have no idea about. Life isn't all parties, groupies, and getting our rocks off. It's about hard work, punishing schedules, creativity, and making music. We don't have the luxury of nine-to-five, Monday through Friday jobs, we work when everyone else doesn't."

I had heard Kane's voice raised in frustration before, but never in anger, and the passion in his voice when he defended his position left me with goosebumps.

The effect of his response not only affected me, but my baby too, because as soon as he raised his voice my baby woke up and became very active.

Anger I could deal with. "Oh my. You make it sound so appealing. You forgot to mention the hard drugs, booze and debauchery that goes with the lifestyle."

I knew I sounded bitchy, but I couldn't afford to be anything else. I was three weeks from giving birth and I couldn't ever entertain anything that made his work sound anything less than frivolous.

"Will you give me a fucking break here?" Pushing himself off the sofa his body almost vibrated with temper as he ran his hands through his hair and paced the floor.

My mouth dropped open at the sight of his strong physique as he threw his head back then forward again to look at me.

Kane shook his head and turned to find his jeans and just like the last time I'd seen him do that, I figured he was about to run.

Sitting silently, I watched him dress and when he was done he surprised me by sitting back down and staring me out. After a few seconds he held up his hands in question.

"What? Did you think I was leaving? Sorry to disappoint you, Jo, but there are some things in life that are too important, and I made that mistake with you once already. You may not think it, but I'm a guy that learns not to take the same course of action twice."

Sighing heavily, I wished things could have been different. I stood and walked over to him. "I get that you think I'm vulnerable. I don't get why you'd want to be saddled with a single mom when you can have any woman you want, Kane. I think you only think you want me because I've said no. When you realize that, you'll be much better off living your life the way you want."

Glancing up at me, his warm blue eyes held mine and riveted me to the spot. "If I can have any woman I want then I want you. Don't lie to me, Jo. You feel this, don't you? This connection we have, yet you're fighting it with everything you have. Why the fuck are you doing that? Why do you think we can't have it all? Me, you, the baby? A good life?"

"Because I'm not a dreamer, Kane. My feet are firmly on the ground, right where they need to be. I'll say it again, look at me?" I gestured with both hands to my bump.

"I'm looking, and my eyes are wide open, baby. I'm not going down without a fight this time. I'll tell you that right now. I fight for what I want."

Getting up, I turned away from him and took a step toward the door. Kane caught my hand. "Wait," he said as he stood up and stepped closer, placing his hands on my shoulders. "I know this must be tough on you, Jo. I get it. That I came from nowhere and that I let you down as a kid. I want to make your life easier. Let me do that for you at least."

"With money you mean? I'm not your charity case, Kane. I'm managing fine on my own. As soon as Ellie arrives my mom is going to take care of her and I'm going back to work," I lied, thinking that my future would actually be form-filling for disability welfare and fighting for medical services for my baby.

"You're happy to do that when what I can offer you—"

"Thanks, but no thanks. I don't want to be beholden to anyone, Kane. I can do this just fine with a little support from my family."

"You are so fucking exasperating, you know that? You weren't like this as a kid. We never argued."

"You weren't a rock star and I wasn't about to be a single mom. Things change. People change. Get out while you can, Kane, I'm not what you're looking for. One day you'll realize that." I shrugged him off, swallowing back my tears as I went back to the kitchen to prepare lunch. I felt thankful that he hadn't followed me because I was a mess.

Ten minutes later I was still carrying out the chores on Mom's list when I heard our heavy outside door bang shut and Kane's car start in the driveway.

My heart sunk to my stomach and I burst into tears because my contradictory hormones had taken over and I was bitterly disappointed. And despite my sensible reasoning I was depressed at my success in pushing Kane away.

I thought that after mulling over what I'd said, Kane had probably decided I was right, I wasn't worth it, and he was never coming back.

Chapter Twenty-Two

TWICE

Sniffling my way through creaming the potatoes I felt even more depressed than I had before he had shown up.

Most women would think I was insane for saying no to a knight in shining rock star clothing, with a ripped and tatted body who rolled up and offered to take care of her and another man's child.

Then again, I wasn't most women. I know there were many who would be as frustrated with me as Kane was, but it had taken every ounce of strength I had to do what I'd decided.

If I gave in to someone who I'd slept with twice to make it easier all round, then I wouldn't have been the girl my parents had raised.

No one would take a risk on a guy based on our history if they were faced with the harrowing circumstances I faced.

Less than three hours after Kane left, my parents arrived home with my eighty-year-old grandmother. "I take it Kane went home to change?" my mom asked.

"Not sure, he left while I was doing the food," I answered, trying to maintain a level of honesty.

"He didn't say when he'd be back? Jacob will be home in less than an hour and I wanted to eat at 2:00 pm. Grandma doesn't like to eat too late these days, her digestion is better when she eats her main meal around lunch time," Mom said.

"For me too, Mom. If I eat too late I can't sleep. I can relate to that heartburn she's complained about for years," I replied.

A knock at the door was followed by Kane walking in without waiting to be invited. I couldn't believe the relief that washed over me that he had come back and I hated the ping-pong feeling my emotions were throwing at me.

"I haven't missed anything, have I?" he asked, making eye contact with my gran who sat more upright and suddenly acted twenty years younger around him.

"At last. You are the famous Kane that stole my granddaughter's heart. No wonder, look at you. What a stud. I'd take a shot at you myself if I was ten years younger. Pity you didn't come back for her before she fell with child," she said, her eyes casting a disapproving glance at my bump. My heart nearly fell through the floor.

"Grandma!" I was horrified that she would say such a thing, two things, actually.

Kane's instant wide grin looked so fucking sensational and it lit up his face. It made me feel weak at the knees. "Well I've come back for her now, but looking at her, grandma, I can see where the good genes come from. If you were ten years younger she may have had stiff competition."

Grandma fluttered her eyelashes and placed her hand over her heart, giggling. "Oh my, you can't go saying things like that to a woman of my age, be still my beating heart," she said in a flirty tone and raised an approving eyebrow in my direction.

I swear the years fell away from her in that moment and I got a glimpse of the girl she once was in her personality.

Jacob entered the room as she said that and commented deadpan, "And you don't want to be saying that at your age either, Grandma. Be careful what you wish for because it may just do that. On second thoughts go right ahead, I could use the inheritance as a down deposit to get away from this lot once and for all."

Mom came out of the kitchen and scolded Jacob and the rest of us for laughing and informed us, in her efficient tone, that dinner was almost ready.

Jacob organized drinks for everyone as we headed through to the dining room where Dad had the turkey already set before him.

Mom had placed the trimmings down the center and I wondered how the hell I was going to get through lunch without my grandma embarrassing me further.

Kane pulled a chair out for my grandma. "Oh, and he has manners as well, Josephine," she said, using my full name, smiling her approval. I stared at her deliberately and shook my head slightly.

When I glanced over at Jacob he was cackling away to himself and I could see he was enjoying her totally fangirling over Kane.

With my grandma seated, Kane pulled out a chair for me and once I sat down he sat in between us.

Turning to me he placed his hand on my back, and a small shiver ran up my spine. I fought the feeling and sat straight-faced.

"Are you comfortable?" he asked attentively. I nodded and lifted the red napkin from my place setting, shook it out and placed it over my lap.

My heart pounded excitedly from his simple touch as his hand remained on my back.

It was only when my dad spoke to him that he slowly slid his hand away and brought it in front of him. Instantly my heart stalled and ached from missing his touch after it was gone.

"Bet you never thought you'd be having Thanksgiving with a rock star, Grandma," Jacob stated, grinning at my gran. She turned her head to look at Kane again with a twinkle in her eye.

"Don't you believe it, I was a wild child in my day," she threw back at Jacob, and winked at Kane.

"Did you just hit on him?" my dad asked his mom, his jaw set firm in an oddly scolding manner.

"Maybe," she said chuckling, giving Kane a naughty smirk. Call me Ethel, by the way. It's been a long time since I heard my name trip off a sexy, hot man's tongue. Kane laughed loudly.

"Damn at least I'm being hit on by one of the women at this table," he said, turning to stare into my eyes with a sexy smile that creased the skin around them.

The connection we shared when we looked at each other was too intense so I looked down at my lap.

Matt arrived and I was thankful for the distraction while he kissed all of us women at the table and quickly took his seat next to Jacob.

Kane put his finger under my chin and lifted it for me to look at him. "Sorry, I didn't mean to embarrass you," he murmured, while everyone else was still chatting.

My dad interrupted by saying, "Maxine, do you want to say grace?" I looked way from Kane to my mom glad for the excuse not to answer him.

Grandma grabbed Kane's hand while he slid his hand into mine. Closing his fingers firmly around it, he gave it a little squeeze.

"Thank you, Lord for the people around us, for this awesome Thanksgiving food, and for the health you have given us to enjoy this day. We also thank you for the love you have given us in our hearts for the people we share this with and for bringing Kane into Josephine's life when she needed him the most. Amen."

My heart almost stopped when I heard her add that. Mortified, I tried to pull my hand away but Kane clamped his fingers tighter and gave me a slow smile. "I'm really honored to be spending the day with you all like this. It definitely beats anything else I've done lately."

Jacob scoffed and replied, "Then you've not been doing it right, buddy. I've seen all those hot chicks hanging off your arm in the media. We'd have to be blind not to."

Kane was still holding my hand at the table and I had kind of got used to it as I waited for my father to finish carving the turkey, but with Jacob's reminder, I tried again to pull my hand away.

Gripping it tighter, Kane looked to Jacob and shrugged, but had the good grace to look slightly embarrassed.

"What can I say, Jacob. I'm a free agent. No hot woman to come home to, so the record company and promoters think it's a great idea to shove me in front of a camera with anything that is the flavor of the month in celebrity land."

"So you haven't slept with all those women?" my grandma asked bluntly, while I cringed in my seat. She'd obviously done her home-work, and I silently cursed Jacob for teaching her how to surf the internet.

Kane kept a firm hold on my hand and chuckled as he shook his head. "I think you've been around long enough that you should know never to believe everything you read in the press, Ethel."

"So you haven't gotten jiggy with any of those women? I find that hard to believe for a hot, young stud like you," she said, looking appraisingly over her half-spectacles.

Kane actually looked a little uncomfortable and shifted in his seat, his hand leaving my palm to run through his hair as everyone waited with baited breath for his answer.

"Well like you said, I'm young...a hot stud...I wouldn't call myself that, but Ethel, surely if you were one of those women in question you'd want any man that was asked what you have just asked me to be evasive. To confirm or deny in answer would ruin the reputation of either those in question or myself."

"Jesus, he's clever," she chuckled and swatted his arm. "Bag him, quick, Josephine before someone else does."

"Bag him? Grandma...really?" Jacob was creased up at the table and my mom sat straight-faced. It was clear she had nothing to contribute that would make my grandma shut up.

Dad looked the most uncomfortable of anyone at the table and I totally got it. This was his mom pushing for answers about a rock star's bedroom secrets. As if that wasn't enough, the rock star in question was the son of his late best friend, Samuel Exeter.

Mom suddenly found some inspiration and quickly changed the subject by asking my grandma about a hospital appointment for her knee, which had been her favorite topic of conversation up until Kane's appearance in her life.

Grandma was thankfully distracted by that question and the rest of the lunch went relatively smoothly, but I found myself yearning for the way Kane had held my hand so possessively.

Toward the end of lunch, Kane's cell rang and he pulled it out of his pants pocket.

Glancing at the screen he gestured the ringing phone at us and said, "Excuse me I need to take this." He rose from the table and made his way from the dining room, but not before I saw the name Catherine accompanied by a beautiful girl's smiling face shining up from the screen. Whoever she was, she was a timely reminder of why we'd never work.

I felt like crying and that was stupid because I'd already made my mind up that Kane wasn't someone who was in my league and I didn't trust the lifestyle he led, no matter how good his intentions.

As soon as he got the call, the pit in my stomach grew wider and I struggled to keep my emotions in check.

Reacting before I began to cry I rubbed my stomach and pleaded tiredness. I excused myself and headed up to the sanctuary of my room before Kane had finished his call.

When I closed my bedroom door my tears fell. My situation was hopeless as far as any feelings I harbored for Kane, but I consoled myself with the thought that my life wasn't really only about me anymore, my baby came first.

How could I even think about any man and carry another's child? How could I even entertain the notion of a normal life when I was carrying a sick baby?

It was all a mess, but I'd found the strength to get as far as I had at that point, and I knew I'd continue to take one day at a time, climbing over every hump necessary to take care of my daughter when the time came.

Being strong also meant allowing myself time to grieve for what I couldn't have and I cried for my lost opportunities in life to bring up my child.

Then I spared a thought for all of those women for whom child bearing hadn't come easy. I was thankful for the gift of a child no matter what they were like or how it was conceived, and reminded myself that everything happens for a reason.

Since Kane had come into my life it had been full of change and discontentment.

Reconnecting with him had created emotional turmoil which had left me feeling more than a little restless. With a few weeks to go to the most difficult chapter in my life I regretted that complication.

~

I must have fallen asleep and woke to the sound of soft knocking on my bedroom door. "Is everything alright, Josie? You've been up here for almost three hours." The light was all but gone outside and when I squinted at the clock it was 5:10 pm.

"Yeah, Mom, sorry, I didn't sleep well last night and lunch wiped me out."

"I'm making some turkey sandwiches with the leftovers, come down and rescue Kane before your grandma tries to elope with the poor guy. He's been fabulous with her all afternoon, but I think he could use some young company.

Jacob went over to Ann-Marie's house to help her with some imaginary emergency. "I wish he'd just admit that he's seeing her. Your father and I don't care that she's divorced with two children. She's lovely and by all accounts her husband wasn't a good man."

Stretching a little, I rolled onto my other side and sat up on the bed. My hip was stiff from the weight I was carrying and when I stood I felt sore. I let out a groan and my mom came over beside me and hugged me.

"It must be tough without Elliott, hon. You are doing a grand job of keeping that baby safe, you're a brave girl."

Hearing my mom say that made me feel dreadful. I was a fraud. Tears sprang to my eyes and I was choked because I wanted to tell her, but I had no clue where to start.

Stepping back, I mumbled that I was just going to freshen up and I'd be right down as I made a hasty retreat to my bathroom. As I stood in front of the mirror I had no idea what to feel or what to think.

Kane wasn't going away from my thoughts no matter how much I tried to shut him out. And still I knew that in two days he'd be gone again.

Chapter Twenty-Three

FLIRTING

*L*eftover turkey and cranberry sandwiches on homemade crusty bread was the best comfort food ever.

I ate two whole sandwiches when I realized that I had plenty of room from dinner.

I hadn't actually eaten very much because I had been so aware of Kane sitting next to me, and I was eaten up with anxiety about what my grandma was going to say next. The woman had killed my appetite. I had managed to look as if I'd eaten without taking much in.

Fortunately, grandma had started to look tired, her energy levels zapped by the fact that she was an early riser, the journey to our home, all the heavy food, and her endless flirting with Kane.

It was ridiculous that my parents made the two hour journey each way, and the hour they'd spend either collecting her things together to bring her to us or to settle her back when she got home again.

Soon after we'd finished eating my dad started to prepare her to leave, stating that he wasn't driving after 10:00 pm because he'd been up since 6:00 am that morning, and if she didn't leave soon she would have to stay over.

It was weird how her personality changed from the flirty, vibrant senior to the frail old lady in a sentence with her son's stern warning.

Twenty minutes later they were in the car, my grandma having kissed Kane not once but three times and an extra hug.

"Until next time," she said, before my dad closed the door and sighed with relief that she was finally installed in the back seat of his car for the journey home.

I smiled as I waved her off, but inside my stomach was flipping over and over because it meant another one-on-one session with Kane. Frankly, I was beat both emotionally and physically.

"Now I know where you get it from," he said, chuckling as we stepped back into the warmth of the sitting room. I wandered over by the fire and sat on the chair nearest the fireplace.

"Get what?"

"Your fire. Your grandma is a hoot. She opens her mouth and whatever she's thinking just falls out," he commented.

"So that's what you think I do?" My baby kicked out in protest when I hugged myself defensively.

"Damn, Jo, strip off that armor for fuck's sake. How am I ever going to know the real you again if you won't let me in?"

I dropped my arms, aware that my unborn child was as restless as I was. None of this was good for her.

My anxiety levels had been through the roof since Kane called and the anguish had continued ever since. The moment I set eyes on him my baby had begun to kick like crazy. I'd been suffering heartburn and felt upset for the majority of the time he'd been at the house.

Nothing felt normal while he was around, and in my last weeks of pregnancy I needed normality more than ever.

"We should talk." Kane stood, pushing his hands deep into his pockets as he wandered over to the window.

Without turning around, he took his hand out of the front pockets and shoved them in the back ones. Flexing his back like he was stiff I heard him take a deep breath.

"If there was a guy...a good guy...hell any guy around who was taking care of you, Jo, I'd back off. There isn't. No. If I'm being completely honest with you. I'd say I was lying about that last statement. I don't want to back off. I've thought about you every day since we were together. I've hated the way things went down between us and we shouldn't have gotten drunk, but we did, and now I've got nothing in my head apart from you. What I mean is I'm sorry about *how* it happened but not sorry that it did."

I looked him up and down but he never turned around. "You may not have been here, Kane, but you have still been right in front of me —most days with a different woman on your arm, since you left my place. I'm not angry about that, it's your life. Women, music, and what else was it?"

"Music, sex and good conversation, Jo. If you're going to throw quotes back at me at least get them correct." Spinning on his heel he walked over and picked up his leather jacket. "Is this really what you want?"

Kane stood frozen with his black leather jacket scrunched in his fist. His knuckles were white from the tension of gripping it.

"Have it your way, Jo. I'm not going to beg. I came here to tell you how I felt. I've done that and even in your condition you won't hear me. I'm no quitter, Jo, but I can see I'm upsetting you, and out of consideration for your condition and the baby I'll leave you alone."

I stood up and stormed toward the door after him. "You rock in here like you own me, telling me how I feel and why I should be with you, but you're not listening, Kane. I don't want you to beg. You're a great guy, Kane, just not great for me. You think because I'm pregnant you should take care of me? Listen to me, because I'm only going to say this one more time. The life you lead doesn't interest me. It would depress me more to be around all those women that act like my grandma did today and wonder if that day was the one where you give in and take them up on that offer. I'm pregnant and I care about you, but I'm not desperate for someone to take care of me. I don't really know you. For all I know you are an alcoholic and may have many STDs. No matter how good you look that's not an attractive package."

Spinning on his heel to face me he leaned in close to my face. He was seething at my attack.

"Let me tell you, I am *not* an alcoholic. Yeah I drink, last time I heard that was legal, right? And as for STD's, I have never been with a woman without a condom. Who's to say you're not the one with the STD? You're pregnant after all. That doesn't happen without an exchange of bodily fluids if my sex education at high school was on point." Watching Kane's normally bright eyes turn dark and dangerous worried me. I'd pushed him too far.

"You know what? This is a waste of time. You are a waste of my time. You're fucking nuts. I was a fool to think there could have been something special here. Your hostility toward me is not warranted, Jo. Think about that. I'm going to go to my hotel now because I am clearly not wanted around here, and I'd hate to think I was upsetting your unborn child by my presence. You know where to find me if you wake up in a more rational mood tomorrow."

Kane left the house without looking back. I stood by the front door until his tail lights grew smaller and my tears blurred their orange glow until there was nothing.

I released the breath I didn't know I'd been holding. Once again, I'd got what I wanted...to be left alone. *So why does my heart feel like it's breaking?*

For all of my life Kane had been the one person who drew out my rawest emotions. Ever since the day we left Germany, leaving him after his father's funeral.

Crying in bed on my twenty-first birthday and all the horrible dreams and worries I had about him in-between.

All of those sad times in my life were around him. That night the depth of those feelings of loss was with me again. *It would be so easy to give in and give myself time with him, but the consequences when it failed would devastate me...us, there is only me to think about. I can't, I have to stay strong.*

During the day that followed my parents asked me question after question about Kane and what had happened after they'd left with my grandma.

Eventually, I tired of it and snapped at them, telling them nothing was going on and I wasn't his keeper.

Despite regretting my outburst the day before there was no way on earth I'd ever admit I'd been wrong to have behaved the way I had, but

I was sorry I had hurt him with the horrible things I said. He hadn't deserved my wrath, it wasn't his fault I was in the predicament I had found myself in.

I found myself staring out at the driveway at every opportunity during that day, willing Kane to come back. I wanted him to defy me for behaving so unpredictable toward him then chided myself for wondering why he would even bother.

Kane had it all. I figured he'd probably woken with a clear conscience that morning after my rejection the night before.

I'd behaved so spiteful for someone who was ordinarily a level-headed person, and if I was being honest, I had definitely made Kane the catalyst for dredging up all the anger I had suppressed in order to cope with my situation. *Why do men have sex and are able to walk away while women like me are left with the consequences?*

For the first twelve hours since I'd gotten out of bed that day I'd felt a huge irritation that Kane had swept into my life for the second time and disrupted the equilibrium I had fought to achieve after he'd left the last time.

My whole existence had changed in the past eight months and when I looked back, from that day, I absorbed the fact that my life had never, and would never, be the same again.

Why couldn't life be easier? Unfortunately, from my experience, we didn't get choices of what happened in our future, but it was predestined from the previous choices made by us somewhere in the past.

By 8:30 pm that night my gut was rotting like it had been twisted in knots and the blood supply had been cut. The flesh inside was slowly dying and I cursed Kane again for ever coming back. If I was frank, I couldn't have blamed him. When he never showed, it taught me how serious he was about all the stuff that he'd said during the previous two days.

I allowed myself to imagine what he was doing, and pictures of parties and glamorous women appeared in my mind. The whole thing was ridiculous and I was torturing myself about something that I couldn't change.

Life was much easier as kids, but unfortunately it never stayed that way.

Kane Exeter hadn't just touched my heart, he'd seeped into every chamber. He was ingrained in every artery and vein by then and my head had been filled not only with those precious memories from our childhood, but the way his gorgeous lust-filled blue eyes darkened as he slid his cock roughly to the hilt inside me, and the roll of his tongue around mine.

It had been eight months since I'd been with him, but every time I tried to erase the memory of the way Kane had touched me, that firm, possessive touch, it made me weak.

The way he wound my hair around his hand and extended my neck as his other hand gently squeezed my throat while his wild animalistic control commanded my body, I felt a pulse in my core.

I couldn't think of one of those things in isolation without the whole chain of movements of every stroke he made on my body coming to mind.

Approaching 10:00 pm, I couldn't bear the wait any longer, but deep down I knew all along that he wouldn't come back, so gave up and went to bed. I was appalled by my brattish behavior but I just couldn't control my rage around him. Or was it passion disguised as rage?

Whatever it was Kane brought out the worst in me, but then again, the weight of what I was carrying, not just physically but emotionally, had begun to weigh me down. I was a girl with a huge burden and nothing in my world was right.

I wasn't ready to be a mother. I wasn't ready to take responsibility for another human being, when I couldn't even take responsibility for owning my own feelings. And I definitely wasn't prepared to take on the care of a sick baby.

Sliding as easily into bed as someone with a belly my size could, I was torn in half. I hated him for that—for coming back and making me feel what I'd never be able to have.

The crushing, tight feeling that gripped my chest made my heart stutter irregularly as my throat closed in and I felt like I was suffocating again. My heart was broken.

Missing beats was only one of the symptoms of my baby's condition, but I had to admit that some had also been missing in mine since Kane Exeter had walked back into my life.

None of what had happened in the previous forty-eight hours had supported my fragile mental state, and the way I responded to Kane's visit was less than dignified.

I spent another restless night trying to sleep, a habit I had formed since Kane had taken over every thought I had.

The dissatisfaction of knowing I would probably live the rest of my life without him; devastated me.

Eventually, after hours of self-depreciation and loathing, I talked myself back to the position of hope and thought he may have been giving me breathing space again.

I even appeased myself with the hope of a slim chance that he'd call in before he left town.

If that happened I'd decided I'd tell him about the baby, and all my fears about the future and his lifestyle, how he reacted to that would be his call, but if he left and didn't call after that, at least I'd know for sure that he'd never come back.

~

Waking with a start, my heart raced and I cradled my bump and felt my baby active in there. My heartbeat was still fast and I had a feeling of dread that made me uneasy.

My thoughts turned to Kane and I crept downstairs at 5:00 am because I had a sudden thought that I shouldn't wait for him to come to me.

Guilt had taken its toll on me and I had an overwhelming need to apologize for the way I'd treated him. Sitting at the desk top computer I began to write an email to explain my feelings instead of being angry about the things I could not change.

Hello Kane, I don't know how to start this except to say I'm sorry, really sorry. For the previous eight months I have struggled with my feelings on many levels, especially what we did, and how reckless I was with you. You made that effortless for me to do. Since then my whole world has changed in countless ways, and I have no control over my life at present. I wasn't prepared in any way for your unexpected return nor the depth of my feelings for you, I've honestly never felt this way before, nor since. Although Elliott and I were in a new relationship, I had begun to develop feelings for him, and that made what we did even harder for me to understand. I had never regarded myself as someone who could allow a moment of passion or lust to overtake my rational thoughts. Yet, that's exactly what happened with you. In those intimate moments we shared, nothing had mattered but you.

Being a girl that doesn't trust easily, I've never been one that had sex with someone without an emotional tie. I viewed what had happened with us as a betrayal even though it was Elliott's choice to push me away. My behavior left me both embarrassed about that and regretful that I had maybe thrown away a second chance at an amazing lifelong friendship with you, for the satisfaction of knowing you intimately. Like I said, I wasn't prepared for that to happen, nor the range of emotions that touched on everything from shame to ecstasy. Those feelings were incredible and memories I'll never be able to erase from my mind.

Allowing myself to be caught up in the seductive charm you ooze instead of my usual rational no-nonsense approach to life fills me with remorse and makes me wish that things were different for us now...but they're not. My situation is what it is and I have had to adopt a hard exterior to keep myself from further hurt by someone as tempting as you. I had thought my barriers were pretty impenetrable from growing up in a military family where I learned to create personal buffers, yet you managed to creep under my skin in a whole different way from that of when we were kids. And from my perspective it's a dangerous way. The thought of allowing myself to have thoughts of anything but friendship with you scares the life out of me.

There is nothing in common between us, apart from the army connection, Kane. The only music my family ever had time for was Matt's tuba and Jacob's trombone efforts with the marching band back when we were kids. Seeing you again the other day has stirred the strongest feelings I have ever experienced, but I can't afford to entertain them without you knowing all the facts and finding some solution to the lifestyle you lead. I'm not trying to change you, Kane, I'm trying to make sense of what all of this means. Please don't make what I'm facing any harder than it already is.

After pouring my heart out, I scanned over the email I'd written and felt pretty miserable because I was allowing myself to chase dreams based on two sordid nights of passion with the man, from the boy who had been everything to me as a child.

Another wave of doubt washed over me and I figured again it was all pointless. I had to let him go. Thinking I had temporarily escaped to a fantasy world, I pulled myself back to reality.

I closed my computer without sending the email. Kane Exeter functioned on a completely different planet because my world wasn't about fame, fortune and fun.

I was a pregnant and soon-to-be a single mom with an extremely sick baby and my focus had to be centered there. By 6:30 am I had concluded that any notion of a relationship with him was absurd and went back to bed with a heavy heart.

Chapter Twenty-Four

FADE TO BLACK

Saturdays were always quiet in my house, my parents usually spent the weekend at my grandma's place and Jacob didn't come home.

I loved the stillness of the silent house and used the time to take a leisurely bath before I settled down to do a little work for Dad at my laptop.

There had been no word from Kane and although my heart felt bruised, I was glad I had come to my senses and hadn't sent the email. It would have been like pouring gasoline on dying embers since he'd decided to stay away.

Sinking myself into work was a necessary distraction and being able to work right up to the birth was one of the few fortunate things I had going for me. As I began to do some audio work a new email message alert from Candice showed up on the bottom of my page. *Answer your phone please!*

My phone vibrated on the side at the same time. I smiled at the drama and swiped to accept her call.

"Josie? Where are you? Did he come and see you? Do you know what happened?"

Confused by her anxious tone, I had no clue what she was taking about. *Did he come and see you? Kane?* I never had the chance to tell Candice that Kane came to visit.

It had happened so suddenly and with it being the Thanksgiving holiday, she'd gone to New Jersey to visit her parents. I hadn't called her because I knew she'd planned an all-day marathon shopping day on Black Friday with her mom.

"Who? What are you talking about?"

"Kane. God. You don't know, do you?" The tone of her voice was loaded with a mixture of emotions. Worry, anxiety, stress, and fear.

"What is it? Is something wrong?" My heartbeat accelerated and shock waves radiated from the center of my chest until my fingers and lips tingled from the effect of a sudden adrenaline rush.

"Oh God, you don't. Kane was found badly injured in his suite at The Drake Hotel this morning, Josie. The news sites are saying he was stabbed and left for dead."

The impact of her words made me freeze. My mind went completely absent of any capable thought and I stared at the faux caramel-colored silk drape by the window. It was the only thing that was registering with me.

"Josie, are you there? God. Is anyone with you?"

Still I said nothing. I had no questions, no thoughts. Nothing. It was as if my mind had closed down, completely traumatized by her words.

Maybe it was my way of protecting myself from further information or maybe it was because my aching heart just couldn't take any more bad news. I was a jinx.

First Elliott and then Kane. My baby. All of those people suffering and all connected to me.

"The latest report was about twenty minutes ago, it says he's alive, Josie. Critical, but alive."

Still staring blindly at the curtain, I slipped into another dream-like episode, then my mind gave me the first rational thought since Candice had spoken to me. *Where is he?*

Suddenly, panic squeezed my heart and I couldn't breathe, my mind flashed to an image of Kane in a hotel room covered in blood and the weirdest, most peculiar feeling came over me and my head buzzed.

It had felt like I was outside my own body from the floating feeling in my brain, and something instinctively told me to lie down. I remember doing that right before everything went black.

"Josie! Josie! Wake up!— Call an ambulance." I heard Matt's voice calling. My eyes were heavy and my head ached as I opened them in time to see Jacob enter the room with his cell to his ear and his other hand running through his hair. He looked worried and I felt confused.

"What happened?" I croaked.

"I think you passed out, honey, are you okay? Let's sit you up, okay?" Slowly, Matt helped me upright and I sagged back into the cushion at the back of the sofa.

"Is it the baby?" I shook my head no and sat confused at what was going on, and why I'd passed out.

I watched as Jacob told Matt to get me some water. He pressed the cold glass into my hand when he returned then guided it toward my lips. "Sip it, Josie."

As soon as the freezing liquid touched my lips my memory was jolted.

"Kane!" The wave of nausea rolled my stomach as I searched Jacob's worried face.

"Kane was found in his hotel room, he's critically ill." Speaking those words just about drained me. Fear and worry filled my mind and I hated myself. *If it hadn't been for me he wouldn't have been there.*

"What? Where did you hear this?" Jacob asked, but didn't wait for my answer, instead he began searching for something then crossed the room in the direction of the TV.

"Candice." I was struggling to explain myself but in truth I had no more news.

"Quit with the questions, Jacob, can't you see she's in shock?" Matt pulled out his phone and swiped the screen while Jacob grabbed the TV remote and turned to the twenty-seven news station.

Jacob's cell began to ring and he pulled it out answering it and using the remote at the same time to scroll the news clip trailers at the bottom for news.

"Turn that off." Matt scowled then went over to Jacob and shared his screen with him. Jacob glanced at what Matt showed him and looked sick.

"Fuck."

"What? Is he dead," I screamed hysterically, and tried to rise from my seat, but Matt pushed me down gently and sat next to me for a second.

"No...not dead. But it's really bad." Jacob replied.

Matt rose again and shoulder barged Jacob for answering me before walking over to the window.

"Ambulance will be here any minute. Do you have anything you need to take with you, Josie? We want to get you and the baby checked out after passing out like that." Matt's attempt to divert the conversation didn't work.

"Just tell me what's going on, I need to know." My voice was full of determination. I *had* to know if he was okay. For the first time since I'd heard the news I'd started to feel. Tightening in my belly caught my breath and a wave of emotions, full of anxiety, worry and fear made me burst into tears.

"Ambulance is here," Matt informed us as he walked to the door to let the paramedics come inside.

I felt like protesting but with the knowledge my baby was less than healthy, I wanted to know she was okay too. "Get my bag from my bedroom it has everything in it. I'd hate to be stuck there without my own things." I was still crying but functioning better than I felt.

Jacob ran upstairs and the paramedics checked me over. Initially they were going to leave me at home but I slipped my birth plan to him and when he read my expression and then the notes he quickly backtracked and said that he thought it would be a good idea to monitor the baby since I'd fainted.

Safely installed in the ambulance with Jacob, Matt left me to take his car and follow us to the hospital. I was glad that Jacob stayed with me for two reasons.

One, we were twins. We had this thing going on where one knew how the other felt most times, and so I knew he would have an idea of what Kane's situation would mean to me.

Second reason was because he was much less resistant to my whiles and would cave easier and tell me exactly what was happening with Kane. I was right about that.

Matt called Jacob while I was having tests and Jacob went outside to take the call. When he came back I pressed him to tell me the truth advising him that keeping it from me was only making me imagine much worse.

Jacob then told me that Matt had managed to get through to the hospital and speak to Kane's

Uncle Dennis. He explained who we were and that Kane had spent Thanksgiving with us.

Apparently his uncle and aunt were aware of this so he wasn't guarded in the information he gave to my brother. According to him, the last person to enter the room was a room service attendant shortly after 10:00 pm on Thanksgiving.

Kane had arrived back to his room and ordered some alcohol. From his account Kane was alone and a little curt in his manner, but tipped him and closed the door after a polite goodnight."

The morning after, a Do Not Disturb sign was left hanging on the suite door and no one figured anything was amiss.

It wasn't until a few hours ago that his PA, Catherine, who he checked in with twice a day, alerted the hotel that she hadn't heard anything from him since the Thursday when she called to inform him about an engagement, and had heard nothing since. That's when they suspected something might be wrong.

When Jacob told me the news my heart almost fell out on the floor. I thought my head was going to explode under the band of pressure squeezing my brain.

All day long I'd been cussing him for not coming, imagining the worst of him, and he'd been lying injured.

My stupid misplaced pride wouldn't allow me to pick up the phone and call him to say I was sorry. *If Kane dies it'll be my fault.* Ashamed of myself, I tried to get off the bed to go and find him. I knew enough to know we were in the same building. *What if he dies?*

My worrying thoughts made me feel distraught and I bawled like a baby. Jacob looked helplessly at the nursing staff.

The young dark-haired nurse shrugged and shook her head. I took that as she had no words of comfort because if she did know anything she may have said so. I think that was the worst part; that no one was even trying to reassure me, and their silence and pitying glances gave me a greater understanding of the gravity of Kane's injuries.

No one had listed them to me, and selfishly, I hadn't asked because the harrowing news that he was in intensive care meant his life was under threat. So just when I had felt my life couldn't be more emotionally stressful it got so much worse.

Strapped to the Cardiotocograph monitor or CTG as the staff called it, I lay watching the flat line on the paper scrolling down from that which represented my womb, while the wiggly line recorded my baby's heartbeat.

Listening to it ticking along then suddenly becoming slow, then fast, soft and loud or a missed beat suddenly made everything real. I felt alone and frightened.

"Jacob can you sit here." I pointed to the chair and he immediately came over and sat down.

Reaching out he held my hand and squeezed. "I know this is hard for you, Josie, but you just have to concentrate on you and the baby, right now." His worry was etched on his face. "The docs are doing everything they can for Kane."

"I need to tell you something. Something I should have told you from the beginning."

Jacob stared with a puzzled expression on his face. "What's wrong, Josie? You're scaring me."

It must have been the look on my face as I gasped for air and tried not to break down in tears as I told him what I'd been hiding.

"It's my baby—she's sick." A strangled sob escaped from my throat and I wailed loudly. All the months of holding my secret in came pouring out of me. I was in an emotional meltdown. "It's her heart...listen."

Jacob looked at the tracing of my baby's heartbeat and looked back to me. "I could hear it wasn't right, Josie, but I thought that was because you were upset." I shook my head unable to bring words to our conversation.

Nothing I said would change the fact that my baby's heart wasn't the same as all the other babies out there.

Jacob bounded from his chair and wrapped me in a tight hug, kissing the side of my head, and rubbing my back.

I felt his body shake as grief tore through him, his shoulders heaving as he gasped in air and buried his face further into my neck. "God, Josie. What does this mean? Is she going to die?"

Even though I had tried to prepare for the possibility, she wasn't if I had any say in the matter. "She's fighting, Jacob. Every day she's fighting. They will operate not long after she's born to try to help her." I looked to the nurse in the room for support and she picked up the cue straight away. "Maybe we could leave Josie to rest for half an hour? We can a chat about her baby's needs if you'd like, Jacob?"

Jacob nodded. "Why did you do this on your own, Josie?" I knew from his question he thought I was selfish.

I felt selfish after I'd seen his reaction. I'd had months to prepare for this and he had a couple of weeks at the most. "You let me take you shopping for—"

"How would you have treated me, Jacob? How would anyone have treated me, knowing I was carrying a baby that may not survive?"

"So you carried the burden alone and protected all of us from worrying?"

"If I thought it would have changed anything I'd have told you all that first day when I'd found out. But I haven't been alone. Candice knew."

"I have a million questions, but I'm going to do what the nurse asks and let you rest." As he was going out of the door he turned and ran his hand down the metal plate on the door. "I'll break it to the others. Leave that to me." His voice was sad, full of sorrow.

Swallowing hard, he gave me the smile of a brave man and followed the nurse who had already left the room. I laid my head back on the pillow and breathed deeply.

For the first time since I'd found out I was pregnant I didn't feel alone.

Candice had always been there but having my twin, the other half of me, sharing the burden of knowing Ellie's fate felt like a massive relief.

Chapter Twenty-Five

FEAR

Once I had told Jacob about the baby, I was desperate for news about Kane. I had been trying to keep calm so that the baby check-up would be fine. I wanted to see Kane, I needed to go and find him.

About twenty minutes later the professor, who had been taking care of me and the baby, came in to see me.

Lifting the paper he put on his reading glasses and studied the trace before he sat down on the chair beside me.

"Josephine, do you remember when I said that we had to keep the baby in utero for the optimum time?" I nodded and thought he was going to tell me that I needed to rest more.

The previous couple of days hadn't been easy and the shocking news about Kane had almost wiped me out.

"Yes, I do."

"So I know you are only coming up to thirty-six weeks, but my instincts are that it would be prudent to deliver your baby tonight. This trace on the report is beginning to look ominous and it tells me your job in keeping your baby growing inside is done. I'm going to set things in motion for a caesarean section sometime this evening when the operating room is available. I need to contact Professor Miriam, the pediatric heart surgeon, and bring her up to speed. You remember her from your scan and when we mapped out your plan?" I nodded again, too frightened to speak because everything was suddenly real.

The massive dark cloud that had followed me around since the day I'd found out about the baby was about to burst.

When he handed me his handkerchief I realized I was crying again. I'd gotten so used to the feeling by that time that it had become one sad, grief-stricken emotion rolling into another. I was powerless, tired and broken down both inside and out.

"Can I go and see Kane?" All the time I'd pushed him away, thinking this can't possibly be what he wants in life, I'd been thinking for him. And to think it was too late to tell him how I felt was killing me. When the professor looked puzzled I expanded on why. "Kane Exeter, he was brought in this morning. We're close friends."

The professor's brow creased. "The young man who was attacked?" The use of that word made me feel terrible inside.

"Yes."

"I'll have a volunteer take you up to the care unit, but I can't give permission for you to see him. That would be the unit specialist's decision, not mine."

Standing to leave, he looked down at me and his eyes softened a little. "You've been very brave to make the choices you have in this uphill battle, Josephine, your baby is going to need all your attention from now on."

It was a warning. I knew what he was saying, but if my life was going to be even more different from the moment they took me to the operating room, I wanted at least to know that Kane was going to be okay, because I knew after my baby was born she would become my sole focus and get everything she needed from me.

An orderly arrived to take me to see Kane. Jacob was accompanying me while I was being wheeled into the elevator to go up to the floor Kane was on, my heart was in my mouth. *What if he's disfigured?*

I didn't know what to expect, and to be honest, I didn't care as long as he lived.

When I saw the way everyone stared at me as I got out of the elevator I had to stop myself from freaking out. The expectant look from the guy who was introduced to me as his uncle Dennis was strange.

What was stranger still was that he seemed to know who I was. The way he looked at me made me feel like I should have been asking questions, and for a moment I thought that perhaps he thought I didn't really care.

None of it mattered. The only thing I wanted was to see Kane for myself. "Hi, Jo...Kane's still unconscious. I'm sure he'd be fighting hard if he knew you were here. He's told me all about you. He thinks the world of you, you know." I didn't know what I'd expected him to say to me, but it definitely wasn't that.

As I stood up from the wheelchair, he led me into the room where the high-tech machinery whirred, the cuff around his upper arm puffed out automatically as the machine beeped its way to a final count.

A long tone signaled his blood pressure and pulse, recorded on a digital screen. Another monitor up above showed an EKG reading of the normal pattern of his heartbeat but every now and again there was an occasional rogue one that spiked higher than the rest.

My anxious gaze became fixed on Kane once I had my nerves in order. Fear made me tremble with shock, but at the same time I felt relieved that his face seemed as beautiful as always.

A flashback image of him asleep on the sofa came to mind. Almost perfect apart from the white concertina tubing with the valve that came out of his mouth and the sound of a regular puffing noise of the machine it was attached to causing the positive pressure in his lungs.

Walking closer to the bed, I noticed a large glass bottle standing on the floor near it. It was half-filled with bloody fluid that had drained via a clear plastic tube coming out of it that disappeared under the thin sheet covering him up to his neck.

Seeing the nurse record all his vital signs while Kane lay motionless ripped my heart to shreds.

Thinking back to the day of him sleeping on the sofa again, and remembering how amazing it felt to have that voyeuristic view of him in his natural unconscious state was nothing like the man I stared at in the room.

Watching him in his relaxed state as he'd slept peacefully was nothing like the stiff, stilted position they had laid him in on the bed.

A chair hit the back of my legs and I realized I was visibly shaking. "Sit down, Josie. I know it's hard to see him like this," Dennis encouraged.

"What happened...I mean how bad is it? Is he going live? H...he's got to live. I never got the chance to tell him..." I sobbed as tears suddenly streamed down my face.

Hesitantly, I reached out and slid my hand under his. It was warm and I decided to turn my hand around so that his hand was cupping the back of mine.

The ventilator puffed in and out and I found myself involuntarily breathing in time with it.

"CCTV shows a guy arriving at his door just before midnight. Unfortunately, he was wearing a hoodie that prevented the police from identifying him so far, but they are checking the CCTV images out on the streets for eight blocks in all directions. We are hoping that they catch the bastard."

"What did he do?"

Dennis looked to the nurse taking care of Kane and she responded. "Kane has three puncture wounds and two others. Two deep in his left lung, one that narrowly missed his kidney, one that grazed his upper right arm, and we think he grabbed the weapon because he's got a deep gouge on his right hand. His breathing difficulties are a major concern, but we're not sure whether he has any lasting brain injuries. He had a heavy knock to the head, but they can't see any bleeding, he just hasn't regained consciousness. The ventilator is to optimize the pressure in his lungs at this moment in time. I'm afraid we are in the watch and wait period according to the doctors."

My heartbeat pounded as I absorbed the terrible news of his injuries as I fought the panic that came with the news of how uncertain everything was.

"Can he hear me?" A million thoughts converged in my brain at once and I suddenly couldn't think again for a minute.

"We encourage relatives and loved ones to talk to patients like Kane. Sound is the last sense to go, so there is every chance that he may hear what you're saying depending on whatever level of consciousness he's in."

Staring blankly at Kane as the nurse spoke, my tears blurred my vision of him lying on the bed and I desperately wanted to tell him what I felt because I felt there may not have been another chance.

"I know this is a lot to ask, but can I have a few private minutes with him? I may not be able to come back after today." Rubbing my bump carefully I looked first to Kane's uncle and then to the nurse."

"No, I have to stay I'm afraid," the nurse replied assertively.

Dennis placed his hands on his knees and pushed off them as he stood up. "Pretend she isn't in the room, Josie. My Kane is a natural performer so he wouldn't mind there being an audience."

Leaning over he patted Kane's hand still holding mine. "Be right back, buddy, I'm sure you'd prefer this pretty girl's company to mine anyway." Kane's uncle attempted a smile in sympathy. I didn't deserve that. If I hadn't been so stubborn and indecisive Kane may not have left and wouldn't have been injured at all.

Closing the door quietly behind him, Dennis stood at the other side of the glass and I turned and sat motionless while I tried to imagine Kane's smiling face.

I couldn't really make out his lips or the natural shape of his mouth with the tube in place. His eyes looked the same as they did when I had watched him sleeping at my place, and I tried to focus on those to give me the courage to say what I wanted to.

"Hi, Kane. God..." A sob choked the start of my speech and I stared at his unresponsive frame lying in the bed. He looked so vulnerable and I'd never seen him like that before.

I swallowed back the tide of emotion and I tried to find the right words to say what I felt in my heart, thinking that it may be my only opportunity. I wondered at the same time if I'd left it too late. Maybe he wouldn't even hear me, or if he did, would he remember?

"I'm so sorry, Kane. Christ, I'm so desperately sorry. I wish to God that I didn't have this stubborn streak in me, but I do."

I had words on the tip of my tongue and once I said them it would be a public admission of my feelings for Kane.

It was time to tear down the barriers I had created to protect myself and disclose what was in my heart. "I love you. I'm *in* love with you. There. I said it."

I stared at him but there was no reaction. No spike of excitement in his heartbeat on the monitor like a scene in a movie. Just the constant, rhythmic puff of the ventilator helping him breathe and the same steady beeps echoing in the room.

"I think I've loved you since second grade, since you let me play soccer and put me in as the goalkeeper. I know now that it was because there weren't enough boys, by the way," I laughed softly. "What I mean is...there's always been this...thing. I don't know what to call it but we had it, and when you talked about the connection we had when you came back it all felt pretty surreal. Fantasy...like white glowing unicorns and fire dragons. Anyway, I'm not going to hash over all this stuff, but I want you to understand how I feel. Twelve years, Kane. From kids to adults...that was more than half my age of time we lost. And when you came back you were no ordinary man. You were a fucking rock star...you *are* a rock star."

Glancing at the nurse I felt annoyed that she was eavesdropping on my intimate conversation. *Bearing my soul is difficult enough without having someone who could repeat what I say to the press.*

My heart dropped to my belly with that thought and I figured none of it mattered anymore.

"I know I frustrated you by turning you down. Believe me I frustrate myself. Try to understand this. In less than two weeks I had two guys I cared about. One I loved, one I could have grown to love. One who had been everything to me as a child, and one who never got the chance to be everything. We'd slept together once, Kane...once and you were asking me to run away with you."

A rare moment of self-pity rose from my gut and crushed my chest. "How did I get to be so unlucky? Every time you got close to me you went missing. First in Germany, then after your mom died, and now..."

Another wave of emotion stole my speech and I swallowed it back. "I slept with two men twice, one died and one is fighting for his life right in front of me. I'm pregnant at twenty-two and I've never had a man inside me without a condom. I don't know how that happened. And on top of all that, I've hurt and kept things from everyone I know.

I'm heartbroken. Hell, even my baby's heart is broken." I sobbed again for a minute then wiped my nose and took a deep breath.

I looked to the door to draw some strength from my brother, but both he and Dennis were gone. Looking back at Kane I knew I had to be honest about my baby and tell him the whole truth as I knew it.

"You asked if this baby was yours. Honest to God truth? I don't know. I don't want to know. It wasn't that I wanted to keep that from you, it was more about protecting you from the hurt and pain you would feel inside, knowing what I do about her. I hadn't thought it all through properly and what it would mean to her in the future. That's why I said it was Elliott's. He's not here anymore to be hurt by it. Life is going to be very different after today. Life for the Carmichael family is about to get massively complicated. I wish I had more time to tell you all the things you mean to me. I wish I had the guts to just go with what you want. I wish I could just let you love me and feel at peace about that. You made me incredibly happy and desperately sad with your offer and the way you kept telling me you wanted me. I felt you make love to me, Kane. Really felt it. I may not have the experience you do, but I can definitely tell the difference between being fucked and what we did. You turned me on my head...my life on its head, but you snuck back into my heart again, and I have to accept responsibility for that. It's my heart after all, it's me that decides who to let in, right?"

Moving my hand from under his, I reached over lifting it to my face and spread his palm across my cheek. I leaned into the soft strength of it. His touch felt familiar and I could smell his scent. Even unconscious, he managed to comfort me.

"They told me my baby is sick, Kane. I've known for most of the time she's been inside me. She's probably going to be fragile all her life...if she makes it. In fact, she's going to need major surgery and I'm scared to death that she won't survive. She's so sick they offered me a choice to keep going with my pregnancy, Kane. It's the only real choice I've been given in my life since the day you came back. I choose her. I love you, Kane...I didn't have a choice about that," I sighed as the tears dripped from my face to the bedsheet staining it.

"I wrote you an email this morning but I never sent it. That's how fucked up I am—that I couldn't even explain to you face-to-face how much I really care, but I feel everything about us is so impossible. Especially now. But I really need a friend, so I need you to fight hard and get well...I've never been in a room with you before where you've had nothing to say. It's painful."

I burst into tears again, my throat closing completely and turned to see Jacob and Dennis both entering the room.

"Josie, they want you downstairs, honey," Jacob said softly.

Slipping Kane's hand from my face, I placed a long kiss in his palm and closed it.

Placing it back on the bed, I walked back out to the wheelchair and sat down. I couldn't allow myself to look at him again because I knew I'd be so overcome with grief that I may not have been able to face what I had to do next.

As Jacob pushed me out the door, I caught sight of a policeman guarding it. I hadn't noticed him before. He stared straight at me with a haunted look on his face and tears in his eyes, and wondered if what I'd said to Kane had been even less private than I'd thought.

The orderly pushed me back to my room while Jacob walked alongside holding my hand.

We never spoke and I think Jacob was thankful for that. I could see the worry etched on his face at what he'd learned earlier and the fear in his eyes about what the next few days and weeks would hold. I wondered how we were all going to get through it.

Chapter Twenty-Six

PROUD

My mom was waiting by the bedside when I returned to the room, her tear stained face was more than I could take and I hid mine in my hands.

Drained from crying so much, I had nothing left in me to say how sorry I was for all the heartache I'd caused. *Everyone must hate me. What did I know about making decisions of this magnitude? If I told anyone everything that had happened in the space of the past year in my life, no one would believe me. But it has happened and I'm worried that the distress I've felt up until now is nothing compared to what may be around the corner.*

Soft familiar hands smoothed my hair and removed mine from my face. My mom's eyes were forgiving and held nothing but love in them.

"Josie, I feel distraught that you've carried the weight of this terrible situation on your own. No one should have had to do that, and the fact you felt it necessary not to tell us says something about your expectations of the advice we'd have given you. What you've done took real guts. You didn't take the easy way out of this, and you protected us from worrying about you and the baby all this time. How you've gotten through this I have no idea. I'm exceptionally proud of you right now."

Her arms wrapped around me tightly like a warm blanket as she cried softly into my hair. Instead of crumpling into a heap of pity and sorrow I drew strength from her words and straightened in the chair. My mom stepped back and looked seriously into my eyes.

"It's not been easy, Mom, believe me. There have been so many times when I've come close, but seeing Matt's reaction back at the house, and Jacob's and your reaction to my news today, has helped me to feel that although this is a sudden shock for everyone, it was the right thing to do. Now all of you still have the strength that I don't to help me and my baby through this."

Jacob's head turned in the direction of the door when the air in the room shifted and my doctor and Professor Miriam came into the room, followed by my dad. The doctor looked around him and then to me. "If I could just have a few minutes with Josephine please—"

"No, they can stay. This is my family. I need them to hear what the plan is." I sounded confident, but that's not how I felt inside.

"Very well, Josephine. As you are aware I have taken advice from my pediatric cardiologist colleague here and she has looked at the CTG reading of your baby's heart from earlier. The operating theatre is booked and I understand from your brother you have not eaten anything since at least midday." I hadn't eaten anything since a slice of toast at 8:00 am that morning.

My obstetrician looked at my mom. "It's the policy of this hospital's trust that any baby who presents with this condition is delivered by caesarean section to put the least amount of stress on the heart and to support the baby by having a team present at the time of birth. The team is to be led by my colleague here who will begin the process of managing the baby's oxygen levels. After birth there is a valve that closes between the left and right side of the heart, taking the baby from the fetal circulation to the adult one."

The doctor saw my family's confusion and clarified, "It's the term used when the baby is breathing air outside the womb. By giving the baby an infusion of artificial hormone, Professor Miriam will keep the valve between the left and right chambers of her heart open and allow the blood to flow from one side of the heart to the other instead of via the circulatory system alone. This will increase the oxygen level as much as we can until the cardiologist can place a stent, via the baby's groin, into the heart. It inflates a small balloon or shunt, and keeps the value open until surgery to correct the vessels. We expect the surgery to take place within the first week."

Watching my family sit silently, listening, their eyes flitting between the two doctors and me, made me feel sick. I hated that they were going through this, but glad that I had their support to face it all.

~

Less than two hours later, I was gowned up, pre-medicated and wheeled down toward the operating room.

My heart pounded inside my ribcage and I had never known fear or apprehension like it.

I felt as if I'd been plucked out of my life and had been asked to play the main character in a horror movie. I prayed for a hero to swoop down and take me away from everything that was all too real by then.

I Kissed Mom, Dad, Jacob, and Matt, before the anesthetist's assistant wheeled me through to the anesthetic room. The two doors I'd been pushed through closed automatically behind me. Kind eyes stared down with concern.

"Hi, am I calling you Josephine or something else?" He'd been the only person in the medical team that had asked me what I answered to. The anestesiologist's team who had asked for my consent to the surgery had referred to me as Josephine and I never corrected them. Maybe I had wanted them to be detached from me.

"Josie."

"Perfect. You can call me Micky. Except you're going to be busy... but I just thought as we were trading nicknames you should know mine." He had no idea how much that tiny piece of normality, in my sick and frightening situation, lifted my heart. "We'll be keeping you awake for the delivery as per the birth plan, Josie. We don't want anything to compromise the oxygen levels. The spinal anesthetic works quickly and as soon as we take you through to the OR your baby will be born in the first five or so minutes. Depending on how you respond after that the whole operation should be completed within half an hour."

While I was being wheeled in and transferred onto the table my whole body felt numb. The environment was eerily quiet for the number of people in the room.

The anesthetist dipped his head to speak, "It looks scary, Josie, but everyone in this room is here for you and your baby—they're a great team."

A green drape was raised like a barrier from my chest and I could no longer see anyone apart from the surgeon's head in front of me.

An obstetric nurse who had been with me from the time I'd arrived at the hospital came and sat on a stool by my head. "Okay, Josie, the team is ready, you're about to be a mom, honey."

Tears trickled down the sides of my eyes and ran into my hairline under the paper cap I wore as I lay there feeling the weirdest dull sensation of someone tugging and pressing deep inside me. It wasn't long before I felt the rough, weighty pressure of her leave my body.

Seconds later there was a lot of activity and the bloody covered face of a baby was held above the drape. "Congratulations, Josephine, it's a girl," someone said. *It's a girl. My girl, my baby girl—Ellie.*

Listening to the hive of activity going on in the room, I knew they were already working to help her. I hadn't heard my baby cry and my throat was slowly tightening with emotion and anxiety.

I couldn't even bring myself to ask if she was okay for fear of being told no.

The poor nurse sitting next to me had no words either, and each time my eyes met hers she gave me a forced, almost constipated-like smile.

Turning my head in the other direction I was surprised to see that the anesthetist wasn't there, but seconds later he reappeared from beyond the drape.

"I was just getting an update for you. She's holding her own, Josie. They have the infusion going and her oxygen levels aren't too bad, but they are going to move her via the portable incubator to the NNICU. Once you are checked over and we've signed you out of recovery you'll be taken to see her. Well done, you were brilliant."

I had no clue why he thought that, I had laid on my back petrified through the whole horrible birth.

~

Eleven hours after Ellie had been born I was transferred, while still on my bed, to meet my daughter for the first time. She was half a day old and I had never even held her.

Entering the unit, I expected the pandemonium of babies crying, hungry, or dissatisfied because their mothers weren't with them.

What I found was a quiet, serene environment—a soothing stillness that was almost spiritual. The calm made me feel less afraid than I had been in days.

A plump doctor with huge, kind brown eyes, walked toward me smiling.

"Hello, Josephine. Congratulations, your daughter is beautiful. She's been stealing my staff's hearts while she waited for you to get here."

I had been determined not to cry, vowing to stay strong for my daughter, but the tears rolled at her kind words despite my best intentions.

Spraying my hands with sanitizer, she nodded to one of the other staff who was wearing cartoon scrubs.

Placing a clipboard on the side, the nurse named Angela, noted on her name badge, wandered unhurriedly toward me with the same calm that surrounded me.

"Ah, there you are, Mommy. Ellie has been settled and is waiting to meet you."

Nodding her head, the orderly wheeled my bed into a side room and immediately Angela followed with a portable, clear plastic incubator.

The shock of dark hair she had surprised me but I fell in love at first sight. My heart squeezed with emotion at my beautiful baby.

Somehow, I had expected blonde hair, like Matt, Jacob and mine, but I couldn't have cared if she had hair or not, I was just relieved to see that she appeared to be breathing.

Ellie's skin color was a little darker than I had expected. Her dark mauve lips and cyanosed coloring were sure signs of the problem she faced. Her head was encased in a little Perspex box-like thing and the nurse was quick to explain that it was to focus ambient oxygen in the incubator around her airways.

"We don't want to disturb her right now, Josie, her oxygen saturations are steady and handling babies like Ellie can cause some stress, but you can put your hands in and comfort her. We encourage skin-to-skin contact wherever possible."

Ellie looked normal sized, but I was scared to touch her. However, Angela's encouragement was exactly what I needed to hear.

I wondered how many other mothers were worried about touching their baby for the first time because it was an unnatural feeling to think like that. At least—I had thought so.

From the very second my finger traced the skin on her leg I knew my heart would never be the same again.

Her soft, delicate flesh was so precious that panic rose in my chest at the thought of what she had yet to face.

For a few minutes I stood there just staring at her, taking all of her in, learning and memorizing every feature about her.

My bond with my daughter grew stronger the moment I touched her. A thin tube fed the hormone to her vein, keeping her body fluids at just the right balance. An oxygen monitor, attached with Velcro, shone a red light making her tiny foot look transparent.

Eventually I had to leave her behind, but in better hands than mine, because at that point I didn't have the skills necessary to keep her alive. It was that fact that helped me to close the window on the incubator and allow them to take me back to my room.

My family were all still in the corridor when they wheeled me back in the bed and Candice had joined them. I wondered which one of them had called her and suspected Jacob, because he was the closest to her at work apart from me.

She was distraught because she had thought it was her fault that Ellie had been born early. The nurse reassured her that this wasn't the case.

Initially the staff tried to send everyone home and wanted me to rest, but I insisted on talking to them because I was anxious to hear how Kane was doing and give my family an update about Ellie.

Angela had taken some pictures of her for me and I shared them with my parents. There wasn't a dry eye amongst us when we saw how fragile she looked in them.

No one had been back to get an update on Kane, so once I had persuaded Matt to take my mom and dad home for the night, Jacob went to find out the latest news.

I was so worried about everything, and I was in pain from the birth wound which didn't help matters.

Candice and Jacob volunteered to stay with me, and even though the hospital policy had stated fathers only, my circumstances had afforded me an exception to their rule. If I was being honest, that first night I wouldn't have known whether they were there or not.

After I'd been given a morphine shot for the pain, the pain subsided, and my thoughts turned to Kane again, but I must have passed out from the drugs because I don't remember Jacob coming back before I fell asleep.

Pain cut into my unconsciousness at the same time as I felt the blood pressure cuff inflate. Cracking an eye open, I saw Jacob asleep in the chair by the window in the dim light of the room.

A nurse was silently recording my chart at the bottom of the bed near to where Candice was sleeping soundly on a pull bed.

When I tried to move, a pain seared through me and my body felt battered and bruised.

Slowly the nurse came closer to the bed and took my left hand, opened the small cap on my cannula, and inserted a needleless syringe.

I watched the liquid drain from it and within seconds I felt the pain subside as my head swam.

∽

If anyone ever said to me that caesarean births were an easy way out, I'd punch them the fuck out because it most definitely wasn't.

Every time I felt one area of my body settle down and become comfortable, another wanted attention.

Emotional overload from worrying about my baby and Kane, my engorged leaking breasts, the bleeding, and a healing wound was a ridiculous combination of things to deal with. I concluded from my first-hand experience that God was most definitely a man.

As the days passed I was thankful for small blessings. Ellie seemed that little bit stronger, putting on weight, and pooping like it was going out of fashion.

I began to feel more optimistic about her survival if the operation went well, but on day four the baby blues kicked in and my thoughts turned darker again.

Ellie's operation was set for day six and Kane was still unconscious. His condition was described as stable. I was taking one day at a time all the while the two people I loved most had that label. I could live with that.

Chapter Twenty-Seven

CANCELLATION

Changing position wasn't easy with a healing wound, and although it wasn't as painful as the day before, I still woke every time I moved.

Jacob was sitting in what was now his usual position in the chair, awake. "You okay? Do you need anything?"

I smiled softly at his concern, he was a great brother. "I think I just need to stand. My butt hurts from lying down, and I want to go and see Ellie. How's Kane?" I whispered, looking to Candice who was still flat out asleep.

"Should I go get the nurse?"

"Why, are you too weak to help me?" I snickered.

Jacob stood and walked over to the bed. "I just don't want to hurt you," he answered in a concerned tone.

"You won't," I reassured him. Gingerly he helped me from the bed and I wandered over to lean on the window ledge.

"I'll ask the staff if you can go to the unit to see your baby."

"Will you come with me?"

Holding the handle of the door he hesitated and smiled. "Thought you'd never ask," he replied with a grin, but I knew him better than that because even in the subdued light I could see how worried his expression became.

"Jacob you never answered me. How's Kane?"

"Just the same...but same is good, right?" The same answer was starting to chew away at me.

It took another twenty minutes before we finally arrived in the unit to see Ellie.

The staff were amazing as usual and Jacob looked like a scared rabbit as his eyes bugged out at all the equipment, and tiny babies weighing not even a third of Ellie.

Deep down inside, I felt the way he looked. Going through what I was going through was tough, actually, tough didn't even cut it.

"She's so beautiful." Jacob had tears in his eyes. He stared silently and swallowed uneasily. "She's gonna make it, Josie," he said with a reassuring tone. He couldn't know that for sure, but he had wanted me to feel better. I connected with the helpless look he gave me and the determination in his low gruff voice.

On sight, the bond was already there for him with her, just like it had been with me and Ellie.

"The surgical team is coming to see Ellie this morning, Josie." Angela reached out and laid her palm on my upper arm in a comforting gesture. I nodded slowly and opened the little porthole between me and my little girl. She was warm despite wearing nothing but a diaper.

Stroking her soft skin, I tried to speak normally to her. "Good morning, precious. How is my baby girl today?" The monitor beeped as she stirred and my eyes were immediately averted away from her to it. "It's okay, Jacob, it does that a lot." It was my turn to soothe my brother's worry. He looked like he was ready to run.

A small entourage of white coats came through the door headed by the surgeon, Professor Miriam. When she saw me standing by Ellie's incubator she gave me a warm, sympathetic smile and wandered over to me.

"This is Ellie Carmichael's mother, Josephine," She addressed the others. "Ellie was scheduled for surgery on Friday, but we've had a cancelation and she's doing well, so we'll be going ahead tomorrow." A cancellation? Did that mean someone else's baby didn't make it?

My heart missed a beat and I felt sick. Turning to look at my baby again, she looked fine, peaceful and relaxed, and I thought for a second, *why can't she just stay like that? She doesn't look like she's in pain.* But I knew that was my conscience not wanting my baby to suffer.

It was a purely selfish thought. The thought of a petrified mother that didn't want to face up to the reality of dealing with everything that was coming her way.

I knew the professor wanted to discuss my daughter with her team and part of me wanted to stay and listen, but I also knew if I did I'd have been scared to death, so I got into the wheelchair and asked Jacob to take me to see Kane.

My heart was aching so badly about everything that had happened and I was so overwhelmed with all the thoughts I had running through my mind.

One half of my brain wouldn't allow me to think while the other half seemed to dredge up the most terrible points of what had already happened, what was happening right then, and most difficult of all, what could happen in the future.

When we arrived on Kane's floor, a different policeman was stationed at his room. He stood from his chair and told us we could go no further. Jacob explained who we were and the policeman turned to look through the window.

My eyes followed his to where Kane was still in pretty much the same position as I'd seen him the last time, except his Uncle Dennis was sitting on a chair leaning forward with his head and arms resting on the side of his bed.

A moment later, Dennis stirred and looked behind him, I guess us talking had drawn his attention. Standing, he stretched the kinks out of his bones, his eyes centering on mine.

His body language became alert and he walked toward the door. "It's fine. This is Josie and Jacob. They are close friends of Kane's." The guard nodded with a relieved smile and left to sit down again.

"How are you feeling?" Dennis asked.

"I'm fine. Can I go in?" I asked, sounding anxious.

"Sure, I think he'd like that."

"What have the doctors said?"

"They ran some tests yesterday, and there was some reaction but he didn't wake up. They saw it as a positive sign though," he said, monotone. He sounded as if he didn't believe it himself.

I shuffled slowly from the wheelchair and entered the room. Just as before, the atmosphere felt quiet apart from the beeping machines and the puff of the ventilator.

Dennis walked up next to me and said, "They're taking him off the ventilator later. His breathing is stable and they've taken the chest drain out. They're not concerned about his breathing now."

"That's good." I stared absent-mindedly at Kane's beautiful features and had to touch him. I squeezed his hand, and still he lay totally unresponsive.

"So, she's here. My baby. Ellie. She's the most beautiful baby I have ever seen, Kane. Dark brown hair, huge blue eyes, average weight, average length, but her heart isn't average...I wish it was. They just told me she's having surgery tomorrow..."

My voice trailed off, as had happened so many times before, my throat squeezed closed and I swallowed back my tears.

"Wake up, Kane. I miss you. I need you to wake up so I know that you know I love you. I don't care what people think, what you do for a living or anything else right now. I just want you to know how I feel."

Leaning toward Kane was painful but I did what I had been thinking about since the last time.

Holding his head in my hands I inhaled deeply, filling my lungs with his scent. I kissed the top of his head repeatedly as thoughts of him ran through my mind.

I couldn't find the words to say what was in my heart. There were so many feelings but my emotions crushed them. Stepping back, I lifted his hand and laid it over my heart.

"I never wanted your life—thinking yours and mine were so different, that I'd never be able to be comfortable around the circles you mix with—but it seems you've stepped into mine.

I had looked at my life as ordinary, and when it comes down to it, we are just the same kids as we always were.

We're just living with extraordinary circumstances. I'd much rather have the worry of groupies than what I'm facing right now, and I'd rather deal with women hitting on you, than watching you like this."

A commotion drew my attention to outside the door and I saw that his medical team had converged and it was time for a reassessment of Kane's condition. I kissed his hand and whispered, "I don't know when I'll be able to come back, Kane. My baby is going into the OR tomorrow, but Jacob will keep me updated. Please, honey, please, please, wake up."

As the doctors had all huddled around the desk to the side of Kane's room, Dennis escorted Jacob as he pushed me back to the elevator. "Does Kane know that Ellie is his baby?"

I was sure the look of shock on Jacob's face reflected my own. And I knew for sure he hadn't heard me tell Kane the last time I had visited.

I stuttered before saying, "H...he's not Ellie's father." Intrigued as to why he would say that.

The elevator arrived and I stepped inside with Jacob. When the doors closed he turned to look down at me. "Kane?"

I shook my head vehemently. "No, Jacob, I don't know why Dennis said that, it's Elliott's baby."

Jacob gave me a lingering look then looked at the door when the elevator car stopped on our floor. Taking his hands out of his pockets he pushed the chair back in the direction of my room.

For the rest of the day I was desperately worried about my baby's fate and spent as much time as I could with her.

Everyone in the unit seemed to know what was happening with her, and I'd never been hugged by so many people in one day.

As each member of staff coming and going from their shift came to offer me words of comfort, I drew a little more strength from them.

If unity and will alone could have made my baby well, it would have happened from the positive vibes we received.

My parents came and went, and I saw them briefly, but somehow seeing their desperate, grief-stricken faces made everything much harder for me, especially at a time when I had to stay strong.

It had been the longest day of my life, yet not long enough when I thought of what the following day may bring, and by 8:00 pm that night, everyone had gone home, including Candice, when I asked for some quiet time alone.

Although Jacob was even more stubborn than me and flatly refused to leave.

"I'm not leaving you here on your own. You don't have to talk to me, Josie, but I'm not going home."

True to his word he didn't make a sound, just sat staring sometimes at me, sometimes at his phone.

Around 9:30 pm I felt exhausted and got back into bed. I'd done too much for a new mom after surgery, and my wound ached. I lay as comfortably as I could, but my head was filled with fear and anxiety again. I prayed to God, for what seemed like hours, to take care of my baby because her life was in his hands.

Waiting with Ellie for the team of people I had to trust with her life was terrifying. Twice during the night I'd vomited due to my guts twisting when I thought about her plight that day.

I'd been told to prepare myself for a long day ahead, but I'd been doing that since I had first learned that Ellie wasn't perfect like all the other normal babies. She was perfect on the outside, more than perfect to look at, with the kind of beauty that brought tears to my eyes.

It broke my heart that she had to suffer just to exist. By the time they came for her I was a blubbering mess.

I tried too hard to be brave, but when it came down to it I was just plain petrified. I would have sold my soul for my daughter not to have to face surgery.

I felt like a failure because instead of escorting her to the OR they just wheeled her away and I sat watching Jacob take my place. He'd volunteered to stay with her until they said he couldn't.

My mom and dad were waiting outside the neonatal intensive care unit doors and when I walked out and saw them I just collapsed into my mother's arms.

Matt had apparently gone with Jacob and I was thankful for such a strong family.

When my dad suggested a walk to the cafeteria by way of distraction, I figured it would be better than all five of us staring at each other in my room while we waited for news.

Feeling drained and scared I agreed to anything at that point, especially to forget the feeling of facing such a harrowing experience alone.

Dennis was sitting in the canteen when we arrived and called us over to sit with him. He mentioned he had sent me a text telling me that they had removed Kane's ventilator and that he'd opened his eyes briefly then fell unconscious again.

Apparently, the heart monitor reacted at the same time so it wasn't due to a spasm but to real activity.

My heart squeezed at the fact that Kane didn't have all the support around him that I did, and if it wasn't for my tiny sick baby, I'd never have left his side.

Dennis asked how my baby was doing, Jacob told him she was in surgery, it was then that Dennis asked to have a couple of minutes with me on his own.

If I'm honest I was in no fit state for conversation, but I was curious what he wanted with me. Did Kane tell him he suspected he could be the father? Maybe he was thinking, *when Kane knows that Ellie is sick he'll be glad he never pursued me to find out.*

Both my dad and Matt became very protective telling Dennis that it wasn't the time, but I was saved when Dennis' cell rang before he could say anything else.

Checking the screen, he swiped to accept the call and stood to listen. I watched his body language change and without another word he ran for the canteen door.

Jacob looked at my face and knew instinctively that I thought it had something to do with Kane, so he headed straight out the door behind him.

Chapter Twenty-Eight

EXHAUSTED

*W*atching my brother leave to go after Dennis gave me another panic attack at a time when I couldn't have taken another piece of bad news. I broke down at the table, sobbing again, feeling completely helpless.

My dad's loving arms wrapped around me. "Come on, let's take you up to your room." His voice, which had always protected me, calmed me down. Gently, he helped me to my feet and guided me by the elbow in the direction of the bank of elevators.

The wait for information seemed endless and the pressure of waiting to see if my daughter survived the risky surgery almost tore me apart. Eventually, the female surgeon knocked on the door and came into the room.

"Great news, Josephine, Ellie has come through the surgery and is doing amazingly well. I'm cautiously pleased with her progress and the perfusion of oxygen is now almost normal at ninety-seven percent."

I was grateful that she delivered the news without a pause like I would have expected from someone breaking bad news.

All of us in the room exhaled in unison. A beaming smile on the doctor's face gave me real hope that I hadn't realized I'd been denying myself.

I heard myself ask, "Can I see her now?"

"Sure, but only one person can come with you. We don't allow visitors for the first few days because of the risk of infection and we like to create a quiet, peaceful place for her to recover from her ordeal.

I looked to all the expectant faces, Mom, Dad, and Matt, and my dad said, "I think Ellie's mom needs her mom right now."

～

No one should have to see their baby the way I saw Ellie. Tubes and monitors surrounded her from the moment she was born, and that didn't change immediately after surgery.

My mom cried and held me, noting how beautiful she was and how vulnerable her condition had made her since the day she'd been born.

We held each other and wept silent tears. Our visit was brief because they preferred her to have some time in silence and dim lighting to optimize the environment for her to recover in a calming atmosphere. Not that they asked us to leave or anything, but we were both extremely inadequate.

I was mentally and physically exhausted.

The toll from before the birth, Kane's attack, and my inability to face what everything meant had shattered my heart into a million fragments. But still I continued to be swept along in an incredulous set of emotionally battering circumstances.

Jacob was waiting when I got back to the room. "How's Ellie?"

Mom filled my family in about her condition then asked, "How's Kane?"

My heart stalled because like I said, anything else, and I'd have gone into complete meltdown.

I held my breath as Jacob nodded and his eyes flitted toward me. There was something concerning about the way he looked at me, and the panic I'd been fighting hard to control almost tore free while I waited for his reply. "He's awake. Groggy. That's what Dennis' call was about."

"Is he okay?" I asked, with note of urgency.

"He asked about you." My heart lifted with that news. At least his memory was intact if he could recognize Jacob and ask about me.

"But is he okay?" I asked again. My instinct was to run upstairs and see him; however, my body was all but done. I had no strength left for another ride on the emotional roller coaster.

"Seems to be...still a little confused about what happened, but yeah, he's doing okay." *Men are useless at giving details.*

Mom, Dad and Matt all looked pleased at the news about Kane as well. I was exhausted and had a job persuading my parents to go home. I needed to sleep because I was still recovering from my surgery. Matt looked visibly relieved when I asked him to take them home.

For a normally unaffected kind of guy, the impact of knowing how sick my baby was, just about wiped him out.

My twin was the one person who had accepted everything I told him and rolled with the punches after his initial shock when I first told him about Ellie.

~

When I woke the following morning, I had a blinding headache. The nurse said it was probably stress from the day before and helped me to feel more comfortable with lighter pain relief.

Jacob had pushed me to see Ellie and I spent the morning with my baby, sitting by her bed. She was being kept unconscious to help her recovery and the medical team was impressed with the progress she'd made.

After several hours of immobility, I felt stiff and was persuaded to leave for a while to have some rest. Jacob arrived to take me back because it was still too far away from my room to walk.

I had tried so hard to keep Ellie as my sole focus, but if I was honest, Kane had always been there in my mind. Trying to deal with both situations had been too much heartache for me to bear.

As Jacob approached the elevator with me he had been talking about Ellie's progress, but when he pushed me into the car, he pressed the button for Kane's floor. "I'm taking you to see Kane, Josie."

My heart squeezed when he mentioned his name. It wasn't that I didn't care; it was more that I couldn't allow myself to because of Ellie's condition.

Glancing up at him I nodded, feeling relieved that someone was telling me what to do. I had felt that if I had said I wanted to go that people would think I was paying more attention to a friend when my focus should have been on my baby.

Seconds after I rose from the wheelchair when we arrived outside Kane's room his head turned and his eyes connected with mine.

A smile stretched across his face and instantly wiped out the visual of the last memory I had of him with tubes and wires everywhere.

He sat forward on the bed and winced a little when he leaned down for the bed adjustment control to adjust the back of the bed so he could sit up.

Dennis stepped out of the room to join Jacob as I entered.

"Hey, babe. How's the baby?" His deep voice sounded croaky and thin, much weaker than I was used to. Tears sprang to my eyes and a feeling of relief washed over me.

"Hi," I said, feeling a little shy, although I had no idea why. "She was so sick. It's been a journey...no it's been hell," I answered honestly, and my voice cracked with the emotional wave that engulfed me.

"Thank God you're okay. Did they say how long before you recover fully? I mean is there any lasting damage?" The instant reprieve from worrying about him, at least, gave me a temporary sense of elation.

"Not that they know of, they had some concerns about my brain, but if they were monitoring what goes on up there I'm not surprised," he said, chuckling with a roguish grin.

"Jesus, Kane, I was so scared," I admitted.

"Crazy fucker wanted my nuts because his girl kept sharing my picture on her social media. I guess some guys just know when the competition is out of their league and only a kill will solve their problem." He chuckled again, and as sick as he was, that twinkle of mischief in his eye showed me his spirit was far from broken.

The way he shrugged what happened off took my respect and adoration for him to a new level.

"Glad you've still got your sense of humor," I said as I smiled at him.

"And my dick...still got that," he said, patting the thin bed sheet. "He wanted to cut that off too, that's what he told me right before I fell backward and bumped my head. Must have knocked myself out at that point and scared the bastard shitless. Makes no sense to me why he would have run at that point, I was sure he was gonna finish me off...but the cops figure he thought he had...left me for dead they said." There wasn't an inkling of fear in his speech and at that moment I had thought he was the bravest man I'd ever known. "Anyway, enough about me, I want to know about you."

Kane's face fell to a serious expression and he waved me over toward his bed. "Can you sit here?" He patted the bed beside him and lowered it a little for me to perch my butt on. It wasn't that comfortable but I did my best.

"I won't be able to sit like this for long," I warned.

"What I've got to say will only take a few minutes," he advised and I looked at him feeling a frown forming.

"There's never gonna be a right time for this, but I need to do this now while it's fresh, Josie. Who knew the trip we'd both be going on when I made that call to you? I'm gonna ask you four questions about some stuff I want cleared up right here in this room, and I want the truth. Bullshit almost killed me last week. Life is short. Shorter than any of us truly know. We built our friendship on honesty, right?" I nodded, wondering what he was going to ask, but already knew the answer to one of them. I had been a fool to think he would never ask about Ellie again.

"Do you love me?" It wasn't the question I was expecting and my heart stuttered.

"Yes." There was no hesitation. Kane's hand reached for my head, pulled me toward his lips and gently kissed my forehead.

"Are you in love with me?" He was right, this wasn't the right time for this, but I answered.

"Yes, I am."

"Believe it or not, I'm madly in love with you too, Jo. I'm so far gone I almost died trying to tell you that." My heart flipped over and I stared numbly at him because I felt sick at what I'd put him through, but in my defense, I did have just cause. I hardly knew him apart from what I'd seen on TV and the way he was around women, and the lifestyle he led, wasn't anything I ever saw myself adjusting to. However, everything we'd gone through since then made me think that life would have been a breeze in comparison to our reality."

Kane took my hand and threaded my fingers in his. Closing them softly he squeezed a little then lifted them to his mouth and pressed a soft kiss on my knuckles. In a quiet, hurt voice he asked, "Why did you lie about Ellie being mine?"

My heart almost stopped for a beat and I stared into his eyes hoping he could feel my pain. "It wasn't to lie to you, Kane. It was to set you free. I was screwed up after what happened with you and Elliott; then he died. Don't you think it would have been easier for me to come after you to take care of us? If I had said she was your baby, would you have just believed me?"

"Probably. You'd never lied to me before."

"So there you have it, Kane. I could have taken the easy way out. Perhaps saddled you with the responsibility for someone else's baby, but then I'd have been embroiled in a life where me and my baby were tied to, one that I had no wish to be a part of back then."

"And now? You'd be part of it now?"

"Yes, no...I don't know. I love you, Kane, but I have a child that will always come first."

"I never had you marked down as ignorant, Jo, so don't start disappointing me now." I gave him a puzzled look as he scoffed at me.

"Do you know who Ellie's father is for sure?"

"In truth? No. Does that make me proud? No. Of course, it doesn't, but I had to do what was best for my baby."

"And you think having no father is the best thing for your daughter? If you think that, it's one fucked-up selfish attitude you have there. Doesn't she have any rights? What happens if she grows up and wants to know the story about how she was conceived? What if she comes asking me to be tested and blames you for not being honest with her if I am her father?"

"She was sick, Kane. I was carrying a baby that I didn't know would survive. How could I come to you with that? Why would I hurt you by giving you that burden to carry?"

"And what makes you think you can behave like a martyr and make decisions for everyone else?"

"Alright. What if she's yours? How are you going to handle that? Look what happened to you. You can't even keep yourself safe. Why would I put my child in danger by associating her with your world? How would we live? Where would we even live?"

"Fuck, I don't know, Jo. Wherever you wanted, however you wanted. I really do love you. Probably been holding out for you my whole life if I'm honest. But I'm so mad at you I could push you off a fucking building right now. You know why?"

Kane was still held my hand, the anger from his temper vibrating from his body into his hand and I tried to pull mine away.

"Stop...I said I could, but you know that I'd never hurt you. It doesn't stop me being royally pissed off with you. Dennis," he called out, looking to the door. We watched Dennis as he came inside and closed it quietly behind him.

"Tell her what you told me," Kane said to his uncle. Dennis shoved his hand into his pocket and looked at his feet before looking back at Kane then at me.

"About two years before Kane was born his mom, my sister, Carly-Anne, was pregnant. Healthiest mother-to-be I ever saw. No problems whatsoever in her confinement and when her baby was born it was an easy birth. About five minutes after she was born she looked navy blue in color. Helena was her name and she lived for about four days. Kane's dad was on a tour of duty at the time so Carly-Anne was staying with my wife and me until after the baby was born. When they realized how sick Helena was, they transferred them to a fancy high-tech hospital in New York, but the baby died on the way. They said it had something to do with the tubes in her heart being crossed over or something when they did the autopsy. They told us it was rarer in girls than boys. Yet, when Kane here was born, he was as fit as a horse."

I tried to stand up from the bed, horror-stricken at my decision to believe it was Elliott's baby and keep Kane out. His fingers tightened around mine. "Stop. Just stop, Jo." His voice was quiet and calm. Too calm since he knew what I'd done.

"I don't blame you for any of the decisions you've taken. They're pretty fucked up but I get you. You're the same girl I knew back in the day. Always trying to keep your troubles to yourself and never wanting to upset anyone. But to throw the words back you've been slinging at me these past eight months, we're not those kids anymore, babe. I'm mad as fuck with you, Josie, but I can't find it in me to hold this against you. Apart from how deep my feelings run for you, how can I stay mad? Look what you did for me? Carrying the burden of a sick baby on your own? While you've been trying to soldier on, there are times when you must have felt life wasn't worth living. I get that, Jo. I get your bravery. You are most definitely from military stock."

Kane dropped my hand and I stood. Facing him wasn't easy with all that I'd learned.

I felt ashamed I'd judged him so harshly. I was the girl that had always been meticulous about planning and keeping my decisions sound, and if Dennis was right, I had made a catastrophic error in not telling Kane I was pregnant.

Edging his way to the side of the bed I saw him wince, but he held his hand up to stop Dennis when he reached forward to help.

Even though he'd almost died less than a week ago, Kane's independence and pride wouldn't allow him to accept help.

We were two of a kind. Standing in front of me, Kane tenderly brushed my hair away from my face and tucked it behind my ears.

Cupping my face in his hands, my throat closed at his gentle caress. I had found I coped better when no one touched me since Ellie had been born. Glancing down at me, the seriousness in his eyes crushed me.

"I know you, Josie. Way better than you think. Coming from a military family you learn habits that die hard. One of those is sucking up all the negative feelings, and locking them away. You took on the worry of Ellie alone, that was fucking heroic, babe, but one hero in my life is more than enough. Heroes, by definition, are people that usually act alone, they do stuff above and beyond what is reasonable and they don't think about the consequences to themselves. My dad was a hero, babe. I don't want another one to grieve over. I'm tired and my head hurts, but this had to be said."

"I'm sorry." There were no words to describe all the feelings that were relentlessly hitting me in waves, but the one thing I was certain of was that Kane's feelings were real. He was dignified and careful with his words when I doubted I'd have been as forgiving as he was.

If Ellie had died and he was her father, then I could never have lived with myself.

"I said I didn't care whether I'm Ellie's father or not, Josie. She's a part of you and I'd love her no matter what, but I think it would be a good idea to find out for sure, especially with what my uncle knows." Nodding my agreement, I closed my eyes and allowed myself to accept that we all needed to know for sure.

Chapter Twenty-Nine

TRYING TIMES

Spending time with Kane had made me realize that there was so much more to talk about, but the timing was off.

Nothing was as important as my baby, but Kane was a close second. He was the adult after all.

When he asked me if he could visit her with me I felt so confused because our emotions were running high and I didn't want to make another mistake.

I needed some breathing space to absorb what Dennis had told me, and of course I agreed to the paternity test.

Whether or not Kane was with me, Ellie deserved to know who her father was and if he was still alive. I'd been scared to face the truth about her paternity, but when it came down to watching both Ellie and Kane fight for their lives it was the turning point—to think I could have lost either one or both was more than I could have handled.

～

Candice couldn't stay away for long and back at the hospital the following morning. Talking to her and Jacob helped me to explore my feelings without feeling pressurized one way or another.

It must have been hard for Kane but he gave me the space I needed to think things through, and I gave permission for the paternity test in return.

The day after the paternity test he'd called to say he'd been discharged from hospital and was on his way to see me. Minutes later I heard a commotion outside my room.

Opening it wide I saw a small crowd of excited fans around him asking for autographs and taking selfies with him.

Despite what he'd been through Kane was grinning and joking around behaving as charismatic and flirty as he'd been before the attack. I watched him in awe as he moved effortlessly around them and wondered how he could still do that?

Kane had almost died just over a week before when an insane, knife-wielding boyfriend had taken his anger out on him because his girlfriend was doing exactly what those girls were doing.

Glancing down the hall toward me he smiled, that same sexy smile that stole my heart, and excused himself.

Kane's uncle Dennis intervened, making space between the well-wishers and fans as Kane turned to walk toward me. A young girl of about sixteen darted in front of him, stopping him in his tracks and hesitantly waved a pen and paper at him.

Kane flashed me a gorgeous grin and a wink, turned and gently took the paper being shoved at him. He murmured something to her and gestured the pen at me, then wrote on the paper.

Handing it back, she glanced at it with her brow bunched, then smiled widely and looked up adoringly at him.

By the time he reached me, I had to ask, "What did you write to her, she looked like she was about to pass out.

"Kane Exeter." He smirked wickedly. "I'm taken now...if you'll have me? And, I know what a ball buster you are...I can hardly give her my number now, can I? But I did ask her how her day was going."

All Kane's cockiness and confidence was still there, and I wondered how he had the nerve to stop and talk to those girls as if nothing had happened, when being famous had almost cost him his life.

"Aren't you scared? I mean after what..." My eyes searched his face; the thought was too painful to even contemplate.

"I'm human and I'd be lying if I said there isn't a part of me that's not. But no one is ever going to stop me doing what I do. I'm the only one that makes that kind of decision about my life. But to most of those fans out there, I'm not the Kane Exeter that you know. I'm their escapism from real life. Hell, if you told some of them that I shit glitter and it smells like roasted marshmallows, they'd believe it. My problem isn't them; it's the ones who go to lengths to discredit what I am, those who are jealous of what I'm achieving. But I am the only one who will decide when to get off the ride. No one else."

I admired his resolute approach to his future, but at the back of my mind were the TV images of famous people killed in public by crazy people. John Lennon being the most notable one because of his career choice being the same as Kane's.

"Can we have a few minutes, Dennis," he asked as Dennis reached the door.

"Sure I had no intention of coming in anyway." He glanced at me and smirked. "It's no fun being around you two, the angst kills me. It's like a scene from that movie his aunt keeps making me watch...*Twilight*." Shaking his head, he wandered over and sat on the chair near the door of the room opposite mine. Kane laughed and continued to watch him. "Have at it then, I wasn't planning on sitting in a corridor all day."

Without answering him, Kane ushered me into the room and closed the door. His face changed and became solemn. "Sit," he commanded, in a gentle tone. I thought he was suddenly behaving a little weird then I realized he had the DNA results.

"Do you want to or should I? I mean I don't need any proof, but..." he gestured to the envelope. Personally, he was stronger than I was. He had acted so cool and collected in front of those people and yet he was carrying life-changing information around in his pocket while doing so.

"You." My voice was barely a whisper as my heart thudded hard in my chest, missing beats while he slowly and deliberately peeled the envelope open. He glanced at me; the look in his eyes told me that he desperately wanted her to be his.

Suddenly I was so nervous I began to shake uncontrollably. Finally knowing who Ellie's father was after months of uncertainty was mind-blowing.

As he slowly took the paper out I silently pleaded with God to let Kane be her father. I didn't care what he did or if he was around all the time, but I could see how much he wanted to be a part of her life.

I had put off letting him see her—I wanted to know either way what his vested interest was even without the result. I knew he genuinely wanted her regardless, just like he wanted me.

Unfolding the paper, Kane studied it for a moment with his brow knitted, his eyes reading left to right then he folded the paper again and stuffed it back in the manilla envelope. Taking a deep breath, he held it to his chest and closed his eyes, and for a split-second I doubted his right to stake his claim.

Opening his eyes the weight of the contents had clearly affected him because he swallowed a couple of times as he stared straight at me and shook his head. "I never doubted she was mine, Josie.

As soon as Dennis told me about my mom, I knew she was mine. I've been patient, more patient than I have ever been in my life with you. But now you know the truth. Can I see her? My baby...*our* baby?"

"That's it? You're not going to scream at me? You're not angry that I kept it from you?"

"Would that make you feel better? Would it change anything? No. And yeah, I'm as pissed as fuck at you for doing it all on your own, but I get you, Jo. I've always been able to get you. What's done can't be changed, but it's how we go forward that matters. I got this now, that's what's important." His serious stare carried the weight of responsibility.

"No, Kane, I don't need a caveman, *we've* got this."

Kane never showed me the paper at that point, but frankly, I didn't need it. Ellie without the tubes and monitors was the spitting image of Kane. Same color hair, huge blue sparkling eyes, and his beautiful full lips on her perfect little rosebud mouth.

Kane came over and knelt on the floor beside my chair and winced. He sat back on his calves to face me. "Josie, I swear to you, I will cherish you and Ellie with all that I can be if you'll give me the chance." I reached out and stroked his cheek and he rose on his knees and kissed me gently.

Within seconds it had deepened and a soft, breathy moan escaped my lips as our tongues began to explore. Kane suddenly pulled away, coughed, and winced again. "See, even when you've just had a baby, you manage to take my breath away."

There was no reason not to agree anymore. Anything he wanted he could have, but that was only if he treated us with respect. I felt that even though I hadn't known him long as an adult, he'd treat us with more than that.

When I asked him if he wanted to go right then to see Ellie, the smile on his face stretched wide and his hand was on the door handle before the sound of my words had died in the room.

Kane had refused security once he'd left his room and reassured everyone, his uncle was all the support he needed, I disagreed.

On our way down to Ellie, Kane met three well-wishers who had heard what had happened to him. I figured the world probably knew what had happened, and although they were fans, it had felt unnerving when people he didn't know had walked straight up to him, shook his hand, and asked how he felt like they'd known him all their lives.

My mind turned to Ellie and the dangers she had faced, and how she had survived. With each passing day that followed her surgery, she came more to life and acted like the normal baby she appeared to be.

I never realized that I hadn't heard her cry properly until she wouldn't stop one morning. It made me anxious, but the nursing staff were quick to reassure me it was a wonderful sound, because babies used a lot of energy crying, and Ellie didn't have much of that before her surgery.

From that point on my confidence grew by the hour, and taking Kane to the unit on that particular day marked a watershed, because I already knew what he was going to find out—Ellie was being discharged from the Neonatal Intensive Care Unit, or NICU, to my care, and back to my room. For forty-eight hours, I was going to take charge under the watchful eyes of the staff, so that I felt confident when we went home.

Approaching the door into her room, Kane's hand squeezed mine.

"Fuck." He was nervous, his normal swagger and cocky tone stripped away, my big alpha male had the vulnerability that had led me to accept that he'd do me no wrong.

"Kane, you're a father now, you can't swear around her." I snickered at the worried look he gave me then he smiled lopsidedly.

"I bet you were no better the first time you saw her." He was right. I was just as unprepared as he was, and I'd carried her around inside me for eight months.

My heart squeezed tightly as he entered the alien environment. Kane's worried face was worse than Jacob's had been the first time I'd brought him with me.

All the staff looked confused that Kane had come with me, only the doctor who took the DNA from Ellie knew Kane was the father.

"Hi, honey, we don't normally allow people who aren't related into the unit. You know how protective we are of our little ones with their fragile immune systems," Angela said, but eyed Kane up and down like she'd devour him in a heartbeat.

"Kane's related, Angela, he's Ellie's father. He's just been discharged from the high dependency suite upstairs."

Angela's eyes bugged out because until that point I'd been the poor single mom with a sick baby. Now she was looking at me like I was a rock star's girlfriend and baby momma. I snickered because I was exactly that.

Kane looked a little lost with the hand-washing routine and sanitizer, but once he was ready I took him by the hand and wandered over to the open cot she was in.

"Kane, this is your daughter, Ellie. Ellie, honey, this is your daddy." Tears pricked my eyes in an unexpected wave of emotion that caught my throat and me completely by surprise. "Sit on the chair, Kane, and open your shirt."

Sitting in slow motion his eyes never left her. "My shirt?"

"Yes, baby bonding is important and skin to skin contact is the best there is for a little one like Ellie."

He never protested, just undid his buttons and pushed the sides wide. My breath hitched when I saw the scars on his left shoulder and just below his collar bone. I knew it was rude but I couldn't help star-ing. "Oh God, Kane," I said shakily, holding Ellie mid-air.

Looking down at his chest he scoffed, "I'm fine, they just make me look a little more badass. Come on, please give me my daughter, I've been dying to meet her."

As he motioned with both hands for her, I laid her on him and watched as our baby's hand made contact with her father's skin. It was as if she knew his significance in her life.

Instantly Ellie's little hand opened from the closed fist it had been in to a flat palm against his warmth as she nuzzled against his smooth skin before lying contentedly still against Kane's chest.

I watched Kane inhale her scent for the first time when he bent forward and kissed her tiny head. The way he handled her with confi-dence despite his injuries touched my heart.

One strong hand splayed in a gentle, protective hold, while his other softly explored her fingers and stroked her cheek with the back of his index finger.

Kane's blue eyes brimmed with tears as he glanced up, looking directly at me, and I witnessed the emotional tidal wave he'd been bravely holding back.

Swallowing roughly, he bent to kiss her again, all the while treating her with the delicacy of the precious baby that she was. Seeing them together cemented my thoughts and grounded me. *We're going to do this no matter what.*

"She's so fragile. A little angel right here on Earth," he uttered, almost to himself. Slouching down a little he closed his eyes and held her quietly there for a long while.

I imagined what was running through his mind at that precise moment, and remembered what I had felt when I held her for the first time that way. I'd never be able to articulate into words what I had felt as I'd tried to absorb the collision of words and emotions too deep to fathom.

An hour visit with Ellie almost wiped us both out; it was an emotionally draining time. Kane was too quiet as he walked me back to my room.

Dennis had called asking if Kane was ready to leave, but Kane had told him to go home as we had a lot to talk about.

He was right we had a lot to talk about, but despite his excuse to his uncle once we were alone he looked tired and barely said a word.

An uneasy silence grew between us and Kane grew restless until it seemed he couldn't keep his thoughts to himself any longer.

"Jo. Are we really gonna do this? Gonna be a family?" My heartbeat rapidly accelerated because sensed a note of doubt in his voice.

My heart pounded in my chest and for a moment I thought he had changed his mind about taking responsibility and dealing with someone like me.

"Do you still want that?"

"Absolutely. With everything in me, babe." Relief washed through me and my heart rate began to settle down.

"So what's wrong?"

Inhaling deeply, he sighed and ran his fingers through his hair. It looked even better than before he did it. He looked so hot and appealing, but appeared to look troubled at the same time.

"This isn't easy to talk about, Jo, but I need to get this off my chest. We've always been honest with each other and I don't want something that comes back on us later. I'd never have brought this up but sometime in the future someone may have something to say about Ellie. Right after I left you I had a one night stand. You had said no to me and for me to go. I went with it and tried to forget you because I thought that's what you wanted. I met a girl in a bar when I got back to Boston. It's no secret how I was. I'm sorry, I was hurt when I left you. And I was single. Anyway...she came back to Cody's place and we...I thought it was one night. Just like many I'd had. You know I wasn't a saint. So, about three months ago the same girl rocked up and told me she was pregnant."

He stopped talking and sat on the chair, placed his hands between his open knees and rubbed them nervously together.

"Cody, Zander and I were eating dinner in this diner in Boston close to the record label studio. Anyway, she saunters in with a bump, saw us and headed straight for us. Cody nudged me and asked, "Did y'all use a rubber? 'Cause I know I did." Zander looked to me and looked at her then said, "Never fucked that one. You know I ain't into redheads." I stared at the girl and looked back at Cody. "Sure. Never been bareback in my life," I answered him confidently, thinking it was most probably Cody's, because if anyone is sloppy about sex it's him."

"Thing is she never stopped walking, came right up to the table and said, "Y'all—I need money to get rid of this kid. It's sick." I was disgusted by both myself for ever being with her, and the nonchalant attitude she had about the life she was carrying.

Cody turned to me and asked, "Wanna go halves with me?" I shook my head no, and asked her what was wrong...she said the kid had a bad heart, her words.. not mine. I offered her medical attention, telling her I'd arrange for her to see a good doctor, and get a second opinion, but I was confused as to how someone would know their baby had that kind of a problem before it was born. She refused to discuss it, saying she just wanted to be done with it. Cody opened his wallet and pulled out five hundred dollars, in hundreds, then dug into his backpack and pulled out a thick roll of more hundreds, handing them to her he said, *"Do what you gotta do, and get your life back,"* it made me feel sick."

Kane swallowed and ran his hand through his hair again before looking at me. "I jumped up and reached over to grab the money from the table—I wanted to make her see sense, but Cody stood up and blocked my way, he held me back when she ran out the door.

By the time I reached the sidewalk the car she was in had pulled away from the curb and I never saw her again. I was too late, but it dawned on me why she had stuck out. It was because she reminded me of you."

"Thanks—a pregnant hook up reminded you of me?"

"No, I only remembered her because of you. There's a difference."

"I'm only bringing her up because she's been on my mind since I found out about my mom's baby and Ellie. When Dennis told me about Ellie, my mind went back to what she had said. Then I thought if she had told me the truth then, Ellie must be my baby. I used the same strip of condoms I'd used with you. I'm not proud, but I can't lie either, the condoms must have been faulty. I'm telling you this not to hurt you but for a much bigger reason." He pulled the envelope out of his pocket. "99.99 percent likelihood...no room for doubt. If we do this, Jo, I won't have more kids. This is the only reason I'm telling you about her. Ellie's condition is on me and I'm never putting another child through what Ellie went through. Or you for that matter."

"Kane. This isn't even up for discussion. We have Ellie. I don't ever want to go through that again." It hurt to hear his story that someone else may have been carrying his child, but I understood why he told me.

Kane exhaled heavily. "I'll take care of it...if you're serious...what if..."

"We lost Ellie? God forbid that would ever happen, but I wouldn't want her replaced." Standing up, he made his way across to me and hugged me as tightly as he could and as much as I would allow.

"Can I stay the night?"

"No, you have my parents to take care of. Go and break the news to them and come back in the morning. I want some time to get used to doing this on my own. I want to be able to do that from the beginning."

Kane nodded, reluctant to leave but he kissed me gently then hovered over Ellie's cot. "She's pretty incredible." A smile crept over his lips. "Like her mom."

Turning to me he stroked my nose like he did when we were kids. "I'll be here bright and early—7:00 am, okay?" I nodded and smiled while I watched him leave.

As soon as he left the room I missed him. When I looked at Ellie she seemed to smile. Okay it was probably wind, but I felt hope for our future for the first time since I knew I was pregnant.

Chapter Thirty

CRYING

When my parents got over the shock of Kane being Ellie's father, my dad made the comment he made all those years ago after Kane's dad's funeral—Kane and I would find our way back.

"Life is strange, sometimes there are things in our future that were always there, it's only when we look back that we realize a plan was already forming and our destiny had already been written," he mused.

I stared in disbelief at my dad, that something so profound had come out of his mouth. It was the first time I had ever heard him say anything that wasn't backed up by hard evidence.

The man I knew normally regarded everything in life as purely anecdotal otherwise. It was like he'd swallowed a bottle of hippy pills or something.

"What I mean is you and Kane...from the time you were little you had this affinity for each other." I liked that description of us—affinity. He was right, we had.

Our home wasn't big but Mom and Dad welcomed Kane to stay while we figured things out, and Jacob moved over to Matt's. Or so he said; Kane and I knew he was more than likely staying with his girl,

Ann-Marie, he just wouldn't admit there was more going on there, though we knew there was.

It felt weird that Kane was sleeping in the next room to me, it wasn't as if no one knew we'd ever slept together, we shared a child. But we were both physically recovering from wounds, and psychologically I wasn't in the best place for anything romantic. I was in love with Kane, but I was also trying not to be afraid to love him if that makes sense.

As we all tried to learn to live with our new situation, Jacob made a comment one day to Kane about how fucked up our situation was, but Matt interjected on our behalves.

"Nah, it's fuckin' rock stars, Jacob. They never do anything like the rest of us." It was Jacob's blunt insight and Matt's matter of fact response that gave me the acceptance I needed to move on.

Moving forward meant facing worries and being in touch with fears and doubts.

Kane hadn't put a foot wrong since we'd been home and appeared to take Ellie and our whole situation completely in his stride. I had marveled at his strength until one night, when I was taking fresh towels to his room and entered his bathroom, I heard a noise.

At first I thought he was humming and smiled, but when I saw he was in the shower with his hands over his eyes facing into the spray as it beat down on him, I realized he was crying.

My heart felt crushed under the weight of his grief and I understood how difficult life was for him with the changes he'd made to be with us.

When he removed his hands and turned he saw me standing there. I was glad that he didn't try to hide is feelings when he said, "I'm happy here, Jo...with you and Ellie. I'm just adjusting to having a baby I love more than life itself who's so tiny and been through so much, you know?"

Placing the towels down I opened the door, fully clothed, and stepped inside the cubicle with him. Both of us stood holding each other and I cried along with him until the water ran cold.

For the first five weeks of Ellie's life, Kane was still recovering from his ordeal, attending physiotherapy, and focusing on his voice and breathing exercises. It was remarkable how quickly he regained his strength.

Kane's physio said it was his positive mental attitude and determination that helped that along. While Kane concentrated his efforts on getting better, I settled into a routine with our daughter.

By Christmas all three of us were physically healed, and emotionally more settled. My optimism was at an all-time high.

From the second week we were home Kane's cell rang regularly with enquiries about his health from his bandmates, PA, record label, and promotions companies. I was glad they showed concern.

All the while he continued to brush them off I was happy, but I knew it wouldn't last. I was nervous about that and as scared as hell that he'd put himself out there again after what had happened. But I was learning to accept that it was Kane's choice to do what he wanted with his life.

As long as he gave us respect and his decisions didn't overshadow mine and Ellie's lives.

Meanwhile, fatherhood suited him down to the ground, he was the doting father.

Some nights I'd awoken to the sound of soft singing coming through the nursery monitor in my room.

When I had gone to investigate, I'd found him nursing a diaper-clad Ellie close to his bare chest, while he sang her some lyrics that I had suspected mimicked what he was feeling at the time.

When New Year's Eve arrived, my parents left for a cruise they had booked the year before for my grandma's birthday.

It marked a watershed, leaving Kane and I alone with Ellie for the week.

Nerves kicked in the moment their car left the driveway because it was the first time we had been on our own since I had seduced him in my apartment.

The most private time we'd had up until then had been a few hours at a time. I had expected him to get fed up with our domestic arrangement.

I had expected him to push me for more because it couldn't have been easy for him to change and live my mundane lifestyle after his previous year's success. He didn't and he had never complained. Instead we used the precious little time we did have alone, talking, getting closer, and sometimes we made out.

Ellie was a great baby, she slept from 6:00 pm until around 03:30 or 04:00 am, waking once to feed in the night then sleeping again until 07:00 am.

One night, when Ellie had gone to bed, Kane had started on dinner while I had a soak in the tub.

It was ridiculous, but I felt so shy. With everything we'd been through I still felt shy.

Softly, Kane knocked on the bathroom door but didn't wait to enter. I curled up in the tub when I saw his head peer around the door and he smirked mischievously.

"Babe, you don't have to do that. I've seen it all before remember? Actually...I remember, hmm," he teased, wagging his eyebrows. He even managed to hum flirtatiously.

"I was coming to tell you dinner was all set, but seeing you in there like that, all wet and naked, it jogged my memory that I've never seen you in the tub before. Can I get in there with you?"

"What? No," I giggled. "I'm just getting out, if you would just—"

"Shh, Jo, you're flustered and babbling. It's cute, but I've been so fucking patient these past few weeks...I don't want to have sex with you, that's your move. I just want to hold you and feel that intimacy. I've been craving it since the day I held your hand in that hospital room. I've had plenty of skin to skin with one of my girls and not enough with the other. It's been killing me."

Without waiting for me to answer, Kane loosened the buckle on his belt and undid his pants. He grabbed the sleeve of his T-shirt and pulled the whole thing over his head. I'd never seen anyone take a T-shirt off like that before or so quickly.

My eyes fell to his already hard cock then traveled up his legs and over his abs, continuing up to his face. He was a stunning man, even after weeks of recovering from the attack, he was still as taut as ever. I empathized with the craving of an addict chasing the next fix. He was so alluring, his smile was seduction without effort, his body a shiny coin waiting to be held.

His hand slid to his cock and he stroked it a couple of times then smirked at me. "What can I say? He definitely likes you, Jo." He continued to stroke himself as he made his way to the side of the bath.

Kneeling beside me he took my chin between his thumb and his index finger, pulled my face closer and kissed me.

There was nothing gentle in the kiss. It was full on passion, hunger and need. His tongue lashed against mine as his other hand swept around the back of my head and pushed me closer. Kane broke the kiss and stood.

Initially I thought he was going to get in, but he bent down and lifted me clean out of the water and carried me back to his room.

My hands flew to my belly, to the ugly red scar that was there. Gripping my wrists he held them away from my body as he examined the healed wound from the birth.

"Don't ever be embarrassed about this. I never want you to feel ashamed of the way Ellie was born. When I see this, it reminds me of the length you went to that ensured her safe passage into this world. It's something you should wear with pride. It fills my heart...reminds me how proud I am of you and it's a badge of honor. Not many girls would have taken the choice you did, and if they did, I doubt they'd have tried to protect those they loved for the time you did, Jo."

Pressing his closed lips to my belly, he peppered kisses along the scar, taking his time to cover every inch of my skin.

Moments later his lips slid to my thighs, first the left then the right. "Trust me. I won't hurt you, I promise," he whispered. "I just need to taste you, Jo." His mouth and hands slid over my wet skin until they met at my knees, trailed up my thighs and spread my legs apart.

A finger traced my pussy, and that tiny touch after so many months, was like the spark of a lit fuse within me.

My whole body came to life as an electrical charge coursed through me and pulled at my core. "Oh," I moaned, my legs slightly vibrating with tension and anticipation of his mouth connecting with the soft lips between my legs.

Kane inhaled deeply. "Fuck, I love you." The passion in his voice took his pitch an octave lower, raising his level of seduction. The effect was incredibly enticing.

When he lowered his mouth his tongue swept delicately over my clit and my butt jerked up to meet his mouth. His tease made me desperate and he snickered.

Glancing up, his eyes connected with mine as a smile played on them. "Damn, I should have asked, is it okay if we fool around?" he questioned with a smirk as he dipped his head and swept his tongue the length of my entrance.

Feelings I had almost forgotten fizzed erotically through my body, while shivers and goosebumps of delight ran rampant over my skin and through every vein of my being.

The way his hands explored as his mouth devoured was a combination handled with a level of expertise and care I had only known from him.

It had been a long time since I'd felt them, it was like a second awakening of lust and desire I had never expected to feel again.

The sensation built so quickly inside me until suddenly a burst of white light behind my eyes was followed instantly by an explosive orgasm so heady I thought I might pass out.

My whole body quivered uncontrollably as Kane held my legs tighter and continued his delicious assault on my sweet spot.

When he eventually stopped, he slid up on the bed beside me and held me so protectively that a wave of emotion gripped me by the throat and I cried.

"It's okay, Jo. You're just a bit overwhelmed, babe. I've got you," he murmured quietly into my ear. Kissing me tenderly on my neck and shoulders he pulled the comforter up over us and lay quietly while I wept silently.

I must have fallen asleep and when I woke, Kane was kneeling by the bed in his T-shirt brushing my hair gently away from my eyes. "Come downstairs, babe, it's almost 9:00 pm, dinner is ready."

I wrapped myself in a bath robe and headed downstairs. I felt bad that he had given me pleasure and I had been so selfish.

A wide smile greeted me as I entered the sitting room and my heart leapt in my chest. The room was in semi-darkness with the glow of the fire and a small tiny lamp the only lighting.

My parents had a log fire which burned all winter long, and Kane had refueled it. It glowed brightly.

Kane sat, Indian style, on the floor and beckoned me to sit down beside him. Burritos weren't what I'd normally eat on New Year's Eve, but they were perfect because I was sharing them with Kane.

"So this year kinda sucked and was wonderful at the same time, huh?" His eyes twinkled with warmth and I could see the flames from the fire mirrored in them.

"Sucked? I think that is putting it mildly." Kane gave me a look of concern.

"Most of your shit is down to me, huh? I'm really sorry for every-thing that happened. Ellie aside, I could never be without her now." Fearing Kane was with me out of some sense of duty, I had to pose that question.

"Is that why you're here? Because you feel responsible?"

He huffed a huge sigh, "You mean are you a pity fuck? You know me better than that. I'd never stay with someone out of a sense of responsibility. It has to be love. Life is fucking short."

"You keep saying that. What if you decide you prefer something else, would you change your mind because 'life is short?' " I cringed because I had used inverted commas to emphasize his words.

"Do you doubt I love you? I'm here because I love you. I'm not here out of responsibility, I swear. Look…I was going to do this tomor-row, but I can't wait since you feel in doubt…wait here." He left the room and ran upstairs then came back carrying a brown business-type envelope.

"Open it." I looked inside and recognized hospital headed notepaper. It was an appointment for a vasectomy the following week. "I'm really serious about this, Jo. I will never put you or any other baby through what you went through, but what I want to know is, are you with me on this?"

"Of course I am. It's a huge step but if you don't want to risk—"

"We don't want to risk…I want to know, Jo. Will you marry me?"

"Because of Ellie?"

"Fuck no. What does it take to make you understand, Jo? Because of us and Ellie. I love you, and I love Ellie. I could never imagine being with another woman now I'm with you. Do you know how hard that is? I've not been laid for almost two months and I don't fucking care. Well I do, my balls are blue, and my cock and my hand have their own courtship going on. What I'm saying is *you* are what's important. *Ellie* is what's important. My own needs come after. Only after you guys are happy can I ever allow myself that pleasure. See?"

"So this is how you propose to a girl? No shooting stars and chocolate? A vasectomy appointment?" I snickered.

"Sorry, babe, stabbed rock stars and burritos, we never do anything lame and cheesy like that." Kane grinned widely and I was so in love with him, I didn't really care how he proposed, I just couldn't resist a final taunt.

"So no cheese, huh? From where I'm sitting that makes you a liar, Kane, because there's a mountain of cheese on these burritos."

Kane swung me around on the floor and climbed over me like he used to do when we were kids. "So, do you surrender? Am I enough of a Prince to take you on horseback to Nirvana?" he asked with his sexy smile that made me think he could take me any way and anywhere he wanted.

"Would answering this marriage proposal be seen as an agreement given under duress?"

"Well I could always fuck you into submission if you prefer," he countered playfully, although the way he said it was gruff and I could hear the frustration in his voice.

"I do. I mean I will...the...I do will come later, right?"

"I think you were thinking about me fucking you when you answered. You want me to do you? What is it they say? The first answer is usually the most honest thought?" Kane's eyes darkened with desire. I was scared because it was my first time after giving birth, but I had to show him how much I wanted him.

"Let me up," I said, pretending to be annoyed. Kane immediately released my wrists and moved over to the side of me. Sitting up I turned on him and pushed him down on his back.

"Fuck, Jo. That was hot. Are you gonna do me now?" he taunted playfully.

"I am." I smiled seductively, opened my bath robe and sat astride him. His cock was ridged beneath his jeans and I began to dry hump him. He grabbed my wrists and quickly changed my position to place me on my back. His hand reached for his buckle and he stopped.

"I can't. I'm not risking it, I can wait until I know you're safe," he replied with a stern look.

"I am safe, Kane. I had an implant inserted after Ellie was born. Just like you, I never want to face that again. The risks are too great at one in forty, and I'm just thankful that Ellie survived. Seconds after my disclosure, Kane unbuckled his belt and stood to pull his jeans off.

Kneeling beside me he grinned, his sexiest boyish grin, and bent over to kiss me. There wasn't a hint of gentleness in it.

Raw passion and lust had turned him almost animalistic in his possession of my body. I moaned loudly into his mouth as his hands worked their magic all over every trigger point I owned.

"You have no idea how long I've wanted this moment again with you," he admitted, his voice deepening with his desire as he pulled my legs up onto his thighs and ran the wet tip of his cock over my clit and down to my entrance. "This is a first for me," he disclosed as he nudged the tip inside.

I watched his reaction and he watched mine as his cock slid deeper inside of me. His eyes were cloudy with lust, but widened again before half closing when he felt me hold him tight, just like I felt him stretching me.

"You are an amazing woman, Jo Carmichael, do you know that?"

"I do, but you so deserve me." I smiled slowly, and he chuckled.

"If I hurt you, you gotta say, okay?"

Kane rocked forward, slid back then did it again before he picked up his pace and got a little faster. I knew he was holding back because I could feel the tension in his shoulders and arms as he tried to take me as gently as he could.

The strain on his face made me want to take charge so I rolled him over and sat above him again. He was deep to the hilt and I rolled my hips frantically, taking him much faster than he'd been taking me.

"Shit, I'm gonna come," he groaned, his eyes widening as he stared up at me while his hands ran up and down my sides.

Suddenly his body went stiff and I felt his warm come spurt inside, his cock pulsing rhythmically as his face displayed his contorted pleasure. His eyes closed as his hands gripped my hips as a sign to stop, and when I did, his face instantly relaxed. He opened his eyes and reached up grabbing my hair and winding it around his hand.

Tugging it, he pulled me forward and down onto his chest and kissed me hard. "Damn, Jo. I love you."

Chapter Thirty-One

FOR THE RECORD

*I*t was a new year, and a new start. I was nervous about where we went from that point on, but we used our days to bond with our baby and our nights to make love.

I wanted Kane in my bed because I was done denying what he meant to me and how alive he made me feel.

"Ellie...her name? Did you really believe he was the father?" I glanced at the sad look he gave me and my heart fell to the floor.

"I led everyone to believe he was, Kane. Personally, I wasn't sure, but we've been through all of that. You both had used protection and I hadn't been with any other guys. Ellie's not named after him." I sat up quickly and looked down shocked at my realization.

"Oh God, Kane...no, I'm sorry, it didn't occur to me that you'd think that way. Helen was my mother's mom, my grandma. Ellie was the name she went by, but you wouldn't know that because she died when I was only four. No one mentioned her when we were kids. She'd been ill for a long time before I was born, and when she died, my mother's way of coping was not to talk about her."

I couldn't have been more stupid if I tried, I'd never have called my baby after a guy that treated me the way Elliott had.

"Well, fuck! I like her name a lot better now," he said, giving me his heart-stopping smile. Reaching over he pulled my head forward and kissed me.

Kane's kisses were an art form. He put as much effort into them as he did into his music. His tongue and mouth were everything from soft and gentle, playful to seductive and from hungry to passionately devouring. I never knew what I was going to get until the moment we were kissing, and I couldn't get enough of him.

"Your parents come back tomorrow," he said, sounding deflated.

"Yeah." I felt sad that our time alone was coming to an end, and as if on cue, Ellie began to cry. Kane pulled a funny face and butt shuffled his way down the bed. The mattress dipped, bouncing me when he headed to the nursery.

"Aw is my little princess missing her daddy?" he cooed. Moments later he returned with our wide eyed bundle of joy who smiled widely as her daddy cooed dotingly at her.

Placing her in-between us, he held one hand and I held the other as she lay awake, contented to have come between us.

"Listen kid, you'll go back if you start being a cock blocker, there are plenty of hours in the day for you to play with us, but come night time...that's when the sky is dark and the moon is shining...you are supposed to sleep like a log, got it, baby?"

I giggled at his serious but calm tone. "Stop saying things like that, Kane, she'll become insecure."

Ellie cooed and we both looked down at her in time to see a huge gummy grin that stretched right across her face. "I think she's laughing in your face, Kane. I've seen how she's got you wrapped around her finger already."

Kane's smile grew wider as he sighed deeply. "To think I had no idea about any of this three months ago," he said as he slid his pinkie finger under her hand and stroked the back of it. "I really love her...like I'd die for her right now so that she could live a healthy life, Jo. Thank you for putting my name on the birth certificate, Carmichael-Exeter has a ring to it, dontcha think?"

"Why didn't you challenge me about being her dad when you first saw that I was pregnant? You just accepted what I told you."

"I asked you, and you'd always been honest with me, Jo. But I wasn't sure you were honest that day. However, I felt your fragility as well. That vulnerable side of you that always stopped me from pushing you further, even as kids. I guess I never forgot when to push and when to leave well alone. For the record...I was coming back for you."

Leaning over our baby he placed a small kiss on my forehead and wrapped his hand around my hair.

"I know none of this is conventional, Jo. Our lives have been ruled by others, who knows what would have happened if we'd been able to see each other growing up? My thoughts on that are that I'm thankful we didn't. We might have been high school sweethearts, but then again maybe immaturity and lust would have gotten in the way of us being who we are now, what we feel now...what I feel for you and Ellie. Things are going to be different for us from now on, and I promise you're not going to lose sleep on my account. I've been thinking a lot about our future. Lying in bed at night with a hard-on has its advantages; all that lost sleep makes for productive thoughts. I took the liberty of contacting some realtors over the past few days and they've sent some property links for us to look at. If you feel ready to make that commitment to me, we'll go and see some places together. If not, it's time I had a firm base to come home to." He glanced down at Ellie who had fallen asleep again. "Are you happy to be with me? You said before you weren't happy about my lifestyle—"

I placed my fingers to his lips. I wasn't sure I was ready to live with him just like that. We hadn't even dated properly.

"Being with you, us here...with Ellie, my heart is so full...at peace. A few months ago, I thought it was broken beyond repair. I know what I said before about the life you lead. I meant it at the time, Kane. I knew no better then, but since then I've grown in so many ways and faced so many challenges. I know I'm strong enough for most things life wants to throw at me now. We've both known the heartache of the things we can't change, the people we can't have those last words with again, the wasted feelings of anger and regret, and I'm done living my life in the quiet."

"Why do I sense there's a 'but' coming?"

I smiled because we used to know what the other felt as kids, and it showed me he still had that ability.

"This is all too soon. It isn't that I don't want to be with you, it's just that I'm cautious of being hurt, or that we've arrived here at this point because of Ellie and what's happened. It all feels so fast. Too fast. I used to think making ends meet and the occasional party night with Candice was living, but you changed that. You crashed back into my life and obliterated any chance that I could settle for that normal existence again. To have those few days with you was magical. My heart has lived a hundred lives in terms of the emotions I've survived since then. The incredible high of being with you and the desperate lows that followed, with Elliott, the worry about Ellie, and that horrible motherfucker that almost took you away from me, made me realize just how fragile life's journey can be."

"Don't you see that's exactly why I don't want to waste time? I know what I want. And that's you and Ellie, us."

"You have no idea how that feels, Kane, but it's going to take me some time to heal and regain my strength from what I've been through, and I'm not going to lie, what you do for a living worries me. It's like painting a huge target on your T-shirt and saying come and get me. I never want to go through the pain of seeing you that way again."

"You and me both, babe," he muttered seriously. "I promise I'll be more careful in the future. I never wanted a guardian or security detail, preferring to live like any other man, and until what happened with that guy I'd achieved that. My freedom is important, but now that I have my girls, I want to make sure I stick around to see what it's like to sleep with a sixty-year-old, and chase lanky homeboys with my shotgun when they come calling for my little angel here."

I glanced up at his face and his lips stretched into his easy, sexy smile that made my bones melt again.

Kane fell quiet and I wondered what was going on in his mind, I could see him thinking as his eyes ticked over my face. "What? What is it?"

He sighed heavily, and I knew by the serious look and the way he chewed his lip that I wouldn't like what was coming. "I had something to tell you, but with what you just said, I'm a little reluctant to share it with you."

I shifted my position and stared at his serious expression.

"You have to tell me now," I pleaded.

"I was going to wait until your parents were back, but I'll have to cut out tomorrow to meet the band, so I'm afraid I'm going to spoil our last night alone...ish," he said, smirking down at our little miracle lying between us. "We've got a gig that I really want to do, it's the big Veteran's charity gig at Sheep's Meadow, Central Park, on Memorial Day, which is a huge deal for me."

Kane ran his hand through his hair then picked up my hand and placed it in his. I felt tense and resisted the urge to shout at him. "Rehearsals start in a couple of weeks and my physiotherapist is building my strength to help me get fit for the set, it's only four numbers so fifteen minutes tops, time-wise."

I stared at him in silence because I was dumbstruck—numb that he'd put himself out there so quickly again, and deep down I wasn't ready for that.

Saying I would try to accept his lifestyle while in the safety of my bedroom, and living the reality of it, was an entirely different feeling altogether.

My heart squeezed and felt heavy as it filled with every emotion I felt but couldn't express in words.

My throat burned with tears that I was determined wouldn't fall at his news. Part of me was afraid for him, worried about his safety, while the rest of me was in awe at his bravery.

I focused on the part where he was willing to do what he believed in despite the risks. More than that, he wanted to do it, and that gave me a greater understanding of what his music meant to him.

"I'm gonna be fine, Jo. How many times does a guy get attacked with a blade in one lifetime? Unless he's a soldier, a samurai warrior, or a musketeer." Watching me carefully, he smiled a half-smile that showed me he wasn't sure how I was taking his news.

"Okay," I mumbled softly. If that's what you want..."

"It's what I need, Jo. It's what we need. We can't let some crazy fucker win the rights over how we live our lives. If we all did that then no one would do anything. What happened to me was a freak incident, and to show all those crazies out there that they are never gonna win pulling shit like that, I am getting right back out there and grabbing life by the balls."

Swallowing back my emotions didn't last long, my throat was on fire and was shutting down as tears filled my eyes until they overflowed.

For months, I had been an expert at sucking my emotions up and living a lie, but I was crap at hiding my feelings from Kane. "Just a sec," he said, and crept off the bed, lifting Ellie and holding her like she was made of China. I watched him padding out of the room, naked, with our baby in his arms and heard him settle her into her crib. "Shh, there's my precious angel. Daddy's gotta have Mommy time, so you gotta stay in here until we catch some sleep. Trust me; I've seen Mommy when she's cranky. It's ugly." I smiled through my tears and heard him kiss her before he reappeared at the door.

Settling quickly back into bed, he tucked his arm around me and pulled me down onto his chest.

"Trust me, Jo, I need to do this, babe. Proving this to myself gives me my life back." Bending forward, he kissed my head and wiped the tears from my eyes with his free hand then dried it on the comforter.

Once again he wound my hair around his hand and repositioned himself before he looked me straight in the eyes.

"Babe, life is for living, I know you've been through a fucking awful time...with all that you've witnessed. But we have to make our own way in life, not be governed by what someone else confines us to. Who knows what medical bills we'll come up against for Ellie in the future? I want us to be prepared for all that, God forbid it ever happens."

As he bent his head to kiss me I placed my fingers across his lips. "Yeah, I understand and I'm so proud that you want to do that, Kane, but I don't want a hero either, remember?"

Kane stared darkly at me and nodded. "And I'll do everything in my power to make sure that's not in your future."

Pulling me tightly against him, Kane held me tight, stroking my back lightly with his fingers and I found his gesture comforting as we lay in silence. I understood his motivation; a concert that benefitted ex-servicemen was close to Kane's heart. I fell asleep wrapped in his arms thinking of our future.

The first of the year had been a turning point for sure, and my optimism remained high. Something I would have found close to impossible less than six weeks earlier.

Kane continued to share our home, sneaking into my bed at night and returning to his first thing in the morning, after my parents returned from their vacation.

He was true to his word about preventing another situation like the one we had faced, and went ahead and had his vasectomy.

The first two doctors he spoke to were reluctant to do the procedure for someone so young, but he found a third that was sympathetic, and with the medical history of Ellie and his sister, he was offered some counseling before they gave him his right to go ahead.

Six weeks after Ellie's birth, and barely a week and a half into the new year, Kane had his vasectomy.

I couldn't help but laugh when he grumbled that they lied to him when they said he could go back to work the next day. *Elephant's balls* were how he described his swollen testicles to anyone who would listen about his harrowing ordeal at the hands of the surgeon.

I snickered when my mom suggested he date my grandma because they would have a field day talking about their aching body parts.

Although we all laughed, the significance of the choice we'd made wasn't lost on any of us.

It wasn't a difficult decision to make when we knew the potential consequences of bringing another life into the world. And although Ellie seemed to be progressing well, there were no guarantees for the future with her health.

Kane milked the sympathy of his minor surgery and it was a week before Valentine's Day, before he regained his natural swagger in the way he walked.

From my perspective life was moving forward and Ellie was growing fatter by the day which was a great sign that she was thriving. With every medical check-up, we held our breaths and celebrated every positive milestone she met.

Kane doted on the both of us, ensuring we had everything we

needed, transporting us to Ellie's appointments and working the band rehearsals around us.

Despite Ellie being a winter baby, she remained healthy during the winter months, and it was a harsh winter.

Thick snow covered the ground on Valentine's Day and I sat nursing Ellie over my shoulder, staring at the beautiful pure white wintery scene outside the window. It was picture postcard pretty, and sitting by the fire with my baby snuggled up to me, felt awesome.

Chapter Thirty-Two

DUMBSTRUCK

Kane slept late on Valentine's day, he'd been up with Ellie during the night so I'd left him in bed to rest.

Although we hadn't discussed what we were doing after rehearsals I had figured he'd take me somewhere romantic for dinner.

"Not sure what time I'll be back, Jo. The guys want to grab a couple of beers after rehearsals. I'll try not to be late." Kane kissed the top of my head then Ellie's and gave me his heart-stopping smile.

I willed my mouth to mirror his, but inside my world seemed to cave, devastated that he was skipping out on that day.

My heart ached at what he said, and I don't know what I was expecting from him on Valentine's Day, but it probably wasn't that.

The most romantic day of the year and I figured he most likely had no clue. Not once did he mention doing anything for it during the previous couple of weeks.

From my perspective his life was getting back on track while mine had just changed from mundane to the one he was on and a whole different destination.

Softly the front door closed and I heard him crunch his way over the snow to his car. I held my breath when I heard the dull thud as he pulled his car door shut.

I exhaled shakily as I heard the machine fire up. Fresh tears ran down my face with the sound of his car engine dying off in the distance.

Disappointment was something I'd become accustomed to while I had been pregnant but with Kane, it was clear, he was being true to his word and was going to live his life his way.

I felt his thoughtlessness was an inkling of what I could expect in my future and felt demoralized because it confirmed my worst fears about his lifestyle.

I had neglected my feelings on that, thinking it wouldn't matter and a new reality dawned on me and my heart fell to the floor because I couldn't imagine myself fitting in. *It seems like I'm never going to learn my lesson.*

Concentrating on my baby, I tried hard to suppress my discontented thoughts about Kane's attitude. It was the first time he'd let me down, and despite Ellie and my situation, there was no way I was standing for a sloppy relationship with a guy purely because he thought it his right of passage as a rock star.

Kane could go fuck up some other poor female's life, because Ellie had fought hard to have a good life, not one where her mom can't take care of her and advocate for her because she's an emotionally weak woman in a fragile relationship. *Okay you are getting a bit ahead of yourself. It's beers with his band, and he's been with me constantly since we came home except for appointments for himself. Stop it, Josie, he deserves to relax and have a little downtime with the boys. But it's Valentine's Day. It would appear nine weeks is my shelf-life.*

It had taken nothing to shatter my fragile confidence with him.

All day long my mind beat me up, soothed my soul and beat me up again, and by the time my mom came through the door I was behaving so highly strung she was losing her temper with me.

"Josie, I don't know what's gotten into you today. You are so snippy. Go take a bath and maybe change your clothes. It'll make you feel better." *Is she saying I'm a mess? Is that why Kane is in no hurry to come home?* I almost screamed *what's the fucking point? Kane's out there having a good time and I'm the one that's left holding the baby,* but I knew that would sound clichéd and dramatic.

I was glad that my mom wasn't mollycoddling me because anger was better than feeling sorry for myself.

I took her advice and soaked in the tub, but nothing was defusing my irritation at how thoughtless Kane was being.

After fifteen minutes my mom knocked on the door and once I'd hidden most of my body she came into the bathroom carrying my naked baby.

"I think Ellie should have a bath with her mommy," she suggested. After feeling my tepid water, she lowered Ellie into my arms. I lay back to let her lie on my chest. Her eyes were wide open, trusting and innocent. Just looking at her I could feel the rage in my body subside.

Gently I cupped the water in my hand and ran it over her back and shoulders.

Ellie cooed and nuzzled against me and within seconds nothing else mattered. I only kept her there a few minutes then carefully laid a warm towel from the rail onto the bathroom floor and stepped out of the bath to lay her on it.

Grabbing a bathrobe from behind the door, I tied it carefully around myself and wrapped Ellie in the towel before taking her to change for bed.

Once Ellie was in bed I was gritting my teeth again, feeling beyond annoyed that at 6:30 pm I had a long night ahead of me waiting for him to show up. *What if he doesn't come home? Does he even see this as home?* He talked about buying somewhere close by but never mentioned it again. *Perhaps he changed his mind.*

When my mom finally coaxed me into telling her what the problem was, she didn't become loyal and sympathize, instead she spoke in the stern manner I'd been used to as a child and asked me if I was giving up on Kane.

When I didn't reply, she nodded at my bathrobe and asked, "Is that what you want him to see when he does come back?" I turned and looked in the mirror. I saw what she saw, a girl who had already given up without a fight.

Around 7:00 pm I was applying some lipstick when I heard car tires crunch over the snow in the driveway and was furious when I looked out and saw he'd driven home.

Drinking and driving was illegal and his complete disregard for life set my mood right back where it had been all afternoon.

I didn't trust myself to face Kane at that moment and I went to check on Ellie. A few minutes later I felt stronger and taking a deep breath I left her nursery.

Kane surprised me when he stood on the stairs with a huge bunch of red roses, wrapped in clear cellophane and tied with a huge crimson bow.

My initial thought was that he'd been told what day it was and the flowers were compensation for his screw-up, but then I noticed the expensive black jacket, crisp button-down shirt and dress pants he was wearing.

"Where have you been?"

"I've been gone all day and all you can say is *where have you been?* No I missed you darling, or what beautiful flowers, babe, or wow, you look hot in those threads, honey?"

Once he'd started speaking I knew he hadn't been drinking and I didn't understand what was going on. "You look beautiful, by the way," he commented with a panty-melting smile. I shook my head and felt all the animosity I'd been carrying around slide straight out of my pores.

"You remembered?"

"Remembered?" He looked down at how he was dressed then to the flowers and finally at me. "Valentine's Day, you mean? Like I could forget? Men have been hung for less, babe." He smirked at me sexily.

"So where have you been? You didn't have beers with the boys dressed like that," I questioned.

"Get your boots on, let me show you," he coaxed, walking over to me and kissing me lightly on the lips. "Don't worry Ellie's not going anywhere, she's down for at least seven hours, right? And your mom is going to take care of her if she wakes in the meanwhile."

Less than ten minutes later, Kane had driven down a side track and pulled over beside a house that was warm and inviting.

272

Red brick with pillars over an entrance walkway led up to a ruby-red painted door with silver hardware. "Who lives here?" I asked, even more confused because I had thought with the way he was dressed we were going to a fancy restaurant for dinner.

"I do. Welcome to my new home." The shock of what he said made my heart shatter. "I wanted to share it with you. Come on," he said, pulling the handle on the door and running around to my side.

All I could think as he led me inside was that he was leaving me. Since he had a place of his own he was moving out.

Swallowing nervously, I stepped inside and was surprised at his taste in décor. Three large, comfortable, brown velvet sofas; a roaring real flame fire, and a smattering of rustic oak wooden furniture.

There were carpets that were a few tones lighter than cream in one half of the room and the part leading to the kitchen was in oak wood as well.

"It's great. I'm sure you'll be really happy here," I enthused, but felt like I was having an out-of-body experience that I was even there at all. I had no idea that he'd found somewhere, let alone bought it.

"I intend to be." He smiled at me while pulling my coat off my shoulders. "Let me show you around," he said, pulling me by the hand. "Kitchen," he said, passing it and entering a long passageway.

"Guest bedroom." He motioned toward a room, throwing open a door as we went past. "Family bathroom." Again gesturing toward a room, throwing open the door.

I barely got a glimpse of the massive square Jacuzzi with mosaic tiling and tiny lights embedded around it before he pulled me further.

"Guest bedroom two. This one has a bathroom but when you've seen one you've seen them all, right?" He grinned and I wished I could have felt happy for him. I was happy for him, but sad for myself.

"This is a mini gym. There is a cross-training machine, a rowing machine, a treadmill, and a couple of bench press areas. I had an awesome sound system installed in here, and there's a projector that's aimed at that wall over there."

I was about to say something when he pushed open the double doors at the other end of the room and the opulence of the adjoining room took my breath away. It looked like a fantasy with a massive four-poster bed that looked like it had come directly from King Henry VIII's castle in England.

The thick, white silk bedding must have cost him a fortune and the chaise longue that stretched the width of the bed looked stunning.

It was totally me once, but the thing that made my jaw drop was that it took me straight back to a heartbreaking moment I'd shared with him when we were kids.

Kane eyed me suspiciously then grinned mischievously. Leaning over toward me, he crooked his index finger under my chin and closed my mouth. "I think you know this room," he murmured softly.

My eyes scanned every detail and when I saw the fireplace with the tall silver candelabras either side I knew he'd remembered. "You did this? Really? You made this ridiculous room for me?"

"Ah, you remember, thank God." He smirked and pulled me into his chest for a tight hug.

I glanced up in awe. "How the hell do you remember this?" I stared incredulously at him, then around the room again, speechless. Everything was just perfect. Crazy but perfect.

"We'll come to that a little later. Come on, there are some rooms on the other side of the house, two play rooms, one with a bar, pool table, gaming machines and shit, and one that's a pamper room. Down the far end there's a little cinema room with half a dozen chairs in there. But in here..."

His words trailed off, as he paused to look into my eyes for a moment while he pulled me toward a door that he hadn't opened. Turning the handle, he pushed the door open wide and it was almost a replica of Ellie's nursery at home.

"I know it's still early. Don't think I missed that little wig out session I witnessed when I mentioned looking for a place. I figured that if I waited for you, it wouldn't happen anytime soon. You are one hell of a procrastinator, Jo. So, I took the initiative and went ahead hoping that if you came and saw it you'd know how serious I am about us."

"Thank you," I whispered. I was much more grateful than I sounded, and felt terrible when I thought how angry I was with him. All that time he was making a home for us.

"You don't have to move in with me. I just wanted you to know how *all in* I am with you and our daughter. I can wait, Jo. I'll wait for as long as you need, but I need this space. I need to work and I can't do it without feeling like I'm in the way at your parents' house."

A knock at the door interrupted him. He jumped to his feet and ran to the door. It reminded me of the day at my apartment. "Jesus, you're Kane Exeter," the delivery girl exclaimed.

Kane gave me a sly glance before turning back to her. "Nah, I wish. That guy isn't as good looking as me, but you're not the first to say that," he replied with a huge grin on his face. Taking the food from her, he handed her a ten dollar bill and closed the door.

"Dinner is served, princess." He smiled and placed the brown paper bags on the table.

I glanced at the branding on the bag. "Fast food, Kane?" I giggled.

"Not just any fast food, come here and sit down beside me." He dropped to the floor on the carpet and beckoned me to do the same, so I crouched down then sat, Indian style, to face him.

"Do you remember the day you drew the picture in your bedroom of your prince's castle, Jo? Your prince was tall and dark, and you told me he looked a lot like me." He laughed and slid alongside me, nudging my shoulder as he reached up and lifted the brown paper take-out bag between us.

Kane took a burger out from a box and bit a huge juicy mouthful. Turning to me, he grinned again, his mouth full of food he mumbled, "How am I doing?"

My heart was beating out of my chest because he was re-enacting the vivid memory from the last day we were together in Germany as kids, right down to the ketchup that splattered his face when he had taken a bite of the burger.

"I love you," I said as tears sprang to my eyes.

"Yeah you told me that at the time as well...I remember it like it was yesterday."

I reached up and placed my palm on his cheek, wiping the ketchup with my thumb. "You have no idea what this means to me, Kane."

"And you still have no idea what you mean to me, Jo. I don't know how else to show you how desperately I want this with you. Wait here."

Rising to his feet he made off down the hall and came back with a huge white envelope with a red heart on the front.

"Happy Valentine's Day, babe, I hope you like your gift."

My eyes never left his as I fumbled with the seal and opened the card.

I broke our stare and looked down as I pulled out a fabulously cheesy card with two cute kids, a boy with brown hair and a smaller blonde girl with her hair in a ponytail.

Tears blurred my vision because it was similar to the card he'd sent me for my twenty-first birthday.

Glancing up to meet his gaze I saw love and warmth in them as well as a naughty glint that made him as sexy as hell. He was chewing his lip and I felt his anticipation as I opened the card.

My heart almost stopped, as the shock at what he'd given me ran in all directions through me. My eyes darted to his and he was still biting his lip, but the trademark grin slowly replaced his worry.

"Thought you may have needed that for reference...in case your memory was a little blurry," he taunted.

Inside was the picture I had drawn the night before we left Germany. It was my dream bedroom from my prince I was going to marry when I grew up's castle. The positions of the furniture were exactly where I'd drawn them in his room.

"You gave it to me as a parting gift after we sat on the floor eating burgers. It's one of the few things I have left from my childhood, Jo. That and your letters."

"I don't know what to say..."

"Then do you mind if I do?"

I giggled, still awestruck, "Sure."

"You don't really want to sleep in a room like that, do you?" he asked, chuckling. "If you don't mind me saying it's fucking hideous, but I'd do it if it meant you were here with me."

"Are you being cheesy or romantic?" I teased.

"Both, it's Valentine's...I can be as cheesy as fuck and still be sexy in my prince's suit," he laughed as he gestured toward his attire.

I giggled raucously. "Damn, that's what the suit was about."

"Yep, the suit is right there," he said, tapping the wonky prince image I'd drawn in the picture. We both laughed as Kane sat back down and nudged me with his shoulder. "Well, Jo. Am I your prince? Does Jo go to the ball, wear the magic slipper and get fucked every which way by the handsome, drop-dead, sexy-as-fuck, can't keep your hands off him, want to suck his cock until it dissolves, prince?"

I roared with laughter and it felt amazing. For that night, at least, we were just two normal young people reminiscing about the good old days.

Kane became serious and explained he'd picked the house for its location, less than five minutes from the cardiac unit at the local hospital, ten minute car ride to my parents' place and ten minutes in the other direction to the airport.

It was clear Kane had given our future a lot of consideration and as soon as I'd seen the bedroom he'd gone to all the effort to replicate, I knew I had been a fool to say no to us moving in with him.

Chapter Thirty-Three

CONFIDENCE

*P*acking our things for the move felt exciting. Instead of my heart feeling heavy it felt excited and full of anticipation.

Every day since I'd met Kane again had been a journey, and even with my reservations about his lifestyle, I felt more equipped to deal with any issues that arose.

Ellie grew stronger by the day, and had survived her first cold. And at almost three months, her heart doctor was happy for her appointments to be moved from the two-weekly reviews to three monthly ones instead.

My daughter's doctor's confidence in her gave me confidence to move our lives forward. She was sleeping through the night by that time and life suddenly felt much easier.

Moving home had felt right, I'd be lying if I said I hadn't felt some degree of worry, but then I think the deep thinker in me had always been a bit of a worrier, and that hadn't helped.

Kane was awesome during the move, he'd arranged everything to be right where it needed to be and had changed the bedroom furniture to a style more in keeping with the house. He informed me that his prince's suit was available in his closet for me to rip off any time I found a yearning for it.

Those first few days after I moved in were idyllic as we planned and discussed small details together to make the house our home.

Three days after our move Kane began to focus on his band again, and true to his word he worked with the physio who drove him hard, too hard in my opinion for someone who'd been so ill.

At the same time rehearsals started up for his comeback gig and all the things I loved about Kane's personality seemed to shine. It was then that I realized the full impact of his ordeal and what he'd been missing during his time out in recovery.

At first I felt sick and apprehensive about him being attacked again, but when I saw how excited he was about performing in New York, I couldn't help but get caught up in his enthusiasm.

Watching how animated he became when he talked about it was enthralling. He came to life when he described his thoughts and feelings about getting up on that stage, and that helped me accept that he was born to do it.

Being good at a job you like and having a need to share a talent were two entirely different things, and for Kane he most definitely had a vocation.

Kane's band manager was amazing in that he arranged for all the band members to come to Maryland and practice in Baltimore so that Kane could stay at home until the actual event day. And with rehearsals and physio he had a full-on schedule.

I worried that he was taking on too much, too quickly, but he reassured me he was feeling fine.

Mom and Dad thought I was worrying needlessly and persuaded me to go with him to a couple of rehearsals, and although it was hard to leave Ellie with them, I took them up on their offer. The first time I left her I felt dreadful, but with regular calls and texts during the afternoon I began to relax.

My parents weren't unskilled, and usually it was me acting on advice from them when taking care of Ellie so I knew she couldn't be in safer hands.

Candice was a star too, always there with encouragement and often kept Ellie amused while I was getting ready to go.

Kane was delighted I went to hang out and listen to them practice.

All the band members were on their best behavior and there wasn't a groupie in sight.

Catherine, his PA, seemed genuinely warm. She was at ease and friendly around Kane and a pang of jealousy shook me that I tried to shrug off, but I couldn't help having Elliott's voice in my ear, *No one is just friends with Kane Exeter.*

On our journey home that day, I was quiet. Getting out of the car, Kane picked up on my mood. "Are you okay?"

I nodded, because to say that I was would have been speaking a lie.

"Alright, out with it. Something's bugging you. Is it Cody? Because I warned him about how he behaves around you."

Pressing me for an answer made me understand that if it was going to work between us then I had to speak my thoughts. If I held them close to my chest then he'd start to do the same, and that wasn't the kind or relationship I wanted going forward.

"Catherine."

The expression on Kane's face was pure confusion and I knew before I even asked him what the answer was, but I had gone that far so I had to continue. "She's very...easy around you...comfortable. Did you...I mean have you—"

"Did I fuck her? Is that what you're asking?" My heart jolted at his crude question, the beat of it raced as I held my breath while he looked at me with concern.

Walking around to my side of the car he slid his arm around me and pulled me close to his chest, kissing my head.

"If that's what you're asking, then the answer is no. Rule number one in this business, you never shit where you eat. And for the record, I stopped shitting the day I saw you at Thanksgiving. She's my PA, Jo. Nothing more. She's a great girl with a great boyfriend. Don is an ice hockey player, so he travels a lot for games, their relationship works well and they are just about as in love with each other as I am with you. So... no, Jo. Catherine is someone who 'does' for me but I don't do her."

The relief was instant. I never wanted to be someone who was the jealous type, but I wasn't kidding myself about how Kane looked, everyone that got close to him wanted to paw him in some way.

Guys patted his back, hugged him or gripped him by the shoulder. Women clung onto his arm, touched his hand, patted his chest, or put their hand on his leg when they spoke. It wasn't just talking, most of their conversations were laced with intent.

Kane took it all in his stride, guiding a wandering hand away while still answering their questions. No one could be near him without touching, my grandma included.

"I have no secrets from you, Jo. And yet, there is a distinct possibility that we'll run into someone that I've been with, but they were a fuck. Not a relationship. I'm sorry if that sounds blunt and I know it hurts you to hear that. I can't change my past, but I can control my dick, babe. My future is with you, not some chick that wants to fuck a rock star for kicks. No one knows me like you, Josie Carmichael, and I want it to stay that way."

"Sorry," I mumbled, feeling ashamed that I brought it up. But his words still stung just as much as if he had slapped me.

"What the fuck are you sorry for? It's natural that you'd feel awkward. I'm glad Elliott's dead, because he was the one guy I never wanted to meet, and I did. The thought that you'd let him inside you made me so fucking livid that my whole body shook with temper when I saw him sitting with you. I never want you to experience that, but I can't prevent it, Jo. Everything that happened before has been put to one side. You are 'the one' my one—*mine*."

Kane pressed his lips together firmly, his steely blue eyes becoming hard while his tone sounded frustrated and determined at the same time. It was really hot when he said *mine*.

My heart flipped over in my chest because the possession in how he said it meant everything to me, and I accepted that if he could prevent any hurt from affecting me he'd do it.

~

Weeks and months rolled by as we found our feet as a new family, and still our little girl continued to thrive. Seeing her grow and react to her world, reaching her milestones, gave me more hope. There were even some days I almost forgot how sick she'd been.

Neither Kane nor I felt complacent about her health. We both knew that our world could change on the spin of a dime, because the memories still burned in the back of our minds from those first days after she'd been born.

If I had to carry that burden I was glad I shared it with Kane because his love for us carried me through anything we faced, and we faced it together.

Watching the way Kane behaved with his boundless energy and his zest for life, it was hard to imagine what could have happened if that guy who attacked him had taken him from me.

As the charity concert drew nearer, I saw more and more of the Kane Exeter in public that I'd first recognized on TV.

A few days before he was due to perform we traveled to New York, my mom traveling with us to watch over Ellie. I couldn't have gone all that way and left her behind.

I was anxious enough about Kane and I knew I'd have to focus as it was the first real test to my strength of character around the music culture.

Once we arrived in New York I felt as if I'd stepped out of my life and into a fantasy. In public, there were hardly any traces of the normal man I knew, and the people we met were anything but sincere, all gushing compliments and praising Kane like he was stupid and couldn't see through their façade, but he never once called them on it.

Instead, he smiled his sexiest smile, remained the charismatic rock star, and thanked each of them kindly, but always kept us moving along.

How he did it I had no idea, and the fact I was with him did nothing to deter the 'touchy-feely' behavior of the people we met.

I'd have felt ignored but for the fact that Kane kept whispering things in my ear like, he loved me, I smelled awesome, and asking me if I was okay. But it wasn't about me; this was all about the man I loved, and watching him work his magic.

During the months leading up to the gig I saw a change in the attitude of Cody and Zander, the two most outspoken members of the band. Andrew, the lead guitarist, had always been a quiet man who emanated angst and mystery, but he was polite.

I had the feeling he was careful about what he said around me.

Cody was the hardest to tame, but underneath the whorish behavior was a man who had attachment issues. He tried too hard to be noticed and when the attention was given he shrank in size instead of growing taller when the spotlight fell on him.

Zander was funny and blunt. If he had a filter I never saw it. He wound Kane up like a coiled spring. It was funny to watch because as soon as he went too far, Kane became the alpha that he was, and Zander sloped off to lick his wounds.

Being around the band without all the glitz and frenzy of the live performance I'd seen before gave me a different view of Kane's band-mates, they were just ordinary guys who had made it big, and in my opinion had no real direction of what to do next.

When Zander spent a little time around Candice at our place he was quite sweet on her.

According to her, the feeling was mutual but she played hard to get with her treat them mean keep them keen attitude. By the day the band was due to perform they no longer intimidated me—but I think my presence intimidated them.

Kane explained that it was the first time a female had entered the inner sanctum of the workings of the band.

During the night before the concert, I felt Kane's restlessness.

We'd made love once and afterward he was still hard and not able to settle so he fucked me a second time and then got up and showered. His adrenaline was pumping and nothing was helping him settle.

I wasn't sure if it was due to the concert or what had happened to him the last time he'd been in a hotel room that kept him awake.

Eventually, I lay him on the bed and massaged him until my hands were sore and he finally fell asleep.

I crawled alongside him and wound my arm around his waist, my face close to his skin and inhaled his scent, exhausted but contented that I'd been able to relax him enough for him to rest. *It has got to be daunting to go out there after what's happened to him.*

A knock on the door woke me to find Kane bare-chested, hair messy and looking every bit the rock star image most women imagined first thing in the morning.

"I'll be leaving around 2:00 pm." I heard him mumble as he closed the door and wheeled breakfast into the room. I realized that Tony, the guy who'd been hired to protect Kane, had arrived along with breakfast before Kane had opened the door.

Knowing someone was there to protect him like that was reassuring and scary in equal parts because it emphasized the risks Kane took to bring pleasure to so many.

"Good morning, beautiful." He beamed his gorgeous, sexy smile as he climbed on the bed, trapped me tightly beneath the covers with his limbs and sat lightly on me . "Doesn't this feel better than when we were kids? Me sitting on top of you?"

A naughty look that warned of his desires affected me right down to my core and he bent forward to kiss me.

"Don't, I haven't brushed my teeth yet," I mumbled, turning my head away from him.

Kane grabbed my face and turned my head to make eye contact. "My tongue has been inside you, I've licked every fucking inch of your body, and I've loved every second of it, Jo. Not even morning breath can keep me away from you." He chuckled and moved his mouth to mine.

I pursed my lips in refusal. Kane's tongue pierced my lips and thrust deep into my mouth sending a pang of desire shooting through my body. I moaned involuntarily as his tongue teased and coaxed and within seconds I was responded like he was my only source of air.

Pulling back, he broke the kiss and smirked wickedly. "Damn, Jo, I expected more of a fight there, you're getting too easy." Crawling off me, he laughed softly and flung back the comforter. With a quick, sharp, smack, he playfully slapped my bare butt, bent forward and nibbled it. "Fuck, girl, I'm insatiable around you, get up and eat before I ride you into next week and make you bow-legged," he said as he walked away.

Shaking his head, he ran his hands through his hair like it was painful to leave me alone. I laughed and shook mine, enjoying his playfulness, and relished the thought that the nerves he displayed earlier seemed to be gone.

"Are you ready for this, Kane?" I asked as I slid into the chair by the place he'd set at the small table where he'd laid the breakfast out.

"I am. Can't wait to get out there." His easy, beautiful smile reached his gorgeous, bright blue eyes. "Are you?"

"Am I?" I had no clue what he meant.

"Yeah, are you prepared for this? For being famous by default. Ready for your prince to be a king for the day?" He smirked at me, and I knew he was self-mocking from what the papers had said by calling him *The New King of Rock*.

"Don't get above yourself, Kane, Elvis was the king."

"Yeah but he's dead, and the show must go on." He gave me a grin that melted my heart. He leaned across the table and took my hand in his. "When I'm up there today, I want you standing right at the side where I can see you whenever I turn around. I'm not just going out there for them, Jo. I'm going out there for us, you get that?"

"I do, and I can't wait to share it with you." Kane's smile was as wide as I'd seen it, pleased that I was with him one hundred percent for his journey back to his rock star performance.

Chapter Thirty-Four

I GOT IT

I got it

We arrived at Sheep's Meadow, Central Park, hours before Kane's performance, but Kane, being the music buff he was, wanted to listen to some of his favorite bands before his spot.

Hedonism, as concert headliners, were the last band scheduled to play.

Kane took me to sit in a cordoned-off area. He was dressed in a plaid shirt, shades, and baseball cap that reminded me of the day I first saw him at the airport.

It was obviously his public disguise and although I'd seen him dress like that plenty of times, I'd only ever seen him wear that type of clothing in public when he wanted to shake off attention.

Tony, *The Henchman* as Kane called him, sat beside Kane and I sat on his other side. I knew there were a few more Tonys dotted around us that had been provided by the event organizers, so I felt easier knowing they were all watching him.

It turned out that I enjoyed some of music from the bands and Kane tried patiently to teach me what he thought was clever about their music while I became his willing student.

There were various other artists around us, some who Kane knew on sight.

All of them respected each other's privacy in public. Of course, some were more recognizable than others, their appearance unable to be disguised. I felt lucky that Kane seemed able to slip under the wire the way he did most of the time.

As the day wore on I could feel his itch—the moment observing was no longer enough, he became restless.

A few hours before his band was up on stage, we left to eat with them before their performance.

Watching how alive Kane became when he spoke about the other performances to his band told me so much more about the kind of man he was.

Everything he said was positive and supportive and if one of the others said something that sounded negative, Kane was quick to converse with them.

Although validating their point sounded much more like constructive criticism.

With fifteen minutes to go, Kane and the band had changed into their stage gear as their manager and the stage manager clued them up on some final arrangements.

A few people I'd never seen prior to that point came in with packs of equipment.

Minutes later, two ear pieces hung down the front of his open neck shirt. He turned, his eyes seeking out mine in the room full of people.

Making his way to me, he hugged me tightly, clasping his hands at my lower back. He swayed me gently from side to side and smiled lovingly down at my face.

"So, Josephine Carmichael, are you ready for me to rock your world?"

"You already rock my world," I replied, smiling slowly back at him.

"And you rock mine, babe." Kane dipped his head closer. "I love you so fucking much, Jo," he murmured into my hair then kissed my head. Leaning back to look at me, his smile was slow and deliberate. "Ready to fangirl?" He laughed as his he stepped back and grabbed my hand. "Alright guys, let's show them how it's done."

Instantly I was being tugged along the corridor and into a space below the right side of the stage. "Up here, babe. Catherine will show you where you need to be so as I can see you."

Kane kissed my closed mouth, turned and headed over to the rest of his band while Catherine smiled and gestured the way she wanted me to walk.

"I'm nervous for him," Catherine stated, and I immediately connected with her feelings.

"Me too, my heart is in my mouth," I replied. That was nowhere near the emotional chaos that had taken over my body. Anyone would think it was me that was facing tens of thousands of people.

"Kane is a total pro, Josie. Takes everything in his stride, he just needs to get this one over with and everything will be back as it was for him.

"Did he tell you he was nervous?" I asked because although he'd had his fitful sleep the previous night, he hadn't shown his nerves that day to me. I viewed him more as excited and keen than nervous during the day.

"Oh, he's been pretty subdued today, for a gig this size, he's normally gearing up the boys and reassuring them, but I haven't seen any of that."

Catherine's words made me understand Kane had been thinking a little more about what happened to him. *Or he was worried but had put a brave face on for me.*

Suddenly a short, fast paced riff from Andrew blared out of the massive speakers and I almost jumped out of my skin. The roar of the crowd erupted like a sound wave that grew in volume.

Kane stepped out of the darkness and into the hot spotlights, waving his bare arms above his head.

The noise went to a whole new level. Andrew's guitar solo continued, but in a muted form as Kane walked to the front of the stage with his hands open as he palmed both sides of the microphone stand.

"Good evening, Sheep's Meadow, it's an honor to be here tonight." The cacophony from the people would have raised the roof if there had been one.

"It's been a long day today, have you all been having fun?" he asked, grinning at the camera that beamed his face to the crowd on the huge screens all over the park.

When he asked them that question, the noise, even in that outside space, reached an insane level of decibels as the fans screamed their affirmative replies.

"Well, alright then, glad to hear you've been entertained. I'm Kane Exeter in case you don't know me, and I hope you all swapped blades for your shades for this gig."

The audience went berserk, cheering and whistling for Kane as he made light reference to the knifeman who almost robbed him of the moment with them.

"Alright, yeah, pretty fucked-up, huh? Well never mind because I'm still here and our band Hedonism are going take the curtain down on the night with the final songs of the gig. I hope you'll join in with me 'cause...I guess it's been a while, and I might be a little rusty,"
he joked.

Nodding his head to Zander to cue the music, three clicks with his sticks then he and Andrew hit the first note in sync and my heart nearly fell on the floor.

My legs buckled as they reacted to the instant noise blaring out from the speakers. And even though I had anticipated the loud sounds when they came, I hadn't expected levels that were so deafening that it affected the rhythm of my excited heartbeat.

Missing beats added to the experience, which in turn, fueled my adrenaline as deep vibrations rumbled rhythmically along the stage boards toward me. I was living their music—it invaded every cell in my body causing tingling in my extremities and a buzzing sensation to collect deep within my chest.

My heart continued missing beats as the thrill of their performance sucked me in until my head, heart, and soul became connected to the music they made.

Being at the epicenter of their performance and not in the crowd instantly made me a fan of Hedonism.

I turned to look at the sea of faces, young and old, their bodies bobbing in time to the music and I stood in awe watching the effect four young men had on thousands of people, and I got it.

Suddenly, I understood what drove Kane, being a rock star didn't have anything to do with how he lived—it was what he lived *for*.

As soon as I heard the words he sang and the way he commanded the attention of all those music lovers, and how he did it, so naturally, it moved me.

I'd been scared to step into his world because I had judged his life based on a few hearsay articles written by people that lived by a code that sensationalized the rock music culture.

I'd been brainwashed with preconceived ideas of a lifestyle I knew nothing about. I felt ashamed that I had almost missed the opportunity to experience his world first-hand.

My eyes scanned the stage and instantly locked onto his. He was swaying his hips, grinning at me between verses, blowing me kisses.

My heart leapt that the boy I'd loved as a child could love me back, as a man. Right there and then I knew I'd never want him to do anything else.

Kane was a warrior, thankfully not a samurai one, as he once joked, and he had the courage of his convictions to stand up and refuse to be anything but who he wanted to be.

Four numbers later the last guitar note died and the disgruntled crowd chanted for more.

They weren't happy with the taste they'd been given and the air was thick with an expectation that craved to be filled.

Kane and the band ran off the stage and he came barreling into me, grinning, his body vibrating, practically buzzing with exhilaration from being able to share his music life with others.

"Well, babe, what do you think?" he asked as he dipped his knees to look directly into my eyes, and I swear he saw my soul.

Those crystal blue eyes that had been full of comfort and love during my darkest hours, held everything that I held in my own heart about how I felt about him. A slow smile that melted my heart crept over his face.

"It was alright I suppose—"

Kane lifted me off the floor and wrapped my legs around his waist while he slapped my butt playfully.

"I thought we agreed we'd never lie to each other?" he questioned.

His intense stare and wicked grin hinted of the night of dirty sex ahead when he got me home.

"What do you want me to say?" I giggled as he squeezed my butt and ran his hand up my back to the nape of my neck, squeezing it tight. I shivered.

"Say yes, Jo."

"To what?"

"Marry me, make me happy. You can do this." His eyes ticked over my face and he held his breath expectantly.

I shook my head trying to find the right words but nothing would come, I wanted to say so much more than yes, but when I saw the frown and how his eyes had begun to narrow, I realized he probably thought it was a rejection.

"You're right, Kane. I can do this...I want to do this. I can't wait to do this with you. When I saw you out there today, I got it. You've always said you got me, but it's taken me a long time to understand what that meant, but today I did. So, yes, Kane, it would be an honor to marry you."

Exhaling shakily in relief, his breath became my air once again as he dipped his forehead to rest on mine and his eyes became the window to his soul.

"You won't regret it, babe. Trust me; whatever life throws at us, we know we'll beat it. We already have—life is short, sweet and hellishly difficult at times, but we've already been there and survived this far. That gives us a head start on everyone else, who would dare mess with what we have. The US Army, life and death situations, and crazy knifemen couldn't keep us apart, Jo. I don't rate the chances of anyone else, do you? I had planned to ask you this question tonight, straight after the performance like I have, and if you'd said no to me, I was prepared to go to that press conference and announce my retirement because you and our baby are more important than anything else to me." My heart tightened that he had been prepared to give it all up.

"In the beginning when you came back, I had only seen one interview with you in all your flirty, charismatic rock starness on TV, and I won't lie, all I saw was a player. A beautiful unattainable man that I'd loved when he was a boy, but a player nevertheless. My impression of musicians was that they were all about women, booze, drugs and... hedonism. It's not. Those habits are personal lifestyle choices of individuals, not some stereotypical image of what you are supposed to fit into. What you did out there wasn't about any of those things. It's about who you are and how you express yourself to others, and you are so fucking kick-ass awesome in that expression. And what I felt was beyond..." I sighed deeply thinking of my next words. "You leave me so breathless. I'm pinching myself right now. So yes, Kane, I do."

Kane flashed me his heartbreaking smile and pressed his lips to mine. "I swear it, Josephine Carmichael, my soulmate. I'll never let you regret it, because I'll make sure to remind you of my fucking kick-ass awesomeness and make you feel beyond...oh and I promise to leave you breathless, with alarming regularity." He winked and waggled his eyebrows. A huge grin spread over his face that made me want to kiss it.

Our courtship was practically non-existent but my dad was never more right when he told my mom all those years ago he wouldn't be surprised if we found our way back to one another.

It had taken us all those years before we did, but Kane was right too, if we'd known each other growing up we may have missed this... and that would have been another tragedy.

EPILOGUE

Kane

FIVE YEARS LATER

"You do believe me don't you, Daddy?"

Glancing at the total destruction in the playroom, I initially saw red. Red nail polish that is.

Our two, white Scottish Terriers, Misty and Bob, had their paw claws heavily manicured, and if I had to pass judgment on the effort she'd put in, she hadn't done a bad job of that.

I chewed my lip and tried not to laugh when my eyes met hers because she was just as easy to read as her mom had been around that age.

Ellie looked like me, but her behavior and mannerisms were all inherited from my wife, Josie.

Some days it freaked me out because being with them was like living in the past and the present at the same time.

My heart squeezed at the familiarity in her voice, the way she moved, and her innocent open stare that gave away all her secrets. And, just like her mom, she made a terrible liar.

She'd been productive I'd give her that. My little budding beautician had taken Jo's mascara and done a great job of coloring three of her dollies' hair with it.

The red nail polish bottle sat open and balanced precariously on the side of her cartoon branded dressing table and two of her own big toes had been painted way beyond the nail and past the first knuckle.

Foundation make-up was rubbed very diligently into the floor all around her. Jo's make-up bag was lying at the side of her leg if any evidence were needed as to who the culprit of the mess was.

I fought to keep my face straight and I tried to find the words to chastise her without saying something that would make me laugh.

"I'm not sure that I do, young lady. You're telling me that Misty told you to do that to Bob? Then told you to paint your toes as well?"

"Yes, she did. Naughty Misty," she said, in a shaky voice, her lip quivering, and her huge doe brown eyes, like her mom's, brimming with tears.

I had to fight all the protective feelings I had for her, I hated seeing her cry. She and her mother owned my heart in equal parts. Being a parent at times like that sucked.

I picked up a dolly that was lying face down and turned it over to look at its face and my heart cracked wide open.

Ellie had painted a red line down the center of the doll's chest, right between the plastic breast mounds.

It was a jagged attempt to make her dolly look just like her. I crouched to the floor and scooped her up in my arms, swallowing hard at how, as young as my baby girl was, she'd noticed the difference in her body.

Josie and I had never tried to hide the start Ellie had had from her.

We always told her that since she was just like any other child now, it shouldn't stop her from being anything that she wanted to be.

Maybe except for something that put excessive strain on her heart, like an international athlete in training or something similar.

Walking over to the chair in the corner of her room, I sat and placed her on my lap. "Your dolly has the same special line on her chest; you want to tell me about that?"

Instantly her little mouth pouted and she looked to our dogs then nodded again. "Misty said Dotty wasn't a real dolly because she didn't have a heart, and I couldn't make her understand that she *was* a real dolly.

The only way I could make her believe me was to do an operation on her, so Misty wouldn't argue with me anymore. Because if she had an operation then she had to have a heart in the first place." *Damn she's so smart.*

Seeing her upset, even though it was at her own doing, crushed my heart and I found it so fucking difficult to do the heavy dad part with her. I was saving that up for when she was a teenager and the lanky boys came calling.

I shuddered to think about that part, but I knew I'd be a kick-ass threatening figure if anyone thought they were getting into her pants.

We heard footsteps on the wooden landing and Ellie's body stiffened as her mom came through the doorway, her eyes widening as they darted around the room.

"Uh oh," Ellie said, in a melodic sing-song voice.

Jo, my gorgeous soulmate, stood with her jaw hanging and her eyes bugging out of her head still clutching the door handle tightly. Once she had absorbed the initial wig out from what she saw, her eyes softened and she shook her head.

"Don't tell me, Ellie...did Daddy put you up to this?" she asked as she spoke to our daughter like she was the sensible one in the room. I sucked in my lips as I tried to keep it together.

Jo was doing the duck lips thing with her mouth as she tried to keep herself from laughing, and I had to look at the corner of the room to keep myself in check and not burst out laughing as well.

"Oh, no, Mommy, he had nothing to do with it," she replied, sounding all protective. "It was stupid Misty over there." She turned to look at our innocent dogs and narrowed her eyes. "See what you've done, Misty, you almost got Daddy into trouble."

At that point I'm afraid I lost it and laughed heartily at our little kid defending my honor. It was too cute.

"Kane, stop that! You are incorrigible." I lifted the dolly in my defense and Jo's eyes immediately focused on what Ellie had done.

"Misty, what have I told you about getting these guys into trouble," Jo asked, immediately changing tack; her mock anger directed at the poor dog that had done nothing except be patient, and have her claws painted.

"Now, Patricia is going to have a *big* mess to clean up thanks to you."

Patricia was our housekeeper. Jo went on to lecture Ellie via the dog about all the dangers of playing with cosmetics and Ellie joined in, indicating her level of understanding, before Jo told us that she'd come to get us because dinner was ready.

Getting out of the chair with Ellie in my arms, I walked over to my wife and slid my hands around her waist. Her upturned face had a look in her eyes that told me how much she adored me and I hoped she read the same look in mine.

Josephine Carmichael stole my heart with a picture she shoved into my hands as fat tears ran down her face. I was almost ten years old then and she was almost eight.

When I had met Jo as a six-year-old there was just something about her that drew me in and tied her to my heart. Her crooked smile with one big tooth and one missing mesmerized me.

Josie was beautiful with the face of an angel. Her brothers used to get pissed when she wanted to play, but in truth, I'd have rather played with her than them, and eventually I never hid that fact.

All these years later, with all that we've done and who we've become, my heart is still hers. It will always be hers.

Our past wasn't perfect and our reunion even messier than I care to remember, but the joy Jo brought to my life with her love and our beautiful baby with her missing beats, made me so fucking grateful for my second chance.

I'll admit I was worried that she'd never let me in again, and if I could go back and have a do-over it may never have worked out like it did.

My only regret was the months that Jo was pregnant that I never knew about, because she carried that weight on her own.

My heart burns when I think about how that must have felt for her, but I can't let it consume me. It is what it is, and she made that choice which was her right and her right only, at that time.

During the past five years, my Jo has found that the worries she carried about living with someone who does what I do as my job, were unfounded.

Sure, there is excess and vulgarity in the music industry, and yes, I was part of that for a while, but for every rock star that's clever, they realize pretty quickly when it's time to grow up.

The seedier side that's on offer can get old rapidly and finding a 'Jo' becomes harder every day.

No one that does what I do, with the fame that follows from that, can be sure the one they're with is there because of you, and not what you do.

Luckily for me, my Jo was there from the beginning, and I'll do everything in my power to make sure she's there at the end because come hell or high water, she's mine forever.

The End.

OTHER TITLES BY K.L. SHANDWICK

THE EVERYTHING TRILOGY

Enough Isn't Everything

Everything She Needs

Everything I Want

Love With Every Beat

just Jack

Everything Is Yours

LAST SCORE SERIES

Gibson's Legacy

Trusting Gibson

Gibson's Melody

READY FOR FLYNN SERIES

Ready For Flynn, Part 1

Ready For Flynn, Part 2

Ready For Flynn, Part 3

OTHER NOVELS

Missing Beats

Notes on Love

ABOUT THE AUTHOR

K. L. Shandwick lives on the outskirts of York, UK. She started writing after a challenge by a friend when she commented on a book she read. The result of this was 'The Everything Trilogy'. Her background has been mainly in the health and social care sector in the U.K. Her books tend to focus on the relationships of the main characters. Writing is a form of escapism for her and she is just as excited to find out where her characters take her as she is when she reads another author's work.

FIND K. L. SHANDWICK ON SOCIAL MEDIA

- **KLShandwick.com**
- **Twitter**
- **Facebook**
- **Bookbub**
- **AllAuthor**
- **Instagram**
- **Amazon**
- **KL's Hangout Group**
- **KL's Newsletter**

Printed in Great
Britain
by Amazon